THE ADMIRAL

THE ADMIRAL

A novel by Martin Dibner

Doubleday & Company, Inc., Garden City, New York

All of the characters in this book
are fictitious, and any resemblance
to actual persons, living or dead,
is purely coincidental.

For Paul and Ed

A portion of this novel was written under a residence fellowship at the Huntington Hartford Foundation in California. The author wishes to express his gratitude to the Foundation's directors and staff, and deeply regrets that this remarkable sanctuary for creative artists no longer exists.

contents

~~~~~~

*"What is the duty today? It is to fight.
What is the duty tomorrow? It is to win.
What is the duty always? It is to die."*

EXCERPT FROM THE DIARY OF
ENSIGN HEIICHI OKABE,
KAMIKAZE SPECIAL ATTACK CORPS.

one

U.S.S. GLOUCESTER

1

All that day the ships ran south and west. Toward dusk they made for Tjilatjap. The Dutch and British anchored in the fairway and the American cruiser *Gloucester*, hardest hit, tied portside to the rotting quay. With her lines secured, her skipper, Harry Paige, quit the bridge and went below.

Word of the morning action had reached the local Dutch and Javanese. They came out of the wretched shacks and bars and stood on the dock in the shadows of godowns to look at her.

On *Gloucester's* damaged decks, the sailors went about their in-port duties. Fuel hoses coupled to the dockside manifolds swelled with the gush of oil. Cargo nets swung out on booms and dull-eyed men jockeyed stores on board and stowed them in the empty holds. Queues of ammunition handlers passed fresh clips to the gun crews who racked them in the splinter shields of their battle stations. Corpsmen carried the stretchers of wounded through the open hatches from sick bay below. Sweat dripped where blood had run that morning.

The captain reappeared, jaunty in a fresh white uniform. His face shone red. His executive officer, a sawed-off Viking of a man named Olsen, met him and walked with him to the quarterdeck. They stood for several moments in the simmering heat. Olsen seemed nervous and did not look directly at the captain. At the foot of the gangway, a small brown man in chauffeurs' suntans stood by the

Dutch resident's vintage phaeton. It was an awesome relic. The kind they use in funerals, Paige thought gloomily. Flowers to the cemetery. He stared round his ship's blown decks.

"I'll be an hour, Oley. No more."

He saluted and so did Olsen, and Paige trotted down the gangway. The chauffeur held the door and the captain climbed in. The Rolls nudged through the crowd, its ancient horn blasting. The captain in the tonneau sat erect, ignoring the stares of the crowd. A corpse under a wilting wreath of white carnations, he thought. *SYMPATHY* in musty gilt embossed across my chest. The car cleared the docks and the native driver stepped on the gas. Thick dust swirled as they climbed in silence through twilight and jungle to the resident's house on the hill.

"I make no deals," Paige said. "All we want is permission to bury our dead in your cemetery and two steel rails to repair the ship."

The fat Dutch resident mopped his face. "Is it asking so much to evacuate my wife and me from this stink hole?"

"Without orders, yes."

"You would leave us to die? Surrounded by traitors and spies? Any moment, Captain, tonight, tomorrow, the Jap will drop his bombs on us."

"And on my ship as well."

"You have guns. You can fight back." His voice rose, shrill with fear. "Safe-conduct, Captain. I beseech you."

"I run a warship, not a pleasure boat. You've got a Dutch admiral out there. Ask him."

"Onderdonck? Damn him, his answer is no. 'Remain at your post like the rest of us,' he told me, 'or you die like a deserter.' Van Gelder, may he rest in peace, he never would have treated me like this. You are my only hope now, dear Captain Paige. Otherwise by morning we are all dead."

Paige looked at the bustle of activity around him. The resident's wife, a quivering tower of clinging pongee, was supervising a small army of servants packing crates of furniture and dishes and loading them into lorries.

"You're in good shape," Paige said. He swallowed the rest of his drink. "What about the graves and rails?"

"For our safe-conduct, yes."

Paige was on his feet, leaving. The resident held him. "My gin you drink. My good Dutch cemetery you want. And my steel rails worth their weight in gold. But for our lives you don't give a damn. Big-hearted Americans!" He pushed his belly against Paige, blocking the way. "It's money you want, isn't it? Gold, eh, Captain Paige? For two Dutch lives?"

He grabbed Paige's sleeve. Paige yanked free and went out to the veranda. He could see the lights of his ship over the village roofs a mile below and a longing filled him, an old longing sailors know. Why must it always be like this on land, filthy and clinging with crud? And never at sea?

The resident followed him, taunting. "How much, Captain?"

"Save your money and rails for the Japanese. I'll bury my dead at sea." He started down the wide steps.

The resident clung to his arm. "Sweet Jesus! Listen!" He looked with swift hate at his wife inside who was shouting orders at the servants. "Yes! Forgive me. I beg you. Bury your dead here in the good Dutch earth."

"It's asking too much," Paige said coldly.

"Not at all! We are honored. Gin, rails, whatever you need." He glared at his wife. "God bless America!" He wiped his eyes. "Please," he said.

"I'll send a working party for the rails."

The resident grabbed his fingers and kissed them. Paige's stomach turned. The man was mad. He had to get away.

The resident pushed him into a cane chair. "A farewell drink." He clapped his fat hands. "Captain Paige's drink. Chop chop!" He collared a sweaty houseboy. "Half a dozen bottles of the best gin."

He chattered madly. The drink tray arrived and Paige sat trapped for an agony of minutes. The resident's wife in rising anger barged about like a loaded tanker that had slipped her mooring. She blasted foghorn orders at the sullen servants in a mixture of Dutch and Javanese.

Her husband, pale as ashes, bemoaned his predicament and drank his gin like water. Any moment now, he babbled, the Jap would swoop down and take over and tear up his precious fields of tea. They will plant chocolate, he whined, to feed their savage hordes. The end was near. It was a privilege and an honor to spend these last hours man to man with a brave American sea captain. His admiration was boundless and he would die bravely. His hands smelled of garlic and he begged the captain to stay for dinner.

Paige was drunk now and the spicy smells of *rijstaffel* challenged his resolve to go. The resident offended him but you cannot hit a man who has just delivered two priceless steel rails and the promise of peace in the good Dutch earth for the ship's dead. It had been a bad morning at sea and the gin a blessing. He had sat long enough now and his ship and men were waiting. He did not care to hear another word about the resident's troubles with his sharecrop planters or their goddam chocolate and tea.

He declined to dine and rose to go, avoiding the resident's pudgy hands. He bowed goodbye to the wife in passing. Her smile was death. The hell with her and down the steps he went, light as a feather.

The resident snuffling waddled behind nursing two bottles. The houseboy followed with the rest of the gin. His eyes were openly contemptuous and Paige yearned to slap him. He settled in the tonneau and they laid the six green bottles by his side.

Such a way to die, he thought.

The resident mounted the running board and leaned close to Paige's ear, triumph in his brimming eyes. "I'll show her," he muttered. "The German bitch. She put me up to it."

Paige smiled and patted his arm. The resident began to cry. He swept his arm in a circle. "My life and my death . . . look at it."

Beyond him lay the plantation fields of his smashed world fed by the sweat of countless brown bodies. Slyly, the driver raced the twelve-cylinder motor. "My beautiful tea," the resident whimpered. For a fleeting moment Paige felt sorry for him. He stuck out his hand. "Thanks and goodbye."

"Goodbye and good luck!" The resident almost fell as the car lurched ahead. He waved to Paige. Tears streamed down his face. His wife appeared out of the dark of the sitting room. A funeral barge, Paige thought. Furious words spilled over sweatstained pongee. Dutch and guttural English, the worst of it. He waved back. He didn't give a damn. The hell with them. He had his graves and his rails and a half-dozen bottles of the best Dutch gin. He did not look back.

The driver sat through all of it with insolent calm. Paige caught a glimpse of his brown face in the mirror and was startled by the intensity of loathing he saw there. A house full of hate. A Hun bitch and treachery in the servants' wing. No wonder the resident drank. Drink provided the sole escape from that sweaty pongee tower of hate. Her big loose breasts under the thin fabric had excited Paige. He hadn't seen or touched the like of it since Manila six months ago. A brief image of his own wife in bed in Georgetown, U.S.A. came and went and he cursed softly.

A monster, that resident's wife, tits and all. Nagging and carping at the sullen gooks and driving them like slaves. The sight of them scurrying about like frightened ants, filling the huge packing cases and lugging them out to the lorries began to seem funny to Paige. She had been mad enough to kill, while he and the resident sat like lords of the manor on Doomsday, lapping up the excellent gin.

Let 'er go. God bless her. Let 'em all go. Rats from a sinking ship. How that house had stunk! Greasy food and gook sweat and fear. It had stunk so much of fear you could scrape it off with a knife. It was on the two of them like a sticky shellac, enough to turn a strong stomach. Paige belched and the driver's back straightened as though he had been shot.

The sun had long ago melted behind the hills. The sky was streaked with color. The car bumped down the winding dirt road. Warm air soothed his itchy flesh. He closed his eyes and sat quietly hearing the first sounds of his ship's repair crews. Above it the resonant throbbing of many insects wafted in from the hills.

The car arrived at the gangway. The driver leaped out and held the door open for Paige. Paige sat for a while not moving. It would be nice to bash the treacherous bastard's nose, he thought. And anyone else who happened to be around. And head on out to the Dutch flagship and hang one on Onderdonck, the stuffy Dutch admiral who had taken command a week ago when Van Gelder was killed.

He vaulted out of the seat so suddenly that the driver had to duck. "Get those bottles to the officer of the deck. On the double— every last one of 'em!" He spun and lowered his head and plowed through the crowd. "Gangway, you gooks. Gangway for the American Navy."

Olsen was waiting at the quarterdeck, oddly pale, and Paige thought: *More of his troubles, I don't need.* Before the exec could say a word, Paige told him to stand by for the rails and see that the gin was brought below. He turned and grinned at the gangway sentry. "Put a bayonet up that driver's ass if he doesn't hurry, sailor." And reeled below.

During his absence the wounded had been carried in litters by teams of corpsmen down the gangways to the quay and stacked like pies in wooden freight cars. Square crosses hastily applied to the gently curved roofs still dripped red paint. Back and forth the corpsmen went, stumbling and cursing, pushing their burdens into the freight cars whose insides were still damp and stained with native sweat and ripe with the smell of rice and tea.

One wounded sailor trailed a bloody bandage and cried for his mother. Another wept without reason. No one seemed to notice. When the wounded were all aboard, the train started for the hills with a clatter of wood and steel. Some of the crew stopped work to watch their shipmates go. Their eyes were filled with envy.

The groans of the wounded were finally lost somewhere in the dark hills. On *Gloucester*'s deck amidships the chow line shuffled through the snarl of power lines and cables and the tireless umbilical sucking of fuel hoses. The men moved listlessly sniffing the drifting steam for something more than its promise of beans again and wormy bread. There was little talk. They had seen the sailmakers below with palm and needle putting the stitches to yards of canvas shrouds. On the fantail a dirge of hammers rang as the ship's carpenters shaped the coffins for the dead.

It was February 1942. The tide of conquest swept southward. Riding its crest were the armadas of jubilant island men confident the world was theirs. The Emperor's planes had found the proud ships that morning and the ships had run. The stubborn men in the ships began to understand the truth of it. They had got this far on luck alone and time like the failing light of day was running out.

2

~~~~~~

They patched her up as best they could. Broad-cheeked Javanese and Sundanese workers streamed aboard and sweated over her damaged hull side by side with the ship's repair parties. Cutting torches spat. Drills and saws whined and sang. Chipping hammers chattered. Welding arcs and floodlights flung grotesque shadows, the moving shapes of naked-waisted men. Showering sparks hissed in the dirty green water and died quickly. Below in sick bay, men died more slowly.

In his cabin forward, Captain Paige penciled the finishing touches to his report of the morning action and sent it to his yeoman for typing. The paperwork of command confounded him. Until this morning's battle, paperwork had been all the fighting he had done.

He hung away his whites and poured himself a generous splash of the resident's best and stripped to the waist and thrust his face through the open port hoping for a breath of air. His eyes were sun-squinted and blue, set wide above a blunt nose. His skin bore the look and feel of wind and sea and too much wine and sun. His pale hard body contrasted sharply with the deep color of his neck and face. His chest was hairy, grizzled and splotched with an ugly heat rash. The length of his flat-bellied torso gleamed with perspiration. An anchor was tattooed in blue above the vaccination on his upper arm, entwined with a length of chain and a faded red U.S.N. below. He was forty-two. The sea had made him fifty.

He drained the glass and poured another and squeezed the juice of a lime into it. Some of his anger had ebbed. All he felt now was a hopeless disgust directed generally at the joint command and specifically at Onderdonck. What the hell was the use in running? he wondered. The Nip will find us wherever we go.

That morning when the enemy planes had finished their work, Paige had begged permission by blinker and flag hoist to press on, to engage the Japanese invasion force as originally planned. Onderdonck had refused and ordered the retirement to Tjilatjap.

Paige knew the dream of a mixed fleet had been doomed from the start. Joint command, precarious on a hilltop in Bandoeng, had cooked it up in a desperate effort to slow the violent tide of empire. ABDAfloat, they named it. A hooligan fleet if ever Paige saw one. The ships, hastily assembled from convoy and patrol duties, were Australian and British, Dutch and American, as ancient as those freight cars, their armament outmoded, their power plants and deck machinery sorely in need of overhaul.

Van Gelder in tactical command was able and courageous but he had nothing to work with. Common code books were lacking, signal books a confusion of wrong meanings. A scant twenty-four hours was all that ABDA was granted in which to establish a common denominator in communications, gunnery control and battle tactics. The barrier of language seemed insurmountable. Liaison officers were hastily assigned to each ship to translate the orders of the admiral and to coordinate it with joint command. Finally, shakily, ABDAfloat put to sea from Surabaya, to meet and engage the invasion force.

The Japanese controlled the air. Each day brought winged death. Van Gelder had done his best and had gone down with his ship a week ago. Now the showdown this morning near Makassar Strait had been the last straw.

The bombers had come in waves, pretty as a Hokusai print. The attack was precise and savage and *Gloucester* bore the brunt of it. Paige skippered her through near misses and splashes but his luck could not hold forever. A 500-pounder smashed its way through the bullet-ripped decks of her mainmast superstructure. Angling aft it exploded against Turret Three, cremating her crew. The damage control parties fought the fires and the bombers returned for a final sweep over crippled *Gloucester*, strafing her decks mercilessly. A burst on the bridge killed Donaldson, the gunnery officer, and the sorely needed Dutch liaison lieutenant, Hofstadt.

With the bombers gone and fires under control, Paige, still hot for battle, rejoined the scattered force, reported his damages and urged the admiral to resume pursuit of the invasion group. His request was turned down and the run was made for Tjilatjap.

During the run, Paige inspected his damaged ship. His men had behaved well under fire and he was proud of them. The count of dead came to thirty-seven. It would be touch and go, he knew, with the dead on board in the heat of day. But a burial at sea by Navy law meant stopping all engines and he'd be damned if he'd slow by half a knot and risk his ship again. So he issued the order to prepare the bodies for sea burial in the event the fleet did not make Tjilatjap that night. Each body was weighted with an eight-inch shell and sewn into heavy canvas and carried up the ladders to the shade of an awning rigged over the fantail.

She had always been a taut and happy ship. Until this morning no enemy fire had touched her. Now the sight of her ruptured decks saddened the men. They slung their hammocks on the open decks or slept sprawled on thin blankets in the hot spaces below. Paige did what he could to comfort his men, walking among them and speaking lightly. His presence was all they asked of him.

Lookouts scanned the sky and gun crews stood by their weapons in uneasy rest. Loaders stacked the empty cartridge cases and racked the fresh clips hoisted from the handling rooms below. Sick bay corpsmen labored to free the remains of men glued by blood and sun to the steel sides of open gun nests. Flesh tore badly from the twisted metal. The stiffened bodies swelled in the sun. The chief boatswain supervised a party with nose rags and hoses to keep the smell down. Paige finally came face to face with Turret Three, unwilling to admit to himself he had been avoiding it.

He stood silent before the gaping hole. It was hard to believe one bomb could do that much damage. The blast had sprung and cracked the two longitudinal beams that supported the main deck. The weakened girders presented a serious threat to the ship's structural integrity and he knew then he would have to do something about it and do it fast in Tjilatjap. Cooler now, he admitted to himself the Dutch admiral may have been right.

And so they had come to Tjilatjap.

He sipped his drink morosely. Tjilatjap. He had his steel rails and a burial ground and if he never saw Tjilatjap again it would be too soon. A vermin-infested hell hole riddled with fever and treachery. A half-assed harbor with a jury-rigged floating drydock, stinking of Borneo oil. It was too damn bad they had not stayed and slugged it out with the Jap. Anything would have been better than this dung heap.

He frowned at the natives bunched on the quay. Goddam gooks. Nip spies with transmitters in their filthy thatched huts. He drained his drink and considered another and decided what he needed more than anything was to get off his feet before he fell off. He had not slept in thirty hours. He sprawled full length on the sagging davenport directly in the draft of the electric fan.

He was bushed. The fight had been a beaut while it lasted and he had loved every minute of it. The tour of the ship had been something else. A duty that had to be done. It had taken two hours and it hadn't been easy keeping the likable grin frozen in a sincere way. Or to rack his brain quickly for the right name to go with the familiar face here and there. And sick bay had been a bloody sight and still was. He closed his eyes. Thirty-seven dead. It could have been worse. Look where poor old Van Gelder had ended up. And Donaldson and the Dutch lieutenant and all the others.

He lay there thinking like that, and resting.

On the quay outside, the natives watched impassively. They wore rags and bright sarongs. Their smooth faces shone like wax in the glare and shadows flung from the decks above. They too had been surprised and trapped by the enormity of war. Their hate for it had begun months ago when the white man came in his ugly steel ships with coarseness and whisky to ruin the fishing and violate the women. His greed had mutilated their paradise and they would not forget it. Now they reasonably believed in the triumph of the Japanese to the north. The panic in the eyes of their haughty Dutch resident filled them with a secret pleasure, a justice they attributed to the gods. It gave them face to witness Caucasian fear. The presence of a confusion not their own was an ecstasy almost too intense to bear.

This crippled American warship was the first they had seen to support the rumors of Japanese might. They pressed as close to the ship's side as the hardfaced dock sentries permitted. They could see with their own eyes the canvased corpses in a long crooked row near the fantail and they could see the carpenters sawing through piles of pine boards and nailing them together.

But it was the wreckage of Turret Three that awed them. It was a terrifying sculpture of twisted metal flung skyward round a huge scorched hole. They had never seen anything like it in all their simple innocent lives.

Death they knew. Death was commonplace. But this accidental artistry of shining steel tooled by violence into an image of living agony dazzled them more than the holiest relics of their temple. A sleek barrel ripped open laid bare the secret of its rhythmic rifling. Wheels and levers of gleaming brass were amulets before their eyes. Delicate dials behind splintered glass shone like jewels in the blue glare of cutting torches. And everywhere the solemn shapes of empty shells. All the tools that dealt in death, shining and divine, a gift hurled from the heavens. They could not tear their eyes away. Its alien and holy presence struck wonder and a curious longing in their hearts.

On the fantail deck the steady hammers of the carpenters drove the nails deep.

3

~~~~~~

The medical officer came calling on the captain. He sank heavily into a chair and fumbled for his cigarettes. His surgical gown was smeared like a butcher's apron.

"Bad?" Paige inquired.

"It's never good."

"Smoking lamp's out, J.J. We're still fueling."

The doctor stared stupidly at the unlighted cigarette in his fingers. "How much time we have here? I need medical supplies."

"I've requested forty-eight hours. We could use a week." He sat up and yawned. "Go on. Grab a smoke."

"Bless you, my lord."

"How's it going in sick bay?"

"Two more dead."

"Christ. Who?"

"One gunner's mate. No dog tag. His rate's tattooed on what's left of his ass. And his girl's name, Ethel, in the most interesting place. Chief thinks it's Mulloy from Turret Three. He's checking. The other one is Benny, the nice Chamorro kid from the wardroom pantry."

"The wardroom never got hit."

"He was an ammunition passer aft." He smoked thoughtfully. "That should be the end of it."

"Too bad. Benny was studying law."

"Celestial navigation would've been better." He sighed. "Sick bay's jammed. I got maybe eight or ten ambulatories who should really be off their feet. What about the dead topside?"

"We bury 'em at dawn in the Dutch cemetery."

"I hope we stuck the right names on the pieces we put together."

"Who'll know the difference?"

"I take pride in my work."

"Navy surgeons are a pack of butchers who couldn't make it on the outside." He took the doctor's cigarette and sniffed it. It stunk of ether and he passed it back. "What's the total wounded?"

"We put sixty-two ashore. I think we can handle the others."

"If there's any doubt, they'd better go, too."

"What's up?"

"This new Dutch admiral. He worries me. I got a hunch he's scared and he'll order us to shove off on short notice."

The doctor rose, nursing his cigarette. "Then I sure as hell better get hot on those supplies."

"And get word to Oley he's got two more dead to take care of."

"Okay, Skipper. Thanks for the smoke." He paused in the doorway. "You better get some shut-eye. You look bushed."

"Look who's talking."

"About Oley," the doctor began and stopped.

"What about Oley?"

But the doctor merely shrugged and went out. Paige watched him go, thinking: J. J. Lefferts, Commander, U.S.N., M.C. (Chancre Mechanic), *U.S.S. Gloucester*. The Marine sentry came in saluting, trying not to sniff the delicate tobacco aroma. The Dutch liaison officer had come aboard earlier to replace dead Lieutenant Hofstadt. Could the captain see him now?

Paige caught a glimpse of a white blouse and white shorts in the half dark of the passageway. Sure, he could see him and he wondered where Olsen, whose job it was to welcome new officers aboard, could be.

He grabbed a tattered bathrobe from his locker, irritated because he needed a shave and shower and because his exec was not on the ball. The Dutch officer stepped over the coaming, saluting stiffly. Paige was surprised to see a young man no older than his own son, David. Hofstadt had been forty.

The skipper's cold appraisal seemed to fluster the visitor who blushed to the roots of his plastered blond hair. His baggy shorts flapped in the fan's path like wash on a windy line.

"Lieutenant Doorn," he announced and clicked his heels. "Royal Netherlands Navy."

Paige bowed gravely and plucked a loose thread from his robe.

"Admiral Onderdonck sends his compliments and regrets the loss of your brave men." Click.

Doorn's shrill schoolboy English was thickly accented and difficult to understand. Doorn himself was as delicately tinted as a picture postcard of tulip time. A hell of a way to save the Dutch East Indies, Paige thought. What's a pipsqueak like this supposed to do? Stick his finger in the dike?

"The admiral requests that you make the necessary burial arrangements with our resident here for our beloved Lieutenant Hofstadt."

"All arranged, Lieutenant."

"I beg your pardon, Captain?"

"He's being buried with our dead."

"A great honor, Captain Paige."

"Honor hell. They're beginning to stink."

"At what hour is the service, Captain?"

"Dawn."

Doorn cleared his throat and began to read a file of dispatches he had brought with him. "Admiral Onderdonck acknowledges receipt of your damage report. He wishes to inform you he will hold a conference for all ship commanders aboard the flagship at 2200 tonight."

"Very well."

"He regrets he must refuse your request of forty-eight hours for repairs. The fleet will get under way at 0600."

Something inside the captain let go. He yanked the file from Doorn's hands and read the dispatch himself, ripped it from the file and crumpled it. He paced the cabin, punching a hard fist into his palm. "What in hell's the matter with him! I need a minimum of forty-eight hours, damn it!"

"That's the message as I received it, Captain."

"I've a hole in Turret Three as big as a house, you hear? And I'm repairing it for sea before I move one damned inch from here."

"Yes, Captain."

"And thirty-nine dead to bury by morning."

"We too have our dead, Captain."

"Nobody asked you, damn it! What the hell's the admiral's rush? Where the hell can we go? I'm staying, you hear, until that turret's repaired."

"Do you wish me to tell that to the admiral?"

"I'd like to tell you what I wish you to tell your admiral."

The belt of his robe had loosened. He pulled it tight and stalked about, his head bent, his chin whiskers scratching his chest. He felt a hundred years old and sick to death of defeat and the stink of fear and the sight of dead sailors' insides in the sun. The scar tissue in his sunburned face ached and he thought of corners where fists had driven him and he had bludgeoned his way out. There was no out here.

His eye caught Doorn at stiff attention. He yearned to hurt him, to whip him with words, to send this rosy-cheeked schoolboy back to his yellow-bellied admiral with his hairless tail between his legs. He thought of David. It calmed him.

"Look, young man," he said. "None of my crew has had four straight hours of sleep in the last sixty. They've been standing watch on, watch off since Pearl Harbor. And eating wormy bread and washing their skivvies in sea water and living with spick itch and malaria since Christ knows when. They haven't made a liberty port or had a drink or a piece of tail in so long they've forgotten what it's like. I lost four good officers this morning. One of them would have made admiral had he lived and maybe President of the United States, he was that good. And two chiefs and thirty-odd enlisted men and all I've gotten in return is you, Lieutenant Doorn. For which I'm grateful, believe me, because without you I sure as hell wouldn't have the faintest idea of what goes on in the mind of your fine, honorable, and highly respectable Admiral Onderdonck."

"Thank you, Captain." Doorn's eyes were moist with devotion.

"Have you seen Turret Three? You could run the whole Jap fleet through it and not scrape paint. If it's not patched before we clear for sea sure as hell we'll sink with the first heavy swell we hit."

"Captain—"

"Just shut up and listen while I say my piece. I've got working parties round the clock shifting ammunition forward to Turrets One and Two where it can do some good. I'm praying there's

enough ammo in this half-assed depot of yours to make up for
what we expended this morning. We got us a small army of
third-rate gooks on board, half of 'em probably Jap spies, and they're
patching a torpedo hole and only God Almighty in His infinite wisdom knows how that torpedo went through the starboard side of the
hull at the waterline and came out the portside without damaging a
hair of anyone's head or even so much as cracking a cup and saucer."

"Yes, Captain."

"There's a repair party aft pumping out a ruptured fuel tank.
My evaps are shot. I'm low on chow and feeding three useless
plane pilots and their radio gunners who have no planes to fly.
Half my searchlights are smashed and once this bucket gets under
way I doubt that her damaged deck and hull plates can stand the
strain. I won't bother you with the details of turbine, engine, and
boiler failures. Or human failures due to gunfire, wet pants, and that
incurable Oriental illness called lakanuki." He smoothed the wrinkles
out of the dispatch and scribbled the ship's name and his name
and rank across the bottom. "You've been patient and polite,
Lieutenant Doorn. Now go tell your fucking admiral my ship will
be ready to get under way at 0600."

Doorn saluted. His fumbling fingers clipped the dispatch to the
file. Paige glared at him. "You got your pound of flesh. Now
scram."

"The sickness." Doorn groped for the words. "It is required I
make full report to Admiral Onderdonck where there is a serious
sickness."

"I reported the dead and wounded. Nobody's got time here
to be sick."

"You spoke of an Oriental illness, Captain . . . ?"

"Ah. The *Oriental* illness. Yes. By all means. The Oriental
illness. You are right. This must be reported to the admiral."

"The name of it, Captain. Again, please?"

"Lakanuki." Paige spelled it out, lingering on each letter. Doorn
carefully wrote it down.

"There are many cases on board, Captain?"

Paige nodded. "Spreads like wildfire. We're doing our best to
control it." He watched Doorn write it all down. He began to feel
better. He grinned at Doorn. "You're a capable officer, Doorn.
Very thorough. Admiral Onderdonck should be proud of you."

Doorn blushed furiously. "Admiral Onderdonck has already told me how proud he is having *you* with us, Captain Paige."

"After my conduct this morning?"

"He admires your spirit, Captain. He told us so." And smiling boldly added, "He saw you at Antwerp in 1920."

"So did twenty thousand others. Now run along."

"He told us about your broken hand and how you went on to win the Olympic crown."

"Moose shit," Paige said and turned away.

The color drained from Doorn's cheeks. "I meant no harm, sir." He saluted the captain's broad back and marched stiffly out of the cabin.

Paige wanted to call him back, to clap his shoulder and apologize for his rudeness and pour him a slug of the good Dutch gin and sit him down and tell him all about Antwerp and the broken hand and how he had clobbered the Limey favorite. The unexpected mention of it had sprung like a tune of glory in the depths of his despair. My Christ! Why not? Was there no room for honest sentimentality in this smelly cabin in this doomed ship of dead and wounded in this tropical stinkhole of a piss-poor port?

He went to the passageway and watched the young man's skinny legs and the flapping shorts disappear up the steel ladder. He thought again of David. He scratched the frayed sleeve of the old bathrobe, the same one he had worn into the ring that shining day in Antwerp twenty years ago.

Maybe there hadn't been twenty thousand people but they had screamed like a hundred thousand. And a Belgian high school band misplayed *Anchors Aweigh* so bravely you had to forgive them and the big Limey favorite had to be carried feet first from the ring while Paige rode the shoulders of men.

The pipsqueak Dutch lieutenant had brought it back sharp and clear as though it had just happened. And he had given the kid a hard time. Why, Paige? Why must you lash out and hurt? "Be damned," he muttered and the Marine sentry said, "Sir?"

"Do you suppose," Paige said, "a Dutch kid would know a moose if he saw one?"

"I wouldn't know, sir," the sentry said. "I'm from Texas, sir. Ain't never seen a moose, sir."

Paige grinned. "Find Commander Olsen. On the double."

He tried the davenport again. Sleep was impossible with the topside racket. He was too charged with memories of Antwerp to rest. Action. That was it. He leaped up and pawed nervously through the disordered pile of papers. The Dutch admiral was right. Ready or not, he had to get the hell out of here into the open where his ship could fight. He tossed the papers about. A Christly mess. No sense to touch a thing. What the hell good was paperwork with the whole damned ABDA lashup already on its way to the bottom?

Everything gone to hell and the war just begun. The Nip like greased lightning and nothing to stop him. The *Boise* piled up on an uncharted rock in Makassar Strait and the *Marblehead* shot to pieces and her turbines fouled and God alone knows where she lay now, right side to or bottom side up. Manila gone and Singapore doomed and all that hellish convoy duty down the drain and the little men clawing at Java.

In the blood of the morning the last of his scout planes had gone into the drink and on the fantail the remains of the dead were mustered for a dawn burial.

The end of the line, he told himself. All those peacetime years of waiting—for this. The need for glory was a steel-bright thing inside him, fashioned out of schemes and dreams in the drab peacetime years. Now his time had come.

He slammed his fist across the littered desk. He'd be damned if he'd be cheated of it. Not without a fight. Here it was on a silver platter. Thank God for that, he told himself. Thank God for war in my time.

He bunched his fists and smacked them together. The impact shivered his biceps. Silver rattled on the dinner tray. He danced on his toes, feinting and jabbing, driving his arms in short punches. Action. That was it.

"Lee Chin!"

His steward's face appeared at the pantry opening. Paige ducked and bobbed and peppered the air. "Lee!" he rasped.

"Yes, Captain?"

"Rig the punching bag on the double."

"Yes, Captain." Lee Chin skulked about, beseeching Buddha for guidance.

"On the double, damn it!"

Lee Chin scurried around the door and dug into a steel locker

and brought out an inflated leather punching bag. Paige had
stripped to his skivvy shorts. He shadow boxed, ducking and feinting.
Lee Chin moved circuitously toward a corner of the cabin where
a fixture had been welded to the overhead to support the circular
hardwood backboard. It was a precarious approach. The captain
closed in, his fists cutting short ugly arcs dangerously close to the
terrified steward's face.

"How yellow can you get?" He danced in, swinging, grinning.
"Get it up there, damn it."

Lee Chin was by nature and religious preference a peaceful soul
who detested violence in any form. His years at sea with Paige had
taught him to resign himself to this occasional ordeal of Occidental
savagery. He weathered the close barrage of fists and words, not
without a blow or two, accidental or otherwise, to his person and
pride. The captain's words pained him as much as the stinging
blows. They rained about his head. His eyes filled with tears. He
desperately screwed the knob into the socket with trembling fingers.
He managed a shaky smile, a pretense of good-natured enjoyment,
reminding himself of what the captain often preached: Exercise,
Paige said, was good for muscle tone and skin and liver and teeth
and bowels. Lee stayed cooped up in the pantry entirely too much
and his body was flabby and useless and he ought to be ashamed of
himself. He was. Abjectly so. He knew he needed exercise, that
good and clean and somewhat hairy American ritual.

It was the captain's order that Lee Chin fight back and take a
swing or two at the captain. Lee Chin would die first. All he could
do was submit and pray that the honorable knob would secure itself quickly and surely in the honorable socket so he could quickly
and honorably get out of the honorable captain's fucking way.

At last it was done and he fled but not before the honorable
captain dealt him a parting clout across the side of his head, a teeth-
rattling punch that would have worried Dempsey. Lee Chin staggered into the pantry, his ears ringing. He sobbed his relief, out of
breath and brimming with renewed love and devotion for his
captain.

Paige now turned his full attention to the bag, hammering it
with expert rhythmic blows. Back and forth it rocked, right and
left, drumming against the polished board with the precision of
a Prussian soldier. And the captain rejoiced because in his heart

he loved the swift unquestioning obedience of bag and muscle and men.

War was forgotten in this concentrated onslaught, and rancor for the admiral and pity for the resident and fear about his future, all forgotten. The dead above and the wounded below and all the dismal urgencies of his command dissolved. He stood on his toes and the beads of sweat puddled and ran through the coarse fur of his hard-ridged belly. He swung and swayed, exalted, snuffling now and slapping his nose and blowing a fine wet spray, his feet and thighs quivering like a dancer's. Eyes half-closed, ears tuned to the thumping rhythm of the bag, hard fists flying, he was ecstatic and supreme. He was deep in the delight of split-second timing and filled with a giddy sense of power, when he heard the pistol shots.

His fists dropped instantly and he was at the open port in two leaps, scowling into the dark. A cluster of natives was bunched in the light and shadow of the storage sheds, attentive to the spectacle of Turret Three. They did not seem disturbed and could not have heard the shots.

He swung round to the pantry. "You hear those shots, Lee?" Lee had not heard anything except the thumping leather bag and his own pounding heart. The captain crossed the cabin, picked up a towel in passing, and spoke to the sentry outside. The sentry had not heard the shots, either. Had he found the executive officer? The sentry nodded. The executive officer had just phoned to say he would report to the captain's cabin in a few minutes.

Paige stood near the open port and rubbed the towel over his body. He had damned well heard something that sounded like .45-calibre pistol shots and somebody damned well better report it and damned soon.

He sat on the davenport and rubbed his damp head and listened, his trained ears sensitive to the normal clamor of work tools and yard machinery and the hum of the ship's insides. His body tingled and his mind was free of the languor induced by the resident's gin. Fifteen more minutes with the bag was what he needed and a stinging salt shower and a few hours in the sack. He felt his jaw. A shave would help.

Those damned shots. He picked up the phone and asked for the quarterdeck. As soon as he heard the duty quartermaster's crisp voice he changed his mind and hung up. Why the hell

am I so panicky? he wondered sourly. If anything's wrong, they'll
come to me.

He paced the cabin, regretting his jumpy state of nerves. He
would have liked a cigarette but did not care to disobey his own
orders. His phone rang and he grabbed it. It was the ship's operator
passing along the respects of the executive officer. The executive
officer wished to apologize to the captain for the delay in reporting.
It would be another five minutes until he could report to the
captain's cabin unless the matter was extremely urgent. If so, then
he would report immediately. Sir.

Paige cursed. "Tell him to get here when he can." He hung up
scowling. Where the hell do these sailors pick up the fancy language?
He had spent six months trying to explain to the men that he was
an easy skipper. He ran a fighting ship, not a finishing school for
Sea Scouts. Plain language was the order of the day. He tried to
drill that idea into the thick skulls of everyone aboard, officers and
enlisted men, and he gave not a hoot in hell if they were Academy-
trained or mustangs or feather merchants or Asiatics. He knew
damned well he had done a good job of morale, yet there would
be one of these seagoing choirboys who had to do things the
tight-ass way. According to the book. Amos Flint's way, full of
gobbledegook. He chuckled, remembering that Olsen, his executive
officer, had spent a year in battleships with Admiral Flint before
joining *Gloucester* and it could account for his stuffy persistence
to regulations. He would have a word with Olsen on *that*, among
other things.

He went to the punching bag and poked it a few times but his
heart was no longer in it. Those damned pistol shots. He stretched
out once more on the couch. Lee Chin came out of the pantry
with the captain's supper on a silver tray. He set it on the table
and quietly left. Paige got up and poked among the dishes. Nothing
tempted him. He went to the open port and stared out past the
network of cables and wire and the clamor of repairs to the ruins
of the old fort. Beyond the fort the whitewashed village seemed
blue in moonlight and the native *dessa* was dark and silent behind
its towering bamboo hedge.

On the hillside the lights of the resident's house still blazed.
Paige picked up his binoculars and watched the wife in her night-
gown still directing the final loading of the lorries. Paige put down

the binoculars and poured some coffee into a cup and wondered if he would ever see home again.

He tasted the coffee and spit it back and roared for Lee Chin, who came running. "Your goddam coffee's cold, Lee." He smothered Lee Chin's excuses in a stream of vile curses and demanded hot coffee on the double. He stared moodily out of the open port. Four months ago the Dutch resident had put on a show for the visiting Americans. A *gamelan* had played its delicate music of gongs, drums, and cymbals. A troupe of nubile girls had performed the *legong* and there had been a clever shadow puppet play. Now it was hostile faces and steel rails and a place to bury the dead.

He could see the Oriental profile of Lee Chin through the pantry opening. The steward was pouring fresh hot coffee into the silver pot. His lips moved and the sight of him sulking and muttering both cheered and saddened the captain. Pray, you sweet heathen bastard, he thought. We need all the help we can get.

The yeoman returned with the typed battle report. Paige read it carefully and signed it and instructed the man to deliver a copy at once to the radio shack for transmission to joint command and the original by motor whaleboat to Admiral Onderdonck in the Dutch flagship.

A paper had fallen from his littered desk during his workout. He picked it up and smoothed it and read it. It was a copy of a dispatch he had sent a month ago to his father-in-law in Washington.

> TO: ISAAC HOLT BLATCHFORD, COMMODORE, U.S.N.,
>   NAVY DEPARTMENT, WASHINGTON, D.C.
>
> FROM: HARRISON PAIGE, CAPTAIN, U.S.N.
> SUBJ: CHANGE OF DUTY
>   1: FIFTH REQUEST RE: INFO MY ORDERS TO CARRIER
>   COMMAND. WHY THE DELAY? ACKNOWLEDGE.

Nothing had come of it. Nothing ever would.

His own carrier. The sweet, mother-loving sound of it! He tore the paper to bits and stared unhappily out at the teeming dock. It would have been nice, he thought, to skipper a carrier just once before he died.

4

~~~~~~

Olsen arrived hangdog as ever. Paige waved him to a seat and poured coffee.

"I heard pistol shots, Oley."

Olsen sipped and avoided the captain's eyes. Paige sat heavily. The fan's breeze splayed the frayed tassel of his robe. He studied it. Grass skirts. Antwerp, he thought. Blood. Poor Oley. Quietly now.

"What about it, Oley?"

"Can't even finish a cup of joe, Captain?"

"Oley, what happened out there?"

Olsen drained the cup and winced. "It was Stick."

"What the hell's he done now?"

"It's all squared away."

"I'll throw the book at the crazy bastard. That was a .45. Where'd he get hold of a .45?"

"You want the full report, Captain?"

"I want to know what the hell happened, Oley."

Olsen sighed and set his empty cup on the green baize and came to exaggerated attention. Paige watched dumbly, sick at heart. Olsen saluted, his eyes rolled upward.

"From: Commander Olsen, executive officer. To: Captain Paige, commanding officer. Subject: Incident in Tjilatjap harbor facility, 27 February 1942. 1. Aloysius Wilson, nickname Stick, chief quarter-

master, former Annapolis towel boy, did on this date load himself
to the gunwales on torpedo juice, source unknown ha ha, and did
jump ship, no liberty being provided, and unobserved by dock
sentries, OD, sky lookouts, security patrol and other personnel responsible and otherwise, took off up the beach like there was a
fireball up his ass and grabbed ahold of a passing gook girl, name
and occupation unknown, the United States then being in a state
of war."

"Sit down, Oley."

Olsen sat and wiped his eyes.

"Who had the deck?"

"Newell. The new ensign we picked up in Darwin."

"The one they call Sourpuss?"

Olsen nodded.

"Who got shot?"

"Nobody."

"Damn that Stick. I'm busting him back to seaman second so
fast his ears'll whistle."

"Stick's okay, Captain. Everything's four-oh."

"I've been too damned nice to that overgrown Dead End kid.
He took a shot at her, that it?"

"Nobody shot nobody, Captain, is what I'm trying to bring
out. Newell, the OD, saw Stick with this native broad not twenty
yards from the ship on the other side of the freight tracks in a palm
grove near the storage sheds. He was bare-ass naked and in the
act of boarding her and she was screaming blue murder. Newell
sent a man to break it up. Stick broke the man up. Newell lost his
head and pulled his .45 and fired a couple of shots. Stick still
wouldn't let go and Newell went down there—"

"He left the quarterdeck?"

"—and ordered Stick back on board and Stick said some nasty
things and Newell clubbed him."

"He struck an enlisted man? The officer of the deck?"

"Just once."

"Why the hell wasn't I informed?"

"This is in the way of a report, sir, you might say."

"Might say my ass. What the hell's going on with these guys?
Thirty-seven dead on the fantail and they carry on like it's Fourth
of July at Coney Island. What are we running—a warship or a
three-ring circus?"

"Newell reported the incident immediately and the dock sentry lugged Stick back on board."

"What about the girl?"

"Took off like a deer."

"Where's Stick?"

"Below, sir, sleeping it off."

"I want him here on the double."

"He's in rough shape, Captain."

"What did Newell slug him with?"

"The butt of his sidearm. It stunned Stick but he's no worse off than the butt of the .45."

"I'm holding a captain's mast and I'm throwing the book at him. And I want a word with that OD."

"He's still got the deck. I'll send him down when he's relieved."

"You'll get him a relief and send him down now. I never heard of an officer striking an enlisted man."

"He's new, Captain."

"He's a trigger-happy bastard. Somebody could have got hurt. What's his division?"

"Fourth."

"Gunnery?"

"The AA batteries."

"Can he replace Donaldson?"

"Not qualified, sir. But Hurley can. He was Don's assistant. We can take Hurley off of the five inch and put him up in fire control where we lost Don and this Newell can go to Sky One to run air defense."

"Is he Regular Navy?"

"Reserve."

"You feel he can handle air defense?"

"He'll have to. There's no one else."

"Christ."

"That ain't all." Olsen seemed to brighten. "We're just about out of eight-inch ammo. The gunners are hunting all over the ammo depot here."

"We below required minimum?"

"We're at it, period."

"What else, Oley?"

"We logged a new Dutch liaison officer aboard."

"He checked in. What else?"

"A working party's ashore digging graves. The rails are aboard. We're topping off fuel and what ammo we can scrounge. All hands not otherwise occupied are scraping and painting."

"Tell 'em to knock off. Last thing we need now is a paint job."

"There's rust all over this bucket, Captain."

"The hell with it. Let the men rest."

"Is there time for a liberty party?"

"Not a chance. We get under way at 0600."

"Just as well. They've about had it."

"Damn it, Oley, who hasn't? Don't for Christ sake let it get through to the crew. Hear?"

Olsen saluted. "Aye, sir. That be all, sir?"

"All yard help over the side by 0500. General quarters 0530. Set sea details 0545. Under way 0600. Muster the burial party 0500 when the gooks leave. What about the starboard list?"

"First lieutenant reports he can correct to within five degrees, maybe less when we're under way. His repair party's still pumping and just reported plugging the hole where the torpedo went clean through."

"Very well. Good report, Oley. You're a good man." He scratched his chin. "One thing."

"Yes, sir?"

"Smile. You look lovely when you smile."

Olsen smiled woodenly. "How's that, sir?"

"An undertaker would swoon. Listen, Oley. Better move the burial ahead to 0515. Let's do it in style. Muster fifty men in dress whites on the dock. And the ship's band, what's left of it."

"That slices the 0600 deadline kind of thin, sir."

"I'm a fast man with a Bible. Make it a hundred hands. Let these Dutchmen and their gooks see how we Americans respect our dead. Anything else?"

"Just this new ensign, Newell. I checked his service jacket. He put in a couple months at antiaircraft school in California. He did fine. And Donaldson spoke highly of him."

"Don? He did? That's very good."

"His orders have been on your desk for endorsement ever since he came aboard. You might want to check him out yourself."

"I'll get to all that paper crap sometime, but not right now." He passed a hand across his eyes. "You may as well know, Oley, without Don or even with him, we're in real trouble. Here this

Dutch admiral's pulling out and we haven't even started repairs. It can only mean the Nip is moving his airfields close in and can strike whenever and wherever he pleases."

He had stripped off the robe and wet his face and began lathering it. He saw that Olsen had not moved. "That's it, Oley. And for Christ sake, cheer up. We got us enough dead men this trip."

He shaved and stood under the coarse dribble of lukewarm water that was his shower. Oley's had it, he thought. Nutty as a fruitcake. Twenty-four hours more, please God, and nobody's going to be the wiser.

He worked the soap to get a thin lather under the hard water, thinking, Christ, no Nip admiral or captain'd put up with this. In the Imperial Navy they shower in straight sake with perfumed soap held between the thighs of smiling towel girls who rub 'em down and soothe 'em while the admiral recites Oriental poetry. Well, Mister Paige, they're not doing bad at all for a lot of seaweed eaters and poets, are they? Look at your bloody Turret Three. They hit hard and shoot straight and how cocksure they are of winning this war! So cocksure they can stand under a shower of sake being rubbed down by bowlegged naked towel girls while Harry Paige has to settle for a dribble of sea water and a crumb of soap that couldn't lather a fart in a typhoon.

And cranked the fresh memory back through his mind: mast high when they strafed and in Sky One poor Don Donaldson defiant with a .50-calibre machine gun blistering his hands and back in Washington, Frisco, and Pearl the goldbraid on its soft ass while Harry Paige says Amen over thirty-nine boys in the moist Dutch earth.

Letters to the next of kin, fighting the bloody paper war and where the hell were the planes they promised, the fighters and the bombers and the men buried in the bloody war of the red-taped Potomac.

I piss in the Potomac, he told himself, and did.

He remembered Shanghai and Hong Kong and the wire service boys trying their damnedest to know what was going on. But nobody knew anything except how to drink champagne and eat Szechwan duck and pooh pooh the pompous Nip and brag that the mighty *Lex* was on her way with a hundred planes and more to come and hooray for us.

Moose shit. He knew. An Army freighter four days out of Manila on December 7 with fifty-four planes on board could have made all the difference in the world. But some brass hat scared shitless behind a polished oak desk pressed the panic button and the freighter turned back. Oh he knew all right. He had seen the planes that could have saved Manila and Corregidor unloaded on the docks at Surabaya where they did no good at all.

He had seen the wreckage of *Repulse* and *Prince of Wales* off Malaya where the spunky Limey admiral, Tom Phillips, had tried to smash the enemy's eighty ships headed for Singapore and instead had got his own fleet smashed. And let us not forget the oil ablaze at Nichols Field and the sadness at Cavite where nine thousand died and the smooth brown ground of Clark where peacock-proud MacArthur's air force was caught with its pants down.

How now brown down. Turret Three and a finger in the dike, the captain shouted as he staggered down the stairs. Antwerp and the rosy-fingered dawn. I'm a son of a bitch, he said to the latherless lousy soap, and under way at 0600 for nowhere.

5

~~~~~~

The executive officer scratched his fingers up and down the shower curtain. "Captain, I have Chief Petty Officer Wilson with me, sir, in accordance with your instructions, and Ensign Newell standing by."

"Be right out, Oley. Get word to the heads of departments I'd like to see them here in twenty minutes. I'll be finished with Stick Wilson in sixty seconds."

Olsen threw a smart salute at the shower curtain and spoke kindly to Wilson and went out. Wilson stood swaying in the captain's cabin just outside the open bathroom door. He was a short, barrel-shaped man in soiled whites, still drunk, his broad freckled cheeks rimmed with a gummy red beard. Narrow bloodshot eyes blinked sullenly at a wisp of steam escaping from the shower. His arched nostrils sniffed delicately like a querulous hound dog's.

"Stick?"

"Sir?"

"Reach in here and soap my back."

"Yes, sir." Wilson reached through the coarse muslin and began to soap the captain's back. A ghost of a grin touched his cracked discolored lips. The old man was feeling good. Everything was going to be all right. Four-oh. "This is lousy soap, Captain."

"Never mind the soap. You fouled up again."

"Yes, sir."

"You're not getting away with it this time, Stick."

"No, sir."

"I've been too damned easy on you. This time you've gone too far."

"Yes, sir." His roving eye had found the gin bottle on the captain's sideboard. His soaping arm slowed as he schemed.

"Higher. And quit stalling."

"I got soap in my eyes, Captain."

"Too damn bad."

Wilson pawed the air. The soap dripped on the captain's head.

"What the hell you doing?"

"I can't see so good."

"There's a towel in my cabin. Use it and be quick about it. I'm not through with you."

Wilson dropped the soap, glided straight as an arrow to the gin, tilted the bottle and was back soaping vigorously in seven seconds.

"Your eyes better?"

"Oh yes, Captain. Thanks, Captain."

"That's enough soaping. Stand by while I wash off and I'll be with you."

"Aye, Captain."

Wilson leaned against the door frame and closed his eyes and allowed his tongue to slide with slow joy over his lips and as close to his chin as it could reach. Ain't war hell? he thought sweetly. He began to snore.

The captain stepped out of the shower and toweled himself vigorously. "How long you know me, Stick?"

"Sir?"

"Damn it, stand at attention!" Like gelatin stiffening, Wilson complied. The captain leaned toward him and sniffed. "You smell like a goddam Back Basin rum bum." He sniffed again. "Been swapping with the natives?"

"I wouldn't do nothing like that, Captain."

"Steal it?"

"I wouldn't steal nothing from nobody, Captain."

"How long you know me, Stick?"

"Since Annapolis, Captain. When you was champ."

"A long time, Stick."

"Yes, sir."

"Always treated you fair and square? Gave you the breaks?"

"Always, Captain."

"And this is what you do to me."

Wilson looked crookedly at the naked captain and down again. Paige tossed the towel to him. "Dry my back." Wilson rubbed the captain's back. "I'm going to teach you respect, Stick. You were a lousy little roughneck sniping butts on Baltimore's south side when Spike Webb picked you up and gave you a job."

"Yes, sir."

"The best damn towel boy the Academy ever had! Twenty years later you don't have enough dignity or self-control to be a towel boy third class in a Shanghai cat house. Look at you! A pot belly like an old man. How old are you?"

"Thirty-one."

"Thirty-one *what!*"

"Thirty-one years, Captain, sir."

"How long you been out here?"

"Seven years, Captain, sir."

"Knock it off, Stick."

"Yes, sir."

"You're no damned good, Stick."

"Yes, sir. I mean no, sir."

"You're a hell of a good helmsman, Stick."

"Thanks, Captain."

"You were great out there this morning."

"You too, Captain."

"Be damned if I'm going to have a drunk and AWOL helmsman under my command. I'm ashamed of you and I'm ashamed of myself for having faith in you and trusting you." He winced. "Go easy there."

"You got hit, huh?" Stick dabbed the towel gently over a huge purple bruise. "You fell or something?"

"One of your crazy goddam turns."

"It's you who gives the orders, Captain."

"Here, give me the towel and tell Lee Chin to lay out my dress whites in the bedroom."

Wilson grinning went to the galley and spoke to Lee Chin and came back. "You're sure keeping in good shape, Skipper. Working out with the bag now and then?"

"Don't brown nose me, Stick. I'm holding a captain's mast on you. You are charged with stealing a quantity of spiritous liquor—"

"Me? I never stole no liquor!"

"What the hell were you doing in my gin bottle? Building a clipper ship?" He rubbed his face vigorously. "All right. You handled the wheel damned well this morning. We'll let you have that one on the house. Now hear this. You are charged with drinking on board a United States Navy vessel, jumping ship, chasing and attacking a defenseless native girl on foreign soil, resisting arrest, disobeying a superior officer, using obscene and foul language, and conducting yourself in a manner unbefitting a member of the naval service, the United States then being in a state of war."

Lee Chin bustled in and draped the captain's trousers on a bedroom chair and did things with brass buttons and black and gold shoulder boards and the captain's gold aviator's wings and campaign ribbons. Paige put on socks and drawers, trousers and undershirt, all starched stiff and white. He softly cursed the ship's laundry. Wilson stood sullen and eyed the gin bottle.

"It wasn't my fault, Captain."

"The hell it wasn't. It took the gangway sentry and a bosun's mate and a couple of shots from the OD's .45 to tear you away from that poor innocent girl."

"Can I say something?"

"It won't help, Stick. You're guilty as hell."

"Can't I even defend myself?"

"You can try, but I haven't got all night."

"That gook girl's innocent as my ass. Last time we made a liberty here, she took me for everything I had."

"You mean you know her?"

"Like the palm of my hand. And poor she ain't. What with the Limeys and Dutchmen, she owns half the joints in town."

"Go on."

"That night you had them native musicians on board? You know, with the gongs, bells, and whistles? So she gives me the one-man tour of the island and takes me for every red cent plus a cat's eye ring I picked up in Manila, a genuine gold watch I won in the radio shack's floating crap game, and my St. Christopher medal."

"For services rendered?"

"Sure, when you get right down to it."

"And you got right down to it."

"It's what it's for, ain't it? Not just to pee out of?"

"What were you trying for tonight—a rebate?"

"All I was after was my St. Christopher."

"Come on now, Stick."

"I swear to God, Captain! You don't expect I'm going to put to sea in this tore-up old rustbucket without it!"

"It's the goddamnedest excuse for jumping ship I ever heard of."

"It's the God's honest truth, Captain. At heart, I'm a religious person. I don't give a damn for the money or the ring and she can keep the lousy gold watch. It's the St. Christopher I was after, so help me God."

"Did you get it?"

"I almost had my mitts on it when your OD clobbered me." He stared sullenly toward the passageway. "She's still got it."

The captain tucked his undershirt inside his trousers. "I've heard enough, Stick. You're a disgrace to the CPO's. You've messed up in every port we've made. You've been at sea too long and you're too damned Asiatic for my taste. Men died in this ship today. Have you no respect for them? The dead?"

Wilson hung his head. Lee Chin helped the captain into his starched white tunic and began buttoning it. Paige studied his reflection in the mirror. "Just for the record, Stick, so you won't bear any grudges, Commander Olsen tried to cover for you. But I happened to hear the shots and asked the questions and got the answers and the decision is mine. You've endangered the morale and safety of your ship and shipmates and it's my sacred duty to deal out the required punishment." He reached to the dresser and transferred his wallet, a handkerchief, a penknife, and a key case to his pockets. He pushed his gold class ring onto a finger and picked up a round enameled medal on a thin gold chain. He held it a moment, then tossed it to Wilson who caught it. "That's for excellence in ship handling. You can wear it in the brig."

Wilson was still staring at the captain's St. Christopher medal when the executive officer appeared. The captain gently propelled Wilson into the cabin. "Oley, I've just held captain's mast on Aloysius Wilson, chief quartermaster."

"Any punishment, Captain?"

"Three days in the brig on bread and water."

"I'll notify the master-at-arms." Olsen saluted. "Ensign Newell's outside, Captain."

"Very well, I'll see him in a second."

"Stand by for the master-at-arms, Stick," Olsen said. "In the passageway." He went to the phone.

"A word before you go, Stick," the captain said. "An old proverb. 'Sharing makes all men brothers.'"

Tears welled in Wilson's eyes. "Your personal St. Christopher, Captain. I will never forget."

"I mean the native broad. Take him away, Oley."

6

Tod Newell in the passageway tried to remember everything exactly as it had happened. His recollection of the brief and violent contact with Wilson was fresh enough but still bewildering. He was new to deck duties and public displays of violence dismayed him. The sight of a naked man attempting rape was shocking, but it did not seem to fall within the scope of his responsibility as officer of the deck. His orderly mind hastily reviewed his duties as set forth in the reliable pages of *The Watch Officer's Guide*; *Naval Customs, Traditions, and Usage*; and *Naval Leadership*. He had read these texts with intense concentration and committed much to memory. None of the tenets seemed to apply here and Newell decided to regard the strange business as a local native custom and best ignored. But the duty bosun's mate had recognized Wilson as a member of the crew and pointed out to Newell the nature of his responsibilities. Newell had no choice then but to order the gangway sentry to break it up and bring Wilson to the quarterdeck.

Wilson brushed off the sentry with a backward sweep of his thick arm and the man fell. The girl's screams blended with the shrieks and whines of shipboard repair tools and for purposes of succor may as well have remained unuttered. To all this Ensign Newell bore startled witness.

He ordered the bosun's mate to the sentry's aid, a decision delayed by the uneasy awareness that any step taken was subject to scorn and ridicule by the salty enlisted men and Regular Navy officers who made it clear daily he did not belong here.

The action in the grove beyond the storage sheds and freight cars gave him a poignant certainty they were right. He did not belong here and he cursed the authors of *The Naval Watch Officer's Guide*; *Naval Customs, Traditions, and Usage*; and *Naval Leadership* for not preparing him for such a situation.

To his horror, the bosun's mate, like the sentry, fell before the hammer blows of the enraged interrupted Wilson. Newell was alone now. The duty quartermaster had gone to the bridge to wind the chronometers or compensate the alidades or correct the gyrocompass error, or something. Newell often did not clearly understand what it was they said when they approached and saluted and requested his permission to perform some vague duty somewhere.

Obviously what was going on in the grove could not be tolerated and Newell, quite certain he must not desert the quarterdeck, went to the head of the gangway and drew the heavy Colt from its holster at his side and cocked it and aimed skyward and shouted a warning at Wilson. To his intense astonishment two shots fired themselves before he knew it.

The report, blanketed between the din of repair tools and the staccato testing of submersible pumps amidships, was heard by a repair party near the galley deckhouse. Their contemptuous looks embarrassed Newell and with a final sense of outrage he shouted to one of them to come running on the double.

A chief watertender arrived, the classic enlisted man's expression of silent contempt in his wary eyes.

Newell unbuckled the web belt from his waist and thrust it into the chief's arms. "Stand by as officer of the deck," he ordered and before the astonished man could object, Newell was bounding down the gangway.

No one was more surprised than Newell himself when he reached Wilson and ducked a wild haymaker and swung the Colt and dropped him. Together with the sentry and the bosun's mate of the watch, he led Wilson, dazed and profanely resisting, back to the quarterdeck. He sent him below in the custody of the master-at-arms and thanked the bewildered chief watertender for taking over.

All of it had happened in less than three minutes. He sent for coffee and ordered the bosun's mate to check the mooring lines fore and aft and told the quartermaster to enter the details of the incident in the log.

Now in the captain's passageway, Newell nervously reconstructed these details and wondered what the captain's reaction would be.

Wilson meanwhile had come out of the captain's cabin, and Newell in an effort to be both comradely and salty, said, "Sorry I had to do it, sailor," and Wilson, barely glancing up, said, "Fuck you, sir."

Wilson's head was lowered as he mumbled the words and Newell in shock was not sure whether it had been that or "Thank you, sir." The master-at-arms, Krueger, jerked Wilson's sleeve but not before Newell caught the conspiratorial grin. He dared not look the sentry in the eye. He stood numb with embarrassment and watched Wilson and his escort clatter down the ladder. Wilson's words still rang in his ears. He was wondering what page of the *Watch Officer's Guide* covered the situation, when the captain's orderly returned and told him the captain would see him now.

He stood at the desk and faced Paige whose sharp eyes missed nothing. "Relax, Ensign Newell. You're wound tight as a clock."

"Sorry, Captain."

"I'm the one should be sorry, neglecting to welcome you aboard." He waved Newell to a chair. "Get a load off your feet."

"Thank you." Newell sat.

"We've got two minutes, Newell. Why'd you fire those two shots?"

"Captain, it happened before I knew it."

"It just went off? Like that?"

Newell nodded dumbly.

"You might have killed someone."

"I fired into the air, Captain."

"A waste of ammunition."

"What should I have done?"

Paige grunted. "You should have shot Wilson between the eyes." He avoided looking at Olsen who stood directly behind Newell and was grinning insanely. "Why'd you leave the quarterdeck?"

"Wilson refused to obey my order. There was no one else on watch I could send."

"Where was the junior officer of the watch?"

"Making his inspection rounds."

"So you deserted your station."

"I turned the deck over to a chief and was back in three minutes."

Paige frowned. No one had told him about the chief. He glanced at Olsen. "How about that, Oley?"

"Permissible, Captain, in an emergency situation."

Paige looked at Newell with more respect. "Considering you're new to the Navy, we'll let this one go by. But in general, Ensign, an able OD doesn't need to resort to his sidearm to be obeyed and he doesn't desert the quarterdeck. While he's there he's in virtual command of the ship. He has the junior deck officer to help him and a quartermaster and a bosun's mate and as many messengers as he needs. He has the authority to order all hands to general quarters or air raid defense or abandon ship or anything else he feels the situation calls for. But he's responsible for his acts just as I, as commanding officer, am ultimately responsible for whatever acts anyone commits while the ship is under my command. So I'm making damned sure my watch officers know what they're doing. Right, Oley?"

"Right, sir."

"I'm told you struck Wilson."

"Yes, Captain."

"You know you're forbidden to strike an enlisted man?"

"Yes, sir."

"Oley, give him chapter and verse."

"Superiors of every grade are forbidden to injure those under their command by tyrannical or capricious conduct or by abusive language. Authority over subordinates is to be exercised with firmness, but with justice and kindness."

"Thank you, Oley. A very serious dereliction of duty, eh, Oley? What's your opinion?"

"Self-defense, Captain?"

"No excuse. It's the duty of the senior officer present to suppress the disturbance and arrest those engaged in it."

"That's what I did, Captain Paige," Newell said.

"And clobbered Wilson while doing it." He rubbed his chin. "What'd you hit him with?"

"The butt of the pistol, sir."

"Anyone see you hit him?"

"The girl, maybe. It was pretty dark, sir."

"I'm not trying to defend Wilson, understand. He asked for it. But we go by Navy regulations."

"I understand, Captain."

"How long you been aboard?"

"Three weeks, sir."

"Stood many top deck watches?"

"This was my first."

"How come a top deck watch the first time, Oley?"

"He qualified in Darwin while waiting for us, Captain."

"What ship, Newell?"

"*Blackhawk*, Captain."

"Shoot anybody on the *Blackhawk?*"

"No, sir."

"Too bad. She's loaded with more screwball Asiatics than Hong Kong harbor." There was a gleam of affection in his eye. "Any special training?"

"Antiaircraft school, Captain."

"How long?"

"Four weeks."

"What armament?"

"Twenty- and forty-millimeter, sir."

"That's a big help. We don't have either calibre on board. What else?"

"I've put in for advance navigation school."

Paige snorted. "You don't expect to get out of here alive, do you?" He swung around. "Where are his orders, Oley?"

Olsen fished the papers out of the pile. Paige read them, holding the sheets close to his face. He looked up suddenly. "Next of kin: Thomas A. Newell?"

"Yes, sir."

Paige's eyes searched Newell's for several long seconds. "What the hell you doing out here?" he snapped.

"Sir?"

Paige flipped the file onto the desk. "Didn't your old man have a cushy job for you back at the plant?"

Newell flushed but said nothing.

"You must be out of your mother-loving mind." He stared at Newell. "You're the tennis player, right?"

Newell nodded.

"Quarter finals, semifinals, but never a winner, right?"

Newell remained silent.

"I'm right, ain't I? Riggs trimmed you in '39 and Mulloy in '40. Next thing you know, Oley, they'll be sending us one-legged ballet dancers. What else qualifies you for war, besides tennis?"

"Small craft, sir."

"You mean destroyers?"

"Just sailboats, I guess, on Long Island Sound."

"Take him away, Oley, before I burst into tears." He turned to Newell. "We don't have time for society playboys out here, Newell. I lost a damned fine gunnery officer, Commander Donaldson. I'm shifting the gunnery department around and whether I like it or not, you're ending up as air defense officer. You just better to hell forget about tennis and toy sailboats and learn how to shoot those guns. Oley, get him squared away with Hurley and Latham so he can tell muzzle from breech. And if he so much as lays a finger on another enlisted man, it's a general court-martial."

Paige stuck out his hand and shook Newell's. "You're playing with big boys now, Mr. Newell. For keeps. Don't forget it. And get that chip off your shoulder."

"Thank you, sir."

When Newell left, Paige sat at the big table, drumming his fingers on the green cloth. "I met his old man once, Oley. Any kid's been able to live with that one, should get by out here. But I doubt it. This joker has never had it tough."

"Donaldson liked him."

"He's a born loser, Oley. Soft and spoiled. He quits in the stretch." He closed his eyes. "Okay, Oley. Carry on."

He sat alone, waiting for the others. Newell, he thought. Of Newell, Connecticut. Of Newell Industries and a thousand-acre showplace with a small lake and eighteen holes on manicured greens surrounding an authentic eighteenth-century stonepile called "Newellton." Heavy farm and road equipment. Tractors, bull-dozers, steam shovels, trucks, half-tracks. And lately, in conjunction with the family-owned Todhunter Arms Corporation, mobile ar-mament, gun mounts, tanks, and tank destroyers. Rifles, pistols, automatic weapons, bullets, and powder. Chemistry research and hush-hush military projects.

Now why should a kid named Todhunter Newell, a spoiled tennis bum without the moxie to go the full distance, with the opportunity to do a noble and patriotic job for his country right there in his own back yard, bother to come out here? Why run the risk of being shark bait when his old man could buy him into any cozy stateside billet his little heart desires?

He had met Thomas A. Newell one summer in the thirties. It was during the trial run of a new destroyer being built at the Bath Iron Works in Maine. The destroyer had been fitted out with an experimental Newell Industries product—an advanced type of submarine detection gear and Newell himself had come to witness the runs.

Paige was flattered that Newell knew who he was and at luncheon had nothing but praise for Paige's ring record. "When you're fed up with what you're doing," Newell had laughed, "come and see me. Newell Corp needs a fighting athletic director and sure as hell you'll see more action with us than you're seeing in the peacetime Navy."

Paige had thought about that many times during those peace-ridden years. It was something to play with until a war arrived.

The p.a. speaker blared. *Fueling completed. Smoking lamp is lighted throughout the ship.* Paige reached for his cigarettes. Well, thanks for small favors, he reflected, and struck the match. He was content where he was. Hot as he was. Doomed as he was.

7

The heads of departments, Navy officers of the line, sat in worn leather chairs round the captain's table. Their bodies and minds ached from the sea and the strain of duty was etched in their faces. They had the look of men who played a losing game too long.

Olsen sat alone in a state a qualified physician might describe as catatonic. His eyes were fixed on the deck. Not a muscle moved. These men knew Olsen well and respected him and they did not allow their glances to dwell too long or too directly on him. They knew it could have just as easily been one of them.

There were four of them. Lieutenant Commander Joe Allen alone was not an Annapolis graduate. He was carrying on the duties of the navigator who had come down with dysentery and had been detached from the ship in Darwin. He sat studying the raised lettering of the gold ring on his thick fourth finger. It was a replica of the Academy class rings the others wore except that his said UNITED STATES NAVY. It made all the difference in the world to Joe Allen.

The engineering officer held a silver spoon and traced the outline of the blue anchor on the coffee cup before him. The first lieutenant leaned back with his eyes half-closed listening to the blend of the captain's voice with the staccato of power tools topside, regretting it wasn't Beethoven's Fifth. Hurley, the acting gunnery officer, was dead Donaldson's replacement. He had arrived last from the damaged handling room where he had supervised the transfer forward of Turret Three's ammunition.

They sipped coffee and smoked and listened to Paige give his standard man-to-man talk with the underlying do-or-die a football coach might use between halves to goad his losing team to victory. No one believed it except Joe Allen.

"I'm not beating about the bush, men. You were a damned fine team when I took over from Goody Lord. When Goody was killed at Pearl, the Navy lost one of her best. Well, he left me a fine ship and a crew equal to any in the fleet, bar none. All I've tried to do is to live up to Goody's standard.

"For the past few months we've been in sore need of major drydock and overhaul, not to mention rest and recreation. At 2200, I'm meeting with the Dutch admiral along with the rest of the ship's captains. Soon as I have the hot dope, I'll pass it on to you all. This much I know. We're getting under way at 0600. From what I've seen and heard, and from what I feel, we're not going to make it back." He paused. Their startled expressions gave him a curious satisfaction.

"Let's face it. We're losing this war." He pointed to a chart. "The Nip's closing in from the South China Sea here and from the Celebes Sea and from the Timor Sea. He packs plenty of wallop and he's hitting with everything he's got. He owns the sky. He lands his troops wherever it pleases him to land. He takes what he wants when he wants and we can't do a damned thing to stop him. All we can try to do is slow him down a little. If we slow him here, it allows precious time to beef up our forces in Australia. And when Australia goes, everything goes.

"Now let's take a look at ourselves. Present condition of readiness is pretty bad. We still pack a wallop but one-third of our major fire power is gone. We're helpless astern on long range. The secondary five-inch stuff amidships will have to carry the load. And we're shy almost forty men.

"Air defense is adequate but hasn't proven itself yet against the Nip's high-level bombing. If we had some of this new radar and fire-control equipment we'd be okay, but that's wishful thinking until we drydock someplace where we can get a major overhaul. And we don't have Donaldson any more to run the show.

"Morale. I know the men are dead on their feet. Standing watch-

on, watch-off isn't making things easier. And once we shove off I've
got a sneaking suspicion it'll be battle stations around the clock for
everyone.

"Get word to your division officers I want a thorough inspection
of life rafts, survival gear, all machinery connected with abandon
ship routine. I want all hands to wear life jackets and flash gear. I
want them to carry belt knives and flashlights and anything else we
can dredge up from the ship's stores that'll help in case of trouble."

"Expecting trouble, Captain?" the first lieutenant asked.

"You kidding?" Paige grinned crookedly. "If it don't show up, I
intend to look for it. All outgoing mail should get off before we
shove. A few words is all they need and tell them for Christ sake
to be careful what they write because there's no time to censor it."

"What about the dead, Captain?"

"We bury them at dawn. They're dead and their worries are over.
You and I have got the real worries. Maybe the Nip'll get Java but
he sure as hell is going to buy it a man at a time, a ship at a time. If
the orders were mine to give, I'd quit this hooligan fleet. I'd belt
my way out to the open sea and take 'em where I find 'em. And I'd
damned well find 'em." He smiled bleakly. "Big talk. The smart
move would be to run for cover south and east and refit and come
back fighting. But who's smart these days? MacArthur?"

They were silent. The vibration of ship machinery throbbing and
the steady sound of repair parties topside was all they heard. He
rapped his knuckled fist on the green baize cloth. "Any questions?"

"The charts, Captain." It was Joe Allen.

"What's wrong with them?"

"They're mostly British Admiralty from 1897. Some are German
and falling apart and scribbled all over in Holland Dutch. ABDA
command's supposed to be flying a fresh batch in from Surabaya."

"Nothing's flying in here except Japs, Joe. Let's use what we got
and pray."

"You say under way at 0600." The engineering officer shook his
head. "We got us a power plant in name only. We could spend a
week on the whole lash-up and get no better than maybe seventy
percent efficiency."

"I'm short hands in central station, Captain, and using ship's
cooks for shipfitters," the first lieutenant said.

"Good idea," said the captain, "now maybe the chow'll improve."
He turned to Olsen. "How's with you, Oley?"

"The laundry's run out of starch, sir, but we're carrying on."

Nobody smiled except Paige. "There you have it, gentlemen. We're in fighting trim and ready to give 'em hell." He turned to Hurley. "Any armament left that can shoot, Guns?"

Hurley blushed with pride. It was the first time he had ever been called "Guns."

"Turrets One and Two, Captain. They're still shifting the eight-inch stuff from Turret Three forward. We'll be manned and ready by dawn, sir."

"Now that's more like it."

"We're short maybe a hundred rounds of eight-inch ammo."

"How come?"

"Some of it went over the side when the bomb hit Turret Three."

"What about the ammo depot here?"

"The Dutch stuff doesn't fit our guns."

Paige was silent for a moment, the humor gone from his face. He turned to Olsen again. "Oley, have the ship's sailmaker lay up here on the double."

Olsen phoned the quarterdeck. The slow minutes passed, the officers smoking, whispering, venturing to guess what was in the captain's mind and not caring to look at him.

Chusak the sailmaker arrived, a bald, sleepy man with the pasty look of a shut-in. He stared at the assembled officers through red puffy eyes. "Give him a cup of joe," the captain ordered and Chusak took it and stood apart, a thick finger hooked into the mug handle.

"How many shrouds topside, Chusak?"

"Thirty-seven, Captain." As though he doesn't know, Chusak sniffed to himself. "And two more below."

"Prepared for sea burial, weren't they?"

"Those were the orders I got. The last stitch through every nose." And thinking now he understood why he had been so unceremoniously routed from his sack, went on. "Wasn't my fault, Captain. If I knew it was a cemetery they were going to—"

"Never mind that. What's in them, five- or eight-inch?"

"Eight-inch, Captain."

"Why not five?"

Chusak shrugged. "Sharks is faster than gravity. With an eight-inch shell they sink real fast."

"I don't see that it makes much difference," Paige said.

"It does, sir, really," Chusak said, a professional jealous of his craft.

"Okay, Chusak. Get some extra hands and open those shrouds and turn the shells over to Gunnery."

Chusak bent a little as though an elbow had been poked in his middle. "Now, Captain?"

"Now, Chusak."

"You mean, cut open all that canvas and take the shells out and sew the canvas up again?"

"That's exactly what I mean."

Chusak stared at the others. None of them said a word.

"On the double, Chusak," the captain said.

Chusak departed, muttering. Paige looked at the others. Olsen alone did not drop his gaze. "Good thing they're eight-inch and not five," Paige said. No one said anything. "I know what you're thinking," Paige said softly. "You're thinking what a cold-blooded bastard is Hardtack Harry Paige, to desecrate the dead like that. Well, let me tell you this: Those thirty-seven projectiles'll do us more good here where they belong than in any goddam cemetery. And I'd do it again if it meant the difference between living and dying. So wipe the holier-than-thou looks off your faces and thank God I *am* what I am and maybe we'll have a fighting chance of getting out of here. Any other complaints?" He waited a few seconds. "All right. We remain in Condition Two through the night until morning general quarters. Burial service at 0515, set sea details at 0545, under way at six. When I return from this so-called conference with the Dutch admiral, I'll send word to each of you if there's anything you should know. Meanwhile, knock off the gloom or you'll have the whole damned crew thinking the war is already lost. This is just the beginning. That's all, gentlemen."

They nodded and filed out. Olsen lingered. "Your gig's standing by, Captain. The Dutch lieutenant, Doorn, is going with you to translate."

"Thanks, Oley. You feel okay?"

"Four-oh, Captain."

"You look like death warmed over."

"Thank you, sir."

"Keep smiling, Oley, and get those thirty-seven rounds of ammo where they can do the most good."

"Yes, sir." He turned to go.

"Oley?"

"Sir?"

"About the laundry. Don't worry. We'll pick up more starch in Pearl."

8

~~~~~~

Admiral Onderdonck spoke in the tired cultivated voice he used to
address a class of cadet students. The ships' captains pretended to
listen attentively but only the Dutch understood what the admiral
said. Paige sat near the closed door and behind him Doorn bent
slightly to translate the admiral's words. "He regrets the necessity,"
the young man hissed, "of asking American and British and Australian ships—to stand by him. It is the decision—of ABDA joint
command—and until there are further orders—they will remain in
the area—and defend the Java coast. Our allied nations—are buying
time to survive—at the cost of the ships you command. He prays—
that it is not at the cost of extinction for each of you—but for the
present at least, each unit must be regarded—as expendable."

There was coffee, black and hot, and several liqueurs. Paige sam-
pled them all. He closed his ears to the soft useless words and wished
to hell he could shove off and see how things were going in
Gloucester.

An aide took over and indicated on a large blackboard the disposition of the nearest Japanese carrier-battleship force reported
earlier that afternoon by a PBY on reconnaissance patrol. Other
invasion forces were in the area and plans had been drawn to meet
the situation.

Another aide moved among the officers present and passed out
sealed envelopes with the operations orders for the following day.

The admiral stood near the doorway and as each ship's captain departed, he shook his hand. "*God zegen u allen!*" Paige was annoyed to see tears in the old man's eyes.

It was a five-minute run in the gig across the open water from the anchored Dutch flagship back to *Gloucester*. Paige sat moodily with the long envelope in his fingers idly knocking it against the cushions. He would have liked nothing better than to tear it open and read the admiral's orders for the morning sortie, but Lieutenant Doorn sat facing him with a look of puppydog devotion. Paige reflected on the degree of shock he could generate in that soft face by simply casually taking the envelope and ripping the seal. It was a most impressive seal of musky red wax impressed with the royal coat of arms. You had to give it to the damned Dutch. Win or lose, they sure as hell ran a fancy dress Navy.

When the gig arrived alongside, Olsen was right there on the ball, waiting to meet him. Paige realized with unexpected affection he still had a taut and happy ship and in these calamitous hours it was something to be thankful for. He thought, What a great idea it would be to haul ass down to the cabin with Oley and break out a fifth of the resident's gin and shoot the breeze about the good old days on the China station.

Grinning, he snapped a sharp salute into Oley's blank face and swinging to salute the colors aft saw the hurt look in Oley's blue eyes and knew there was trouble again.

He listened numbly while Olsen told him. Stick Wilson had broken out of the brig and jumped ship and was on the loose again.

A senseless rage made his tongue feel thick. He pulled Olsen by the arm until they were out of hearing of the quarterdeck watch. "If that stupid bastard has to be treated like a mad dog, he has come smack dab against the right man."

"We'll get him back aboard, Captain," Olsen promised. "Give us time."

"This is an order, Oley. Muster a search party on the double. Find him and get him back on board and slap him in the brig. I want him in chains, hear?" Olsen said nothing. "You hear, Oley?"

"Chain him. Yes, Captain."

"For his own good, Oley. In his condition he's liable to hurt somebody."

"Chains. Yes, Captain. For his own good."

"For Christ sake, Oley, how'd he do it?"

"The brig guard left the key where Stick could get it. Then he doped off and Stick jumped ship." He began to laugh. "A little like old times, eh, Harry?" Olsen could not stop laughing. Paige stared at him in horror and stalked away.

The search party caught up with Wilson by following a trail of excited native police, some cowed, others bleeding, helmets awry, all angry. They had made the mistake of trying to stop him. Wilson, drunker than before, had cursed and carved his way with the jagged neck of the captain's gin bottle into the native *dessa* to the sleeping mat of the girl who had his St. Christopher medal. The search party surprised him *flagrante delicto*. In reporting the capture, the junior officer in charge of the search party derived a shameless vicarious pleasure in reporting that the moments of entry were simultaneous.

The prisoner had an odd request. He wanted to see the captain. The captain refused and issued orders to manacle the prisoner's wrists and return him to the brig. No one thought to search the prisoner. By using a file kept for such purposes inside his sock and shoe, Stick filed himself free and tried to jump ship for the third time.

The officer of the deck standing the midwatch caught sight of Wilson's chunky figure in skivvy shorts sliding down a mooring line in moonlight. He made the necessary preparations. When Wilson cleared the rat guard and reached the dock, the gangway sentry instantly clubbed him into a state of semiconsciousness with the butt of his rifle and he was dragged on board.

The captain, awakened again, ordered the prisoner locked in a storeroom, chained hand and foot to stanchions, with a sentry to stand watch for the balance of the night. Wilson, revived, received word of his punishment in a subdued manner. They stripped him to the waist and Krueger, the master-at-arms, cursed him while ring-bolts were welded to the bulkheads. A length of chain was passed through the ringbolts. Leg irons were snapped round Wilson's ankles. Krueger, a thirty-year man with no love for Wilson, observed with pleasure that the small of the prisoner's back rested directly on a dogged-down hatch cover. Its clamps dug cruelly into the flesh.

These were the captain's orders, Krueger told his prisoner. He didn't make the rules. He only carried them out. Nor had he chosen the place or the form of punishment and Stick Wilson could end up with raw holes in his back for all Krueger cared. Wilson taunted him. "How's about the thirty bucks you owe me from shootin' crap last week?"

Krueger sent a smashing kick to Wilson's ribs. "That's the down payment, you crud." He kicked again. "And that's for giving Navy Chiefs a lousy name."

Wilson grinned through bloody cracked lips. "My old pal, Krueger."

"I'm doing my duty is all, so quit bitching."

"Up yours."

Krueger put the heel of his shoe in Wilson's groin and stamped down. The color drained from Wilson's face but he did not utter a sound. "Like it?" Krueger asked.

"You're a real hero, you kraut prick."

Krueger kicked him again. The blood under Wilson's back made a sucking sound. He groaned and passed out.

"What's a matter?" Krueger taunted. "That little bit of gook poontang already beginning to burn?"

Unable to sleep, Paige spent the next few hours writing letters. He cleared a space on his cluttered desk and wrote with a steady, slanted scrawl and occasional flourishes. From time to time he glanced at a blue leather frame embossed with a gold anchor inside of which were the faces of his wife and son.

To his son David he wrote a curiously stuffy and humorless note. Somewhere in the coils of his mind was the misguided notion that Lord Chesterfield's gems of paternal guidance were exactly what every young man should have from his father. He felt he owed the boy something of this nature to guide him, should he, Paige, not return. So he stressed the necessity for excellence in all departments and modestly acknowledged his own failure in several and the deep regret he felt because of it. He pointed up the maternal heritage of being a Blatchford, a legacy of courage and fame through five wars, and the responsibility therein for David to conduct himself with gallantry and honor. In the same way he, the father now at war, hoped to measure up to the challenge so that the name of Paige would shine as brightly in naval history as that of Blatchford and Holt, Farragut, Jones and Decatur. Your ever-loving Dad.

The letter to his wife Felicia was no different from its infrequent predecessors—a terse yet dutiful accounting of his state of health and the automatic inquiry after hers; an interchangeable arrangement of tired clichés invoked by rules and years of censorship and the tradition of naval reticence. He realized the futility of trying to keep from her his whereabouts and the nature of his duty because certainly she had access to such restricted information through her father, the commodore, should she care to inquire.

He put the letter with the others to be mailed at dawn and sat at his desk and for an hour worked smoothly without interruption. He initialed directives and signed orders and when the detail work was done he rose and stretched, pleased that the immediate and possibly final disposition of his detested paperwork was done.

He considered phoning below to inquire after the prisoner in the brig and decided not to. It was almost four o'clock. He stripped and turned in, directing the flow of forced air to carom off the bulkhead and cool his nakedness under the thin sheet.

The noise of repairs at Turret Three had ceased. Heavy welding's done, he thought. The rails are in. Thank God. He rested with his arms beneath his head, his ears tuned to the hum of ship's machinery, soft murmurs in a passageway, the muffled scrape of leather on the ladders as the watch changed. The sense of order comforted him. Sweat cooled clinging in the fan's breeze and joined him to the bedsheet. Stick's a bloody fool, he thought. Let him rot a while.

A bare hour remained until the ship would come to life again. He lay wide-eyed with the empty feeling of a man who knows his time has come and he will not live through another day. He did not care to dwell on that. His conscience was clear. His duty done. If he had sinned, he also had served. Celestial arithmetic was not his line. God & Company could handle that. He would know in the morning when he opened his orders, what the odds would be for or against Paradise.

His only regret was losing Felicia whom he truly loved. He got out of bed and took her letter from the envelope and tore it to pieces and wrote her another so drenched in love he dared not reread it but thrust it in the envelope and sealed it and went back to bed. In all of his life, in all he had done and said, he had never revealed so much of himself, his feelings, his deepest needs.

He slept almost at once, at peace, snoring slightly, his hands clasped under his head, his nakedness revealed and gleaming with sweat. He was a boy again dreaming, a slender boy with a Navy captain's mind and his mother, smiling and younger and more beautiful than he truly remembered her, rocked him with a lullaby.

Sleeping, he smiled. The drunken old girl had never crooned him a lullaby in all her life.

Ensign Newell wrote no letters. Nor did he sleep. He sprawled in his narrow bunk feeling angry at himself. He had stood his first top watch on his first ship. Like the rest of his life it had gone sour. The captain knew. Everyone knew.

Had it really been "Thank you"? he wondered. Not likely from a brute like Wilson. He wished he were dead. Or asleep. He covered his head to soften the snores of the two planeless pilots in the bunks below him. The cabin smelled of sweaty bodies and charred clothes and cordite and the junior officers' "head." A faulty blower rattled pushing warm air through the flaking duct. Newell thought back to the trouble that brought him here.

Amy Trowbridge. Dynasty, they had told him. To mate the Newell wealth and power with the blueblooded Trowbridge shipping fortune would be an alliance to make nations tremble. The first date was so easy it frightened him. "A basic physiological function," said Amy casually dropping her drawers. "As natural, Toddsy, as a bowel movement."

Well hooray for dynasty, he decided later, even if it was ruining his forehand drive. He wondered what else she had learned at Wellesley. The wedding was set for a year from June.

It was the same summer he lowered the boom on his father. After three years at Newell Industries, he was fed up with the indignity of being the boss's son. His bright but unseasoned ideas met a wall of conservative refusal. Rockribbed executive vice-presidents spoke to Newell Senior of the boy's great promise and behind his back did what they could to destroy him.

He bid them goodbye and went back to tennis, Amy, and sailing full time. After a night of too many martinis and too much Amy and a day of shame on the courts at Forest Hills, he drove alone to Boston and enlisted in the Navy.

He made the sentimental mistake a week later of phoning Amy who flew at once to Boston and spoke her piece.

"Just what am I supposed to do while you're out there playing sailor boy? Keep it in moth balls? Sit around and twiddle my thing until Toddsy comes marching home? Do you think I'm made of steel, darling?"

He nodded brightly. "Yes."

"You must be out of your mind," Amy raged, "to go off and do such a childish thing. I've been worried sick and anyway, if you feel obliged to do your duty for your country, you don't need that silly sailor suit. You can do it from the executive offices of Newell Industries. This absolutely insane idea of enlisting as an ordinary sailor when we're not even at war is perfect proof you haven't grown up, you're still a child and I blame no one but your mother. Don't think for a moment I haven't heard how she's babied and pampered and sheltered you and if you think for one minute after we're married she is going to have a single solitary word to say about what you eat or wear or do, you've another guess coming, my dear."

The ultimate *my dear* startled Tod with its inflective resemblance to his mother's imperious endearments. One father is enough, he mused, but two mothers?

He celebrated the rupture with a night on the town in the lively environs of Scollay Square with sailors no less determined to drown in drink than he. He passed the balance of the night with an astonishing blonde whose talents began where Amy's dropped off.

He was hung over the next morning and barely made it to the Navy Yard in time. He was dismayed to be ordered to the commandant's office where a well-preserved visitor in a stiff collar and Brooks Brothers suit awaited him. The gentleman was John Prentiss Loring II, director of the Boston offices of Newell Industries. His business was brief. Newell Senior had delegated him to locate his son and see if there was anything to be done for him.

There was not, Tod said. The Navy was providing employment, food, clothing, shelter, pocket money, and discipline. He felt sorry for Mr. Loring, a gentleman with whom he had in the past corresponded on routine corporation business. Mr. Loring seemed embarrassed by the meeting and embarrassed by the chore demanded of him. Demanded is certainly the word, Tod thought. He knew too well how his father went about these things. He decided not to feel sorry for John Prentiss Loring II because the old gaffer received but did not earn a cool $40,000 a year plus bonuses, dividends, and stock options.

"Go back and tell my father to run his own errands," Tod said. Saying goodbye to Loring gave him a curious feeling in his throat. He could not keep from laughing.

He was transferred from Boston to a sixty-day officer candidate school and emerged with the temporary rank of ensign and a grinding hatred for martinets. His first assignment was to an anti-aircraft gunnery school on the coast near Redwood City where the targets were streamed behind tow planes over the Pacific and he was taught to direct Oerlikon 20-mm and Bofors 40-mm gunnery crews.

His orders came for duty aboard *Gloucester* which, typically, had no twenties or forties. While awaiting transportation in San Francisco late in November 1941, he met with his father for the last time before going overseas. Newell Senior offered to forgive his son on one condition: that he, Newell Senior, would demand of his circle of friends surrounding the President of the United States his son's return to duty at Newell Industries where he was vitally needed for the defense effort. Tod thanked his father and said he preferred being treated like the rest of the guys and that's the way it was.

A week later he was aboard a new fleet tanker enroute to Australia to pick up *Gloucester*. Two days southwest of Pearl, after a week of great tennis at the club, he was sunbathing on the deck of a PT boat lashed to the tanker's well deck. The word was passed on the bombing of Pearl Harbor. Newell went below and took the three tennis racquets out of his foot locker and heaved them over the side, presses, covers, balls, and all.

He lay around Darwin itching for action and standing temporary OD duty in *Blackhawk*. Two weeks later *Gloucester* stood into the harbor. Her decks were crowded with civilian refugees from Manila and Corregidor and all the beleaguered outposts of the Asiatic station. The women and children looked dazed and bereft. The men were old and helpless. *Gloucester*'s war paint flaked her sides and her crew looked underfed and tired. He reported aboard at once and handed to an officer of the deck his orders, now crosshatched with countless endorsements of the interim commands. He was led below to Commander Olsen who bleakly wished him a Merry Christmas.

He would never forget that first night aboard. His ship. Something his old man didn't own or buy for him or demand of him. He lay in the stifling dark close to a dank dripping bulkhead. The sea pounded and the bunk chains rattled and loose gear slid and he was twenty-six years old and had never got past the semi-finals of anything and he had finally run away and it was a long way to run but he knew it would have to be a long way and it was worth every mile of it because he had done it himself. No one had told him to or how or yes or no and that was a damned fine thing for Todhunter Newell to know. It was funny, he thought, remembering what Amy had said about keeping it in moth balls and he laughed about it and cried a little and rolled over in his narrow bunk and made room for Amy.

9

At sea no man sleeps easy. In port as well, a time of night comes sailors dread. The moored ship is still. There is no rush of sea to make it live, no pulse but a throb so faint it shapes the death wish, nothing more.

Men sleep. Men twitch and dream. Men stare at dials and levers, blackness, nothing, waiting for the sea again, green and cold, blue and warm, just so it's sea.

In *Gloucester* this last night the tools of burial were finally laid to rest. Palm and needle, stiff canvas shrouds, pine smooth and clean, bright nails. Small shut Bibles sat like mourners silent and grave. The bosun's pipe was dry and stilled.

The clamor of tools ebbed. From a temple somewhere in the dark, buried in a thicket of palms fringing the foothills, a low throb of music pulsed over the village, rode like a whisper on the night air. Men woke, stirred uneasily and wondered. It was an ungodly hour for ritual in a temple, for the lucent pleading chime and gong blended into a delicate antique melody.

The men in the stifling ovens of the ship and on the warped decks and in watch stations aloft heard this alien melody and found it comforting. It seemed to speak to men everywhere and the men listened.

Pray, it said.

The din of power tools resumed, abrupt and dissonant, drowning the cadence of the temple's soothing *gamelan*. The men could no longer hear the ancient melody. Some quickly forgot it. For others its haunting sound would comfort them forever.

For these men, forever would not be long in coming. For others it had arrived. Thirty-nine pine coffins bore witness, awaiting their rendezvous with worms. They were lined in crooked rows on the open hangar deck amidships, carried there in the night to ease the morning transfer from steel to earth. Guns in the wooden boxes would have served the men better, or bullets or beef or the company of whores. Anything but the useless mutilated flesh and shattered bones stuffed and sewn in canvas already slashed, stripped by need and the captain's orders of their last symbol of dignity, the phallic eight-inch projectile.

In the morning the living too would go somewhere to die, to a place not yet certain by latitude and longitude (but that is how it would finally be reckoned); and no one of them would refuse. Such is the code of good men.

The season of defeat is also the season of the west monsoon and in Java, land of the vertical sun, the rainfall is heaviest. Flora and fauna thrive and the insect life is an excess of pullulant boisterous procreation. Take for example the *Perichaeta musica*, a remarkable worm that eventually grows to a length of twenty inches and is capable of producing melodious musical sounds. It thrives on wood and flesh rot and when its time comes, it too goes somewhere to die but has no awareness of courage or sacrifice. Its only code is survival and it does not really care where it dies or if the melodious music it produces has anything to do with living or dying.

There was music and mourners to bury *Gloucester's* dead that grim dawn, furnished by the full complement of musicians and marchers demanded by the captain. No flags flew. The cargo nets sagged limply, glistening like spiders' webs heavy with dew. The ship's band led the cortege to the cemetery. Torrential rain lashed down as the coffins were lowered into the muddy graves. Because of the rain, some of the instruments seemed blurry and off key.

The sailors were sad and too tired to notice. Several native fishermen wearing straw hats like hoops and carrying nets and spears, watched curiously as the procession slogged by. Some bared their heads knowing the strangers were Christians and this was their custom. Out of respect for the dead they did not comment to each other on the guttural thumping of the instruments, so coarse-sounding and so full of holes, so different from their tinkling delicate *gamelan*.

Captain Paige spoke with a pitchman's ease, not reading from the Bible he held. Rivulets of rain coursed down the cheeks of the men, giving a comic impression that each wept copious tears. The sun rose at 0547. Two minutes later the men were back aboard and the ships of the hooligan fleet stood out from Tjilatjap on schedule, the crews at battle stations, the dead at rest in the earth to thrive.

The sortie was without incident except for a sleepy storekeeper who, on arriving at his general quarters station, observed the blood and pain of Stick Wilson who neither slept nor was unconscious, who could not or would not speak, whose eyes alone expressed his contempt for minor authority. The storekeeper reported the fact to his chief who advised the executive officer who dispatched the master-at-arms, Krueger, who reluctantly released Wilson to the custody of the sick bay.

10

~~~~~~

Captain Paige in his cramped sea cabin on *Gloucester*'s bridge tore open the envelope and looked at his orders. He called for Doorn who arrived almost immediately. Paige thrust the orders at him and the young lieutenant began to translate.

Commencing at 0630, he read, the force would split into two groups. The larger group with the Dutch flag cruiser as its mainstay, would continue eastward and during the night turn north through Bali Strait, its primary mission to intercept the heavy concentration of enemy invasion forces moving southward through Makassar Strait. Its secondary mission was to divert enemy attention from the movements of the second group, but to avoid engagement wherever possible with equal forces of enemy ships-of-the-line.

The second group composed of *Gloucester* and two American destroyers, *Hurlburt* and *Cushman*, would proceed one hundred miles southwest of Tjilatjap to a point north of tiny Christmas Island, to rendezvous with an Allied merchantman convoy. The convoy was bound for Bombay from the Australian port of Fremantle. It had for escort the American light cruiser *Phoenix*, and included the last-minute addition of the airplane tender *Langley*, with a deck cargo of thirty-two sorely needed P-40 fighters, and the British freighter *Sea Witch* with twenty-seven more P-40s crated and in her hold.

Langley and *Sea Witch* would separate from the convoy at the rendezvous point and in company with *Gloucester* and *Cushman* as antisubmarine screen make all possible speed to Tjilatjap where fighter aircraft were desperately needed to meet the inevitable enemy invasion of Java's shores.

Phoenix, temporarily detached from Vice Admiral Herbert F. Leary's Anzac force, would be relieved by *Hurlburt* and would return to her Australian base where support was needed. *Hurlburt* would assume escort duties for the remainder of the Bombay run.

Should the two groups fail to rendezvous, *Gloucester* and her two destroyers would proceed north and east at top available speed to rejoin the flagship group at Surabaya.

The order ended with the reminder that zigzag plans should be in operation and absolute radio silence maintained due to the superiority of communications and reconnaissance enjoyed by the enemy. Should the primary mission prove incapable of accomplishment, and the rendezvous at Surabaya impractical, then the commanding officer of *Gloucester* would assume duties as senior officer in tactical command and be privileged to act independently.

Paige thanked the liaison officer and dismissed him. He issued the necessary instructions to the bridge and sent for Commander Olsen and went out on the open wing deck. Flag hoists snapped at the halyards. A blinker signal clacked. The sea was a smooth glass mirror of sky and emerald hills and the air crisp smelling and washed clean by the night rain. The rakish hulls of *Cushman* and *Hurlburt* veered to starboard breaking the line order of ships, and Paige felt a pang of sadness, remembering the "tin can" life of his younger days.

The OOD reported 0630 and the execution of the course change. The communications officer appeared with translated copies of the Dutch admiral's orders and behind him, Olsen, frowning and gray-cheeked, presented the captain with a mimeographed copy of the plan of the day and requested a word with him alone. "About Wilson," he explained.

The captain had not forgotten Wilson, "Unshackle him and if he's sober slap him in the brig."

"He's unshackled," Olsen said, "and he's in sick bay and Doc Lefferts is mad as hell."

"What's *he* got to be mad about?"

"He says he's got enough casualties without us making our own."

"What's with Stick?"

"His back's all tore up from the dogs on the hatch cover he was spread-eagled over."

"Who the hell said to do that?"

"Those were the orders, Captain." Paige observed that Olsen's loyalty did not allow him to say "Those were *your* orders, Captain." Paige walked into the chart house and sat on the navigator's high stool and watched Joe Allen plot the dead reckoning course on a chart so worn the markings were barely legible. "Christ," he muttered.

"Sir?" The navigator turned and stiffened.

"Not you, Joe." Olsen was passing his cigarettes around and Paige took one and leaned forward as Olsen lighted it. "It's Stick's own fault for thrashing around like a wild man and getting himself torn up like that."

"Yes, sir," Olsen said. The navigator politely turned to his charts. Paige stared through the starboard porthole across the open bridge watching *Cushman* take station. That was the life. Tin cans. He heaved a sigh. "Belay the brig order, Oley. See that Stick gets patched up and back in shape. We're going to need him on the helm."

"Yes, sir."

"Is he really bad off?"

"He's hollering to be let out, sir."

Paige handed him a copy of the admiral's orders. "Here's the hot dope, Oley. It'll be good to get a look at the old *Langley*. Haven't seen her in a dog's age."

Olsen read the orders. "It's about time they brought in some planes. We can sure use air cover."

"If they can clear and level an airstrip," Paige said. "Right now it's all jungle. And how in hell will they land those heavy crates?" His eyes were bright. "Maybe she won't make it to here. Maybe we'll get a crack at the Nip after all."

"Not make it?" Olsen looked confused.

"Forget it, Oley. Get your tail down to sick bay and tell Stick to sober up. We sure as hell are going to need him."

Olsen left. Allen said, "Excuse me, Captain, did I understand you to say the *Langley* might not make the rendezvous?"

"She'll make it. *Langley*'s a hell of a ship. Our first Navy carrier. She was the old *Jupiter*, a collier converted in '22. I served a hitch in her in the fleet war games off Galápagos back in '31, with the

Lex and *Sara*. They were new and fast and even with the wind up her tail the poor old *Langley* couldn't make over fifteen knots. Now she's the workhorse of the airborne Navy. Does all the dirty work, training, convoy duty, and the big flattops get all the publicity. They're the glamour girls. *Langley*'s like Cinderella." He looked away, feeling sad. "I'm damned glad she's finally got the chance to do something. Maybe this time she'll get to the ball."

"You like carriers, sir?"

"It's all there is, in my book, Joe."

"You'll get one, sir, when there's enough to go around."

"If I live that long." But he knew better. He looked over Allen's shoulder at the chart where a penciled X marked the rendezvous point. His eyes followed an imaginary course north and west to Sunda Strait and in his mind he could see the Japanese supply and transport ships hugging the coast like bunched sheep. He thought: I'd be in and out so fast they'd never knew what hit 'em. And took a deep breath and aloud said, "So we play nursemaid to the *Langley*," saying it with such contained passion that Joe Allen looked up startled, "Yes, sir," he said. Paige dragged on his cigarette. "It's a funny thing, this radio silence so far south. The Nip must be a hell of a lot closer than our recon reports seem to indicate."

"We're ready for 'em, Captain." Allen watched the skipper settle his cap more firmly over his ears and move out to the open bridge. The skipper was all right, Allen reflected. Not like some of the trade school boys he came against, snotty and patronizing the minute they found out he wasn't Academy. Half the lousy ensigns fresh out of Annapolis acted as if they owned the Navy. A good thing they weren't all like that. Especially Paige. And Paige loved his ship and that was all Joe Allen could ask of any skipper, even one crazy enough to prefer a carrier to his *Gloucester*.

Paige on the open bridge climbed into his high swivel chair and stared moodily at the broad expanse of green sea. The Dutch admiral's force steamed smartly off the starboard quarter. A bewildering variety of flag hoists flapped on the flagship's halyards. On *Gloucester*'s signal bridge the Morse blinker went *dit-dah-dit* like a jazz-mad insect. All Paige could think of was the waste of it, the mother-loving waste. Like Navy Day in Chesapeake Bay.

The crew secured from general quarters. Extra lookouts were posted aloft and the ship settled down to sea routine. Paige drank coffee, sharing his silver tray with the OOD. Now with his own command he began to feel better, cockier. The morning sun, already hot, slanted across the bridge. The steady look of the men standing watch touched him with pride and out there the tin cans on station port and starboard plowed the smooth sea. He had put the morning burial out of his mind. The feeling of guilt about Stick Wilson became remote and less troubling. Steam rose from the hills abeam to starboard. Soon the land would sink below the horizon and the fear of the enemy aloft would lessen.

Lee Chin appeared from nowhere squinting in the sun to ask if the captain cared for breakfast. Paige became acutely aware of how hungry he was and grinned at Lee Chin and ordered a whale of a breakfast. He lit another cigarette and slid down in the chair and through half-closed eyes watched the shoreline of village and matted jungle dissolve into shapeless green no longer ominous or tragic.

The morning grew to noon in swelling heat. Commander Lefferts climbed the ladder with the change of watch and greeted the captain. He was a plump and usually lighthearted man in his early fifties. There was no chaplain on board and a senior medical officer was the next best thing. He had shepherded the crew through the vagaries and vicissitudes of the China station for more than thirty months without stateside leave, attending to hernias and spick itch, clap and confession and that old Oriental illness with a skill and compassion beyond the call of duty.

He was tired. His face had a nasty gray pallor and the flesh hung from it in loose pouches and under his eyes were startling patches so dark they seemed to be bruises. His wrinkled khaki shirt was open at the collar and the armpits showed pale arcs of previous exertions. A fine spray of bloodstains decorated the length of his left sleeve. He saluted stiffly. Lefferts, a casual man, had never saluted before, and Paige observed with surprise the look of anger suppressed in Lefferts' eyes. With an air of innocence he offered coffee and waited for the worst. Lefferts refused coffee. He had drunk enough in the last twenty-four hours to pay off the Brazilian national debt, he said, and if it would please the captain, could he have a word in private?

That he could, Paige told him amiably, and they retired to the sea cabin. He produced a bottle from a drawer beneath his bunk. "You're looking kind of peaked, Commander. How's for a shot of the Dutch resident's private stock?"

"That's not what I'm here for, Harry, and you goddam well know it."

"Have a shot anyway, J.J., and we'll argue later."

He poured two drinks and Lefferts sipped his and drained the glass and shook his head. "How in hell do you expect to get away with it, Harry? My God in heaven."

"He asked for it."

"But to spread-eagle a man on a hatch cover—"

"I don't know about any hatch cover, J.J., and I gave no order for spread-eagling. Chains and the brig was all. But whatever that crazy son of a bitch got he deserved. He was a raving madman last night. A danger to the ship and crew. Oley's turned in the report and you can see for yourself."

"All I can see is where Stick Wilson's damned lucky he don't need an amputation. Your master-at-arms had the leg irons so tight they cut off blood circulation and Christ knows what else."

"Well, I'm not feeling sorry for the likes of Stick. I'd have keel-hauled him myself had I the strength to get out of the sack. He jumped ship three times last night, just to put the blocks to a gook broad. Now you know damned well, J.J.—"

"All he wanted to do was bring her aboard. To share—" Lefferts stopped and put his hands to his face. Suddenly he was too tired to go on, to even think about anything. Paige offered the bottle. Lefferts pushed it away. "Sorry," he said thickly. He pulled the binnacle list from a pocket. "That's the final count on the wounded, Harry."

Paige scanned the list absently. His mind still heard the word "share" and he wondered about his unpredictable helmsman. He passed the list back to Lefferts. "Any of them stalling?"

"You don't have a malingerer aboard. Not one. Don't ask me why."

"Hell. Stick'll be okay." He grinned. "The sly bastard. He wanted to share."

"That goes for the whole damned crew, Harry. They're with you to a man. Frankly, if I had to put up with what they've endured these last few weeks, I'd have jumped ship myself."

"Think those casualties can man their battle stations?"

"You couldn't stop 'em."

"Good."

"The power of Paige," said Lefferts. "Defies medical science."

"We'll know when the time comes." He put away the bottle. "Now let's get a shot of that bracing sea air. Do you good."

They stood together on the open bridge. Lefferts breathed deeply. Paige was right. The sea air swept across the spray shield and he filled his lungs and his head cleared and he felt right again. He thought back to his youth and his first surgical effort, accomplished with a dull jackknife in a dry California canyon under sycamore and oak.

He was nine and the patient an ageless iridescent lizard doing push-ups in the sun. The severed tail performed its nature-given diversionary antics while the rest of Mr. Lizard escaped. Or was it Mrs. Lizard? he had wondered then. A surgeon should know these matters. He pursued the lizard to find out. So are surgeons born. With dull jackknives and curiosity.

"Ever live in California, Harry?"

"Navy stations mostly."

"I mean *live*. I got me a lash-up in the Santa Monica mountains ten minutes from Beverly Hills. I could be grossing forty, maybe fifty grand a year and keeping a chunk of it. What am I doing out here, tell me?"

"How could you keep such a chunk?"

"Cash. No records."

"You'd last one day, J.J."

"Who'd ever know?"

"You would. You and your damned integrity."

Lefferts stared across the sea at no escape. *Cushman* low in the water cracked along at twenty knots to maintain station. The doctor wondered who was in pain there, who bled, who was dying. How much of Wilson's ankle must go? He wondered how to begin about Olsen. He felt sorry for himself here in the good clean air, abused, no scalpel in hand to steady himself.

"What's the plan, Harry?"

"Rendezvous with *Langley* and escort her load of fighter planes for the hopeless defense of Java."

"You don't think we can defend Java?"

"They don't pay me to think." Paige saw the slight tightening of Lefferts' jaw muscle. "What the hell, J.J., nobody knows what can happen. We carry out our orders, period."

"After *Langley* unloads, then what?"

"Surabaya, maybe. If the Nip's not in there first. The Dutchman's going to let us know." He nodded toward the flagship group now hull down, a scattering of masts like matchsticks. "If they make it through Bali Strait."

"You don't think they will?"

"Who knows?" he snapped. "Who the hell knows?" He examined the fringe of fancy sennit work that decorated his chair. "Pretty, isn't it?"

Lefferts nodded.

"Stick's work. He's a genius at it." He hesitated. "Besides the ankle, how bad off is he, J.J.?"

"Lacerations on his back and butt. Like he spent the night in a meat grinder." He took the fringe in his fingers. "You wouldn't think a roughneck like that could do such delicate work."

"That's Stick for you."

The doctor felt the time had come. He took a deep breath. "There's a sicker man than Stick on board, Harry." He avoided the captain's eyes. "Oley Olsen."

"What's with Oley?"

"He's in bad shape. I made a mistake. I should have requested he leave ship in Tjilatjap."

"All Oley needs is a good kick in the ass. He's sloughing off, is all."

"He's in bad shape, Harry. He needs rest and probably psychiatric help."

"Moose shit. He's just worn out from the pressures lately. He'll snap back."

"He's in no condition mentally to discharge his duties."

"I'm not going to tell you your business, J.J., but I don't go along with this mental crap. We're not running one of your Hollywood actors' schools out here. So knock it off."

"Just the same, first chance we get, Oley should be detached. I'm making out the necessary medical report."

"What makes you so cocksure he needs help?"

"He talks to me."

"What about?"

"His family. His thoughts and feelings."

"Like what?"

"It's pretty personal, Harry."

"Then why does he shoot off his mouth if it's so personal?"

"He has to unload it on somebody. It's not easy. That's the hell of it."

"I never heard of such a thing."

"I'll send you my medical report."

"I won't endorse it. I won't forward it. So forget it."

"Look, Harry. Oley is a fine officer. He's got plenty of guts. Loyalty to you. Wants to do his job. But he can't. He's sick. He's the sickest man on board."

"He was here a while ago. He didn't look sick to me."

"He's got problems at home. He's got problems in his head."

"He's got problems?" Paige laughed. "If I lose Oley, what've I got? Donaldson dead and gone. Next officer in line's Allen. A mustang two-and-a-half striper. If I'm knocked off who's left to run the ship? An ex-enlisted man? Or should we get Stick Wilson out of the brig and let him run it?" He shook his head. "Olsen stays where he is."

"I'd like to help him," Lefferts said, "but it's out of my line."

"Give him a couple of aspirin and a boot in the ass."

The doctor remained silent, stretching his fingers. He studied the soap rash on his hands. Green soap and the scrub brush a hundred times a day did that. He thought of white corridors in mainland hospitals. He heard the starched rustle of nurses, the purr of machines on rubber wheels. He felt the five-fingered phallic stretch of sterile gloves. Poor Oley, he thought. Up the creek without a paddle. He looked at Paige who was staring moodily to sea. "Thanks for listening," he said, and went below.

11

The morning dragged. Men moved about the decks clearing loose gear, testing survival equipment, checking life rafts and floats and the condition of emergency stores. The lookouts were posted in pairs, spelling each other at half-hour intervals to ease the eye-strain of sky-searching.

The chief bosun's mate reported a reserve of two hundred gallons of aviation gas on board. Did the skipper want to dump it? Paige hesitated. They just might pick up a spare SOC from *Langley*. "Hold it and check with me later, Boats," he said.

He caught the signal bridge of the *Hurlburt* flashing a blinker message and wondered. *Trouble already?* His glance from habit drifted skyward. All they needed now was a nosey Nip to knock the mission into a cocked hat. He waited fretfully, waving off Lee Chin who had arrived with his lunch tray. He slid out of the chair and went to the signal bridge where the duty signalman was receiving. Paige stood at the flag bags and waited. The ship's bell sounded noon.

"*Hurlburt*, sir. She's requesting forty-three life jackets and wants to know have we any ice cream."

"Affirmative, first request. We'll advise later when to come alongside. Signal *Cushman* to maintain station."

"How's about the gedunk, Cap'n?"

"Tell 'em to try Schrafft's."

He bolted his lunch and went into the chart house and looked over Allen's shoulder. "How soon?" Allen scratched his head. "We're just about there, Captain."

"What bearing will they show on?"

"One six zero true, Captain."

"There's nothing out there."

"I know, sir. I checked."

"Reduce speed to fifteen knots. Change the zigzag plan to conform to a ninety-degree starboard turn every fifteen minutes. Will that keep the rendezvous point in sight?"

"It should, sir."

"Advise *Hurlburt* to come alongside to pick up life jackets as requested. *Cushman* takes the covering antisub station."

"Yes, sir."

"I'll be in my sea cabin." He started out, stopped. "No, damn it, I'll be on the open bridge."

He watched tight-lipped as the signal hoists fluttered aloft. He had eaten too quickly and would have enjoyed a quick nap, but was certain now he would not rest until the convoy showed. *Hurlburt* made her approach and the transfer of life jackets was carried out smoothly. Paige observed that the customary repartee and good-natured insults between ships did not occur. He smoked several cigarettes and began to wonder whether indigestion could be fatal and how nice it would be right now to have no worries.

At an hour past noon the burning sun hung over them like a gypsy curse. Paige quit the bridge and almost knocked over Lee Chin who had shuffled up quietly to remove the lunch tray. Paige swore and the watch crew looked the other way. He went into the chart house, his binoculars bouncing angrily against his sweat-stained khaki shirt. The navigator was stretched out on his bunk in nav plot. He spied the captain through the open door and scrambled to his feet, stuffing his shirttails inside his black belt. Paige jabbed a thick thumb into the chart. "You're damned sure this is right, Joe?"

"I've checked it out with the orders and this is it, sir." He fumbled to make certain his fly was buttoned. "They're wrong or late." He preferred not to say that they may have been sunk. Paige caught it.

"We'd know if they were intercepted. They'd sure as hell break radio silence." He took off his cap and wiped the dripping sweat-band. "Maybe that silly Dutch kid got his signals mixed. Maybe he never learned to read English and translated by dead reckoning. Maybe he's a Nazi spy and he's got us out here so one of the Nip subs can lay a fish into us." He jammed the cap on the back of his head. "I'm getting the creeps boxing the square like this, Joe."

"Safer than laying dead in the water, sir."

"The whole business stinks," Paige said violently. "It's no damn good, laying to like sitting ducks. One sub is all it takes." He tore the cap from his head again and went to the chart table. Together with Allen he carefully retraced the course and when he was convinced they had come to the rendezvous point as planned he threw down the pencil. It bounced and fell to the deck and he muttered again, "The whole business stinks."

He sent for the OOD. "I want the lookouts on the ball. No doping off. They haven't reported a thing all morning."

"Probably nothing to report, sir."

"The hell nothing! *I've* seen things. A crate. Fish broaching. Plenty. A sharp eye out there, you hear?"

"Yes, *sir!*"

A *mermaid*, he muttered, *a sea nymph. Davy Jones.* You'd think they'd report *something*. He had lied. He hadn't seen a damn thing but you have got to keep those lookouts on their toes. He went out to the wing of the bridge and swept the horizon 360 degrees through his binoculars. He lowered them and glared up at the lookouts aloft. Each man seemed to be searching his sector diligently. One lowered his binoculars as Paige watched. Paige gestured at the OOD. "He's not searching."

"I just gave him permission to rest," the officer said.

"Rest hell! He's on watch, isn't he?"

"He reported the sun was burning the balls of his eyes, Captain."

"You tell him to keep those glasses up where they belong or I'll give his balls something to burn about. What the hell's come over this ship anyhow?"

He stormed into his sea cabin and slammed the door. He rummaged through the pile of papers on his desk until he found the admiral's orders. He read them again though he knew the words by heart. His legs tingled. Any moment now, he thought, a Jap fish is going to plow into the side of this rustbucket. He threw himself on his bunk and groaned. Where is everybody? Why am I alone? Why are they all against me?

He looked at his watch. Thirteen twenty-two. He'd give 'em eight minutes. No more. To hell with orders. No. He didn't mean that at all. He believed in orders, in chain of command, in the respect due authority. But this was no good. He felt it in his bones. And sure as hell he did not want to turn back to Surabaya. There must be a way. There just the hell must be some goddam way.

12

He lay on his bunk with his hands folded across his belly. One thing was certain. The minutes, all eight of them, must live out their seconds one by one, all four hundred and eighty of them. Then he would act.

The communications officer arrived with a dispatch marked SECRET. The duty radio operator had monitored a message from ABDA command to the Dutch admiral. An allied patrol PBY had reported a heavy Japanese invasion force approaching St. Nicholas Point. Paige read it twice and consulted the charts and guessed it must be the Nip's western arm out of the South China Sea.

"Keep it under your hat," he said.

"Aye, Captain." The comm officer saluted and left. Paige looked at his watch. Eight minutes on the nose. He sat up, calm now, the hunger for contact subordinated to the knowledge he was free and could proceed on his own. He scribbled instructions to the signal bridge and navigator and passed the word to his heads of departments. Preparations would be made immediately for *Gloucester* to separate from her two destroyers and operate singly. Olsen was on the phone seconds later, questioning the message. "There's still an hour, Captain, until the *Langley* rendezvous." *He's off again*, Paige thought, *the hard-nosed bastard.*

"Thank you, Oley."

"Is there an emergency of some kind?"

"We're returning to Surabaya via Sunda Strait."

"The orders called for Bali Strait, Captain."

"I know what the orders called for," Paige shouted and hung up.

He did not leave his sea cabin. He could hear the duty signal-man's hoarse voice reading the change of orders advising the destroyers to maintain the rendezvous with *Langley* and *Sea Witch* until dark. If contact was not made, to return to Tjilatjap and await further orders. He lay on the narrow bunk feeling the sweat soak through his thin shirt onto the damp soiled bed covers. The clatter of blinker signals port and starboard made sweet music. Free as a bird, he thought.

The OOD's voice came unevenly through the speaking tube near his head. It announced the departure of the escorts. "Very well," Paige ordered. "Execute course and speed change."

"Aye, sir."

"Pass the word to sick bay to get Wilson squared away on the double. He's standing his trick on the wheel tonight."

The ship heeled and its vibration increased. Fatigue had left him. He peered through the small port at the spotless sky. The ship's clean thrust through the warm sea charged him, as though he himself moved through it. He stripped off his shirt and dropped to the deck and did twenty firm push-ups, slowing down for the last five and barely completing the twentieth, his neck and back muscles corded like rope. He rubbed his face and body with a coarse towel, put on a fresh shirt and a starched garrison cap and quit his cabin and sauntered aft to the signal bridge and leaned against the flag bags. *Cushman* and *Hurlburt* were hull down, their gaunt stacks like eight hazy sticks where sea met sky. Just like that, he reflected with pleasure. No time at all. He looked aft along the cluttered ship's center line where work parties still labored. Beyond them *Gloucester's* wake churned and bubbled, flattening the sea along its edges in foaming eddies, all of it flat to the horizon but crooked as a snake. Paige turned and roared past the startled faces of look-outs on the narrow catwalks, "Helmsman, damn it! Steer a straight course!"

On the smoke-blackened hangar deck amidships a working party chipped paint and swept. Sailors in streakily dyed dungarees checked life lines and the security of life rafts lashed to the sides of deck structures. Paige stared at the sky, cloudless except for a low bank over the mountaintops. If anything would stop them now it must come from there. He sent for the first lieutenant. "What's all the action on the hangar deck?"

"Getting squared away, Captain, is all. Preparing to dry out a mess of water-soaked gear and stuff."

"Belay it. Got any red paint on board?"

"Yes, sir."

"Bright red?"

"Yes, sir."

"Paint me the biggest damn Jap flag you can paint on that hangar deck, fast as you can paint it. Rope it off until it's dry. Get all hands available to turn to." The first lieutenant stood dumb for a moment. "Get going," Paige snapped. The first lieutenant's startled look pleased him. He wondered how long it would take Olsen to find out and if anyone else in the ship would be smart enough to know his mind. Stick, that shrewd idiot, would know in a split second.

The executive officer arrived breathing hard. He started to speak. Paige's expression stopped him. Together they watched the chalk-mark design of the rising sun take form. Painters followed and soon the flag spread glittering and wet in the cleared center of the hangar deck between the catapults.

"What d'you think, Oley?"

"It sure makes us one hell of a target."

"The Japs won't bomb their own ships, Oley."

"How's about one of *our* boys?"

"If we've a land-based plane left that can fly, I'll eat it, wings and all."

"You really think we'll get away with this?"

"Don't you?"

"Frankly, no."

"Why not, Oley?"

"Our colors is why. A plane'll spot the Stars and Stripes in a minute."

"Any spotter close enough to tell the difference won't live long enough to do anything about it."

"He'd report the contact to his base on sight." Olsen's voice cracked. "You're asking for it!" He was frightened and seeing it made Paige angry. It confirmed his suspicion that Olsen was not sick. He was yellow. And worse than that, Olsen did not see the humor of it, the outrageously funny anecdote it would make some day in wardrooms and officers' clubs. Paige became surprisingly

gentle. "Sure, Oley, I'm asking for it." He took Olsen's arm and together they walked round to the shade. "Between you and me, I
don't know what the hell else to do but retire and damned if I
know where to retire to. Now look: They'll be landing troops and
stuff all night somewhere off St. Nicholas Point. We're taking a
crack at 'em, Oley. This is the only way I figure it can be done.
It's a gamble. But I know how the Jap mind works. Show him his
flag and he bows or yells 'Banzai.'"

Olsen's face twitched. "They'll never fall for it, Captain."

"Take a look at the recognition charts, Oley. We look a hell of
a lot like a Nip heavy cruiser from the air. Nobody's been fighting
long enough to be a seasoned observer. And how's about his con-
ceit? He's winning this war and he's so cocky and convinced about
Yankee stupidity, he'd never believe we'd dream up a screwball idea
like this one." He saw that Olsen was not listening. The exec's
worried eyes were searching the sky for enemy bombers. Paige said
abruptly, "That's how it is, Oley. It's my ship. If I'm wrong it'll be
my ass."

"It's every man's ship that's in her, Captain."

"Not as long as I'm in command."

Olsen's look in return upset Paige so violently he wanted to hit
him. "That's all," he said thickly and turned away.

"A ship full of dead men," Olsen muttered and was gone before
Paige could restrain him. He leaned over the splinter shield, his head
throbbing. He watched Olsen now two decks below briskly walk aft
to his battle station. A compact springy figure telescoped to a
dwarf. From the captain's viewpoint, the yellow stripe was a mile
wide.

Inside the roped area the working party was putting the finishing
touches to the painted Japanese flag. Men who lingered were ordered
to their duties by the highly charged first lieutenant. He glanced at
Olsen as he crossed the hangar deck enroute to Battle Two. Their
eyes met and like puppets they shrugged in unison. Captain Paige
on the signal bridge witnessed the exchange. It did little to soften
his stormy mood.

The crew settled uneasily into the afternoon watch. The sun had
begun its downward swing when the first plane contact was reported. A shudder seemed to drift through the ship. Air defense
stations were manned and all hands not assigned to topside duties
were ordered below.

It was a blurry pinpoint in the bright sky, hovering on the starboard quarter, difficult to identify at this early stage, impossible to know if it had sighted the ship. The men stood at their gun stations, waiting for orders. On the bridge and in the air defense command station above, anxious eyes searched through powerful binoculars. Paige had a curious thought just then. *What do I want it to be?* he wondered. *Ours or theirs?*

The plane maintained a respectable altitude and appeared to be on a course slightly diverging from *Gloucester's* course. To Paige's practiced eye it had the vague outline of a patrol bomber. He was not yet prepared to commit himself, but was reasonably certain it must be the enemy.

The air defense officer leaned over the splinter shield above and called down. "Fantail lookout reports it could be a PBY, Captain."

Paige was startled to see Newell's face under the stenciled helmet. He had forgotten that Newell had taken over as air defense officer, that Latham had gone to the five-inch batteries and Hurley was gunnery officer. And Donaldson dead in the warm Dutch earth. And Newell, Christ almighty, a trigger-happy and precious cargo.

"Thank you, Mr. Newell," he said. "Advise your lookouts to hold any reports until identification is positive."

"Yes, Captain."

"Between you and me, if it's a PBY, it's a ghost. We lost the last PBY a month ago. It isn't a PBY we got to worry about. It's whether that Nip baby out there spots us or not."

He remembered the last of the PBYs a month ago, the pitiful remnant of the patrol squadron Admiral Thomas C. Hart had brought to Java from Manila. In the dying hours of the Philippines they had flown back to Corregidor lumbering in under the flaming muzzles of the enemy guns at Cavite and Bataan and had flown out with the last tender cargo of stranded American nurses. Gone now, those gallant Catalinas, into the briny, or belly deep in a jungle, rusting for parts.

Newell called out. The plane had sighted them and had changed course. "Kawanishi flying boat," Newell said loud and clear. "Headed this way."

"You sure?"

"Yes, sir. Same type a *Lexington* fighter plane shot down near Rabaul a couple weeks ago."

Paige was somewhat annoyed by the authority of Newell's pronouncement. Who the hell did he think he was? He steadied his binoculars on the splinter shield. There were the four engines on high, unmistakably head on. He nodded to his talker. "Pass the word on all circuits. The plane is a Kawanishi flying boat and it's headed this way." He called up to Newell. "No firing until you get the word. Understood?"

"Yes, Captain."

"Too many trigger-happy hunters on board."

Newell reddened though he detected an edge of compliment in the skipper's words. "She carries at least one 20-mm cannon and she's heavily armed with machine guns." He went on like a nastily bright schoolboy. "She's larger than a Pan Am Clipper and has a cruising speed—"

"Knock it off," Paige snapped. "It's no time for intelligence reports." He heard the identification pass over the ship's intercom, repeated at nearby stations. Men fumbled with helmets and ammo clips at the gun mounts behind the circular splinter shields. The sun bore down without mercy. For the first time no one felt it. The clean bow waves swept past. The big plane began to climb. Paige watched it, twitched restlessly. Without turning, he called for his talker. "Pass the word. Absolutely no shooting unless I give the order."

His neck began to ache. He called for Lee Chin and ordered hot coffee with plenty of sugar. It was the precise moment, he knew, to prove something to the men. Calmly he sipped his coffee. All part of the legend, he told himself. He nudged Hurley, the acting gunnery officer. "How come this new kid Newell knows so much?"

"Recognition school, Captain, two weeks."

"He'd better hold fire," Paige growled.

"He will, Captain. He's okay."

"This run has got to prove something."

Hurley nodded and nervously pushed his helmet firmly down on his head. The Kawanishi was within visual identity range now. It began to circle like a cumbersome green potbellied bird. An agonizing minute passed. The pilot rocked his wings. The plane dipped lazily and finished its circle and headed away.

Minutes dragged by. "Stand easy at air defense," the captain said to the OOD. "Set Condition Two." He looked down at the painted flag on the hangar deck and bowed to it.

Hurley unbuckled his helmet and wiped the sweat from his head. "You sure as hell proved it, Captain."

"I'll know for sure when Fat Boy's base sends out for a closer look."

It did not take long. They came in high as Paige again called the gunners to man their air defense stations. Newell made the first recognition—Mitsubishi OB-97s. They swept in at 300 miles an hour in two formations of three planes each.

Very businesslike, Paige thought grudgingly. The land-based two-engine bombers roared overhead in flawless formation close enough for him to see the fixed nose guns and the mounts of the turret guns. They circled as the flying boat had done, with admirable style and grace. After a long look, they wiggle-waggled their tapering wings and departed.

"A lovely sight," Paige muttered and passed the word to secure. He went to his cabin below and stripped and showered. The sticky lukewarm sea water calmed his trembling body. He rubbed himself until his flesh was a blotchy deep pink. He would not care to live through another half hour like the last one. He slipped into skivvy shorts and stretched out on the bunk and closed his eyes. Oley and *his* problems. It was too bad, he thought, there had been no ice cream to spare for *Hurlburt*.

His little game had worked and he felt pretty damned cocky about it. He knew his luck could not hold forever. The Kawanishi didn't matter. She was a slow, long-range aircraft and could have come from Sarawak or the newly captured base at Amboina. But the fast and heavy Mitsubishis meant trouble. Their range was limited. They had to have come from an air strip a lot closer than Amboina. They could have come Surabaya where Paige had hoped, God willing, to tie up when he was through with his little surprise party at Bantam Bay. Now if the Nip had taken Surabaya there was no telling where he could go except you-know-where.

He dressed and went to the navigation plotting room and instructed Allen to break out the large-scale charts of Sunda Strait. He sent for Olsen and the engineer officer and elaborated on his plan. He told them the final phase of the mission was to return to Surabaya to regroup with the Dutch admiral's force and then head west to intercept the enemy invasion force coming south from the China Sea. He poked at the chart. "A hell of a lot of time can be saved by taking a short cut up through Sunda Strait. There's one little hitch. That Nip invasion force out of the South China Sea might not want to let us through. Anyone care to discuss it, pro or con?"

He did not look at Olsen. He did not have to. After the business of the painted flag he knew he had Olsen in his pocket. The others stood mute, respectful, ready. "All right, then. We head up Sunda Strait and right on through to Surabaya." He poked the communications officer. "Any interceptions from the *Langley?*"

"No, Captain. With radio silence we can't expect anything much."

Paige addressed the engineer officer. "What can you deliver for flank speed?"

"Thirty-two knots, Captain."

"For how long?"

"Till something gives. Till the glue pot and baling wire runs out." He scratched a sallow cheek. "We're running on this thin Borneo oil, Captain, right out of the ground. It seems to do the job, but I sure as hell can't guarantee what it's going to do under maximum strain."

"We're going to need speed once we enter Sunda Strait and I'd rather not show up that close to land until dark. Once it's dark we can head right in. Far as I know they haven't got around to mining it yet, and we've got a break on an early moonset. We can be through those bastards by dawn and headed for Surabaya before they know what hit them."

"We'll need air cover, won't we, once it's light, sir?"

"Our fighters out of Surabaya will cover us," Paige said smoothly. "Now let's get down to the real details. What about time, Allen?"

"You'll never make it before daylight, Captain," the navigator said.

"Nuts." Paige bent over the chart, irritated at the truth. "These old charts—can we trust 'em?"

"That happens to be a British Admiralty chart of 1897. I've been doing better with the *London Times* atlas. Any way you slice it, Captain, you can't make a night approach and run the Strait and clear Bantam Bay safely before dawn."

"What's this point here?"

"Java Head."

"And this island west of it?"

"Panaiten. On some charts it's Prinsen Island."

"What about hazards to navigation?"

"Your guess is as good as mine. The markings are in Dutch and some of the names are Indonesian, Malay, and God knows what else."

"What's this *Ug. Kulon?*"

"A lighthouse on the island. I hope."

"It's marked as a light all right but damned if I can tell what that *Ug.* means."

"The Dutch kid told me it's Malay for point or cape. You can see, it shows up wherever the land sticks out into the sea."

"Couldn't we save a few hours running between Java Head and Prinsen Island?"

"Sure, but we could also run aground. We have no depth charts. No idea of the currents, or the hazards of navigation."

"Neither did Columbus. How much time do you think we could save?"

Allen worked for a few seconds with the dividers and a pencil and a parallel ruler. "Maybe three hours."

"What's this light blue color mean?"

"Anything from zero feet to six hundred."

"That's not too bad. We'll take soundings as we go. You've got a couple of miles to play around in between those two points, Joe. Hell, you could run the Pacific fleet through it beam to beam."

"We'll be taking a considerable risk, Captain."

"I'll have Wilson on the wheel. Wilson could run the *Queen Mary* blindfolded through the eye of a needle. Have we any other aids to navigation?"

"That light at *Ug. Kulon,* if it's working. Java Head's a thousand and fifty feet and with that and maybe the lighthouse at Flat Cape, we can get a fix." Allen seemed to shake himself out of a dream. "You're not seriously thinking of running it tonight, are you, Captain?"

"I'm seriously thinking of killing Nips, Joe. I want the quickest way to get to him and hit him before he puts his whole damned army on the beach. If there's water in that cut and we can save three hours, I'm for running it." His eyes searched their disbelieving faces. "Look," he said quietly, "it's everything or nothing. Face it. The Nip's got us by the balls, no matter which way we run. How long do you suppose they'll fall for the phony red meatball? We're licked no matter what we do, so we'll do it in style, right?"

No one spoke. Paige struck the table with his fist. "It's my command and I'm calling the shots, but I'm not going to ram it down

your throats. Let's vote on it. I'm for running the cut and slugging
it out. Vote me down and we swing back and rejoin the tin cans
at Tjilatjap."

"Vote?" Olsen protested. "It's highly irregular."

"Moose shit," Paige said.

"I'm for running it," the chief engineer said quietly.

"Me too," said Allen.

Olsen looked at each face except Paige's. "Okay, make me look
chicken. I'm with you all the way . . ."

Paige clapped him a solid blow on the back. "Spoken like a
frigging Annapolis sea scout, Oley. You'll make admiral someday."

"God forbid," Olsen muttered redfaced.

"Now then," Paige said briskly. "Give me a course, Joe, to bring
us off Java Head by dark to run the Strait at a speed that'll place
us off St. Nicholas Point before dawn."

The navigator's instruments moved expertly. His eye caught the
engineering officer's. "Can the engine room sustain twenty-eight
knots for, let's see—seven and a half hours?"

"On two minutes' notice. How long it'll stay there is not up to
me." He pointed to the overhead. "Him up there. It's up to Him."

"Knock off that stuff," Paige said. "She's good for thirty-two and
better."

"Not without a major overhaul, Captain."

"She'll do it. Go on, Allen."

"That's about it, sir. Barring a bad break we can be off St.
Nicholas Point roughly at 0300. Sunrise is 0540. That's two hours
and forty minutes to clear to the east. Of course some of that'll be
in pre-sunrise daylight."

Paige studied their solemn faces. "We'll have the advantage of
surprise and speed. And everybody else is *them*, not us. At thirty
knots we'll be in and away before they know what hit them."

"You said twenty-eight, Captain."

"You'll deliver thirty, mister, or I'll throw the book at every snipe
in the engine room." He punched the engineering officer's thin
arm. "I won't call for flank speed until we make the first contact.
Then stand by to pour on the coal and keep her there." He turned
to Olsen who was distractedly biting the flesh round his nails.
"Hot chow to all hands, Oley, as fast as the galley can dish it up.
Then battle stations and have the men stand easy. Break out dry
rations, so they'll have something to chew on besides each other."

He jabbed them all, his voice charged with the promise of battle. "Come on, now. Snap out of it! If you want your men to think they're attending a funeral, they damn well are. For a few thousand Nips. Now have the OD cut in the squawk box. I'm giving the word to the crew."

They got out of his way as gracefully as they could. He grinned at the perspiring JA talker who manned the captain's circuit. He came in trailing black phone lines. "All stations?" The talker nodded. Paige cleared his throat and pressed the button on the mouthpiece and blew into it, testing. His eyes were bright and he rose slightly on his toes. "Men, this is your captain speaking. We're heading into Sunda Strait tonight. There's a good chance we'll tie into a Japanese convoy on the run to Surabaya. We've got the guns and the guts and the big advantage of night surprise. It's time somebody took a crack at those arrogant little bastards. We're just the crew to do it. So let's give 'em hell. Tomorrow night we celebrate in Surabaya." He clicked off and saw that Commander Allen watched him curiously. "A small fib can't hurt, Joe." He shrugged. "And who knows? We might just make it to Surabaya."

Olsen followed him to a corner of the wing bridge. His face was gray as dust. "Permission to go below, Captain?"

"What's up, Oley?"

"I want to see Doc Lefferts. I'm asking to be relieved."

"Not granted." He turned on his heel and Olsen spun him back. "Permission to go below," he said again. His voice was low and tense. A stubborn glazed look had come into his eyes. Paige glanced round. They were unobserved. He kept his narrowed eyes on Olsen's hands. "When GQ sounds, you had better the hell be at your battle station, Oley. That is all." He saw the pleading in Olsen's eyes and grabbed an arm and thrust his face inches from Olsen's. "I never figured you'd be the one to spill your guts, Oley. I was wrong. You're a stinking coward. One lousy air attack and you crack up in a million pieces. There are sick men below'd give their right arm to be topside. I mean sick men—not stalling like you."

"I'm not stalling, Captain." He tried to move his arms. Paige pinned them to his sides.

"You'll obey orders like everyone else in this ship. When you're bleeding I'll know you're sick and not before. Now pull yourself together or, by Christ, I'll slap you in irons." He saw Joe Allen watching them through the glass of the pilot house. He let go Olsen's arms. They remained limply at his sides. He felt both contempt and relief that Olsen wasn't making something of it. "Go to your cabin and clean up and report to Battle Two. You've got ten minutes."

"Ten minutes." Olsen straightened and wiped his eyes. "Aye, sir." He saluted and turned and went down the ladder. Paige flicked at his blouse as though there were dust on it. Joe Allen looked away, sorry he had seen it.

Tod Newell on the deck below gave way at the foot of the ladder for the executive officer. He greeted Olsen who went by as though Newell did not exist. Newell climbed the ladder slowly. The Navy was trouble enough, he thought. A man in a ship must live in a shell and do his duty, keep his nose clean and ignore anything not immediately and directly his own business, as though it did not exist.

But he would never forget the hurt look of a punished child in Commander Olsen's eyes.

13

It was dusk when *Gloucester* began her approach to Sunda Strait. The ship was darkened. Zigzagging ceased and the course was set north by northwest for Java Head. The crew settled down to nighttime duties, all hands at battle stations and watertight compartments dogged down.

The scuttlebutt swept through the ship like a hot wind. Below decks and topside the crews stood by their weapons, touching up, attentive to the instruments, testing, making needless and minute adjustments. They talked noisily to quiet their fears. Some said the ship's luck had always held and would hold again long enough to see them through the tricky strait to Surabaya. Others swore their time had come. They had heard about the lack of charts and the skipper's determination to run the strait without them. They had stretched their luck too long and sure as hell the Galloping Ghost of the Java Coast would run aground and more than likely sink. The argument raged in fierce whispers and embroidered obscenities. Some men listened and said nothing and prayed. None of them knew what really lay ahead.

Night fell. The ship passed Java Head at twenty-eight knots with Prinsen Island abeam to port. Stick Wilson in borrowed dungarees and pain stood the quartermaster watch, temporarily relieved of the helm. He made the entry in the rough log, noting with a routine curse the shadowy bulk of Indonesian hills uncomfortably close to port and starboard.

Hardly room enough for an alley cat to scratch his ass, he thought sourly. He checked the entry he had neatly printed. *Entering unmarked channel between Java Head and Prinsen Island. Steaming at various courses to conform to midstream; speed 28 knots.*

Entering this unmarked channel gave Wilson an eerie sensation in his crotch. His hand stole down to comfort his genitals. It occurred to him that much of his life had been spent in entering strange places. His total experience at sea and on shore since the time of early youth recalled a variety of channels, apertures, cracks, crevices, bays, inlets, and just plain holes. They had been small and large, dry and wet, hairy and bald, rank and sweet, animal and mineral, living and dead, and there was one thing, he thought, you could say about the bundle of them. They all meant trouble.

It had surprised him when the word had come to report for duty on the bridge. In the brig and later in sick bay he had begun to believe the skipper meant everything he had said. He glanced at the captain's dark shape erect in the starboard chair and in the darkness he grinned. Tomorrow he would needle the Old Man and let him know he damn well couldn't skipper his ship without Stick Wilson on the wheel.

His back itched where soft scabs crusted the lacerated wounds. The real pain circled his ankles where Krueger had tightened the irons. His skin tingled and he began to sweat. He closed the logbook keeping a pencil between the leaves to mark the place. He limped to the wheel and tapped the helmsman, a quartermaster striker. The man jumped. "Relax," Wilson muttered. "I'm relieving you."

"Aye, Chief." The striker wiped his hands on his shirt and muttered the ship's course and speed. Wilson studied the compass repeater, his face reflected in its green glow. Dead on course, he noted. "You're doing okay," he said. "I relieve you."

"It's the carrots, Chief."

"Never mind the goddam carrots. Tend the log."

A good lad, he thought sourly, but if he ever expects to make quartermaster third, he'd better the hell knock off yackety-yakking about carrots.

The striker swore by the magic of carrots and claimed they gave him superior powers of night vision. When there were fresh carrots

on board he begged, borrowed, or stole them and when the fresh
produce was gone, he conned the mess cooks out of carrots by the
can. Wilson knew all about carrots by the can. When he had been
a kid on the streets of Baltimore, two fat policemen had surprised
him one night breaking and entering in the market section of
South Broadway.

He was twelve then, big-boned and tough, and looked five years
older. The policemen knew it would be useless to turn him in again.
He was too young and his tart charm had on previous occasions left
them redfaced as well as flatfooted before the indulgent judge who
sat in the district's juvenile court. This night they had had a few too
many in their routine tour of the saloons and their fill as well of the
whippersnapper's impudence. They would teach him a lesson, they
decided, and told him solemnly the charge was forcible entry. They
dragged him into an alley and held him and stripped a thick carrot
from a fresh bunch and tore down his ragged jeans and rammed it
into him. Sweets to the sweet, they said and cuffed him and sent
him spinning into the dark muddy street.

Even now his sphincters tightened as he recalled the ordeal of
pain. The crude joke had the desired effect. He was never caught
again. He knew he had been lucky. It could have been worse. It
could have been cukes. The hell with it, he told himself.

The shadowy bulk of the captain in repose at the starboard windows brought him back to reality. He recalled the aroma of the
skipper's spicy gin and the honor of scrubbing his back. They could
not keep him in the brig and it made him proud that he could take
all the Old Man dished out and more if it came to more. The Navy
needed him here, right where he stood. He was the best damned
helmsman on the China station and they knew it.

The way he felt right now he could conn the mighty *Lex* herself,
all 888 feet of her, down the Swanee River with his little pinkie on
the wheel. He squared his hat, pushing it over his eyes so he could
barely read the greenish face of the compass repeater. In no time at
all he'd be back in his CPO blues with the hashmarks clean up to
his elbow and nobody knew it better than the Old Man himself.

Paige's thoughts were elsewhere. Automatically they were tuned
to the steady throb of turbines and the swift motion of the shoreline
close aboard. Every motion, sound and smell had meaning. But more
immediately and consciously, he was thinking of the consequences
of his decision to run Sunda Strait. The moment awed him.

He did not regret leaving the rendezvous with *Langley* to the two destroyers. Their skippers were seasoned officers capable of handling any situation that might develop. He was more concerned with the aftermath of his present action. The time would come when questions would be asked. He took a deep breath. There was no sense in trying to kid himself. If it came off, nobody'd have the gall to dispute its brilliance and daring. If it didn't—he shrugged— he wouldn't be around to know the difference, anyway. When the last round was fired all that would matter would be the record. Statistics were what they remembered. He grinned. He would give them a statistic they would not soon forget.

He slid out of the chair frowning, hearing the leadsman call out his soundings. The navigator joined him. "We're getting bottom, Captain."

"Slow to standard speed and try the other side of the channel."

"I'd recommend one-third standard, Captain."

"Standard, Allen. We haven't got all night."

The ship's bow waves calmed. The passing minutes were silent, marked only by the leadsman's cry. The gun crews in the topside stations leaned over the splinter shields and stared uneasily at the shoreline and the swirling bubbling phosphor slipping past the ship's side. Paige fretted. The jungle smells were too close, ripe in the soggy night air. Black rain clouds curtained the hostile stars to the west. He liked that. *Gloucester*'s hull dipped and rose through the long swells, smoother now and without vibration. Instruments seemed to tick louder in the dark quiet of the bridge.

The leadsman sang out, cheery now. Paige breathed easier. A lookout aloft in the foremast reported a faint light. Searching through binoculars, Paige picked up its reflected glow pale off the starboard bow.

"That should be the lighthouse on St. Nicholas Point," Allen said.

"Distance?"

"By dead reckoning, say, twenty-five thousand yards."

The JA talker approached the captain. "Forward control reports a range finder surface contact to port, Captain, bearing three zero zero relative, distance about twenty thousand yards."

Paige stepped out to the open bridge and stared into the darkness off the port bow. He could see nothing to interrupt the faint line of the widening horizon where the Sumatra coast melted into the sea. He looked upward to the steel bulk of the range finder housing that extended over the open bridge and lined up his glasses with the angle of the range finder. He could not find the target. He poked the JA talker. "Tell forward control to verify the contact." He went inside. "Something's out there all right," he muttered to Allen. "All engines full ahead. Alert all hands at battle stations."

Allen gave the order. The skipper studied the faint glow of the light on St. Nicholas Point to ease his mind about the unidentified target to port. They waited to hear from forward control.

"Target verified, Captain. Moving on a northerly course."

"Tell Mr. Hurley in forward control to label the unidentified object Target A and keep feeding us the range."

"Aye, Captain." Allen passed the word. "What's your guess, sir?"

"A picket destroyer and the son of a bitch can give us away." He nudged his messenger. "Have the signal bridge break out the biggest battle flag we own and hold it at the dip."

The JA talker spoke up. "Forward control's tracking Target A, Captain. Appears to be a single ship, bearing unchanged, distant eighteen thousand yards."

"Keeping up with us," Allen remarked.

"Maybe we can slip by," Paige nodded to the talker. "Be sure all information goes to Battle Two." He pushed thoughts of Olsen from his mind.

Shadowy forms round him took life, moving to the business of battle. Below decks men stirred. They had waited a long time. They looked to throttles and brass wheels and sucked in the forced fresh air of the blowers. Enmeshed by catwalks and steel ladders they stood at their stations, anxious eyes on mercury in slim tubes, watching valves, reading gauges. Pumps hammered. Pistons thumped. The whine of generators, the pounding of shafts, the minute gasps and cries of plagued steel and air and steam hard driven, lured their minds from the troubling awareness that they were blind to what went on above. Beads of sweat dripped on hot metal, sputtered and were gone. In their steel vault of oil, noise, and fear they goaded boilers to pressures so intense the instruments rattled and steel plates trembled near the bursting point. All of the racing ship shuddered as she plowed her resolute furrow through the night sea.

On the bridge the vibrations sent the skipper's binoculars crashing to the deck from the coaming where he had rested them. The bridge watch jumped. Swearing, Paige hung the strap round his neck. The JA talker droned the ranges every five hundred yards to Target A as they were reported from forward control.

Doorn, the Dutch officer, appeared from below. He had strapped himself into a bulky life jacket and wore a battle helmet that made him appear more girlish than ever. He approached Paige and saluted. "Can I be of service, Captain?"

Paige stared at first without recognition at the earnest pink face, then brusquely said, "Just stay the hell out of everyone's way."

Signal bridge reported the battle flag at the dip. Paige stepped out to have a look. "Nice night," the chief signalman said, light and easy as though they stood at the corner drugstore.

Paige startled said, "Sure, if it doesn't rain." He noticed Doorn alone in a corner near the flag bags and considered a mollifying word of encouragement, or a light remark on the Indian sound of Ug. But he changed his mind and instead reached out and, curiously, touched the coarse fabric of the battle colors. The stripes were broader than the span of his fingers and the blue behind the stars seemed blacker than black.

He went forward and stationed himself at the starboard pelorus and checked the steadiness of Stick Wilson's steering. The channel ahead, dark and ominous, was evenly parted by *Gloucester's* bow. The navigator touched his sleeve. "We can make out St. Nicholas Point now, Captain."

Paige raised his glasses. The dim shape was barely visible. "See anything else, Joe?"

"The transports and barges are probably on the far side. Don't suppose we'll get a look at them until we've rounded the Point."

Paige swung his glasses to port and searched for Target A. There was no break in the smooth line of horizon. The JA talker came out carrying loops of phone lines. "Gunnery officer reports the range to Target A is close enough for Turrets One and Two."

"Does he think they've observed us yet?"

The JA talker spoke into his mouthpiece. Paige waited. The speaker shook his head. "Negative, Captain. Mr. Hurley says to tell you Turrets One and Two are on target."

"Tell Mr. Hurley to hold fire." He turned to Allen. "Ring up flank speed, Joe. The channel opens up ahead. Set a course that brings us close to the Point without running aground."

"Aye, sir." Allen returned to the pilot house. "Right five degrees rudder. All engines ahead flank."

It was the quartermaster striker, the carrot lover, whose eyes spotted Target A, a faint silhouette off the port bow, almost indiscernible at about eight thousand yards. The ship steadied on the new course and Paige studied the enemy shape almost casually, resting his glasses on the lip of the splinter shield. It was a rakish gauntstacked destroyer, patrolling slowly on a southerly course, port side to *Gloucester*. Possibly the new Nip *Kagero* class, Paige guessed. He wet his dry lips. A sunk *Kagero* this early in the war would be a feather in his cap. Or a hashmark on my tombstone, he told himself.

"Steady as you go." Allen turned to him. "We're on course, Captain."

The JA talker was repeating the ranges to Target A. "Mr. Hurley is asking again, Captain, can he open fire?"

"Tell Hurley to hold his water."

He would let the *Kagero* go. He would wait for the big boys. His largesse and calm surprised and pleased him. So did his total command of the situation. He was conscious of the hair-trigger response his orders received and the attention of each man to detail. How tame they get, he reflected. Taut and obedient and ready to give all without question. Any time now.

The ship strained for flank speed. The hull shook. Gears rattled like loose teeth in a dead skull. The JA talker spoke out. "Signal bridge reports blinker message from the unidentified ship, Captain."

"*What* message?"

"International code. They want to know who we are."

"Ignore it."

"Aye, sir." He cleared his throat. "Lookout aloft reports lights ahead."

"That's more like it." Dead ahead at fourteen thousand yards, the gray masts and superstructure of several ships hull down loomed suddenly. Blinker signals winked. *Dit-dah-dit, dit-dah-dit*. Target A, abeam to port, blinked back. Paige felt the cold sweat along the sides of his head. He motioned to the JA talker. "Hand me that rig of yours, son." He fixed the headset over his cap. "All hands," he said. "This is the captain. We've completed the run through Sunda Strait. The picket ships of the enemy landing force are visible ahead. Matter of fact, they're in our goddam way and we're going right through. Left tackle, I'd say from here, unless they turn tail and run. We'll slug our way through and be out of there before they know what hit 'em. Everything's in our favor. I know every man jack of you will do his duty. God bless you. God bless our ship."

It was very quiet on the bridge. He winked at Allen. "The same jazz that beat Army, Joe, remember?"

Joe Allen did not say anything. Paige removed the headset and passed it to the JA talker. His legs became entangled in the trailing lines. "Keep it clear of me, son," he said mildly, "or sure as hell I'll go on my ass."

Hurley's pleading voice rattled down the speaking tube from forward control. "Range to that can is closing fast, Captain."

"Forget him, Guns. We're going for the big ones."

Joe Allen pointed ahead. "A rough-looking bunch out there, sir."

"Murderer's row," Paige said.

"Why are we holding fire, sir?"

"For the five-inch to get in their licks. Range is still too much for them. If we opened now with the main batteries, we'd give our position away."

"But that picket destroyer's already signaling. They'll be waiting for us."

"I'm gambling on confusion. They don't know who we are, Joe."

In Sky One, Ensign Newell called out the silhouettes. "Farther left a *Sendai* class light cruiser. Dead ahead a *Mogami* heavy. Two points off the starboard bow another heavy, looks like *Tone* class. There are six destroyers—"

Paige cursed. "Knock it off, Professor!" He had moved to the port wing of the bridge. Blinker signals flashed urgently from Target A. She's too damned close, Paige thought, for comfort. A lookout's scream sent the blood racing to his head.

"Torpedo on the port beam!"

"Left hard rudder!" He lunged for the splinter shield and saw the ghostly wake and then another. Sleek death. The seconds dragged. *Gloucester* strained to the emergency turn. The ship heeled. Deck gear slid and crashed. Men stumbled, groping for hand holds.

"Resume base course!" The streaks slithered past, luminous and silent, the closest less than a hundred yards distant. No time to waste now, Paige thought, and stared anxiously at the massed enemy silhouettes ahead. Back on course, *Gloucester* plunged throbbing nose-deep into the roiled sea. A confusion of reports flooded the bridge. The phone talkers yelled for discipline and looked beseechingly to Paige for help. He fought to keep his air of cool command. "Advise all topside stations to report nothing but torpedoes."

"What about ships, Captain?"

"Christ, a blind man could see all those ships!"

The radio officer pushed his way to the captain's side. Paige glared at him. "What the hell are you doing here?"

"Sorry, Captain. *Langley* and the two cans, *Cushman* and *Hurlburt*—" he stopped, his face agitated.

"Report, damn it!"

"They've gone down seventy miles southeast of Tjilatjap."

Paige turned away.

"Thought I'd best tell you—"

"You've told me. Now shove off."

"I thought I'd remind you, you can break radio silence now."

Paige punched his arm. "Hell, yes! Raise ComSoWesPac, Darwin. Give him our position. Tell him we're about to crash a fancy landing party."

"Those words, Captain?"

"Whose the hell do you want? Farragut's?" He thought of famous last words. Why the hell not? Was history for Farragut, Jones, and Perry alone? "Get off a dispatch to CINCPAC in Pearl. Here, give me that pencil." He scribbled rapidly across the clipboard, a slow grin spreading across his face. "That should give Old Nick a turn." He patted the radio officer's behind. "Get if off, genius, before we're all blown to hell."

It was time to present his calling card. He pulled the JA talker to his side and raised the mouthpiece to his lips. He pictured Hurley on the other end, green and brave, trying to fill dead Donaldson's golden slippers.

"Guns?"

"Aye, Captain?"

"Range to the nearest heavy?"

"Twelve thousand yards, closing." There was a pause. "Eleven five, sir. Two targets at that range, port and starboard."

"Thanks, Guns. Label 'em Target B and C." Any moment now he expected the jolt of torpedoes against the ship's side. He nodded to Allen. "Two-block the battle flag."

The colors flapped heavenward, two signalmen clutching the deep folds to clear obstructions.

"Guns from bridge?"

"Aye, Captain."

"Range."

"Eleven thousand."

"Stand by." The seconds passed. "Listen carefully, Guns. Our course is taking us between the two cruisers, B and C. Split your main battery fire. Direct all five-inch mount officers to engage targets as they see them. Once we're through, there's no Turret Three to cover for us. Your after five-inch will have to do the job. Make every shot count. We have got to kill on the way in."

"Aye, Captain."

"Commence firing."

Six tongues of orange flame licked out followed by an ear-splitting roar. In eight seconds, six more. And more and more. Each salvo seemed to burst the heart of *Gloucester*'s men. They cheered and wept. It had arrived at last, this terrible joy.

The guns continued firing for almost two minutes, incredibly without challenge. Through his glasses, Paige observed the first salvo straddle the heavy cruiser to port. The second struck the starboard hangar deck of Target B, setting fire to a scout plane on its catapult. It exploded as the deck crew pushed it to the side to be jettisoned.

On Target C fire flashed in her superstructure. Men leaped and fell to the deck below her canted forward stack. Paige grabbed the JA talker's phones. "You're right on, Hurley. Goddam good shooting!"

He knew it, he knew he would be right. In spite of the picket destroyer's alarm, the flustered heavies had not yet determined who and where the enemy was. From the shore, coastal guns threw heavy antiaircraft fire. Tracers streamed high across the night sky. Paige slapped Commander Allen's back. "The silly bastards think we're planes."

"They still don't know what hit them," Allen said in wonder.

They watched the burning cruisers, under way now, belching smoke, moving apart. Their AA tracers joined the fire from the shore and stabbed skyward. Allen pointed ahead. The shapes of more ships cleared the thick smoke. They raced in wild confusion seeking safety and an enemy to fire on. A brightness of starshells soared upward white as noon and burst too far astern of *Gloucester* to reveal her.

"Range to Target C, Guns."

"Nine thousand yards, Captain."

The stricken cruiser erupted in a solid sheet of flame as she circled for a favoring wind. Her captain raced about the bridge screaming orders as men lowered lifeboats to the water. She listed heavily to starboard and began to drift slowly toward shore.

Starshells burst high above *Gloucester*, fired from a light cruiser several thousand yards beyond Target C. "Take her under fire, Guns. She's Target D."

"Aye, Captain."

Paige stationed himself behind Wilson. "Come left easy, Stick."

"Rudder's left easy, Captain."

"Head between that light cruiser and Target B."

"Aye, Captain."

"We're going right through that hole."

Holes, Stick thought.

"Allen? How soon will we have Target B abeam to port?"

"If they hold relative position and we maintain course and speed, I'd say three and a half minutes."

"They sure as hell don't know what hit 'em. That first can was the only one on the ball."

"It won't take long with these starshells, sir."

"By that time, Joe, I want to be through those big boys and in a position to take a crack at the transports. When do we round the Point?"

"Five minutes, give or take a few seconds."

"Good enough. What course?"

"Probably one-one-zero. Depends where they're landing troops and we won't know that until we round the Point."

"As soon as we've run this gantlet, execute the course change. With or without me. Understand?"

"Aye, Captain."

He peered ahead where *Gloucester*'s eight-inch guns had taken the light cruiser under fire. From the corner of his eye he saw the first muzzle bursts flame from Target B. *Now they know*, he thought, *and here they come*. "Left hard rudder!" He gripped the edge of the splinter shield too late. The enemy salvo struck and the ship shuddered and Paige was thrown heavily to the deck. A rope of pain spiraled upward from his ankle to his knee. Needles of paint flaked from the bulkheads, flicking his face and hands. Glass smashed on steel. The ship pitched sickeningly. *Christ!* he thought. A *hit the first salvo*. "Who said those Nips can't shoot?" He scrambled to his feet and with Wilson flung himself against the spokes of the wheel. Together they slowed and controlled it.

"Head between those two," Paige said pointing.

"Why not?" Wilson was breathing noisily and blood ran from his nose. The others struggled to their feet. Paige moved among them, helping them back to their posts. Pain streaked like fire through his leg. He pulled his talker to him.

"Any report on the hit?"

"No report yet, Captain."

The rudder was over and the ship heeled sharply in her return to base course. A comfort of salvos thundered from *Gloucester*'s Turrets One and Two, whistling, bursting, tearing into enemy steel and flesh. White flame burst to starboard. Target B had lost way and Paige, hobbling to the starboard side, saw that she was dead in the water and sinking rapidly by the bow. Flames hissed and died as the sea swallowed her. Two destroyers swung out to stand by for survivors.

Gloucester plunged on, closing the range abeam of Targets B and D. Both had fled on diverging courses to avoid her suicidal bow. Several thousand yards distant now, they opened fire with their main batteries. Six- and eight-inch projectiles splashed geysers skyward, obscuring *Gloucester* in tons of water. She trembled violently. Her decks flooded and men clung desperately to gun shields and life lines and to one another. Paige heckled. "Where the hell are the damage reports?"

His talker beseeched and threatened all stations. Nothing but near misses was all that damage control reported. Paige cursed. "They're not on the ball. They're missing something."

Heavy shells straddled *Gloucester* once more. Deck plates buckled and steam lines parted, hissing death. The talker shook his head. Nothing, he told the captain. No direct hits.

Through smoke and cordite shreds in the garish light Paige caught the rakish shape of Target A, the picket destroyer. She was low in the water. She had circled the other ships and now raced off the port quarter parallel with *Gloucester* and matching her speed. The concentration of fire from the two cruisers ceased abruptly. It took Paige several moments to realize why. His changing position had brought him directly between them. Their hits had been on each other and *Gloucester* had escaped unscathed. "How lucky can I get?" he muttered.

He studied the approach of Target A uneasily. In taking the cruisers under fire he had neglected to keep cognizant of her relative position and now was dismayed to observe her abeam to port at a distance he estimated less than two thousand yards.

"Hard left rudder, Stick."

Wilson turned an agonized face to his skipper.

"You mean right rudder, Captain?"

"Left hard rudder, damn it!"

Stick's thick fingers spun the wheel to port. "We'll be broadside to that can, Captain, and take his torpeckers right up our ass!"

"Mind the helm," Paige roared, "and your goddam tongue!" He shouted into the speaking tube. "Guns! All five-inch that can bear, take the target abeam to port under fire."

"Aye, Captain."

That's the one baby can screw things up, he told himself. He wiped his clammy hands on his shirt. Stick was right. His outraged reaction to the helm order of a turn to port was natural. Paige had deliberately ordered the wrong torpedo defense maneuver. Normal procedure called for a starboard turn, presenting a narrower target in less time. But Paige knew now the Japanese destroyer skipper was no fool. He alone had detected *Gloucester*'s approach and had challenged it. He alone had been bold enough to launch the first torpedo attack.

He had come along now almost undetected and at any moment would unleash another attack. He would have predicted another evasive turn to starboard and his calculations for the spread of torpedoes would compensate for it.

Paige clung to the port alidade as the five-inch guns blazed away. Because of the radical turn, they were splashing short.

"Steady as you go!"

Wilson fought the wheel, muttering to himself. *Gloucester*, like a plagued steel beast dipped and rose and plunged ahead. Paige fixed his glasses on the sea between the racing hulls, a swift helm command ready at his lips. "Order all lookouts to keep a sharp eye for wakes!" He heard the word passed.

Where the hell were those torpedoes? Had the shrewd Nip skipper outfoxed him after all? Was he delaying his spread until Paige had committed himself to the emergency turn? The range seemed to

___

be closing. His eyes played tricks on him in the darkness. He cursed. If he didn't do something soon, something wild and unexpected, he'd have those fish in his belly before *Gloucester* could answer even the most radical helm. *That smart son of a bitch,* he thought. *That sly yellow bastard. I'll show him who's running this show.*

"Hard left rudder!" He touched Joe Allen. "Light him up, Joe."

Wilson groaned in anguish and put the wheel over. His eyes were glassy with hate. "You'll ram him sure as hell," he cried. He blinked as *Gloucester's* searchlights came on.

"That's the idea." Paige leveled his glasses on the destroyer bridge and studied the distraught movements of the Japanese commander. His reckless helm order had upset the enemy's calculations and his torpedo officer was having difficulty setting up an accurate firing course. Of more immediate concern was the sudden awareness that the two ships were on a collision course and the enemy skipper obviously did not relish the idea of being run down by the heavier ship. He could veer off to port and avoid the collision, or he could hold his course and gamble on a hasty firing of the starboard tubes simultaneous with a hard left rudder to clear the cruiser's clipper bow.

Paige gripped the railing hard. The enemy destroyer held course. In the searchlights' glare he clearly saw the three torpedoes lunge from their deck tubes amidships and slap into the bubbling foam.

"Rudder's still left," Wilson cried.

"Keep her there." He leaned with the turn. *A bit of body English and a prayer,* he thought. He came up sharp on his good leg. The torpedoes were running true. He was helpless to move. The ship appeared to stand still, seemingly anchored where she was, unable to change now that her course was committed. Sure as hell I'll lose her now, Paige thought, just when everything seemed to be working out.

He reached out and gripped the engine room telegraph and in his rage slammed the levers against FLANK SPEED again and again. "C'mon, you bastards! Speed! Deliver speed! What the hell's wrong down there?"

The talker cringed. "Engine room says they don't know where they're getting what they got."

Jesus H. Christ. He let go the levers and shut his eyes. His testicles ached so he had to hold them. He waited like that, every nerve pounding. There must be an easier way to earn a buck, he thought. A cleaner way to die.

The main batteries held fire, waiting for a steadier course on which to base their firing calculations. The five-inch could no longer bear. An eerie silence fell on this violent place in the sea.

A ragged cheer. He looked round and saw where the torpedoes had passed close astern. Where he had calculated they would.

"Steady as you go, Stick!" He coughed and clawed at his throat, grinning insanely, vowing to himself: I'll go to church. I'll pray on my knees to God. I'll drop hundred-dollar bills in the collection box. I'll sing holy hymns in Macy's window.

"Douse searchlights!"

"Steady on"—Stick read the course where the needle quivered—"three-three-seven, Captain."

The destroyer had made her turn to port to clear *Gloucester's* overtaking bow. Heeled over with her starboard deck awash, she was trapped in the turn that slowed her, wallowing in her wake like a puppy on a polished floor.

"Dead duck," Paige gloated.

"We're gonna hit," someone whimpered.

"Come right a hair, Stick. All I want is a piece of her fantail." He grabbed the mouthpiece of his talker's phones and depressed the button. "All hands take cover! Stand by for a crash!" And to Wilson: "Hard right, Stick! *Hard*, you bowlegged bastard!"

His words echoed in the night wind and shrilled back to his ears from the topside squawk box. A stillness followed in which he clearly heard the bridge chronometer tick the seconds. Then silence disintegrated into bedlam as *Gloucester's* bow at flank speed crunched into the enemy's side. The impact caught and flung men and gear in a grinding eruption of metal, wood, and cloth. The night air instantly filled with curses and screams. Sea water rushed past wrenched steel bulkheads. Live steam hissed from burst mains. In the ghastly glare of starshells, fragments of splintered bone and flesh tore cloth and whined skyward. Men were tossed like broken matchsticks into the sea. Scalded and spitted and crazy with pain, shipmate followed shipmate over the side.

Gloucester's bow had struck cleanly. She rose high, dripping men and wreckage and seemed to hang there for several seconds. Then sheer weight and momentum and her churning screws drove her ahead through the rest of the destroyer's starboard side and tore it from the forward section. Paige watched the jagged edge of the enemy fantail pass ten yards from where he clung to the wing of the bridge. A blur of naked-waisted men and the twisted insides of living spaces drifted by. A rack of depth charges churned past so close he could almost reach and touch it. Turning, he watched the last of it settle and disappear into the sea before *Gloucester*'s stern had cleared the scene. He felt an odd twinge of regret. That tin can skipper was too smart to live, too good to die.

He bent, deafened now by the resuming gunfire of the main batteries. The talker shouted in his ear. "Damage control forward reports we're taking sea water, Captain, very fast in the chain lockers."

What were they expecting? A vintage champagne? His leg throbbed painfully. He drew a breath and squinted ahead. Blinker signals winked like Times Square at midnight. "I'm a fox in a hen house," he muttered to Allen. "How soon do we turn that goddam Point?"

"Two minutes, Captain."

"Christ, we'll never make it now."

A commotion on the forecastle deck begged his attention. He nudged his talker. "Find out what the hell's going on down there. Sounds like pistol fire."

"Don't look at me," Wilson said.

Dead astern the cleft destroyer's bow nosed up. The sea flooded her midsection and she settled sluggishly a few feet at a time. The captain flicked Wilson's ear. "If you made the turn when I ordered it, he'd have gone down like a rock."

"More fun this way, Captain. Slow and nasty."

The talker spoke up. "Repair One reports several buckled plates forward from Frame 1 to 8, watertight doors damaged and we're still taking sea water in the starboard chain locker. Paint locker's on fire and under control."

"Casualties?"

"Some men missing from their battle stations forward is all. They're still checking. Damage control reports a hit aft in the plotting room. Nobody got out."

"What was the ruckus on the forecastle deck?"

"Unexpected guests, sir. We took aboard some Japs when we rammed that can."

"Where are they?"

"They ain't, Captain. Not any more."

"Tell Repair One to report when they get that water under control."

The ship slowed and yawed and he knew the damage to the bow was more serious than the report had indicated. He glanced at Wilson on the wheel. "Having trouble, Stick?"

"She's steering funny."

"Try to hold course." Sure, he thought. With your face ripped open and blood in your eyes, try to run home. The big guns below him still thundered. Turret One had taken the *Sendai* light cruiser under fire to starboard. *Gloucester* plunged ahead on her erratic course as Wilson fought the wheel. Turret Two's eight-inch rifles depressed to engage the *Tone* heavy cruiser to port. Her salvos overshot and Paige swore. In a few moments the opportunity would be lost—the crippled cruisers too far aft for his forward turrets to bear. The hell with them, he thought. Bring on the transports.

Shells whined. An explosion, muffled to his deafened ears, sent him to the deck. He sat stunned. Arrows of pain coursed through his leg. Wilson's mouth was at his ear. "She don't answer the helm, Captain."

"Shift to after steering." He struggled to his feet. "All engines ahead slow." He sent the speed signal to the engine room. His JA talker lay dead. Paige removed the headset from the man's ear and wiped away the blood. He fitted the phones on Wilson's head. "Tell Commander Olsen in Battle Two to take the helm. We'll keep the conn here and relay course changes to him."

His ship was in trouble now. About time, he thought, feeling *Gloucester* lose way. She broached to, her port beam meeting the sea amidships. As her speed slackened, her flooded bow dipped low, scooping deep into the quartering swells. The sea broke high slamming tons of water down the length of her forecastle deck and aft.

Got to get those transports. Just one crack at 'em is all. He clung stubbornly to the image. Wilson nudged him. The ship had straightened somehow and her course steadied.

"Steering's aft, Captain."

"How do you know?"

"Battle Two just said so is how I know, sir." Wilson looked hurt.

Paige grinned and jabbed his middle. "Ask the exec how he's doing."

Wilson saluted stiffly and made the inquiry. "He reports every-thing is under control. He sounds funny, sir."

"What do you mean, *funny?*"

"Giggling. Like a schoolgirl."

Joe Allen came out of the chart house, dividers in hand. "We can make that turn now, Captain."

"Let's hope so." He rubbed his jaw. *Giggling?* "Tell Battle Two to come right with standard rudder to course"—he glanced at Allen —"one-one-zero?"

Allen nodded. Paige repeated the course. "Let's see if the old girl answers the helm. All engines ahead full."

Seconds passed in an agony of doubt. Slowly, *Gloucester* com-menced her turn. Paige faced Allen with a look of relief that froze as sudden hell broke loose. The ship shuddered. Amidships a tower of flame leaped high. Debris showered the bridge from a hit on the catapult deck. A repair crew struggled with fire hoses. Some fell screaming. Paige remembered the drums of aviation gasoline he had not dumped. Why the hell hadn't the plane crews taken care of it? Or the chief bosun's mate? What the hell was wrong with the sprin-kler system? Why the hell must he think of everything?

The course change fanned the flames outward from the blistering hull. Fire fighters edged along the slippery canted deck as close to the lashed drums as they could get. Any minute now, Paige thought, they'll be blown to kingdom come. Wherever the hell that is. He turned away. Allen did not miss it. "They'll make it, Captain."

Paige stared at him. "Where the hell are those transports?"

"Beyond that low point, inside the bay."

Paige shouted into the speaking tube. "Guns, stand by for new targets." He peered ahead. "Can't those damned snipes crank up more speed? We're dragging ass."

"Transports off the starboard bow, Captain." Allen pointed.

The shapes of massed merchant ships took form through the haze. Landing barges in a constant flow moved like water bugs to and from the shore. "A course, Allen, on the double." Paige snapped the words in anguish as another near miss rocked the ship. "Got to close range fast."

"One-five-zero, Captain." The word was passed to Battle Two. Allen helped a corpsman drag the captain's dead talker to the shelter of the pilot house. Paige studied the massed armada of troop ships.

"Guns."

"Guns aye, Captain."

"Targets are the transports to starboard, Hurley. Our new course can pile us on the beach but it's giving you point-blank range. You can't miss. Throw everything you've got."

"Yes, sir."

"Commence firing."

Gloucester's starboard side came alive with gunfire. The shrill crack of .50-calibre stuff mingled with the deep boom of the main batteries. Enemy fire still rained round *Gloucester*, scoring, missing, unable to stop her. Thick black and yellow smoke wreathed her decks and superstructure. The stink of cordite and death hung over her. Men fought flames and clawed at wreckage. Round after round spilled from the muzzles of guns while men still lived to fire them.

A thousand yards ahead along the curving shoreline, the confused scene came clearly now to the topside crews in *Gloucester*. Wooden barges were burning and foundering. Small men raced about like stricken ants and plunged into the sea. Enemy AA batteries still penciled useless tracers across the reddened sky.

The thunder of heavy guns quit suddenly. Paige looked below and realized with sinking hope that Turrets One and Two were silent. "Forward control from Battle One. What's happened to your gunfire forward?"

Hurley's voice crackled in the speaking tube, some of the words fading. "Battle One from forward control. Magazines forward report all ammunition expended."

"*All?*"

"All eight-inch projectiles, Captain, and Turret Two—can you hear me, sir?"

"Too well, goddam it. *Report.*"

"Turret Two still has nine rounds on deck from the handling room and that is all. Repeat: Nine rounds of common to Turret Two and that is all."

"Very well." He reached down and gingerly felt his leg. The cotton khaki had shredded and the flesh was numb to his touch. Nine rounds. Three salvos and out. Finis. *Kaput.* "What about five-inch and the machine guns?"

"Still firing, Captain, when they can see targets."

Nine rounds. Nine stinking lousy filthy farewell rounds of common. "Listen, Hurley, we've still got way on. Throw on your search-

lights and flood those transports. Break out every damned bit of
ammo we've got. Incendiaries, armor-piercing, shrapnel, Fourth of
July. But hold back those nine rounds of common until we're so
close you can't miss. Then let 'em have it. Don't wait for orders.
Shoot when you've got 'em where you want 'em. Kill 'em. Repeat,
kill 'em."

Two crippled enemy cruisers off *Gloucester*'s quarters had found
the range and still lobbed their shells. Paige shut his ears to
damage reports. All that mattered now was to stay alive long
enough to finish off the transports.

Gloucester's searchlights from their platforms aloft blazed to life.
The starboard five-inch guns took up their rhythmic thump. The
chatter of the one-point-ones and machine guns followed as Newell
in Sky One gave the order to open fire.

The range to the transports closed slowly. Paige hobbled to the
ladder and pulled himself up to the port wing of Sky One. It was
an unexpected beehive of activity. Ensign Newell, stripped to the
waist and wearing headphones, fed ammo clips to the loaders who
dropped them into the smoking breeches of the one-point-ones.
Doorn, in his oil- and blood-streaked whites, stood beside him and
triggered a .50-calibre machine gun whose fire arched in bursts toward
the nearest transport's open bridge. Neither had observed the
captain and Paige descended quietly. *Be damned!* he thought in
pleased wonder.

Glancing aft he saw for the first time what a shambles his ship
had become. Bodies lay everywhere, now oddly shaped for men.
Gloucester's decks and superstructure had crumpled like tinfoil.
Motor whale boats hung in their davits, smashed and useless.

A shout from Allen sent him limping to the open bridge. A
direct hit had smashed through the thin armor of Turret One. Flame
and smoke poured in dense clouds through the windows of the
turret booth. A repair crew hacked at the dogged-down steel door
twisted on its lower hinge and jammed. "Hurley says the sprinkler
system's fouled up and they can't flood the magazine. Those guys
are trapped in there with the live powder."

"It's too late to help 'em."

"They'll roast alive, Captain!"

"The hell with it, Joe. They're out of ammo anyway. I want
those transports!" He bawled into the speaking tube. "Hurley! The

hell with Turret One. Get along with those nine rounds of common. What are you waiting for?"

Allen shouted orders to the repair crew. They dragged a fire hose to the slitted window of Turret One and directed a weak stream of water through the opening. Another crew pried open the door enough for a man to squeeze through. Three men made it, staggering and choking, before the turret erupted in a stunning burst of white flame.

The concussion shook the bridge and sent deadly steel fragments flying. Fire broke out in the chart house. Paige grabbed charts and flailed at the flames with his bare hands until Allen pulled him away and together they took cover in the lee of the pilot house. Paige covered his face. Allen gently shook him. "We're doing okay, Captain." He stared in horror at the loose shreds of skin hanging from Paige's scorched hands.

Turret Two below the bridge opened fire at point-blank range on the massed wooden hulls of the transports. Three times. Three salvos. Nine direct hits. For nine good men buried in the good Dutch earth, Paige thought. He moved to the rail. He did not need his glasses or a scorecard. Together with Joe Allen, he watched the nearest transport disintegrate. Beyond her burning superstructure, two more transports became solid sheets of flame through which half-naked men ran screaming and leaped into the sea.

"Hard left rudder." The ship heeled sluggishly as the helmsman in Battle Two put over the rudder. Enemy gunfire found *Gloucester*'s searchlights and plunged them hissing to blackness and shattered glass. Paige laughed wildly. "Too late, you dumb bastards. Too late!" He turned away and Joe Allen grabbed him and threw him to the deck. A shell whined over them and smashed into the forward gun director above their heads. Paige dimly heard the wrench of ruptured steel and a terrible roar and that was all he knew.

Bomb splinters showered the bridge. Men fell bleeding, their cries shrill against the hoarse warning shouts and the din of guns. All sound meshed in a grinding crash. The gun director, ripped from its housing, tipped forward slowly and like a monstrous idol toppled. It struck the lip of the splinter shield. Its range finder arms folded like a doll's and all of it struck with crushing force on the welded shell of Turret Two. Paige sat up, his head throbbing. "Steady as you go!" He could not hear himself, felt for his ears, and shouted again. He crawled free, wiping blood, seeking Allen. He pressed shredded palms to his face, nose, ear, panic on him.

Enemy searchlights bathed the bridge in light. The big guns had ceased firing. The ship seemed to right itself, faltered, slowed, began to list. Paige's fingers found his cap. He jammed it on his head thinking insanely *dignity of rank* and in sheer madness caught a fleeting image of Admiral Flint's handsome face in disapproval. About him were the dead and dying. In the naked glare he saw Allen in the chart house bareheaded and unhurt coolly repeating the last helm command to Battle Two. Wilson was gone and for an instant the captain grieved.

Bleeding men crawled from the shambles of Turret Two into the bloodstained arms of weary corpsmen. Some wept. Paige groped for the speaking tube and could not find it. The bulkhead itself was gone. He ripped the soundpowered phones from a dead talker's head and chest. The circuits were dead. No station acknowledged. He tried the engine room telegraph controls. There was no response. Over the gaping hole of the gun director housing he saw Ensign Newell's crewcut head appear.

"Can I help down there, Captain?"

"Keep your damned guns firing."

"I'll try, sir. Everyone's dead up here." He disappeared and the captain joined Allen in the chart house.

"No control here, sir," Allen said.

"You hooked into Battle Two, Joe?" Allen nodded. Paige said, "Give me the phones." Allen adjusted them to his skipper's head. As though nothing had happened, nothing in the world, Paige said calmly, "Battle Two, this is the captain." He waited. There was no acknowledgment. "Battle Two. This is Battle One. Any one there? We want to shift the conn aft. Come in, Battle One."

"Maybe they hear you and we don't hear them," Joe Allen said. Paige held up his hand. "Somebody's there."

"Battle Two, aye." The voice came through weak and blurred.

"That you, Oley?"

"Commander Olsen's gone, Captain."

"What do you mean, gone?"

"He just ain't here, sir."

"Who is this?"

"Linwood, Captain. Yeoman second." The voice cracked slightly. "They're all gone. I'm all alone."

"Stand fast, Linwood. We're coming aft."

A single machine gun fired sporadic bursts above the bridge. Newell in Sky One, Paige guessed. It surprised and pleased him. He tried to raise Hurley in forward control. The line was dead. He pulled off the earphones and together with Allen started aft to the ladder. Another explosion rocked the ship. Paige crawled back to the phones. "Battle Two. You still there?"

"Battle Two, aye."

"Report damage."

Silence. A faint crackle. Paige heard the sound of voices and rushing water. "Linwood? You still there?"

"Battle Two, aye, Captain. They just passed the word from damage control. A torpedo in the engine room aft."

Paige envisioned live steam and scalded men. "Very well, Linwood. Hang on." The ship's vibrations ceased. Strangely, she seemed to glide ahead barely making way. Paige searched the water. All he asked now was sea room enough to sink her in—a deep sea the enemy could not salvage from.

Another explosion sent Paige to his knees. He rolled in pain, his leg live as fire. *Gloucester's* hull shivered with the impact of two more torpedoes, seconds apart. What remained of her insides died in steam. Her bow settled. The sea began her death run through.

A clean fast end, Paige prayed. He felt drained but not unfulfilled. Not weak certainly, the way he used to feel after ten rounds with an in-fighter, a body puncher who hit as hard as he did.

Still captain, he thought hazily. Captain goes down with his ship. He tried to get up. His right leg seemed numb from the knee down. Gingerly, he tried to flex it and closed his eyes against the pain. Where the hell had Oley gone? Linwood. Who was Linwood?

Strong hands helped him. He looked blurrily into Allen's tense face and Wilson's broad one. Wilson. "Where in hell you been, Stick?" He winced as they tried to lift him.

"Flag bags. Where the goddam hit threw me."

"Chasing broads—" he grinned feebly, touching Wilson's cheek.

"You're hurt, Captain."

"Look who's talking."

"We got to get you below, Captain," Joe Allen said.

"Everybody's dead and gone," Stick said.

Paige pulled himself free. "I'm staying." He felt drunk and sleepy. They sat him up. "Resume firing," he muttered.

Stick pleaded. "Time's running out, Captain."

"Shove off," Paige said. "That's a command."

Allen's fingers eased but Wilson's gained strength. "What the hell for?" he snarled. "What'd the Navy ever do for you?"

"He's still in command, Wilson." Allen seemed confused.

"Command, my ass! Command of what? What's in it for the Navy if he stays? A dead hero?" He strained at the captain's arms. "C'mon, damn it!"

Paige heard the words distant over peaceful fields of snow in clean winter air brittle as glass. He smiled, wanting to live, thanking Wilson for those words.

"Joe?"

"Yes, Captain?"

"What is our situation?"

"Dead in the water, sir, settling by the bow. An eighteen-degree list to starboard. All communications disrupted. Enemy torpedo boats have taken us under fire at close range port and starboard."

"Where is Commander Olsen?"

"Don't know, sir. Communications with Battle Two are out."

Paige fell silent. Can't they let me die in peace? He heard the rattle of a machine gun. "That all they got?" he asked Allen.

"That's your trigger-happy feather merchant in Sky One," Wilson said.

Strength seemed to return to Paige. He sat up. They tried to help him. "I'm okay now," he said. The hell with dying, he thought. Who was he to ask for peaceful death? Mahatma Gandhi? He looked at the bodies around him. "Pass the word. All hands, Joe. Abandon ship." Allen stood dumbly staring at the captain. Paige shoved him gently. "Get going, Joe. Abandon ship. We sure as hell can't save her."

The navigator crawled past Paige to the squawk box. His words echoed flatly on the wrecked bridge. "Circuits are dead, Captain."

"Try word of mouth. And quit staring at me like that."

Tracer fire raked *Gloucester* as the torpedo boats raced by. Paige clung to the side of the splinter shield and cursed them. His eyes settled on the burning transports. *Look at those babies burn!*

He crawled into his sea cabin, his leg dragging. Lee Chin kneeled on the deck praying. "Time to shove, Lee. Old Buddha can't help us now."

Lee Chin got to his feet still mumbling prayers. Paige fumbled for some papers and his diary. He rolled them in waterproof packets and stuffed them into his pockets. He pushed Lee Chin ahead of him through the door. Pain coursed through his arms and legs. "Keep low and head for the ladder and get over the side."

"Your hands very bad, Captain."

"Get going, Lee."

"I stay with you, Captain."

"Get a life raft down there and hold it for us." He turned away abruptly and the pain shot through him again and he stumbled. Lee Chin helped him to his feet. Paige bent, cursing pain. Lee Chin took his arm. "You hurt too bad, Captain."

Paige shoved him. "Blame your lousy cooking. Get that raft ready. On the double."

Allen joined him, his arms full. "I dumped most of the classified stuff, Captain. These are the rough logs. Think we'll make it?"

"We'll make it." And he thought: *In the pig's ass.* A bugle's clear notes rang out. Paige stared at Allen. "What the hell's that?"

"Abandon ship, Captain."

"A damn nice call. I never heard it on a bugle before."

"It sure is pretty," Stick said.

A burst of machine-gun fire ricocheted off the pilot house. Smashed glass flew. Allen helped Paige to the ladder and they started down. Dazed men stumbled out of the scuttles, faces and bodies scorched, clothes in shreds. Some fell on the deck and lay still. Others writhed in pain, making pitiful animal sounds. Gunfire rang out on the forecastle deck. Paige and Allen ducked for shelter against a bulkhead. Paige peered cautiously round the splinter shield. Two knots of men were knee-deep in water, braced against Turret One, firing Thompson guns at the motor torpedo boats. The fast boats in formation made a high-speed turn. On the reverse run their machine-gun bursts cut the men down. They toppled into the oily water like smashed dolls.

Lee Chin brought a life raft alongside and held its painter with both hands, his feet braced against the scuppers. The raft bobbed violently. "Hurry, please," he begged. Wilson tugged at the captain's arm. "C'mon, skipper." Allen with his arms full made his way with difficulty onto the raft.

Oil and cordite and the smell of seared flesh clung to the moist
night air. Empty brass from eight-inch shells littered the deck at the
foot of the ladder. Wilson kicked them aside and helped the captain
down to the main deck. Paige gripped the bottom rung. "What about
Hurley's gang in forward control?"

"They got the word, Captain."

Paige stared aloft. "I don't see them." Machine-gun bullets laced
the bulkhead a few feet over their heads. Steel fragments flew.

"Let's go!" Wilson pleaded. He called down to Allen. "He won't
budge, Commander." Allen climbed back on deck. Paige held his
arm.

"Where's Ensign Newell?"

"He got the word, Captain. They must have heard the bugle."

Paige nodded at Wilson. "Get Newell."

Wilson started up the ladder. The roar of boat motors increased.
Allen pulled Paige down behind a ready ammunition box. Lee Chin
took a few quick turns on the painter to secure the line to a
stanchion. The boats came on. He flung himself flat on his belly
but he had waited too long. The torpedo boats roared past, throttles
wide open. Bullets pummeled Lee Chin like a pillow and ricocheted
off the ready box and chunked against steel, inches from the captain's
head. Paige lunged toward Lee Chin's crumpled form. Allen dragged
him to the safety of a passageway. They clung together, their fingers
hooked to the coaming, bodies flat to the slanted deck. "Bastards!"
Paige cried. "Bastards!" Water sloshed over the coaming and rolled
the empty shell casings. They clinked like heavy coin. Lee Chin's
blood ran over them. Paige could not tear his eyes away. "I hope
to hell he knew how to tie a half hitch." He wiped his eyes and
peered cautiously out of the open hatchway. The patrol boats were
a thousand yards away, turning. He looked to Sky One but could
not see Wilson. "He just better the hell bring Newell back."

Allen said nothing. He tested the odd knot Lee Chin had made.
It seemed to hold the raft securely. We just might make it, Allen
reflected. If Wilson would only hurry.

Newell in Sky One heard the bugle call. He had just fired at a
careening torpedo boat and was reloading a magazine. It was silly,
blowing a bugle at a time like this. He saw the gunnery crew climb
out of the top hamper of forward control above him. Hurley appeared, gesturing and shouting for him to go. Newell hesitated.

The skipper's last order to Sky One had been to stay there and "keep those damned guns firing." It was always the last order received you were supposed to obey, at least that had been made clear at midshipman school, where very little else had been made clear. Well, he was doing the best he could. He looked up at Hurley still shouting and wondered if fresh orders would countermand the captain's. War is very complicated, he decided, and the best thing to do is to wait where he was until Hurley and his gunnery control crew reached him.

The deck felt hot through the soles of his shoes. Looking aft, he observed Commander Lefferts climb on deck through a smashed hatchway. He wore no cap. His pouchy skin looked lavender in the garish light. He carried something bright in his fingers. Newell was surprised to see it was a scalpel and his arms were bloody to his elbows.

Fires burned abaft the galley deck house. Beyond the twisted wreckage of the aviation crane amidships men were rigging cargo nets for ladders. Others slipped hand over hand down Gloucester's scaly side into the sea. It became clear to Newell now, what the bugle call had meant.

The men who could make it clustered on the upraised fantail. Others dragged the wounded aft in makeshift litters or carried them in their arms to keep them from drowning. The enemy boats had turned and Newell watched in horror as they raced back and raked the decks with gunfire. Awkward in their life jackets, the men milled about like bewildered sheep. Struck, they sagged and fell and with the curious finality of weighted sacks slid into the sea.

Hurley's crew had started down the tripod foremast. Hurley was the last to go. The torpedo boats in mid-run spotted them. Tracer bullets arched upward. Caught in a crossfire, the men clung for seconds, then fell. Hurley's body came headfirst in a swan dive, arms outstretched, and impaled itself on a finger of ragged steel where the gun director had ripped away. It hung, grotesquely jerking, not ten feet from Newell. Hurley moaned and Newell turned away in horror. As a child he had once found a day-old bird fallen from its nest and dead. Now this. And it was no less piteous.

He was filled with an oppressive rage. He raised the machine gun and rested the barrel on the lip of the splinter shield. The last torpedo boat passed dead abeam when Newell squeezed the trigger. He held it for seconds after the last round had ripped into the boat's hull. Half-blinded by smoke, he watched the helmsman sag and the boat swerve out of control. Weaving crazily it crashed against *Gloucester*'s side, its crew flung into the sea.

Newell raised the machine gun over his head and hurled it down on the smoking wreckage. He went to Hurley but could not touch him to free him. He did not know where to begin. As Newell watched him, Hurley died.

He had talked with Hurley once or twice over coffee in the wardroom. Hurley's wife had worked for Newell Industries in Connecticut before she married him. Her name was Betty Ann. According to Hurley, they had three impossible kids, all girls, all under nine and described by their amiable father as being part witch and full of piss and vinegar. He described for Newell the big old house on staid Chestnut Street in Salem where the family lived while he was away at sea. Some day Newell must visit them, Hurley had said.

Some day he would. They would want to know how it had happened, wanting the intimate details to pass along the gold star route to the Hurleys to come. He would tell them all right. He would make the trip to the Chestnut Street house and sit in its Victorian stillness and tell them. But he would never tell them this, their one beloved man impaled like a slab of beef on a butcher hook.

Wilson's head appeared over the ladder. "The skipper says to get the hell out of here, we're abandoning ship." Newell went to the ladder. Wilson looking over his shoulder saw Hurley and his eyes met Newell's and he shrugged and started down. Newell saw a movement among the dead. It was Doorn, whitefaced and mute. His eyes stared at Newell and seemed to flicker. Newell dragged him gently to the ladder and lifted him and swung a leg over the shield. The dead weight of Doorn on his shoulder threw him off balance and he missed the first rung. His neck muscles ached painfully. He gripped the ladder tightly, his blistered palms tender on steel. *One hand for yourself*, he remembered, *and one for the Navy*. He looked below.

Toward the shore he saw the heavy cruiser on its side aground. Beyond her smoking hull two transports burned fiercely and several barges, beached and gutted, were still smoking. The unholy waste of it, he thought. At the foot of the ladder, he had to step wide to avoid the crumpled bodies of two men.

Why not me?

He knew why not. His father's last words on the Navy Pier in San Francisco had been quite clear: "God will watch over you, son," his father had said. Leave it to Thomas A. Newell, Tod thought. He had arranged it with God, personally.

Two more decks to go. He descended slowly and hesitated, hearing screams. He looked aft and saw the survivors of the machine-gun attack leaping into the sea. Oil on the water had raised a curtain of flame. They swam frantically to escape it, arms and legs thrashing. The fire swept by the wind raced toward them and with a hideous crackling roasted them like cockroaches.

Newell stood transfixed. The scene was intense and pitiless, each detail etched larger than life. He had never witnessed death so swift and grim, so absolute. Hurley's. Theirs.

"On the double, Newell!" Joe Allen, two decks below, had launched the life raft. Paige and Wilson were aboard and Allen joined them and held it close to the ship's side where it heaved violently. Newell lowered Doorn to the deck and unstrapped his own life belt and secured it round Doorn's waist. He brought Doorn to the rail. The effort exhausted him. He dimly heard the shouts of the others but seemed drained of strength and purpose. He held Doorn teetering on the rail. Allen pleaded and Wilson cursed. Newell could not move.

"Get him, Stick," Paige ordered.

Allen steadied the line. Wilson climbed the raft's edge and caught Doorn's limp arm. He tugged hard and Doorn's body slid from Newell's grasp into his waiting arms. Wilson took one disgusted look. "Christ! Don't you know a dead man when you see one?"

He let Doorn go. The body hit the edge and splashed into the sea. Newell watched stupefied as it floated away. "He was still alive," he said. "I saw his eyelids move." Newell started to climb after Doorn's body now drifting along the ship's side gathering oil. The roar of the boat engines drowned Wilson's curses. He caught Newell's leg and yanked hard. Newell like Doorn toppled into the sea. Wilson muttering ducked low and the machine guns fired at another raft a hundred yards away.

Newell sank through thick oil to warm sea and came up vomiting. He struck out in terror, afraid to die, certain he would. His fingers clawed the ship's side slimy with moss and were cruelly raked by barnacles. He held on, heaving mouthfuls of oily sea water and struggled to catch a clear breath. His hands bled from many small cuts.

Someone pounded the thin steel from inside the ship so close to his face, he recoiled. A muffled voice like an echo in a tomb distinctly cried, "God help us . . . oh God . . ." and was lost to Newell.

Hands reached down and dragged him across the coarse canvas of the raft. He struggled to escape. Strong arms stayed him. His insides churned uncontrollably. Weak and dizzy, he yielded and lay there, drained. Allen pushed off. He did not look back when *Gloucester* with a rumbling sigh went down.

She had been a gallant ship. Lying on the bottom, in the ooze that was her final resting place, *Gloucester* threw her last salute. Something burst inside her smashed body. Its violence rumbled upward, pressured the men's ears with the hurtling roar of an oncoming express. Huge bubbles with steel guts burst the surface, geysering upward, reached for the enemy torpedo boats and smashed their hulls like biscuits.

Five hundred yards away the raft tossed wildly in the trough of enormous waves. The four men lay half-stunned, clinging to the safety lines. The seas piled over them. Paige's moans and the suck of the sea beneath the raft were the only sound in the quiet aftermath. It seemed for several minutes the war had gone away. Bodies swirled in widening whirlpools and drifted free. When they could, the men on the raft worked frantically to save them. It was a waste of precious strength. None they reached had survived the explosion and they rolled the bodies back into the sea.

The raft pitched like a cork bob. The shrill staccato of machine guns resumed, much closer now.

Newell tried to sit up. Allen sprawled over him, pinning him. The sound of guns had ceased. The cries of men lost in the darkness grew faint. Newell lay dizzy with nausea, unable to open his right eye. He raised his head and saw the captain and Allen's tear-streaked face and Wilson's beard. He could not see the ship anywhere. It seemed no more than seconds since he had left her. He touched Allen who still sprawled across him. "Where's the ship?"

"Gone."

"The skipper?"

"Out cold." Allen released him. "Behave yourself." His voice sounded strange. "Look for survivors. Keep low. They're still shooting." He carefully wiped the oil from Newell's stinging right eye. Watching him, Newell thought how odd it is that Allen, always calm and dry as powder, should weep.

Two torpedo boats crisscrossed the area in and out of the floating wreckage. Their powerful searchlights stabbed the darkness. The bodies of men drifted by, supported by life jackets. Naked feet protruded, trailing tiny wakes. Newell thought of sharks and nibbled toes. The first flicker of dawn showed in the eastern sky. The sight of it after violent death and the red night revived his spirits. He could breathe now. Keep low, he remembered. Search for survivors. Live. His right eye, gummed shut, was afire with pain.

"The wind's pushing us east," Allen whispered. "We might just drift out of here if the tide won't pile us up on the beach."

They lay still. Newell through his one good eye watched the wakes of the enemy boats. Curled and exotic, he thought, like the plumed tails of ancient animals in the Todhunter tapestries back home. He chuckled insanely and Wilson elbowed him. "Sorry, sir," Newell said. The silence was broken by the lapping of the water against the raft's nose. A voice called out somewhere in the night. "Frigging fool," Wilson grunted. "Asking for it." And turning to Newell said, "Another hero," saying it with such contempt that Allen spoke up sharply. "He did all right, Stick. He did fine." Newell, deeply moved, could not look at them.

"My eye's killing me," he muttered.

Allen probed in the supply box lashed to a thwart and produced a first-aid kit. He swabbed Newell's eye and attended to the cuts on his hands. "You did fine up there, kid," he said quietly.

It's good to feel pain, Newell thought.

Wilson untied two short paddles and passed one to Allen. "Go easy," Allen cautioned. "All those damn boats got to do is spot us once and we're dead ducks." They paddled in silence for a while. The raft did not seem to make much headway. The captain did not stir.

"How much longer to daylight?" Newell asked.

"Thirty minutes, maybe." Allen studied the movements of the distant patrol boats, seen only when the raft rode the crest of a swell. "Once it's light they'll have all day."

A motor whale boat drifted close, bottom up. Bullet holes had sieved her side. A thick body, naked but for dungarees, draped the keel. Allen caught the drifting line and secured it to the raft.

Wilson said, "It's Krueger." He let go the paddle and hauled the line close. Before they could stop him he dove into the water and gripping the strakes, pulled himself up the boat's side. Allen held the line taut. "Go easy, Stick. You're rocking the boat." He turned to Newell. "Stand by to help him get that man on board."

Newell kneeled on the raft's edge. Wilson rolled Krueger on his back. Newell caught a full view upside down of the green-tinged face. The eyeballs were blank in their sockets. "The man's dead, Commander."

"Forget him, Stick," Allen called out. "He's dead."

Wilson ignored them. He loosened Krueger's belt and stripped off his dungarees and shoved the body into the water. It sank at once. Wilson tied the legs of the dungarees around his neck and slid down the boat's side. They pulled him aboard the raft. He set about at once turning out Krueger's pockets. "Nothing," he muttered and fell back. Newell tried to comfort him. "You did your best, Stick."

"A hell of a lot of good it did me. The crummy kraut owed me thirty bucks."

Allen said, "Here they come again." He gently shook the captain. Paige groaned and raised his head. "Lee Chin?"

"Dead, Captain."

"Hurley make it?"

"No, Captain."

Paige rubbed his face. "Poor Lee."

"He tied a good knot," Allen said. "I never saw such a knot."

"A Chink specialty," Wilson said.

Newell crawled over. "Those Jap PTs are headed this way."

"Everybody," Allen said. "Over the side."

"We could play dead," Newell suggested.

"I play dead to no live Jap," Paige said.

"They'll shoot anyway," Allen said. "For kicks."

"Let the bastards shoot."

A searchlight stabbed the water fifty yards abeam. "That's too frigging close," Wilson said.

"You first, Newell. Over the side easy," Allen said. "No splashing."

Newell went in. Allen lowered the captain over the side, holding him under the arms. Paige cursed steadily, his words easing the pain of his wounds. In the water Newell put an arm round to support him. Allen and Wilson slid in and came alongside quietly. The steady throb of motors increased. "Those bastards hunt real careful," Stick said.

"Quiet," Allen cautioned. "Words carry over water."

The searchlight swept over the whale boat and raft, came back and lingered. The four heads remained still as death. The light moved on to a floating crate. "Under the whaleboat," Allen whispered. "Easy . . ."

"This goddam oil . . ." Wilson gagged.

"Strain it through your beard," Paige muttered.

In the shelter of the inverted hull they heard the close approach of the boats. Powerful motors were idling, spitting softly. They heard the gibberish of enemy voices. The seconds dragged until the motors revved suddenly to life. A spray of bullets ripped canvas, sang through wood. Splinters flew. The four men clung to the gunwales, hope dying within them.

A minute dragged by. The sound of motors dwindled. They heard the sharp staccato of machine-gun fire, a single burst, safely distant now. Paige squeezed Allen's hand. "Smart move," he said.

"You okay, sir?"

"Just the damn leg."

"Shall I keep the conn?"

"Very funny. Yes. You keep the conn."

"I didn't mean it as a joke, sir. I'm sorry."

"Carry on, Commander Allen."

"Thank you, Captain. Newell, ease out and take a look around."

Newell held his breath and ducked and came up alongside the raft. An eerie glow from the burning transports hull down reddened the western horizon. The starshell's glare had died. No flares lit the sky. He could see no sign of a torpedo boat anywhere.

To the east the coming of dawn was unmistakable. He did not care to dwell on what it might bring. He tapped on the whaleboat hull. "All clear," he said.

They helped each other onto the raft. It had drifted farther than Allen had expected and he tried to remember how the currents moved here and the nature of the tides.

The coast east of Bantam Bay appeared now as a darker blur. Wilson and Newell paddled. The wind helped. The raft moved slowly. Toward escape, Newell hoped, but the troubled faces of the others made his heart heavy. The navigator sat with the captain, holding him. Allen's bony, oil-streaked body trembled with contained emotion. He stripped away the ragged ends of the skipper's trouser leg and wound tape around the swelling. Wilson stopped paddling and with a low curse pointed to a sudden turbulence scarcely two hundred yards ahead. As they watched, a periscope broke the surface, trailing its feathery wake. The submarine, half-submerged and its decks awash, loomed before them.

Allen dragged the weighted sack of ship's papers to the raft's edge, ready to let go. Wilson gripped his paddle like a club and growled comforting threats deep in his throat. Looking in all directions Newell realized there was no escape.

The raft bobbed alongside. A head, bald and freckled, was thrust through the conning tower hatch, the face pale as a desk clerk's.

"'urry, you blokes. We 'aven't got all day, y'know."

"A bloody Limey," Wilson croaked, reaching up an oily hand.

Allen grabbed him. "The captain first," he said. Glad hands helped them.

All Tod Newell worried about as he clambered aboard was how his father had managed it, this far from home.

14

Rumors of a night engagement near Sunda Strait trickled through the heavily censored press. A lone American cruiser had surprised a major Japanese invasion force and enemy casualties were numbered in the thousands. The invasion of the Java coast had been seriously delayed by the audacious attack. Precious time had been gained for the build-up of allied resistance in Australia. The name of the American cruiser and the extent of damage and casualties was being withheld pending notification of next of kin.

Tokyo said nothing. Washington was evasive. The press scolded editorially for the people's right to know. The truth of the matter was, the American high command was as bewildered as anyone else. It had not yet determined precisely what had happened in Sunda Strait and was immersed in the complex process of evaluating a stream of incredible reports. One reliable statement was on record from the skipper of the British submarine; he had picked up several survivors including the commanding officer of the American cruiser. Another report transmitted by short wave radio had been sent by a lone coast watcher who had observed most of the action from his jungle position east of Bantam Bay. A third report originated with the Japanese admiral in command of the damaged invasion force. He could not know that the top secret Japanese code had been broken. It was a most detailed report and on its astonishing news Navy Intelligence in Pearl Harbor and Washington placed most credence.

A burly four-striper named Charley Miehle was flag operations officer at Pearl. He was awakened a few hours before dawn and handed Paige's first dispatch. He was tempted to tear it to bits. Had his old classmate Paige been there he'd have torn Paige to bits. Miehle was bone-tired. In almost three months he had lost twenty-two pounds. He had not slept six straight hours since the December attack. Now in bed, his precious sleep disturbed in middream, his view of Hardtack Harry's impudence was understandably dim.

He had screened enough of Paige's screwball dispatches to paper a battleship. He knew firsthand his old friend's burning ambition for a carrier command. It was his private opinion that Paige would make a damned fine carrier skipper and Miehle was prepared to do what he could to further that ambition. But not at four in the morning. Not after an exhausting eighteen hours of sunk tonnage reports and missing warships and endless casualty lists.

He sat on the hard rim of his bunk and smothered a curse with a yawn and initialed the outrageous dispatch. The duty radio officer who had brought it asked if a copy should go to the admiral. If things were as Captain Paige indicated, there may have been a hell of a wingding in Sunda Strait and maybe CINCPAC should be advised.

"We'll wait," Miehle said grouchily, "for further reports."

But Captain Miehle, a good officer and attentive to his duty, could not sleep. He sat up and reread Paige's words and scratched his hairy belly. Damn Paige. There was an official limit a punch-drunk ex-pug Navy skipper could go with his practical jokes. There was a limit to his violation of radio discipline. There sure as hell was a limit to the patience of a bone-weary operations officer half-drowned in a sea of red tape. And there still was a month to April Fool's Day. Paige just better the hell be on the ball. Cursing softly, Miehle began to dress.

At the radio shack, he sat with his feet on a disordered pile of water-damaged first-aid kits and stained bundles of BuNav directives. He clutched a chipped mug from which he occasionally sipped coffee. Like Navy men everywhere, he was addicted to coffee. For twenty-two years he had drunk Navy coffee round the world—black gang coffee, gunners' brew, shaft alley juice, old black joe. The best he had tasted had been in chiefs' quarters. This was the worst.

He sat apart from the radio operators, immune to their private wisecracks, and sipped their coffee with a self-pitying look. Some day, he thought sourly, we'll set standard regulations for Navy coffee. Like island pussy, hot sweet and black. But not right now. Right now we'll fight the war.

He checked the reports from *Gloucester* until there were no reports. A fresh series of reports began to filter in from other unexpected sources. An air of suppressed excitement took hold of the duty crew. Their instruments seemed to click and clatter more sharply. The room smelled faintly of scorched rubber and the sweat of confined men. They moved about with a fresher urgency. No one joked.

Miehle forgot about the coffee. He hustled between the coding room and radio center. As he assessed the flow of information, his outrage turned to awe. Now he was wide awake. He phoned the admiral and dispatched a messenger and when the story seemed complete he shoveled the reports into a folder and patted the weary communications officer on his damp bald head. By 0700 he was on his way to headquarters, his cap set at its cockiest angle since Annapolis graduation.

Scuttlebutt, rumors, intercepted reports notwithstanding, Maury Nickelby, Admiral U.S.N., Commander in Chief Pacific, had work enough to do. He was in his shirtsleeves that morning signing his name to a mountain of orders and directives when his orderly handed him the first dispatch. "From Captain Miehle, sir, and he's on the way over." Nickelby read:

FROM: CO:CA30
  TO: CINCPAC/PEARL HARBOR

BRAVELY ENGAGING ENEMY SURFACE FORCE CLOSE RANGE/ NW JAVA ST NICHOLAS POINT BANTAM BAY X MANY CAS CLS DDS COVERING LANDINGS VIA TRANSPORTS AND BARGES X NOW DO I RATE FLATTOP COMMAND X PAIGE

The admiral sighed. "Hardtack and his little jokes." He read it again and put it aside. "Send Captain Miehle in the minute he gets here."

Captain Miehle strode down the long aisle of the temporary headquarters building past a snarl of sleepy-eyed WAVES and through a corridor where a Marine sentry smartly saluted and held wide the door marked CINCPAC. The sentry was a courtesy to rank. Admiral Nickelby needed no one to protect him. He was a remote yet motherly man and no one would dream of harming a hair of his fine gray head. He wasted no time on formalities, waving Miehle to a chair.

"What was Hardtack doing in Sunda Strait?"

"God knows. His last orders were to escort *Langley* into Tjilatjap."

"No alternative?"

"If rendezvous failed, to make Surabaya."

"Did he request change of plan?"

"Negative. After all, sir, there's radio silence out there." He shrugged. "He could have made it to Surabaya."

"You can kiss Surabaya goodbye, Charley."

"I heard."

"Nothing in his orders about Sunda Strait?"

"No, sir."

"The ABDA Dutchman might have set it up as a secondary mission."

"Nice try, Admiral. Face it. Hardtack took off on his own. Again."

Nickelby read over the reports and tapped his bony fingers on the desk. His hands had the weathered look of old harness. He sat in his khaki shirtsleeves and tried to make sense of this madness out of the Java Sea. "Any survivors?"

"A British sub picked up Hardtack and his navigator, a mustang name of Allen. A few others."

"That's all?"

"That's all so far, Admiral."

"Where's Paige?"

"Being flown in from Darwin."

"He all right?"

"A leg injury. Some burns. Nothing serious."

"Get the lot of them into base hospital immediately on arrival. Absolute security until we find out just what happened out there."

"Yes, sir."

"That's a lot of dead boys to explain, Charley. Anything on the credit side?"

"They salvaged some classified stuff including the ship's log."

"I want to see that log. Put Intelligence on the survivors as soon as they're able to talk. Get me transcripts of the reports. I'm worried as hell about no survivors."

"I expect some of 'em made it to the beach."

"You expect too much, Charley. We have no beach on Java."

"Could be some got to Surabaya."

"They'd be better off dead."

"One of those coast watcher reports mentions a pickup but we haven't been able to verify it."

"Let me know as soon as you hear." He turned and studied a huge pin-studded wall map. "How many on board *Gloucester?*"

"Seven hundred and ninety-two, sir."

"What's her full complement?"

"Wartime—just over a thousand. She was undermanned."

"Survivors again?"

"Four are all we have reports on."

"Any estimate of enemy losses?"

"We're working on it, sir."

"Keep me informed, Charley."

"Aye, sir. Admiral Rogers flies out at noon. Want to see him?"

"Why? They've already crucified him."

"He'd like to see you before he shoves."

"What can I say to him? Nice try? Good luck?"

"It wasn't his fault."

"Wasn't anyone's fault. It could have been you and me, Charley, and don't you forget it." He pushed angrily at the snarl of papers on his desk. "Sure. Tell Rog to stop by. I'll have a word with him."

Rogers, he thought after Miehle had gone. Close to the top when the ax fell. Now he'd be lucky to get a tugboat command in Chesapeake Bay. That's the Navy for you. Tight-lipped and tribal. Keeps its sins to itself and punishes its own.

Rogers had been wounded at Pearl that December morning and just now released from base hospital. The other top staff officers had already been recalled. No one man had shirked his duty, no one man was to blame. It was their own hard luck they were the ones on deck when it happened. They would take the rap for everyone. Just as he would have had to, had he been here and others had failed him. His eye caught the glint of gold braid on the shoulder boards of his jacket hung across the desk chair. It had taken a hell of a long time and two wars to build that braid from a

slender ensign's stripe to what it now was. He wondered if the trip
had been worth it.

He thought of *Gloucester* on the bottom of the Java Sea. He
thought of her reported dead. He had known *Gloucester* well.
As a line officer in 1929 he had witnessed her launching at Newport
News. He became her first gunnery officer as a "plank owner" a
year later at her commissioning. Those were Prohibition days. Instead of the customary champagne, she had been christened with
a jug of water. She had been a favorite of Presidents, a winner
of countless fleet awards. Nickelby had lost touch with her as his
professional interests turned to naval aviation. It had been on his
recommendation that Paige had taken over as *Gloucester*'s skipper
until there would be enough carriers to go around.

How should he assess now what Paige had done? Until he had
a more complete estimate of enemy losses, it looked bad for his
old protégé—a direct disobedience of orders, the loss of a valuable
fighting ship and a terrifying waste of men's lives.

And it might well be a stunning victory against overwhelming
odds, a much-needed victory at a most critical time.

Dear admiral, he told himself. Shove your fancy clichés up your
stack. Deep down you know damned well you're preparing your
alibis for Amos Flint. You know damned well what his reaction
will be.

He went to a file and checked the list of ship's movements.
Task Force 16, commanded by Admiral Flint, was at that moment
returning to Pearl from raids on the Japanese bases of Wake and
Marcus islands. High winds and heavy seas had limited the effectiveness of the raids. Maury Nickelby could accurately predict the
stormy mood in which his celebrated sea admiral would return.
Not that he feared anything Flint might do or say. Flint was a small
thorn in his side, but it kept him on his toes and that was where
Nickelby preferred to be.

He winced. Where he had to be. The Jap had taken Wake and
the Philippines and all of the Dutch East Indies and sure as hell
Australia was next unless something was done and damned soon.
Something more than chasing his tail around a few unimportant
islands like Wake and Marcus.

Somewhere in the pile of papers before him were the terse words
of the President and the Navy Commander in Chief in Washington, reminding him that the western world awaited some heartening

word from the Pacific. Which horse do I back? he wondered. Cautious Flint or Crazy Paige?

A matter of luck, he thought, just where fate decides to draw the line between heroism and dereliction of duty.

The admiral flicked the intercom to his flag secretary's desk. "Paige's plane in yet?"

"Put down at Ford Island two minutes ago, Admiral."

"Put a smart yeoman along with Intelligence on him so I get a fast report. I want Paige's medical as soon as it's available. Where's Task Force 16?"

"One moment, sir." Nickelby, waiting, reached for Paige's original dispatch. The flag secretary came back on. "Task Force 16 is expected to clear the net at 1130, Admiral."

"Set up a conference with Flint as soon as it's convenient for him. Send in the summary of his battle reports on Wake and Marcus. Keep shooting me operation reports on Sunda Strait."

He read Paige's dispatch again. You had to hand it to that crazy maverick. He broke the rules but he did it with guts. A style all his own. Flint, on the other hand, was always beating his gums about fighting a civilized war.

What was a civilized war? Nickelby wondered. War was life or death and winning was all that mattered.

Twenty-four hours later the results were on his desk. Secret intelligence in Tokyo bore out the accuracy of the intercepted report of the Japanese invasion commander and the eyewitness account of the Java coast spotter. Before going down, *Gloucester* had sunk by gunfire a heavy cruiser and a light cruiser, and a destroyer by ramming. A second heavy cruiser was enroute to Kure for major repairs. A light cruiser had suffered minor topside damage and had taken an eight-inch shell at its water line amidships, but had remained on station during the balance of the invasion. When last observed, she was still afire and attempting to correct a fifteen-degree list. Two medium transports and a tanker were buried in the mud of Bantam Bay. Another transport had been sunk by gunfire, most of it from *Gloucester*'s secondary batteries. The presence of unexploded six-inch shells of Japanese manufacture on the decks of several Japanese ships would bear explaining at some later court of inquiry at Imperial headquarters. The estimate of casualties dead or missing was somewhere between four and five thousand.

The official Japanese communiqué had nothing to report except the glorious sinking of the American heavy cruiser, *Gloucester*, by submarine torpedoes north of Sunda Strait. She had gone down with all hands during the "co-prosperity sphere landings." There were no survivors.

Nickelby angrily pushed up his glasses. No survivors because survivors meant prisoners and prisoners meant extra bellies to feed and guards better engaged in fighting duties. He scanned the rest of the enemy's secret report. Barges and miscellaneous landing craft sunk or damaged: an estimated seventy. The loss of arms and ammunition, food and clothing, medical supplies was impossible to check but must have been considerable.

He stacked the papers and clipped them and dropped them into a file box. A grand haul, Hardtack, he thought. He went to the window and stared gloomily across the gun-manned tops of temporary buildings to the blue harbor. He felt the wind on his face, hot and damp, blowing out of the south. Off the western shore of Ford Island the hulk of the ancient target ship *Utah* was sorry with rust, *Arizona* a silent tomb. *Oklahoma* lay on her side like some mired prehistoric monster. A salvage crew labored with cranes and engines to right her. Hundreds of cables stretched taut from her sides to the shore. *Gulliver*, the admiral thought, *among the Lilliputians.*

Hickam Field. The Navy air station at Kaneohe. How had the enemy known enough to flatten the one hangar of three that housed the Navy's patrol bombers? Were the same spies sitting right outside his door at this moment typing neatly and obediently on government stationery, waiting with their infinite Oriental patience for the next surprise attack? He cursed softly. They had flown him out on emergency orders smack dab onto this badly mauled island in the middle of the biggest damn ocean in the world. He was surrounded by a do-or-die enemy with wallop enough to send him and his smashed navy to the bottom for keeps. All that was asked of him was to put the bloody pieces together and win the war.

His intercom came to life. Vice Admiral Rogers had arrived and awaited his pleasure. He frowned. Admirals weren't having much pleasure these days. He greeted Rogers warmly. Nickelby had his thumbnail estimate of Rogers, as he did of every flag officer who served him. A nerveless bantam cock of a man—all heart and

no fancy feathers. His official report of the December attack had
been a classic of documentation, cool, lucid, and unbiased. To
Nickelby, who had difficulty in expressing himself via the written
word, it was a work of art. Much more remained to be told. In accordance with the Navy's unwritten code, information of so personal
a nature could not have been included in any official report. Nickelby
meant to find out as much as he could without embarrassing Rogers
into any violation of confidences.

"Good to have you back," he said.

"Just to say goodbye, Nick," Rogers smiled thinly. His eyes had
a dull, almost withdrawn expression. His fingers shook as he lighted
a cigarette. Nickelby could only think, *It could have been me.*
It was hard not to feel sorry for Rogers.

"Any idea what you're going back to?"

"I've heard the scuttlebutt."

"That court of inquiry's mere routine, Rog. It's what they'll
try to do to you after it's over."

"They've already begun, Nick. My orders are delayed but I hear
it's the Aleutians."

"Raise a stink."

"In the spot I'm in? Come off it, Nick. I'm glad for any scrap."

"You did a damned fine job here. You deserve the best Washington can offer."

"Thanks, Nick." He inhaled deeply. "Heads have to fall. Law
of the jungle. Mine'll go along with the others." He watched the
smoke dissipate. "Just the same, there's nothing I can think of,
going back over it day by day, that I'd do any differently now."

"Could we have done any better, Rog?"

"Up to the point of the attack, no. But once the shit hit the
electric fan, that's when we fell apart." He sat up and his eyes
brightened. "It's a funny thing. No one seems to think of that.
Let's face it, Nick, that's where the real trouble was. We fell apart."

"Spilt milk, Rog."

"Can I forget it? Can you?" His words rushed together. "I'm
getting this off my chest, Nick, and you're the one who should
hear it. Because you're next."

"You might regret it."

"Just between you and me, Nick, off the record. Once I'm
in Washington I'll be hamstrung and you know it."

"Okay, Rog," Nickelby said, secretly pleased. "Off the record."

"They fouled up just as badly back there as they think we did here. They just never got the word to us. We were working in the dark half the time. Those smart Far East experts in Intelligence, where were they when we needed them? What about their petty bickering with War Plans over protocol and all those interdepartment jealousies? We didn't know who to believe, Nick. By the time an evaluation reached us out here it had passed through so many hands and carried so many ifs, ands, and buts there was no way at all to assess it properly. Our own noses weren't exactly clean. Everybody passed the buck. We figured it was the Army's job to defend the island with their radar warning net. They figured it was up to us to handle air reconnaissance. Everybody assumed everybody else was on the ball. Nobody bothered to check. That morning we had enough goldbraid off duty to run a coronation ball on Haliewa alone! The Jap was lucky and he was clever and we were caught with our pants down."

"We didn't do too badly, once we got started."

"I'm not questioning the personal courage and sacrifice of the men, Nick. The crews on the old wagons in Battleship Row behaved well. True Navy, if you'll pardon the sentiment. That's the point I'm getting to. Finally. *True* Navy. *Command.* That's where we failed. That's what hurts, Nick. The pros. The trade school élite. Us."

"Give me a 'for instance.'"

"Our carrier commanders. All three task forces were at sea, thank God. These task force commanders knew the score. We had been over the tactical situation of a surprise attack time and again. They had their orders. They got word of the attack the minute it happened. Here was the one fight they'd been spoiling for since Lord knows when. In spite of the confusion and the phony reports, you'd think after all these years they'd know enough to seek out and destroy an enemy force in their own back yard."

"The reports seem to indicate they tried."

"They write their own reports, Nick. Alibis. They carried on like a bunch of school kids with wet pants that day. We had headaches enough here without their endless yapping for scouting information and verification and instructions on what to do. You wouldn't believe what was put out over those ship's radios. Those Japs must've died laughing. They sure weren't dying any other way. And where were our mighty task forces? The carriers? The babies whose fire power and range and invincibility we sweated blood and bullets for and bragged about all these years? Helpless. They had the guns. They had the planes. They had the decks to fly them off. They had the trained crews and they had the ideal situation." The cigarette had burned to his fingertips. He slowly crushed it. "The years of drills. Launch and recover. The war games. The plotting and planning. The politics to keep the battleship admirals from giving us the deep six. My God, the loud talk and the drunken boasts in wardrooms and officers' clubs. And when the big moment came—wet pants."

"Take it easy, Rog."

"I've taken it easy too long." He stood up. His eyes glistened. "You see what I mean, Nick? You have any idea what I'm trying to say? Dry rot, Nick. Deadwood within. We let the people down. All of us. We muffed it. Granted, it wasn't our fault the Japs hit us. That's how wars go. It's the foul-up after it happened that's eating me. What've we done *since?* Steamed around in circles. Broken radio silence. Bombed our own ships. Fired on our own planes. Lost men overboard. Crashed fighters in faulty deck landings. Bickered and carped over seniority and responsibility. We've been carrying on like a bunch of fresh water amateurs when you and I know we're supposed to be the mightiest nation afloat. And we are yet to fire a single shot in anger. Do you call our carrier group a fighting task force?"

"It's supposed to be."

"Hell, Nick, you don't have a slugger among them."

"Tully?"

"Okay. Tully is one."

"What about Flint?"

"What about him?"

"I mean, how'd he behave during the action?"

"Like the others. A chicken with his head cut off." Rogers went to the window. "Flint's an old buddy of mine, Nick, and what I have to say hurts. He's a smart sailor, square and honest and he'll fight to the last man and go down with his ship, head high and a hand tucked in his tailor-made tunic. In full dress, if he can manage it and he probably can. Amos is a Navy showpiece and everybody handles him with kid gloves. If he's the model naval officer in the classic Navy tradition, then I say piss on the classic Navy tradition. I saw what happened to it seven December last.

Nick, I don't want to see any more of our ships go down or
any more of our good men die. I don't want my two daughters,
God bless 'em, to spend the rest of their lives bowing to a slant-
eyed husband in a silk kimono, but that's what's going to happen,
Nick, unless we get us a fleet of skippers who are dirty fighters.
Ball-kickers. Eye-gougers."

"And Amos Flint isn't?"

"On three December, Admiral Flint delivered a deckload of
fighter planes to beef up Midway. Buffalo Brewsters for the Marine
fliers. He headed back for Pearl, scheduled to enter the channel
at 0730 the morning of seven December. Dirty weather delayed
fueling his destroyers. When he was a couple of hundred miles
out, he launched eighteen of his planes for Ford Island. When?
0600. Why? So the world could see that Amos Flint was johnny-
on-the-spot. Did he notify us that eighteen of his planes were coming in? Like hell he did. We shot down five."

"Everybody was trigger-happy that morning."

"Then why the hell didn't his boys shoot at those Jap planes?
They were flying right through them and never fired a shot. And
then we threw together a task force for him, with orders to sweep
the seas and find the Jap attacking force. They found nothing."

"You can't blame him for that. It's a big sea."

"I blame him for overcaution. For lack of initiative. For delusions
of personal grandeur. He's a front runner who can't deliver when the
chips are down."

The admiral picked through the pile of papers on his desk.
"You ever meet Harry Paige?"

"Hardtack?" Rogers relaxed. "What's that crazy son of a bitch
gone and done now?"

"Plenty." Nickelby handed him Paige's dispatch. Rogers read it
and shook his head. "Sunda Strait, eh? He must have taken on
the whole goddam western attack force out of the South China
Sea."

"He did."

"I always liked Harry. I always figured that cocky son of a bitch'd
end up like that, slugging it out. What a way to go."

"He didn't go." Nickelby felt better. He passed Rogers the intelligence reports of enemy battle damage. Rogers read them through.
"All right," he said. "That's one. How many more sluggers do we
own? Where the hell are they hiding?"

"I'm finding out every day. When I find 'em, I put 'em to work. You've been through hell, Rog. Just don't lose the faith."

Rogers looked at his watch. "I feel like Louis the Sixteenth. All I need is a tumbril."

"Don't take any guff from those boys in Washington. They need you, Rog. They need you real bad. And you can do something for me while you're there."

"Name it."

"We need those new carriers. We need 'em fast. If you have an inside track to the top brass or the right congressmen, or whatever it takes to bypass the battleship boys, do it. We have got to push along that program. It's our only chance. This is a carrier war, Rog."

"We've known it all along. You know the kind of thinking we've been bucking."

"No more. The Japs proved how wrong they were. Those old battlewagons out there in the mud were ready for the scrap pile long before the first Jap bomb touched a deck. They did us a favor, Rog. They proved the superiority of carriers and they united the nation fast."

They shook hands. Rogers hesitated at the door. "I'm glad Hardtack made it."

"He made it all right. But he lost *Gloucester* and just about every man on board."

"He's a slugger, Nick. Can you think of anything we need more?"

"Carriers."

"And skippers to fight 'em. You saving one for Paige?"

"I don't know," the admiral said slowly. "I don't really know."

Nickelby's chief of staff, Vice Admiral Getchall, found him a few minutes later deep in thought. It seemed odd. In the ten weeks since Nickelby had taken over as CINCPAC, Getchall had not once known the admiral to take time out for reflection.

"Anything wrong, sir?"

"Anything right?" He straightened.

"Your boy Paige. He's just been logged into a private room in the north bay of Ward B, Navy Hospital. Commander Allen and an ensign named Newell are next door. The only way to visit is through a private corridor and there's a Marine sentry on duty."

"Good. What about the enlisted men?"

"One. Wilson, chief quartermaster. He's there, curtained off."

"Stick Wilson?"

"The same."

"No others?"

"Three died in Darwin. That was it."

"What shape's Paige in?"

"Doctor says good."

"You have his medical report?"

"Commander Touhy's working on it."

"I'm going over there. I want to talk to Paige."

"What about the newspaper people waiting to see you?"

"When I get back."

"They're breathing down my neck."

"Let 'em breathe."

"What about Admiral Flint? His group just cleared the net."

"Set up a date with Flint before the press interview. Say about 1600."

"They're gonna bitch like hell."

"Let 'em bitch." He buttoned his collar and pulled his tie together. "Hold everything until I've got the word from Paige."

He treasured the privacy of his staff car. It was the one sanctuary where he could meditate without interruption. His driver wove slowly through the maze of yard traffic. It was becoming clear now that Paige had lost more than his ship and crew. His decision to run Sunda Strait probably had cost the Navy *Langley* and *Cushman* and *Hurlburt*. The loss of *Langley*'s planes could no longer be reckoned in dollars. It ran to real estate like Java and the Solomons and if things didn't change damned soon—Australia. And what price, Nickelby wondered, do we put on the lives of American boys? One boy—what price? He knew that ten minutes after he'd sprung the sad news to the press corps he'd be hearing the anonymous voice of the vast army of next-of-kin keening the old heartbreaker: *Where Is My Wandering Boy Tonight?* And he would be the one to defend it—to say what had happened was right.

How did I end up here? he asked himself. Is this what I really wanted?

Those years ago when he took the midshipman oath, he had been taught at once the difference between democratic and military leadership. They had handed him The Book. Study it, they told him. The Book said that everyone in a democratic social order is given the opportunity to be the kind of leader he wants to be. But in a military order, leadership cannot allow the luxury of the individual's desire for self-expression.

His sense of justice had rebelled then. He asked questions. He was sternly told that this difference—exactly this difference—was what makes a military society more efficient and therefore superior to a democratic one. Especially in times of emergency when every effort must be directed to the protection of that democratic order and the institutions that support it. To defend it to the death if necessary. To safeguard it against the ravages of the enemy.

In that book in those words. It had come very close to wrecking his career, because he did not believe it then. And The Book went on to say that the willingness and ability to assume and discharge responsibility under such terms was the key to leadership and leadership was the purpose of his military life.

That was what The Book said and he had conditioned himself to believe it. He believed it because he was committed to be true blue Navy, devoted to God and Country and the Old Etcetera. And all of him believed it except that secret part buried away in the dark of his mind, a part of him still boy, still deeply compassionate.

It would take another time and place to bring the truth to light from that dark recess. A place where trout lay in the shadows of a chill pool. A time for man to be boy again and with the strength of innocence question the right of anyone to deal in the murder of living things.

The driver stopped the car and opened the admiral's door. For a moment Nickelby watched the mighty labor of men and heard the ring of steel on steel. It would echo everywhere in the free world.

An eagle in pain, he thought, screaming her rage.

Have I failed myself? He hoped not. Let us say, he consoled himself, that a greater duty calls and strength of innocence is stored like rod, reel, creel, and fly box for the time of the trout.

15

He found Harrison Paige propped in a wheel chair near the window.
The blinds were drawn. The room smelled of rubbing alcohol
and fresh green paint. Dollops of white plaster stiff as cake frosting
spattered the walls and the unpainted baseboard. A look of haste
and make-do was everywhere.

A bosomy Eurasian nurse was feeding Paige from a metal tray.
The admiral observed with satisfaction that she wore an ensign's
stripe on her white starched cap. Seeing the admiral, she quickly
got to her feet. Nickelby absently waved her down. His eyes were
on Paige. He was unprepared for the change he saw and needed
a few moments to compose himself.

He had not seen him in two years. They had both been on leave
in Cavite then, putting in their flying time at the Navy Air
Station. They met last for a farewell drink in the taproom of the
Manila Hotel. Paige had been his robust, wisecracking self, too
loud for some and not caring a damn about it. Nickelby recalled
how arrogant and handsome Paige had looked in his starched summer whites. He was leaving in the morning to relieve the skipper
of *Gloucester* at Olongapo. He had waved a copy of his orders
under Nickelby's nose. "Somebody's shanghaied me, Nick."

"*Gloucester*? It was my idea. I'm a plank owner myself, Harry,
and proud of it."

"I'm itching for a carrier, Nick. You know that."

"Sorry, we're fresh out. Settle for a desk in Washington?"

"Hell, no!"

They drank to *Gloucester* and to the Navy and to the men at sea and finally they drank to each other. That night they drove forty miles into the mountains to the resort at Tagaitay and hung one on. Paige did most of the talking. Nickelby did not mind. Paige's blunt style relaxed him. When it was time to go, Paige struck a vintage fighting pose. "I'm shoving off, Nick. And Tommy Hart and the whole damn Asiatic Fleet just better the hell be on their toes."

That was the last time Nickelby had seen him. Now Paige sat in a wheel chair, his famed fists two bandaged paws in the lap of the white Navy blanket. His cheeks were deep hollows, the skin an unhealthy scarlet, peeling in filmy patches. The flesh of his neck hung in loose folds still tinged green with traces of the oil of his last command. His eyelids were swollen, the lashes rimmed with a dry crust and oozing.

He tried to get up. The nurse restrained him, spilling some food from the tray. She leaned close, dabbing with a napkin. Paige moved his bandaged hands helplessly and managed a wink at Nickelby. "My luck," he muttered.

"Hello, Harry."

"Excuse me for not rising, Admiral."

"Try," Nickelby said, "and I'll knock you flat." He pulled up a chair. "Go on, finish your chow. This is a social call."

Paige coughed, a dry hacking spasm he was unable to control. Liquids dribbled from his mouth. The nurse set aside the tray and held him. Nickelby watched impassively. The nurse wiped Paige's face and chin. He winced with pain. Nickelby could hear his breathing, a noisy asthmatic wheeze. Paige motioned the nurse aside. His eyes sought the admiral's. "Why social? I kind of hoped it would be an official invitation to a flattop."

"You're lucky it's not a general court." He glanced at the nurse who stepped away. "That last dispatch, Harry," Nickelby continued in a low voice. "Who'd you think you were? John Paul Jones?"

"What was wrong with it?"

"Flippancy at a time like that."

"I don't recall any flippancy. All I said was—"

"All you said was how bravely you were taking on the enemy singlehanded. You know damned well every word of it becomes official. Everybody who's anybody, up to the President, has access to official dispatches. And *bravely* was hardly the word. *Rashly* would be a lot more like it."

"I had a sneaky feeling it was the last dispatch I might be sending. So I gave it the works."

"What were you doing in Sunda Strait? Fighting a private war?"

"It's time somebody took a poke at those Nip bastards." He glanced at the nurse across the room. "You'd better shove off, Ensign. The language gets rough from here in."

"I'm used to it, Captain."

"Get going."

"Sir, my orders were to see that you finished everything on that tray."

"My orders are for you to shove off."

She looked to the admiral for confirmation. Nickelby nodded. She retrieved the tray. "He's terribly weak, Admiral."

"He'll recover, I'm afraid," Nickelby said. "Save it." He waited until she closed the door. "Cute little trick, Harry."

"A hell of a lot of good it does a guy with mittens like these. And then there's the potty routine—"

"Just what the hell happened out there, Harry?"

"You read my report, didn't you?"

"Knock it off, Harry. What happened?"

"You mean the rendezvous with *Langley* and all?"

Nickelby nodded. Paige began to cough. The admiral waited, cautious, sensitive, worried. "We hung around almost two hours for that damned convoy," Paige said. "Couldn't break radio silence. The Nip has subs all over the area. I didn't know when the hell a search plane'd spot us. We'd been hit from the air time and again. The crew was just about dead on their feet. We'd been running for days. You know the beating we took south of Makassar Strait the day before, thanks to the crummy Dutchman. Well. No convoy. No *Langley*. I was jumpier than a whore in church. I had lookouts aloft burned to a crisp. For all I knew the damned convoy had never left Darwin. Or the Nips had got to it, enroute to the rendezvous point. I might be next. So the intercepted report on the Nip invasion force north of Sunda Strait sounded like a good deal. I ordered the cans to stand by for *Langley* and *Sea Witch* and we shoved off alone for Sunda."

"You know what the *Langley* was carrying?"

"Fighter planes and pilots."

"We needed those planes, Harry."

"I could have stayed, sure. Suppose I did and the rendezvous came off as scheduled. Sure as hell those Nip planes would have added *Gloucester* to the box score. I'm good but hell I'm not that good! It's a damned lucky break I got away when I did."

"Against orders. Your orders were to return to Surabaya if rendezvous failed."

Paige was silent for a moment. "Nick, that whole ABDA idea was wrong from the start. I had no faith in the Dutchman after Van Gelder went down. I acted as I thought best at the time. That was the situation as I saw it and if I saw it wrong then for Christ sake relieve me and court-martial the hell out of me but don't imply I didn't act in the best interests of the service."

"Just tell me what went through your mind."

"I had to move out. I was a sitting duck. We lost our scout planes two days before off Makassar. I had no plan or position on the convoy's course or anything. And we'd been fighting and losing this damned war every inch of the way. Shipboard morale was lower than whale shit. I could've had a mutiny on my hands."

"Mutiny? Are you that bad a skipper? Your lack of logic and basic horse sense scares the hell out of me, Harry. The particular ship you command isn't as important to preserve as your authority —the authority of command—which is a lot more valuable to us than one ship. Now carry on."

"The minute I got word the Dutchman had ordered a rendezvous at Surabaya I knew we were dead. The Nip had Surabaya all staked out. To go in there would be suicide. I could have headed for Australia but the cans were low on fuel for such a long run. They had to be in range of Tjilatjap."

"You could have made it to Australia on your own."

"In my book, that is no way to fight a war. That's running. I had done all the running I had stomach for."

"You knew the run up Sunda Strait was suicide, didn't you?"

"It was a calculated risk. They weren't expecting any opposition from the south at Bantam Bay. From Surabaya, yes, but not up the Strait. I had the advantage of surprise and darkness. I had big guns and speed. And I had a crew of men sick to death of running. All we wanted was one real chance to hit back. We threw everything we had, Nick. Too bad you weren't there to see it."

"Thank you," the admiral said dryly.

"What the hell! We were as good as licked anyway. I just couldn't see going down with a full load of ammo. I couldn't see sitting around while our whole world was going to hell out there!"

"Take it easy, Harry."

"One more thing." Paige cleared his throat and wiped a loose cotton sleeve across his mouth. "We took three fish before she went down. We managed to get life rafts into the water, and two motor whale boats. I watched those Nips joyride in and out, machine-gunning the men. Cold-cocked murder, Nick. For that alone I'm going to get well. I'm going back out there and I'm going to kill every Nip son of a bitch I can lay hands on."

"It's ships and planes I want destroyed, Harry. Not men."

"I'm going to give you both."

"Why'd you risk it alone, Harry? You could have taken one of the destroyers for antisub escort and maybe saved your ship."

"I could operate more freely alone. The sub risk in the Strait was negligible. Their subs were concentrated more to the east, in the convoy lanes between Australia and India. I had plenty of speed and guns and more range without the cans. Anyway, *Langley* and *Sea Witch* needed 'em more than I did."

"Enemy search planes could have picked you up."

Paige grinned. "One did." He told Nickelby about the red meat-ball. The admiral's face relaxed and Paige knew the worst was over.

"I've looked over the log book, Harry. You traveled at dangerous speeds through poorly charted waters. I noted in particular your passage through a narrow channel east of Prinsen Island."

"Prinsen. Yes." He avoided the admiral's steady eyes. "That was a short cut, you see, and it placed us within range of the invasion group before daylight."

"You took an unnecessary risk running that channel, Harry."

"I figured it saved the fleet a few hundred gallons of oil. With Java and Borneo gone, we're going to have to be careful as hell with our oil, Admiral."

"So to save a few hundred, you lost a few thousand. Plus your ship and your crew. Was it worth it, Harry?"

"Are the returns in yet?"

Nickelby nodded.

"Then you know damned well it was worth it." He grinned.

"Tully always told me it's smarter to shoot first and argue later. That's what I did."

"There's nothing more you care to tell me?"

"I'll stand or fall on the record, Nick."

"Nothing to say—off the record?"

Paige looked at him in genuine surprise. "What's eating you?"

"Just this. You took seven hundred and ninety American boys to their death or worse, Harry. Yet you can sit here and brag about how many Jap ships you sunk and how many Jap sailors and soldiers you killed. But not one word do you mention about the boys you lost."

"It isn't the easiest thing to talk about."

"It's how you feel, Harry, that concerns me."

"I don't know what you're driving at! I did my job."

"Almost eight hundred dead, Harry. Doesn't it reach you?"

"Hell, Nick, you can't make an omelet without busting a few eggs."

"How can you sit there and make jokes? Almost every damned one of your boys is on the bottom or in a stinking Jap prison camp. What the hell are you made of? Can't you *fake* some real feeling?" He got up and paced the room. "I know it's war! I know you were doing your job. But damn it, man, don't you *feel?*"

"We're trained to kill, not feel. I'm doing my job."

Nickelby paced between the window and the bed. The room was silent for a time. He stood behind the wheel chair where Paige could not see him. "The first new carrier's due for completion by mid-May if we're lucky." He spoke brusquely and Paige dared not look at him.

"Which one is she, Nick?"

"*Shiloh.* She's fitting out in Newport News. Put in a month or so for a refresher on one of the carriers here and she's yours." Paige began to say something but Nickelby stopped him. "After shakedown, she'll join up here with Carrier Division Two. Flint runs the show. It's a team. There are no individual stars. Flint issues the orders. Every skipper from tin can to flattop obeys. That's the way Flint operates. So far the records prove he knows his business. Can you work under a man like that?"

"I can carry out orders like anyone else."

Outside the hum and chatter of yard activity mingled with the brute roar of plane motors. A fly buzzed and circled Paige's head. He moved his bandaged paws irritably. "Damn it, Nick. I can obey orders. Flint's or anyone else. You know damn well I can."

"I hope so, Harry. For your sake." He looked at the bandaged hands. "Any idea how long before you can get out of here?"

"Just give 'em the word and I'm out."

"The hell you say. Look at those bandages."

"I don't need hands to conn a ship, Nick."

"I'm not sending cripples out to fight the war."

"You need me, Nick."

"I need every man I can get." He spoke with such sharpness, Paige looked up startled. "I'll give it to you straight, Harry. We're losing this war. Your little clambake in Sunda Strait took guts. Gave us our first real break, but it's the kind of break I can't afford too often. I'm sure you know what I mean." He reached for his cap. "I'm seeing Flint this afternoon. I don't expect him to be too happy when I tell him about *Shiloh*. It means bypassing a few numbers—skippers more qualified by the book than you. And most of them are Flint's boys. But I'm not going by the book this time."

"Thanks, Nick."

"Don't let me down." He settled his cap squarely on his head. "How you coming along on the battle report?"

"Steady. A yeoman takes it down two hours in the morning, two in the afternoon. It's all the visiting they'll allow me."

"I'll see that word gets back to Felicia and the commodore." He paused at the door. "Your boy's at the Academy, isn't he?"

"David. Yes."

"We sure can use those youngsters out here."

"He'll be out in June."

"Like to be there, wouldn't you?"

"You kidding?"

"It may work out, Harry. But you've got to get yourself in shape. Get some beef on you, for God's sake. You look like death warmed over." Death, he remembered. "Any recommendations for citations, Harry?"

"Everyone did his duty."

"I'll be recommending you, soon as the battle report's evaluated. See what you can do for any of the others. It was an outstanding action."

"I'll check and add it to the report." He was thoughtful for a moment. "You remember Oley Olsen? A class behind me?" Nickelby nodded. "He was my exec, Nick. I hate to say this. He let me down."

"How, Harry?"

"Quit when the going got rough."

"Well, Harry, he's dead now."

"That doesn't change things. I had to order him to his GQ station. He made it to Battle Two but that's about all."

"Was Olsen married?"

"Yes."

"Kids?"

"Yes."

The admiral looked uncomfortable and said, "Do what you think is best, Harry. Anyone else?"

"Well, yes. There was a Dutchman on board, liaison officer, a kid really, more in the way than anything. But he picked up a machine gun and fought along with the rest of us. Surprised the hell out of me."

"Recommend him."

"A Dutchman? Sure, if you say so."

"And the three who got off with you."

"I'll need more citation forms."

"I'll see that you get them. You'll want these boys with you again, won't you?"

"If they'd like it, yes."

"Would you?"

"Sure. Especially Joe Allen, the navigator."

"I'll have 'em assigned to new construction, Newport News, after their leave is up."

"Thanks a lot, Nick."

"Anything else?"

"Just my gym equipment. Bar bells and bag and so forth."

"Put in a claim like everyone else."

"Okay, Nick, and thanks."

After the admiral had gone, Paige stared out the window. Can't help it about Oley, he told himself. No one to blame but himself. And I treated the Dutch kid like a dog. He didn't have to do what he did. He deserves a medal. As for Oley, who's left to know the difference except me?

He squeezed his eyes shut. A carrier. Well, Christ, I earned it, didn't I? He leaned his elbow on the buzzer and his nurse came running. She stared at his streaked face.

"You feeling all right, Captain Paige?"

"Something in my eye. I'm okay."

She wiped gently at his wet cheeks. "Can I get you some orange juice?" There was a smell to her, sweet and female, he had noticed before.

"Sure. And the chow I didn't finish."

"The tray's been picked up, Captain."

"Fetch another on the double. Can't you see I'm being starved to death?"

"Yes, *sir*, Captain Paige."

"If I didn't have these damned bandages on my hands, I'd squeeze the life out of you."

"The admiral must have brought you some good news, sir."

"He sure as hell did." She left. He thought briefly of the admiral's good news. Seven hundred and ninety men. The admiral was a piker. Bigger things lay ahead for Hardtack Harry Paige. He'd show 'em. As soon as he got out of here and back out where he belonged.

He began to tear at the bandages with his teeth.

In the guarded corridor outside, the admiral listened to the young Navy doctor. "We're treating his eyes with cold boric acid solutions every fifteen minutes, sir. It's what we call a chemical conjunctivitis. It's an inflammation—"

"His eyes don't worry me. What about that cough? It sounds like hell."

"The cough results from the oil that got into his lungs out there. It's going to be a while until we know he's in the clear. Depends on how much of the stuff he swallowed."

"What about his hands?"

"Second degree burns—not too bad. We had much worse right here last December. He's torn a tendon in his right leg but he's on his back and it should be healing nicely."

"When can he get out?"

"If there are no complications—two weeks."

Nickelby swore under his breath. "What about the others?"

"Doing as well as can be expected. One of them, Wilson, is in trouble. Gangrene in one leg. Bad."

"So fast?"

"He had some open wounds. No telling how he got 'em. We're doing what we can for him."

"And the others?"

"Doing nicely. They were lucky to make it, sir."

"A hell of a sight luckier than the boys the Japs picked up." He stared at his watch. "I'd like to see the others. Just to say hello."

"Of course, Admiral." He led the way down the corridor. Nickelby cautioned the Marine sentry. "Absolutely nobody—especially newspaper people." He spoke briefly and warmly to Commander Allen and Ensign Newell. He spent several minutes with Stick Wilson whom he knew from his teaching days at the Academy. Wilson seemed cheerful and the admiral said nothing about the leg. He figured Wilson would be knowing soon enough.

His driver drove fast to get the admiral back to headquarters. The last thing in the world Nickelby wanted was to be late for a meeting with Admiral Flint.

16

Confrontations with Amos Flint invariably aroused in Maury Nickelby a mixture of envy and irritation. He had grudging respect for Flint as an officer and a gentleman, but it was his fellow officer's sartorial elegance that bothered Nickelby most. It violated Nickelby's conservative views on Navy austerity, and he was painfully aware that Flint's scented presence several times a day in freshly pressed silk gabardine or featherweight tropical worsteds did little to endear him to the hearts of his brother officers in sweat-stained and wrinkled cotton khakis.

Scuttlebutt had it that Flint never went to sea with less than thirty uniforms—seven each of the gabardine and worsted khakis, seven each of dress blues and dress whites. Two sets of full dress completed the basic wardrobe. All were meticulously hand-tailored and cut with an imperious disregard for regulations.

It had never occurred to Nickelby to seek the truth behind the rumor. If Flint needed the luxury of thirty uniforms to fight the war, he should have them. Nickelby considered himself and the naval establishment and the entire democracy, for that matter, fortunate indeed to have an officer of Flint's capabilities on their side. If Flint was prone to radical departures, Nickelby thanked God they were limited to items of dress.

Flint was a cautious leader who planned with painstaking care and moved to attack only when the odds favored him. At this stage of the game, Nickelby reasoned, it was enough to stay alive. The time for daring was yet to come.

Thirty uniforms. His phone buzzed and he stared at it morosely. He knew what it was about Flint, damn him. Flint was handsome and Flint was cultured and Flint was earmarked by Washington for Chief of Naval Operations as soon as the war was done. He was the picture-book admiral, the Navy hero universally loved and admired, whose looks, words, deeds stirred the hearts of women and children and gave lesser men vicarious dreams of grandeur. Nickelby scratched his gray head and reached for the phone. Who'd want a homely and inarticulate sourpuss like myself, he wondered, whose awkward frame my store-bought uniforms seem loathe to touch? The hell with all that, he told himself sternly. The conduct of war is a tragic necessity, not a social career.

"Nickelby," he said.

His flag secretary advised him that Admiral Flint's staff car had just driven up and Admiral Getchall had gone down to meet him. "Send them right in and not a word to the press boys." He reached for his jacket and brushed the dustless shoulder boards and straightened his black tie. Rising, he observed with some irritation that his trousers were hopelessly wrinkled though they had been freshly pressed that morning. He was already on the defensive and he knew it. He walked to the window and glumly observed crisp Flint and his entourage and silently envied the splendor of it all.

The arrival of Admiral Flint at a shore-based Navy establishment could hardly be described as routine. Poseidon at the Acropolis, or Captain Kidd at the court of William and Mary could not have created a greater stir.

Flint stormed a beachhead like a dashing whitecap and riding his wake like flying fish came his devoted aides. He was aware of the effect his entrance had. He planned it as carefully as he planned his strikes at sea. He knew to the glint of his last button the exact image he presented to his awed and stiffly saluting observers and took considerable pains to achieve it.

Several inches of wire stay were removed from the crown of his gold-encrusted cap to give it the rakish look he preferred. No regulation metal stars would do for him. Those that adorned his collar points were embroidered by hand with silver thread. The tapered look from shoulder to hip he owed to the genius of a firm of gentlemen's tailors long ago resigned to the meticulous idiosyncrasies of Amos Flint. His slim waist owed its elegance as well to their cleverness with a built-in supporter that did wonders for his unpublicized pot belly.

The pot belly was the only facet of Flint that shirked the glare of his well-planned publicity. Amos Flint was the salty darling of the society columnists. He was the pet and occasional peeve of political and military analysts. He was the living breathing symbol of the American Navy. To the public at large as well as his aides and the lesser ranks and rates of the Navy, he had the quality of eminence a cardinal might hold over his flock.

Three generations of Flints before him had been Navy officers. The Navy was more a part of him than he was of the Navy. His wife's forebears were pure Navy and if his two broad-beamed daughters could have made Annapolis, they would have welcomed the chance. To his deep sorrow, Amos Flint's wife bore him no son.

Two years and a summer before Pearl Harbor his family had given him a fiftieth birthday party that had covered the Sunday society pages of the Richmond, New York, and Washington papers for a week before and after the event.

The lawns of the ancestral Flint home, "Cavendish," bordering the James River, had been transformed into a flower-packed replica of a ship's quarterdeck—in truth, some fluttery landscape designer's dream of what a quarterdeck might look like. Carnation cannons belched flames of American Beauty roses from their sixteen-inch muzzles. The estate's flagpole became an ivied foremast topped by a revolving searchlight composed of yellow and white chrysanthemums and its halyards carried a *HAPPY BIRTHDAY* signal hoist in authentic alphabet flags.

Along the lawn's edge a simulated pennant made of seven thousand tulips flown in from Holland for the occasion spelled out *Congratulations, Admiral.* By the sheerest coincidence Captain Flint had earned his two silver stars that morning.

No one deserved them more. At the Academy he had commanded his class in the final year as the honorary four-striper cadet lieutenant commander, the highest military post in his battalion. Amos Flint had stood fourth in a class of one hundred thirty men and to this day had not forgiven those three who had topped him. After graduation he served in a variety of destroyers, cruisers, and battleships. He skippered a destroyer in the South Atlantic during World War I.

After a brief tour of duty as instructor at the Academy and another at the Naval War College, he caught the fever of naval aviation and earned his wings. He guessed that carrier planes would win the future wars and he was determined to lead the new breed of Navy sea-air fighting men. No seagoing Flint before him could make that claim and he wanted more than anything else in the world to bring new glory to the distinguished family name.

Now precisely at four o'clock, he arrived at Navy headquarters. He nodded briefly at the corps of reporters bunched in the outside foyer. He greeted two of them with a princely touch of cordiality, saying aloud, "Hello, Bob. Hello there, Fred," and his neatly ordered mind translated the greeting into New York and Chicago press releases. The working press to Amos Flint was no different from the Army—a distasteful but necessary adjunct to his career. He strode past rows of desks between gawking yeomen of both sexes. He wore one fawn-colored glove and idly slapped the other against his thigh. It was a proven gambit of his planned haughtiness to carry his shapely head high and to focus his thoughtful gaze slightly aloft, as though he steered his course by God. It gave him an air of divine preoccupation guaranteed to capture the hearts of every female in range. The office WAVES, loins brimming ardor, barely restrained the impulse to touch him as he passed. A few who had not yet bedded down their first three-striper conjectured giddily on what it might be like with an admiral. This was war. This was the fighting Navy. And Admiral Flint, the right man at the right moment in history, was primed to make the most of it.

17

The two admirals greeted each other across the huge desk. Too sloppy, Flint told himself, for a man locked in a death struggle for the biggest ocean in the world. Too fastidious, Nickelby thought, to suffer the bloodstains of battle.

Captain John Everton, Flint's chief of staff, stood at the big game board and explained the shifting tactical situation in the Marshalls and Gilberts. He moved the brightly marked pieces like toys. Nickelby listened attentively. Getchall at his side sipped black coffee and took notes. Flag officers of both staffs sat around with a pretense of interest and hoped it would soon be done.

Flint was not paying close attention and seemed more concerned with fondling the stitched tips of his fawn gloves. He had created this particular situation at sea and was bored by its repetition in miniature. He had a feeling that Nickelby's greeting had been somewhat cool and wondered why. He was aware of Nickelby's customary envy and found pleasure in the marked contrast between their appearances. Nickelby was too simple, too square, to mask his emotions. He had been a losing poker player as far back as Flint could remember. But now Flint was piqued. He had expected more praise from CINCPAC for the results of last week's raids. He believed they represented the first breakthrough in the solid wall of Japanese victories and offered a possible opportunity to shift from a purely defensive position to a more aggressive one of defensive-offensive.

Easy stages. Step by step, feeling as we go. It gave Amos Flint great comfort and a sense of well-being to know this was how he would win the war, pawn by pawn. It was just too bad Old Nick was so damned miserly in giving credit where credit was due.

Flint could not know that, because of a rash of unfortunate accidents, Nickelby was not entirely pleased with the operations of the newly formed task groups. The success of the mission had been threatened by an inept scout pilot who broke radio silence to report engine trouble, by dirty weather that damaged planes and swept a destroyer sailor to his death. A turret accident had killed a cruiser's gunner and two plane handlers died on the flight deck of Flint's carrier when a crippled plane crashed the barrier.

Yet in spite of these setbacks, the newly devised method of task force operation seemed workable and Nickelby had hopes. His present air of annoyance had also to do with Flint's highly polished half boots, fashioned of sleek leather handpicked in Manila by Flint himself and tooled by a Spanish craftsman who had fled Barcelona after the civil war. They were the handsomest boots Nickelby had ever laid eyes on. They were, unfortunately, a rich shade of non-regulation brown, polished to brass brightness and by contrast put to shame Nickelby's size 12 plain black regulation oxfords with built-in arches, purchased a week ago at Pearl Harbor's ships service for six dollars.

The room was stifling in the hot damp afternoon. The pressures of command and combat had worn tempers thin. The staff men fidgeted, impatient to see the routine business done so they could escape to the coolness of the officers' club. As soon as Everton completed his report, Nickelby began speaking and they knew from his sharp tone, the conference was far from over.

The admirals with their chiefs of staff stood over the charts and the strategy board. Nickelby shot crisp questions at Flint and Everton. He seemed particularly interested in minute details of communications and maneuvering of the task force operation, and noting the unrest among his juniors, took time out to explain his interest.

"The old fleet principle is passé, gentlemen. Whether or not the task force concept will provide a more effective technique remains to be seen. It's up to your units in the field to test it and prove it. So far it seems to be giving us the flexibility we need to cover an ocean as big as this one. The Marshall and Gilbert raids with Flint and Tully's groups were swift, effective, and well-executed. The accidents were unfortunate. We must cut them to a minimum. We plan to continue with our present task force divided into two fast carrier groups. As soon as new units now under construction are made available, we'll be able to operate several fast task forces, with task groups built around the nucleus of three or four carriers."

"How soon?" Flint wanted to know.

"Wish I could say. I've cumshawed every fighting ship I could from the Atlantic Command and they're squawking like hell. Out here the Jap has Singapore and Sumatra and is heading this way. If we can keep him out of Australia another six months maybe we'll be over the hump. We need carriers to do it. Every yard stateside is going full blast twenty-four hours a day. Meanwhile we have to hold the line with what we have and hit 'em when we can."

"We are, aren't we?"

Nickelby smiled faintly. "You're doing fine, Amos. No need to feel offended. We estimate seventy thousand tons of Jap shipping sunk as a result of what Tully and you have done. Plus a hell of a lot of damage to airfields, aircraft on the ground, fuel dumps, and supply depots. While we're on the subject, I want to say the aerial photography is sub-standard. I've sent off a hot dispatch demanding trained men. We're helpless in our raids without good photo intelligence." He turned to Flint. "How'd our fighters stack up?"

"All guts, no planes. The Jap Zero flies circles around our fighters. Turns tighter, is more maneuverable and their pilots are better protected."

"We should have a few changes soon. The F4Fs are rolling in. We're getting self-sealing fuel tanks and 20-mm cannon to replace the 50-calibre stuff." He looked at the men for a moment. "That's about it. I'd like Everton and Getchall to remain with Admiral Flint and me for a while longer. Rest of you can go."

He turned to Everton and Getchall. "This is still Top Secret information. I should have asked you both to shove off with the others, but I see no reason why you shouldn't know." He took a breath. "In San Francisco last week, I was informed Churchill is desperate for anything we can do to get the Jap carriers off his back. His bases at Bombay are vulnerable and the possibility of an invasion of Ceylon and India seems more certain each day." He glanced almost reproachfully at the tip of Flint's boot which extended past the edge of the desk and almost touched his leg. "The British would be pleased for any diversion we can offer the enemy. Your raids, Amos, are one way. The Jap's beginning to find out we can fight back. It seems to me, and I mentioned this in San Francisco, it's time for the Tokyo raid."

Both chiefs of staff looked at Nickelby, startled. Flint stiffened and waited. "With B-25s from a carrier at about 400 miles," Nickelby went on, speaking to Everton and Getchall. "We've kept the plan under wraps. You'll get the details as soon as Amos and I get together on the when of it. We've already figured out the how."

"Maybe you can launch 'em," Everton said, "but how in hell will you get 'em back aboard? B-25s need a few acres of deck to land on."

"We don't land 'em. They fly to Tokyo, drop their load, and land in China."

"The nearest friendly Chinese airfield is better than a thousand miles beyond Tokyo."

"Eleven hundred. They can make it."

"I'm still against it, Nick," Flint said.

"That's what I told 'em in San Francisco. They left it up to me, Amos. We're carrying on." He turned to the two staff officers. "Don't get Amos wrong. He's willing and able to carry out the mission. He just feels it's an unnecessary risk, a waste of time, and the possible loss of planes and men."

"And all for a showy Army publicity stunt," Flint said.

"It could be a hell of a morale builder back home," Everton said.

"The tactical gain is nil," Flint said.

"It'd sure rock the Jap Imperial Command," said Getchall. "They figure the war's just about over."

Flint flicked imagined dust from his boot tip. "We don't have the carrier strength to risk it. It takes one to carry the planes, another for combat air patrol. Add to that supporting cruisers and cans to fill out two task groups and there's precious little left to hold the line."

"Well, there's still a week or two to work it over. Mid-April's the scheduled target date. Snap out of it, Amos. It's my private opinion you're peed off because the Army's involved in it."

"That's right," Flint snapped. "Why give them a slice of the pie? What has the Army ever done for us?"

"What they're giving us is the range," Nickelby said. "We don't have a carrier bomber yet that we can launch outside the limits of the enemy's offshore air patrol that can make it both ways. And since we can't recover B-25s on a carrier deck, these Army lads are willing to go the extra mileage just to get a crack at the Japs on their home ground."

"I still feel we haven't fully explored the possibility of making it an all-Navy operation."

"I respect your devotion to the naval service, Amos. But I don't give a hoot in hell who does the job of winning this war, as long as it's won."

"It'll be won and the Navy will win it." Flint's cheeks had a mottled red look. "Rushing into things half-cocked isn't going to do it."

Nickelby permitted himself the luxury of a sustained study of Flint's brown boots. Silence hung heavily in the room. The chiefs of staff seemed embarrassed. Everton, sensing the personality conflict in the exchange, motioned to Getchall and got to his feet. "Stick around," Nickelby said in a tired voice. "What I have to say concerns all of us."

They are really lovely boots, he told himself, and one day I will ask Amos for the name of the bootmaker. Flint, piqued now, flicked fawn gloves and through the plasterboard ceiling demanded of God witness to his martyrdom.

"You have got to remember, Amos," Nickelby went on. "That the basic job is being done. We were asked to cover and hold the Hawaiian-Midway line and to keep communications clear with the West Coast. I'm satisfied now we're doing it. I intend to hold with everything I lay my hands on and to hit hard when I can. The big mistake before December seventh was our estimate of ourselves and the Jap as fighting men. We were too damned cocky and too smug. We figured we were the unbeatable—the greatest navy in the world. We learned the hard way we weren't. We may never get a chance to prove we can be. And don't think the Jap is going to sit around and do nothing after we show him we can fight back. The Jap is shrewd and dedicated and he knows damned well it's all or nothing and he isn't going to settle for nothing. He's a first-rate fighting man. He's a fanatic enemy, willing, eager, honored, to die for his country. A Japanese commander doesn't think in terms of cost in men. He considers only the objective. And it can be a damned insignificant objective and it will make not a particle of difference.

If this appears to be a form of Oriental insanity to our Western minds, let us not be fooled. It is real. He will fight for his Emperor inch by inch to the last breath in the last man. He knows our weakness is mercy and he sneers at our high regard for human life. He thinks we're soft and we lose face by it and as an enemy are unworthy and contemptible because of it.

"His logic is this: Make the cost in human lives and ships and planes so fantastically high, the American will beg for peace. Interesting theory, eh? How many Americans feel that way, do you suppose? How many would prefer to back down now rather than accept so great a loss in human lives? After all, the Orient is a hell of a way off and at that price, they figure, Japan can have it and the hell with it."

Flint started to say something. Nickelby talked through him, his voice sharp-edged now. "The Japanese haven't lost a sea war in 350 years. They don't intend to lose this one. Their navies are well-trained and well-equipped and they can make-do with a hell of a lot less than our men. They've been preparing for this shindig for a long time and they're prepared to lose ten million men to gain their ends. I repeat: ten million. How many men are the American people willing to sacrifice?"

They remained silent. He turned to Flint. "We must risk the life of every man in uniform if we expect to beat these people, Amos. I don't care if the uniform is Army or Navy, Coast Guard, or Marine. Or 100 percent wool with two pairs of pants. Or whatever the hell it is. I know we're going to risk a lot less if we work together. Don't speak again of Army versus Navy. In a way that may seem odd to you, because you are a loyal and dedicated Navy officer, I find it unworthy. Some may call it treason."

The ordered tramp of feet rang flatly in the street outside. Its measured beat filled the silent room, heavy with the echo of his last word.

"I hate to make these speeches," Nickelby muttered. "And today it's too damned hot." He nodded to Everton and the two chiefs of staff rose and gathered their papers together and left.

It was an occasion rare enough to call for a drink. Nickelby went to the cabinet behind his desk and brought out a bottle and held it to the light. Dust danced on the sheet of the sun. He squinted at the bottle and grunted amiably. "Sun's over the yardarm, Amos. How about a nip?"

"That was a nasty crack to make in front of the others."

"Hell, Amos. You asked for it." He unscrewed the cap and proffered the bottle to Flint. "Long time since we raised a cup together."

"After you, sir," Flint said stiffly.

"Cheers, Admiral." Nickelby tilted the bottle and wiped its mouth and passed it to Flint who grimaced. "Sorry," said Nickelby with a sly grin. "I always forget." He produced a stack of paper cups and ceremoniously poured a shot. Flint raised it. "To the men at sea." He drank it down and dabbed his lips with a folded handkerchief. "I feel the reprimand was uncalled for. And using the word 'treason'—"

"You think that's a reprimand, Amos, you ain't heard nothing yet. That was merely a review of enemy characteristics worthy of the most conscientious Intelligence officer."

"I intended no friction," Flint said.

"Amos, forget it. I'm always shooting off my mouth." He toyed with the cap on the bottle. "What really got me started were those fancy boots of yours. You can't get by with brown boots when regulations call for black. You know that."

"I'm entitled to indulge my privilege of rank."

"What you need is another nip."

"Thank you, no."

"Lovely boots," Nickelby said. "But those yellow gloves. I know an admiral needs something on his bare feet to pace that hot quarterdeck. But gloves?"

Flint's icy stare would have withered a lesser man. "This jungle," he said, "ordains it."

Nickelby chuckled and wiped his lips with a sleeve. Flint watched him coldly and wondered what magic had brought this ungainly man so far. He had been known as a plodder most of his Navy career, low on the list of eligibles and far below the fair-haired boys. His record was adequate but undistinguished. He had a reputation as a reliable troubleshooter but Flint could find little more to be said for him. He lacked the natural social graces Flint deemed essential to a career officer. What then had been the magic? Not his breeding, certainly. He could not trace his ancestry past a stolid Swede farm girl of a mother and an inept Scot father who ran a moldering pharmacy in a dust-bitten Midwest city. Flint knew. He had met them both at graduation. He had thoroughly checked the

Nickelby line in a fit of pique the day in 1939 when Nickelby, to the amazement of most high-ranking Navy goldbraid round the world, had been skipped a hundred numbers to vice admiral and handed the Atlantic command.

His rugged charm? Had he sold Washington a bill of goods on his fleeting resemblance to Lincoln? Flint shuddered. A damyankee *parvenu*, his late grandfather (the Confederate commodore) would have labeled him. A *yahoo*, his late father (the admiral) would have sneered.

"You're right, Amos. It's a jungle. And jungle law says kill or be killed." Nickelby commenced to cap the bottle and hesitated. "Those poor newspaper bastards have been hanging around all day. This'll cheer 'em up."

Flint said nothing. The notion that a drink would be served to a motley pack of freeloading snooping rum-guzzling newspaper hacks struck him as an insult to the service and unworthy of a man with three silver stars on his collar. Stars that could stand a polishing, Flint observed sourly, and a collar so stained with sweat it curled like a withered leaf.

Nickelby unlocked a drawer of his desk and withdrew a thick manila folder. "Operations orders for the Tokyo raid, Amos. You're being detached within forty-eight hours."

"That's damned short notice, Nick."

"We had shorter notice on seven December. Joint Command wants this project under way. So does King George of England. You're from Dixie, Amos. You're not going to let down the King of England, are you?" Flint searched the guileless blue eyes for malice behind the faintly chiding tone. "Those orders," Nickelby continued placidly, "are going to return you to the States and put you under wraps for a while. You will work in close association with units of Army air force command. These units must be trained and equipped for carrier duty and the entire task force operation worked out to perfection. I don't know a Navy officer better qualified."

"I resent having to leave just when things are beginning to go our way."

"You'll be back in six weeks and you'll have a hero's welcome from the free world, Amos. You can't resent that, can you?" He handed the portfolio to Flint.

"Who's my relief?"

"Spike Tully. He takes over tactical command as ComTaskFor 2. Temporary, of course, until you're back. When you finish training the Army, we'll detach *Hornet* to San Francisco and put the Army planes aboard at Alameda and designate you as over-all command, Operation Tokyo."

"That leaves an opening for Tully's ComCarDiv billet. Anyone in mind?"

"Pop Lindsey. He's skippered *Lex* and qualifies for rear admiral."

"Good choice. Pop Lindsey's a gentleman and a savvy sailor. He deserves it. I'd like to recommend Bugsy Gallant to skipper the *Lex*, then. He's been long overdue for a carrier command."

"That's okay and I want a four-striper to go along with him for a refresher."

"As good as Bugsy?"

"Better. Harry Paige."

"Paige?" Flint stared at him.

"Hardtack himself."

"Isn't he laid up?"

"He'll be available in two weeks."

"I can't believe you mean it, Maury."

"I mean it." He fidgeted. "I thought you'd offer some resistance. That's why I sent the others out and laid on the booze, Amos. You're a difficult man to deal with, cold sober."

"Deal with? It's the United States Navy you're dealing with. The American people, Maury. For heaven's sake, have you completely lost your senses?"

"I hope not. We're continuing the present program of exploratory offensive raids against Salamaua and Lae in New Guinea. I'm assigning Paige to temporary duty as an observer in *Lex*. Then I'm detaching him and ordering him to new construction. He'll probably get the first big carrier off the ways."

"*Shiloh?* I'd save that for Gallant. My heavens, Maury, there's a waiting list long as your arm of four-stripers qualified for carrier command. Men a damned sight more reliable and worthier than Paige. Paige's record is black enough—"

The hard glint in Nickelby's eye stopped him. Flint carefully laid down the portfolio and began to pull at his gloves. "May I speak freely?"

"Certainly, Amos. But I must tell you that nothing is going to be changed."

Flint's fingers trembled as he lighted a cigarette. "At least I will have done my duty as I see it by speaking my mind."

"By all means." He restrained a bow.

"I would think, after that blunder in Sunda Strait, a shenanigan I would call it, were it not so tragic, after such a performance, it would seem to me Captain Harry Paige would earn a Naval court of inquiry and not another sea command."

"Why?"

"It was a reckless action undertaken in violation of orders and you damn well know it, Maury."

"You seem to know all about it."

"The word gets around. He lost his ship and every man in it. Yet he managed to save his own skin. If that alone doesn't call for a general court I don't know what does."

"There are details you don't know, Amos." He handed over his staff estimate of the damage inflicted by *Gloucester.* Flint glanced at it and tossed it back. "Unverified," he snapped. "And it still does not excuse the direct disobedience of orders." He milked the fingers of his glove. "As a friend and brother officer, Maury, and in the best interest of the service, I suggest you're making a grievous mistake."

"I invariably try to look with approval on any of my officers who act with intelligent initiative."

"What was so damned intelligent about taking a crippled cruiser singly into the middle of the Jap fleet? My heavens, Maury, you know the man's record! Tail end of his class. Would have bilged out if he wasn't so handy with his fists and fast talk. Ran his first command, a lousy little minesweeper afoul of the channel in Hampton Roads of all places. And that time at Pensacola, do you remember? He was placed under hack for stunt-flying. If it wasn't for his father-in-law, good old Blatchford, he'd never have gotten off. Face it, Maury. Paige is no sailor, no navigator, no leader of men. His grasp of strategy and tactics is z-e-r-o. That he should be selected to skipper the first carrier of a new class is just—well it's what you accused me of, damn it. It's treason."

He was suddenly short of breath and sat down. He reached for the fingers of his gloves. Nickelby watched him, an expression of gentle patience on his homely face. "You seem to know more about Harry Paige than anyone else. Why, Amos?"

"Just because—hell! He's always grabbing publicity, always working some cockeyed angle to get his name in the papers."

"You're not doing too badly yourself."

"It's not my fault if the newspaper boys want news, is it? After all, I'm the fighting fleet. I'm where things are happening. But of all officers—why pick a loud common roughneck—a dangerous show-off like Paige?"

"Because he's a killer, Amos, and it's killers I need. I'm giving the Sunda Strait story to the papers just as soon as you and I are through here. Think they'll like it?"

"They'll be printing a pack of lies. It was a night action, remember. Things look a lot different at night."

"Well, they're getting it. If they're lies, I'll take the rap."

"I'm not questioning *your* integrity, Maury."

"The hell you're not." Nickelby for some unexplainable reason felt obliged to smile. It did not escape Flint. He pounded the desk.

"You said I could speak freely and I will, damn it. I mentioned a few of the black marks in Paige's record. I did it because apparently you had not known about them or in the pressure of events, overlooked them. Do you recall the fiasco for his flying anchor stunt? He overshot and smashed the hell out of the *Idaho's* fantail."

"Hell, that was ages ago."

"It was spring of 1921 during the war games off Long Beach. I remember it as if it happened yesterday. How about his tour of duty at the War College? He made a fool of himself spouting theories, asking ridiculous questions, drinking all night. I tell you, he was a clown. A disgrace. To give a man like that command of a carrier at a critical time like this is, in my considered opinion—well, it's stupid, Maury, and dangerous and I for one would object strenuously to having such a man in any task group under my command."

"Is that all for now?"

"I could go on."

"We'll let Tully worry about it."

"Does Spike have any idea of what he's getting?"

"He will in due time. Right now Paige is recovering from burns." His eyes fastened on Flint's fawn gloves. Holsters, he thought suddenly. Fancy tooled saddle leather, studded with semiprecious stones and the pearl-handled butts of two nickel-plated .45s. He could see them, swinging low on Amos Flint's girdled hips, glinting in the sun. "Holsters," he muttered and Flint's head snapped up. "I beg your pardon?"

"I was thinking this, Amos, and you can have it for what it's worth. Your total recall of every bad detail of Harry Paige's career leads me to believe your concern is personal rather than official. I'm thinking, for example, of Rollo Blatchford's well-stacked daughter, Felicia. I can't remember details as well as you, but I seem to recall you were engaged to her before Hardtack came along and married her."

"Not so," Flint said quickly. "At least not officially engaged." He avoided Nickelby's eyes of pure blue innocence. "I dated Felicia if that's what you mean. My heavens, I dated dozens of Navy juniors. I could have had any one of them."

"You never had Felicia Blatchford, did you?"

"Do you expect me to remember a thing like that after twenty years?"

"You remembered Hardtack's flying anchor fiasco."

Flint reached angrily for the portfolio and tucked it under his arm. "Would you please advise your duty secretary I'm leaving now and to pass the word along to my staff?"

Nickelby pressed the button of the intercom and passed the word. "And Harry's been nipping at your heels ever since."

"I see no reason to continue this discussion." Flint tapped the portfolio. "I presume my staff joins me in this—cavalry show?"

"Roger." Nickelby stared at his watch with an air of annoyance. "Before you go, Amos. In all fairness. Do you want out?"

"Out of what?"

"If you want 'out' of this Tokyo raid just say so."

"You want Paige to have it? Is that it?"

"You're acting like a child."

"You stated before I was the most qualified man for the job, did you not?"

"You are and I did."

"And it's my duty to undertake the mission assigned me, no questions asked. Just as it's your duty to give it to me. Duty, Maury, takes precedence over all other considerations. At least with me. *Noblesse oblige*, you know."

Nickelby sighed. "If you want to turn it down, there'll be no hard feelings."

"I certainly will not shirk my duty. But it's permissible, isn't it, to disagree in principle with an idea and still obey orders?"

"I cannot tell you, Amos, what a pompous snob you are and what a pain in the ass you give me. It would be unofficer-like. Instead, let me say that you have spoken like a true Navy man. I just wanted to be sure you put your heart in the Tokyo raid. It's a winner. It can be as demoralizing to the Jap as Pearl Harbor was to us. It'll put the name of Flint on the lips of every American man, woman, and child with an ounce of red, white, or blue blood in their veins. And you can do the job slick as a smelt."

"Well! Thank you." Flint snapped his gloves over his fingers. "I'll meet with my ship commanders tonight. I'd like to be the first to give Pop Lindsey the good news. We've been through thick and thin together, Pop and I." He looked directly over Nickelby's head at his good Friend and Shipmate, God. "That's about it, then?"

"Unless you want one for the road."

"I wouldn't want you to run out of Dixie Cups, Maury. The newspaper boys would never forgive me." He took his leave in style, head high, stomach in, the clean contours of his handsome face marbled with cold fury.

Nickelby remained standing, his hands locked behind him. I'm getting ornery and creaky, he told himself. "Holsters," he muttered softly. "Nickel-plated .45s with pearl grips. For Christmas. Or the Tokyo raid." His eyes rested on the bottle. He flicked the intercom button. "I'll see the press boys now."

He went to the window. The sun was low in the sky, not yet set and more a blaze than a burial. Colors like those would be cheap and tawdry on anything but a sunset, he thought. Holsters. When the time came he would not forget the holsters. And a medal for Olsen's wife and a dead Dutch lieutenant.

The yard din had not abated and he liked that. Round the clock murder, he thought. Right now it would be noon hour back home and the lunch crowd from Hancock's paper mill at the counter in his late father's drugstore yelling for service and his sister's half-deaf husband taking his own sweet time. He remembered the oil of wintergreen smell and the sucking sound of chocolate syrup drained from its porcelain well. He made a hell of a good ice cream frappe in his day. Folks went out of their way to tell him so. He was fourteen and he called it Maury's Special and it sold for a dime, walnuts, whipped cream, syrup, and all. No telling what a concoction the likes of it would bring today.

The newspapermen were filing in. Nickelby rubbed his jaw and picked up the *Gloucester* report. One thing was certain. When he was through talking to them and they had had a pull at the whisky, it wouldn't be too long before Gabriel Heatter would be booming his blessed words, *There's good news tonight.*

18

Paige grinned for the cameras. "Luck," he said.

A quartet of favored war correspondents had been cleared by Admiral Nickelby for a brief interview and had come to call, shepherded by a Public Information officer. Paige sat naked, propped high in the hospital bed, covered to the navel with a coarse muslin sheet. His arms were thick with bandages from which his blackened fingers protruded. Navy documents and pamphlets were strewn about the bed and side table.

One of the correspondents said he was surprised there weren't other survivors besides the four of them.

"Restricted information," the PI officer said quickly.

"What about it, Captain?" the correspondent persisted. "The scuttlebutt is, you lost a hell of a lot of boys."

"We've died before," Paige said.

The questions flew. The answers were typically Hardtack Harry Paige.

"That's all, gentlemen," the PI officer said. "Captain Paige needs his rest."

The pencils scribbled and the correspondents' heads bobbed admiringly. They loved the captain's style and he made good copy. They soon left, followed by the PI officer. Paige picked up a pamphlet labeled TOP SECRET and continued reading about the new *Shiloh* class carrier, its construction, operation, and maintenance.

A plump pink-cheeked doctor came in followed by a staff nurse. Paige put aside the thick pamphlet and watched as the nurse's scissors cut through bandage. Her closeness excited him and she did not seem to mind when his elbow brushed her. The doctor cautiously peeled back outer layers of bandage. "This may hurt, Captain." It hurt. Paige said nothing. The nurse carried off the loose pile of gauze while the doctor went on probing. "You're doing fine. You'll be out of here in no time."

"When's no time?"

"A couple of weeks."

Paige swore. The nurse returned and wiped the sweat from his face. She was shapely and fragrant and had absolutely no business being around men too long at sea and he wished she would go away. The doctor was praising his good health, saying what a fast healer he was. Burns like Paige's sometimes took months to heal. Paige asked about the other survivors and the doctor said they were doing fine and would be released when Paige was released. All except Wilson.

"What about Wilson?"

"The leg, you know. He's been asking to see you."

"Well, send him in."

"You'll have to go to him, Captain."

"It's that bad?"

"We finally had to amputate."

"What the hell for?"

"Gas gangrene."

"You mean to tell me you butchers had to amputate his leg? Hell, all that happened was, his blood circulation was cut off for a while."

"We received the patient already dangerously ill, Captain. The leg was full of dead tissue and in an advanced state of crepitation and our gas gangrene antitoxin had no effect. He'd have lost his whole leg if we hadn't operated. He'd have died if we didn't get to him when we did. As it was, we were able to save the knee."

"My God, the man was fine."

"Would you care to see him, Captain?"

Paige remained silent, staring at the ceiling, the corners of his mouth pinched and white. "He keeps asking to see you," the doctor went on. "His spirits are low. It would do him a world of good. The nurse can wheel you down the hall."

"Forget it."

Paige turned away. The doctor stood redfaced for a moment, then shrugged and went out. The nurse cleaned up the loose ends of bandage and straightened the medical things on the cabinet and left. When he was alone Paige picked up the pamphlet on carriers and resumed reading where he had left off.

Later during his evening rounds the doctor stopped to chat with Stick Wilson. After a hesitant beginning and prodded by Wilson's demands for the facts, he admitted that Captain Paige had refused outright to visit him. Stick lay back and thought about it for a while. His pale whiskered cheeks seemed oddly skrunken and his eyes were unsteady and bright.

Christ, he thought. He bore no grudge. All he had wanted to do was to let the Old Man know he didn't give a damn about the leg. What the hell was a lousy leg from the knee down between a couple of Asiatic shipmates who shared the memory of Yangtze gunboats and Juggy Nelson, junks and sampans and Japanese whores, and the tap room of the Manila Hotel and battle? All he had wanted to do was explain to the Old Man it was the gook broad on the beach at Chili Jap who was the cause of all the trouble. He wanted the Old Man to know he had jumped ship the last time to bring her aboard so the Old Man himself could have a piece because the Old Man was as human and horny as any of them and hadn't the Old Man himself told him sharing makes all men brothers?

"Doc?"

"Yes, Wilson?"

"What happens to the leg?"

"It heals."

"I mean the other part. With the foot and toes and all."

"We take it out and bury it."

"You already done that?"

"Yes, Wilson."

"Do me a favor, Doc."

"Sure. Anything you say."

"Dig it up, will ya, and gift wrap it and send the goddam thing to Captain Harry Paige. With my compliments."

In the officers' ward down the passageway, Tod Newell awoke to the harsh beat of rain. In his dream it had been flame blistering paint. The need to scream and run awakened him. He looked at

Joe Allen asleep and smiling in the other bed. Allen was regular Navy and rarely smiled and it pleased Newell to see the smile even in sleep. Traces of oil lay in the deep lines of Allen's otherwise young face and the thick bandages on his hands and shoulders and across his chest were rimmed black-green.

Newell envied Joe Allen his untroubled sleep. Dreams for Tod Newell were nightmares filled with the cries of the trapped and dying. Dreams were entanglements of tennis nets (or were they cargo nets?) trapping arms and legs as he sank gagging in warm oily sea water. Last night it had been endless volleys of tennis balls flung at him hard and fast changing without warning into machine-gun bullets that drove him to the back court spinning and scream-ing as they thudded into his middle. He longed for the dreamless slumber of his youth and the solid and absolute triumph of six-love, six-love, six-love.

His daylight hours were spent in an unreal haze of disbelief at salvation and in his more lucid moments with random thoughts of the mysterious wonders of Navy jargon. Take a shaft alley, he would tell himself, playing the game. A shaft alley is a narrow concrete space between tenements, planted with a thousand spears. Flaked out is a lifeless sailor in a shroud filled with dry cereals. The oil king is a Brooklyn version (voision?) of the mythical elfin ruler of Goethe's great ballad and Schubert's song. And why is a smoke stack called a Charley Noble?

So the slow hours passed in the game he played to insulate him-self from the recent images of raw horror at sea. In all his sheltered life the only act of violence Tod Newell had ever witnessed had been the death of a small dog one summer night. Blinded by the headlights' glare, it had blundered into the path and under the wheels of Newell's Buick roadster as he raced to a cup tournament in Westchester.

He had lost that one, too. In the semifinals. Paige knew. It's the game that counts. Shaft alley, oil king, flaked out. And who would be seeded at Forest Hills this coming season? Charley Noble?

Thank God he still had his two hands. Holding them aloft he watched them tremble. A few scabs from torn bits of hot flying metal and a long healing gash from God knows what. But all fingers present and accounted for. And ten toes below.

Poor Wilson, he thought. The nurse had just told him and when he slept on it, it was a dream swollen with a fresh image of the helmsman looking like Long John Silver, with a hole in the deck for the pegleg.

He closed his eyes. Everything was going to be all right and for once in his life he didn't need his father to tell him so. He bunched his right hand into a fist and held it until the trembling stopped. It is a good hard fist, he told himself, and it can still grip a Slaezinger Autograph Special and come summer, by golly, they had better watch their wickets at Wimbledon. Wickets, he thought, playing the game, not knowing a wicket from a winch.

Alongside him Joe Allen, hero, slept on, dreaming of the new cruiser *Gloucester*. His old home was gone and he would miss it but that was the sea for you and the Navy way and here in his dream was the replacement, sleek and tough, her topside decks bristling with the newest Bofors and Oerlikon armament and her bridge and chart room blessed with the latest marvelous machinery of brass and stainless steel under battle gray, an ecstatic world of sonarscopes, fathometers, and holy radar. Heaven at sea in a dream and plain Joe Allen home again and that was why in sleep he smiled.

A nurse wearing the two full stripes of a lieutenant came into the ward followed by an enlisted man. Coiled lengths of black wire trailed from the phone she carried. The nurse went directly to Newell. Her eyes were shining in a way he did not like. Her expression was a lopsided blend of awe and bold scheming.

"The mainland calling long distance, Ensign Newell."

"For me?" He already knew. He had seen it in the nurse lieutenant's eyes.

"Your father."

Not with a war on. He wouldn't dare, Newell told himself.

The corpsman set the phone on the bedside cabinet and nodded at the nurse who picked up the receiver and after listening for a moment smiled brightly and handed it to Newell.

"Here you are, Ensign. Just like home."

He said hello and stiffened hearing Irma Thurston's businesslike voice, Irma being Thomas A. Newell's private secretary and everyone should know that Thomas A. Newell never picked up a phone until the party in person was on the line. And an instant later there was the immediate torrent of Thomas A. Newell's words, strident autocracy crowing in contempt of distance, time waiting for no man. Blurred power swept westward over three thousand miles of outraged homeland teeming with war effort in the factories of furious revenge and across two thousand miles of ocean bottom strewn with the corpses of ships and men and like a tidal wave rose and fell against the ears of Todhunter Newell couchant in the Navy hospital on Oahu.

Joe Allen had opened his eyes. Newell saw that he and the others stood by entranced like bumpkins at a country carnival. He sat in shame letting the strident words spill out and over him and his thoughts raced to the source of it, reawakening the images that had sent him all his life running from it.

Did America realize how much of its daily life depended on Thomas A. Newell? On the Newell Plan? Food, for example, for the maw of America, nourishing, brain-building, body-building sustenance created in the Newell Foundation's scientific kitchens out of seaweed and tree bark, out of waste products and ingenious chemical coagulations to teach the palate of America the Newell-inspired lesson of conservation. Corn pone from surplus silage with added nitrates and nitrites, bilium and bolium. Vitamin-packed gefüllte fish wrapped in pre-digested self-assimilating plastic grape leaves for the highly orthodox Armenian trade. Beans for Boston made from cod.

Did America know its parks and playgrounds were an integral part of the Newell Plan, size and facilities determined on a per capita age group formula conforming to the national norm by race, creed, and color? That the Newell Geriatrics Plan guaranteed happiness through the sunset years and a dignified death involving the deceased's loved ones in nothing more than a routine removal of a minimum of ashes?

Happiness was the key to Thomas A. Newell. Happiness at any price. And his son on Oahu, listening to the modern day Machiavelli in Newell, Connecticut, behind two anterooms of palace guards in his awesome office suite so huge it would shame Hitler and Mussolini combined, could only wonder how he had got his number. How had he managed to bypass wartime priorities and the endless echelons of military rules and regulations and national security restrictions? And on which of his nine colored telephones had he chosen to honor his son and heir while the urgent business of America at war must wait? Who needs armies, Tod wondered, with a man like Thomas A. Newell to run the world, running it from the throne end of a rug deep enough to growl, leaning back in the glove leather embrace of the patented Newell Execulaxor, and ingenious therapeutic armchair wired to take dictation and simultaneously exercise the busy executive's stomach muscles with a vibrating woven plastic webbed belt guaranteed against risk of hernia and sternly unyielding to self-abuse while a sponge rubber spine rest massages his back and neck muscles. The source of man's fatigue is unmassaged neck muscles and laziness, according to *Executive Survival*, the invaluable handbook written, published, and distributed as a tax-deductible public service by Thomas A. Newell and manufactured in accordance with paper conservation orders of the War Production Board to which he was a dollar-a-year consultant.

Looking about in a desperate effort to gather strength to withstand this unexpected paternal onslaught, Tod Newell saw that Captain Paige had come into the room and in a wheel chair sat watching with the others. A goddam vaudeville act, thought Newell in shame, and something happened. Something wild and uncontrollable tore through him and he interrupted his father in midsentence. Speaking harshly into the phone he shouted at the top of his voice, "Shut up and listen for once, goddamit! You don't know what I've seen out here!"

And hung up. The others watched in silence, waiting for the next act, approving, disapproving, he did not know or care and lumping them with his father and the rest of the world, he closed his eyes and raced forward to the net and returned his surprised opponent's uneasy lob with a forehand drive that smashed cleanly to the back court.

He said aloud, evenly, "That's an order," and the serious way he spoke broke the tension in that hospital room and somehow, because of the long-distance call or the defiant look in his eyes or because of what he had seen out there, Tod Newell for a shining moment was in absolute command and they knew it.

The corpsman began coiling the phone lines and the nurse carried away the instrument and Paige said, "Who was that?"

"My father."

"Who the hell does he think he is?"

"God."

Paige chuckled and wheeled the chair to a position between the beds, using his elbows. "I met the old buzzard once. Met him in a Maine shipyard and he thought he was God even then and that was before we needed him. Doesn't give a man a chance to get a word in edgewise, does he? Didn't, that time in Maine."

"He's used to giving orders."

"Well, he's cock of the roost now. Number one, calling way the hell from where's that lash-up? Massachusetts?"

"Connecticut."

"Asking Junior how the Navy is treating you, I suppose. Well, you can tell him from your skipper, we've made a first-class gunnery officer out of a second-rate tennis player."

"I don't think he'd care, Captain."

"Hell, Newell, I'll tell him. You did fine. I had a look at you in Sky One, you and the Dutch kid. You did fine and I'm damned proud of you and to hell with your old man."

He saw the welling in Newell's eyes and turned quickly to address Joe Allen. "I came by for just one reason, Joe. We got the word from CINCPAC I'm getting me my carrier—the new *Shiloh*. I'd like to keep the old team together. Are you with me?" And turned back to Newell. "You too. What about it?"

"I'd be honored," Tod Newell said.

Joe Allen said carefully, "When will she be ready, sir?"

"She's almost ready now for shakedown. A month at the most and she'll be out there where she's needed. I'm sure going to need a navigator, Joe."

"There's a hundred'd give their eyeteeth to ship out with you, Captain."

"I want you, Joe."

"I'm not qualified for air, sir. You'll be wanting a navigator who's earned his wings."

"You never had duty involving flying?"

"Getting airsick is all. I'm a sailor, sir. It's about all I've ever been."

"Goddam it, Joe, you want to ship along with me, don't you? I'm damned grateful for all you've done and I want to keep the old team together. After what we've been through?"

"I reckon so. Yes, sir."

"You can put in for pre-flight as an observer. They have a kind of accelerated lash-up for short timers. We'll get you detached for a priority assignment and by the time we've run *Shiloh* through her shakedown and all, you'll have your wings."

Allen looked unhappy.

"What the hell's bothering you, Joe? Speak up."

"Like I said, I'm a sailor, sir."

"So what? What the hell's wrong with trying to improve yourself? I mean flight pay and all and serving your country where you're most needed."

"*Gloucester*'s the only ship I've ever served in, sir. My first and only duty. I don't know the first thing about Navy air or flying a plane. Ships—"

"You're chicken. Is that what you're trying to tell me?"

"No, sir. It's being asked to do something I know nothing about."

"You don't have to know a damn thing about flying to learn. Hell, you won't be doing any in combat, anyway. It's just another one of those goddam regulations the land-based Navy cooks up to make us sweat. So carriers' senior officers have got to have their wings, and being ship's company you'd have to comply."

"I'd sure like to ship out with you again, Captain. Does it have to be a carrier?"

"Damned right it does. And I want you with me, Joe."

"Yes, sir. I'm grateful for that, believe me. It's just that being up there scares the dickens out of me. Just watching from the bridge when we used to launch those SOCs off of our old steam catapults used to leave me limp as a rag."

"Listen, Joe. Halsey himself went through the aviation course at Pensacola when he was, hell, fifty-one or -two years old. Did it so he could skipper the *Sara*. You think he wasn't scared? He switched from student observer to student pilot, flew everything they had. Took real guts to do it, too. He should have washed out the minute they tested his eyes. And a grandfather, mind you, and a four-striper. There's nothing to be scared of, Joe. It's just a question of what you want to do."

Allen was quiet for several moments. "There going to be another *Gloucester*, Captain?"

"Should be, with all the heavy cruisers under construction. And she's a proud Navy name." He looked at Allen's bent head. "That what you want, Joe?"

"It's more in my line, sir, you might say."

"That's what you want then?"

"That's what I'd prefer, sir. If there's a choice."

Paige abruptly turned and stared out of the window. Joe Allen fidgeted a while. Newell watched, wishing he were elsewhere.

"Captain," Allen said. Paige seemed not to hear. "Sir, if what

1

I said has got you so peed off, then I reckon my going along
is damned important to you and it's what I should do."

"It's damned important, Joe, the three of us alive, after what
we went through, it's a sort of symbol, you might say of the
survival of the American way of life, just us out of that entire company of men."

"I never thought of it that way, sir."

"It's the American way, Joe."

"Okay," Joe Allen said in a low voice, "I'm with you, sir."

"All the way, Joe?"

"All the way, sir."

"Knew I could count on you, Joe. You too, Newell. And congratulations. You boys will be getting another half-stripe and a
couple of weeks leave soon as you're out of here. There's a thing at
the White House—they'll tell you when. The President wants to pin
a medal on us—for living, I guess. Then Newport News and *Shiloh*
sometime in May. The orders are being cut right now. Good luck."

After Paige had gone, Joe Allen was quiet for a long time.
Then he spoke to Newell without looking at him. "The skipper
said three of us, didn't he?"

"That's right."

"What about Wilson?"

Newell told him what had happened to Wilson. Allen closed
his eyes. He was as good as dead now. He had lost his ship and
his luck with it. He would have liked to do something about it
but he was a good sailor and this was the Navy and there wasn't
a thing in the world he could do that would make it any different.
Wings. What a cruddy way for a saltwater sailor to go. He felt
airsick already. Poor Stick, he thought. But he felt sorrier for himself.

19

Captain Paige's love letter to his wife, Felicia, was delivered to her bedroom in the Georgetown house by her maid Lizzie, on a silver tray with her coffee and the rest of the mail.

The tray like Lizzie was a treasured Blatchford heirloom. So was the rundown house and everything in it except Felicia herself who seemed endowed with an enchanting youthfulness that miraculously replenished itself daily. As for the antiques surrounding her, they had been presented to the Paiges on the unpredictable whim of her father from time to time, the excuse being a birthday or anniversary, Navy Day, or possibly an unscheduled celebration of the victory of *Monitor* over *Merrimac*. With the presentation of each piece, the commodore would deliver a sonorous elegy of its history, a pathological ritual that on each occasion the Paiges found themselves less able to bear. It was rumored that this alone was at the root of Harry Paige's long absences from home and the reason behind his repeated requests for sea duty in the Pacific.

Rumor aside, it could certainly explain Felicia's chronic indolence and the extraordinary amount of time she spent in bed. The commodore was a domineering personality and, caught between love and filial devotion, she lived in fear that the sheer weight of her inherited responsibilities were about to crush her to death. She would take to her bed, an imposing mahogany four poster that had known General Washington, and stay there comforted by the radio, the fashion magazines and her priceless Lizzie. Though her father had removed himself to a hotel suite, his possessiveness persisted and his meddling in the routine of the antique-cluttered house dismayed her.

At its lowest ebb, she would lie in bed and indulge herself in longings for a home designed with the spareness of Le Corbusier and the simple forms of Eames, whose genius she admired in the magazine pages that came and went across her coverlet. Her tastes were simple and her single devotion embraced her husband's return. She loved Harry Paige with all her heart. Nothing her father had done through the years, or would ever do or say, could change that.

She sipped Lizzie's strong coffee and listened to the news. "Hear that, Lizzie? A hero's welcome."

"I heard it." Lizzie slit the envelopes with a 1792 G. Aikens skewer and stacked them on the tray. "Like I always said." Lizzie had long ago recognized the captain's gifts and with her special familial privilege often spoke out in his defense, to the commodore's disgust.

"David will be so proud."

"He always was proud, whatever his Daddy done." Lizzie passed the opened mail to her mistress. "The commodore phoned to say he's on his way." At the doorway she turned. "He said to make positive you was up."

"Must I, Lizzie?"

The quality of her mistress's voice made Lizzie look sharply. Felicia was reading her husband's letter, the last mail from Tjilatjap. "Heavens," she murmured flushing.

"Something wrong?"

"Oh no." She spoke softly. "He must have thought he was going to die."

"Him die? Hah!" Her clattered footsteps down the stairs echoed her disbelief.

The letter delighted Felicia. Lizzie was absolutely right. Harry could never die. She believed that and her body wakened, believing it. Beneath the hothouse languor and paleness, there was woman enough for a dozen Harry Paiges. Felicia at forty-plus was as passionate a woman as she had been when Paige had courted her as a Navy Junior. Her failure to take part in the social activities that attracted other Navy wives was cause for much concern from the commodore. Her unusually white unblemished skin convinced him she was anemic or worse and he demanded periodic medical checkups. Felicia submitted graciously, welcoming the change, secretly delighted by clinical politeness in the face of such intimate medical probing. After thorough tests, her gynecologist invariably reported to the commodore that he had not encountered a female, even twenty years younger, in more perfect health. "Why not?" the commodore would growl. "She's a Blatchford and what's more, she sleeps fifteen hours a day."

She loved her bed, lonely as it was, a safe, snug harbor. She understood the fever of Navy wives without their husbands, the fever that drove some to drink or to casual infidelities, and she did not dare to risk it. With David grown and gone, she fought to adjust her daily life to fit her husband's prolonged absences. Being witness to the amorous pitfalls of auxiliary Navy boredom, she had tried to establish a brisk pattern of household duties to occupy her time. She entertained for the commodore and thought seriously of a victory garden. It was going to be a long war without Harry and there must be no time for dalliance.

And here she was in bed at noon again. She turned to the rest of the mail. Invitations to Navy functions. A funny postcard from David at Annapolis. A sale brochure from a downtown department store. An invitation to Hollywood, California, of all things. The front door buzzer sounded.

"That's the commodore's ring," Lizzie shouted up the stair well.

Felicia heard her father puff and bellow as he climbed the stairs. She put aside the tray and muttering a shocking four letter word prepared to welcome him aboard.

One had to see Commodore Isaac Holt Blatchford to believe him. He stood above the silk coverlet of his daughter's bed, a quivering totem of mottled flesh over a vast expanse of blue and gold. Six feet, three inches—he would have preferred the statistic in fathoms—and weighing ("*Displacing*," the commodore growled) a shade under two hundred and eighty pounds. His claret face was fastened atop the totem like a massive ritual mask on a neck so short it was no neck at all but a red-cemented extension of cheek and jowl. His voice like a ship's bell submerged, rumbled from its depths. He wore his hair slicked over a washboard brow, brushed carefully to port and starboard, leaving a baby pink center line.

The Blatchford name, like Flint, was interwoven with ruffles and flourishes in the sturdy fabric of the American Navy. Blatchfords had fought with gallantry and honor on Lake Erie and in Manila Bay. A Blatchford in *Monitor* had faced a Flint behind the grim iron hull of *Merrimac* in Hampton Roads.

In spite of his distinguished heritage, it was Isaac Blatchford's personal tragedy never to go to sea. The fates and his voracious appetite had not fitted him for battle. As a midshipman his weight continually threatened to bilge him from the Academy. He fought each ounce with true bulldog Blatchford tenacity. He seemed to eat nothing and exercise fiercely. He was observed daily trotting countless track miles in all weathers, his body swathed in a blue sweat suit and his neck encased like a leaky steam pipe in layers of USNA towels.

Nothing came of it. What he sweated off he secretly gorged back on. He was capable of intense loyalty to anything but a diet. Stern warnings never failed to stiffen his resolve but not for long. Self-discipline dissolved to reappear in the form of smuggled sweets and starches. His dialogues with Academy doctors and physical fitness trainers were classics of sly pleading, self-castigation and promises. His weakness, he insisted, was unique and deep-rooted. He was descended from a long line of chronic sufferers of overdeveloped taste buds.

Navy medical science had not yet ascended to that pinnacle of specialization. But his plea was sincere and his zeal pathetic and his name was Blatchford and he graduated with his class. Such tribal legacies are not easily dismissed. For his excesses he was committed by orders to a lifetime career in shore-based commands. His friends called him Rollo.

The Blatchford spirit was undaunted. He turned to in true Navy style and made the best of it. In time he became the Navy Department's high priest of protocol, with special attention to personnel and the pecking order. His ponderous weight was felt everywhere the full dress Navy went. His bluff charm masked the sense of failure he secretly knew and created the dichotomy that drove him to extremes of temper. His chauvinistic fervor was of a savagery that could sink leviathans. His envy of the success of others drove him to depths of despair. He drank, but socially only, and never while on duty.

So Rollo Blatchford never went to sea and the battles he won were shore-based and bloodless. One battle unwon was that with his son-in-law Paige. He would never forgive him for stealing away his daughter. He regarded the failure of Amos Flint to win her heart a disaster equal to the sinking of the *Maine*. Those years ago, he had shrewdly evaluated the coupling of the two great names, placing special emphasis on the wealth that went along with Midshipman Amos Flint. He encouraged the match and encountered no resistance from Flint who found everything about Felicia to his liking. But Felicia would have none of it. She had fallen in love with Hardtack Harry, the Navy's hope for an Olympic boxing crown that year. Rollo's reactions were apoplectic and when the wedding was a certainty, his blessings were restrained. Though Harry brought home the Olympic crown, Blatchford would have preferred the cold Flint cash. And since there would not have been house room under the one Blatchford roof in Georgetown for the combined ancestral portraits and heirlooms, Felicia would have moved south to "Cavendish," the Flint establishment on the James, and Blatchford could have fetched a fancy price from some well-heeled patriot for his decaying though classic home.

Paige, having no family or home to speak of, moved in. He rightfully assumed the mortgage payments and the running bills and provided an allotment for Felicia during his years at sea. The commodore moved out anyway, as much in self-righteous anger as in the sure knowledge he could eat less guiltily and to his heart's content elsewhere. His feud with Paige, hidden from official eyes, ran deep—for Paige with puzzlement and diffidence, for Blatchford with a vengeance he probably could not truthfully explain.

His bright eyes were full of schemes as he entered his daughter's bedroom. The sight of Felicia still in bed confused them. "Rise and shine, girl! It's past noon."

"I'm planning a victory garden," Felicia said.

Blatchford groaned, as much to mask a prolonged belch as anything else. He was badly hung over. His efforts to chug-a-lug a magnum of vintage champagne at a wedding supper the night before had come a cropper and it troubled him. His feats of gluttony were already interred in Navy legend and the result of the night's performance seemed as shameful to him as though he had trampled on the Union Jack.

"Had something to tell you," he said. "Let's see now, what it was." She waited while he groped for the scheme. "It'll come," he went on. "Look. Have Lizzie fix me something, eh? A cold drink. I'm dying of thirst." He added guiltily, "A nibble of something. Noon, anyway."

Felicia rang for Lizzie. "Sandwiches and a bottle of ginger ale for the commodore, Lizzie."

"A large ginger ale, Lizzie, and the bourbon decanter."

"Absolutely not, Daddy. Just the sandwiches and ginger ale, Lizzie."

He sat on the edge of the bed. His quick fingers ransacked the remnants of Felicia's breakfast and he wolfed it down before she could protest. "A hell of a night. Ruined my best set of dress blues."

Felicia murmured her regrets. She knew he already had had a lunch and did not feel sorry for him. "Can you remember what it was you had to tell me?"

"In a moment. Something in the morning paper—"

"Dick Tracy is a German spy."

"Not funny, Felicia. I'll think of it."

"About Harry coming home?"

"I've known that for weeks."

"You never told me. I had to read about it in the paper."

"Secrets, my dear. Classified information, you know. Anyway, I've enough on my mind without family problems. Spent time enough last night defending that wild husband of yours."

"The radio called him a hero, Daddy. Just five minutes ago." She brightened, surprised to hear him defending Paige. "Why'd you have to defend him?"

"Family name. Protect David. Bad enough the lad's got to live his life as Harry Paige's son."

"Come off it, Daddy. To the rest of the world he's a hero. You're just carrying an old grudge and you know it."

Blatchford poked among the crumbs. "He lost his ship and just about everyone aboard. Oh yes. That's it! What I wanted to tell you. Among those aboard and saved was the Newell boy."

"Do we know him?"

"Are you serious, girl? That's Newell of Newell Industries and Newell Corporation, his son."

"I'm happy for him, coming out alive. Not many did."

"The point is, I wanted you to know he'll be here and you'll meet him. I've big plans for young Newell."

Lizzie arrived with a loaded tray and Blatchford fell to like a desert rat in the last stages of survival.

"Is Harry going to get the carrier he wanted so badly?"

"Yes, damn it, though I've done everything in my power to keep him from making the stupid move." He refilled his glass with ginger ale. "Battleships is where he belongs. Had him lined up for command of the *Kentucky*. Her keel's just been laid at the Norfolk yard. He could be skippering a brand new battle wagon and be close to home until she's ready. Couldn't want a better break than that, could he?"

"Thanks for trying, Daddy." She meant it.

"But no. The big shot's got to get himself mixed up with carriers. They're no damned good. Vulnerable. Planes crash and smash. And ugly? Those flattop lines are a disgrace to the Fleet. Mark my words, girl, before this war's half over, aircraft carriers will be as obsolete as Roman galleys."

He tore at a sandwich. Felicia looked the other way. "Your lovely battleships weren't much help at Pearl Harbor."

"You're a woman, Felicia, or sure as God is in heaven I'd strike you down for such a remark. Shame on you." He chewed busily. "Can't expect a woman to understand the ins and outs of strategic warfare, I suppose. But we were stabbed in the back at Pearl. Pearl Harbor was a freak, a one-in-a-million chance and the luckiest break the Japanese Navy ever got. And believe me, they'll pay for that treachery, and pay and pay as long as there's an American battleship afloat."

"Is there?"

"And where were those high and mighty carriers when those planes came in? Why weren't they around? Flattops! For flatheads! Never you mind. I'll see to it David keeps his senses about him. No flattops for him."

"Yes, Daddy."

He belched. "Be good to see the Blatchford name on a seagoing roster again."

"Blatchford?"

"David's middle name."

"David hasn't used a middle name in years."

"Why not? He was christened David Blatchford Paige. Anything to be ashamed of?"

"Ask David. He dropped it. Ask me and I'll tell you it sounds pompous. David Blatchford Paige. My heavens, Daddy!"

"Blatchford was good enough for four generations of Navy."

"Well, the fifth seems to be rebelling. Actually, I'm a bit worried. David doesn't seem to be *enjoying* it one bit."

"Have you talked to him?"

"He won't say much. He seems to take a dim view of the whole business."

"I'll have a word or two for him."

"Not until June you won't. No leave, you know, and three years for David, not four. They're rushing the poor things through."

"Biggest calamity since Pearl. And the ninety-day wonders—you've heard about them? Commissioned officers in three months. Can you imagine? *Three months!*" A fine spray of ginger ale swept the silk coverlet. "And who are they? Insurance agents, shoe salesmen, shysters, college bums, riffraff from every walk of life, in dress blues with gold on their sleeves, masquerading as officers and gentlemen. What's the civilized world coming to?"

"Relax, Daddy."

"Civilians are taking over. Giving orders. Running our great Navy. And where do they come from? Four years of loafing, boozing and, pardon the expression, fornicating on college campuses coast to coast. And a well-trained, clean-cut midshipman like our David, after learning from the bottom up, has to take orders from scum like that." He wiped his brimming eyes.

"David will be all right, Daddy. He's a fine young man."

"With Blatchford blood in his veins, why not?" He studied his elaborate wrist chronometer. "Got to shove off. Thanks for the snack."

"There's an odd letter here, Daddy, from a Lieutenant Commander Faygill."

"Public Relations. Real go-getter. Reserve, though. Why odd?"

She rummaged through the mail. "Floyd Faygill. He's inviting me to attend a bond rally when Harry's back in the States."

"What's odd about that?"

"It's in Hollywood, California." She began to laugh.

"You'll go, of course. Your duty, Felicia."

"My dear, it takes infinite strength of character for me just to get up from the bed to go to that bathroom there. Can't you just see me getting to Hollywood, California?"

Blatchford frowned. "Have you had a checkup lately?"

"You had better go, Daddy. Nobody's watching the war."

When he was gone, Felicia lay back utterly exhausted. Poor man, she thought. The whole burden of war squarely on his shoulders and no one knows it. I really should help. Do something. Nothing as ghastly as Hollywood, California, but *something*. The victory garden, perhaps. It had been a harmless lie but now that she thought about it, not a bad idea at all.

Let me see now, she thought. It could fit nicely between the tulip beds and the peonies. Lizzie's husband, Robert, was the man of all work and he certainly must know how to plant silly little vegetables like cucumbers, carrots, corn and tomatoes. Too bad tomatoes weren't comatoes. Then all of her victory garden could begin with the letter "c."

Cucumbers, carrots, corn and comatoes. The contemplation of so rich and alliterative a harvest brought to her mind the less welcome image of her father devouring every shred of it. She shuddered and tried to think of squash and beets, vegetables he did not enjoy. Summer squash would be lovely to look at, yellow in sunshine through the open doors of the dining room.

She was about to ring for Robert and remembered that Robert no longer worked for her. He had taken a job in a defense plant weeks ago, somewhere near Baltimore.

Felicia watched her good intentions fade. The cornucopia of cucumbers, carrots, corn and comatoes, followed by squash and beets, spilled past her closed eyes. Images blurred. She smiled and waved at a parade of Navy wives she knew, driving by in Navy League cars piled high with knitted woolen scarves. Later, they would be serving doughnuts and coffee at the USO and dancing tongue and groove in the arms of perspiring sailors. And even later, who knows, sleeping with them.

She reached for David's postcard that she had thought so funny and read it once more.

> It's no fable Cain killed Abel;
> Each day Cain kills him again.

Such a funny thing, an Annapolis midshipman writing pacifist poems. And when does he find the time? She slipped the card into the drawer of her night table with the others David had been sending. She would rather die than let her father see them. Or

Harry. She had wanted to destroy them but had not the heart. They are fine poems and it's my own son David who writes them and may God help him.

She felt faint. Was Daddy right? Was it time again to see the painfully polite doctors? Harry, she thought. Harry is what I need most. Can you hear me, Harry, scribbler of wild love letters—one? I need you, Harry. Hurry.

And slept.

20

Paige returned to sea alongside the skipper of *Lexington* for the refresher tour of duty and took part in the action against the Japanese bases at Lae and Salamaua. Wilson remained at Pearl, needing time to learn how to live with an artificial leg. Joe Allen and Tod Newell were directed back to the States, to report to the Commandant, 12th Naval District, for reassignment to new construction. They shipped back to San Francisco aboard a four-stack *Omaha*-class cruiser bound for a Mare Island overhaul and refitting. She was a gaunt and rakish vessel, much lighter than their old gone *Gloucester*. Her scarred weathery decks and salty crew made them feel at home. Allen did not talk much. When he did talk it was about the years spent in *Gloucester*. He did not care to think about what lay ahead.

They picked up fresh orders at Mare Island—a two-week leave and the medal ceremony at the White House. Then for Allen, temporary duty involving flying at the Naval Air Station in Jacksonville. For Newell it was a precommissioning detail at Newport, Rhode Island. Then both were to report aboard *Shiloh* in May at Newport News, Virginia.

They said goodbye in front of BOQ where they had spent the night. Newell thought it would be a good idea if Joe Allen would come East with him and spend the two weeks as a house guest at Newellton. Allen had heard enough about the Newell name to know what to expect, but for some reason he was unable to explain to himself, he turned down Newell's invitation. He had friends in Pasadena, he said, and this would be the only chance to visit them. They shook hands and promised to get together in Washington.

"We'll have us a ball," Newell promised and he meant it. He felt lost and alone when quiet Joe Allen, whom he really barely knew, headed for the ferry and the train south.

He was not alone for long. A tall gentleman in well-cut tweeds came over. Newell had noticed him a few minutes ago, chatting with the yeoman who had stamped their orders. He wondered what there was about the gentleman that seemed familiar. The man excused himself.

"I'm addressing Todhunter Newell, am I not?"

"I'm Newell. Yes, sir."

"Barton, Mr. Newell. Congratulations."

"Barton?"

"Resident director, Newell Industries West. The plane's ready any time you are." His card glistened with expensive engraving. Harvey Blenheim Barton, Junior. Tod recognized the style and quality of the business card as top-echelon Newell. A fifty-thousand-a-year executive. The old man wasn't fooling.

"What plane, Mr. Barton?"

Barton twitched his elegant shoulders and produced from his breast pocket a long envelope which he handed to Newell. A conspiratorial twinkle in Barton's eye should have warned him but Newell was reading the papers, a set of official Navy orders.

"I've already got my orders, Mr. Barton."

Barton's smile was steady and the twinkle more paternal now. It reflected the expertise of an executive who doesn't climb to fifty-thousand a year by back-stabbing alone. "These aren't just your father's orders, Mr. Newell. This is an official Navy document amending the orders issued to you. Your ultimate destination is indeed the aircraft carrier, *Shiloh*, in Newport News. But as you can see"—and he pointed to the orders—"your leave is hereby canceled. You are to report for temporary duty to Newell Industries, Newell, Connecticut by any military transportation priority available to Newell Industries. The orders are signed by the Secretary of the Navy." He folded the crisp sheets and returned them to his pocket. "Shall we go? I have a company limousine waiting." His smile was ingratiating and in spite of his impeccable attire, he seemed too servile for Newell's tastes. "Come along, now, young man." He marched off.

Newell saw the long black limousine bearing the familiar Newell Industries device in the parking area some distance away. The time for decision had come. He had weathered dive bomber attacks and machine-gun bullets, flame and oil, and the agony of maimed and dying men. He had had Hurley with him then and his gunnery crew. He had had Paige and Allen and the fighting ship of men. He was alone now. Allen was gone and Wilson and the skipper were gone and he needed their strength. He did not have it and his own was a slender thread.

He picked up his sea bag to follow Barton. He dropped it. "Mr. Barton!" he shouted. "I'm not going. Who does my old man think he is, trying to run the Navy?"

Barton, shocked, turned, and over his shoulder Newell saw his father getting out of the limousine tonneau. The storm went out of his eyes. He could not believe it. He could not accept the fact that his father had put aside the pressing problems of nation and world to fly here to greet his son returned from battle. He swung the bag to his shoulder again and with his free hand waved and his father waved back and Tod was running, grinning, still not believing and dewy-eyed, muttering, *Why, the sweet old bastard, all the way from home just to meet me!*

His father stood smiling, legs apart, the appropriate casual American look of affluence about him, about his rumpled expensive clothes and his white crewcut hair. Tod embraced him. Father pushed son to arm's length and the first thing he said, the first words after the long time of being apart were: "One lousy stripe, son? Was that the best you could do?"

They boarded the plane at Alameda, a new four-engine Skymaster, and settled down for the long flight east. Thomas A. Newell explained that the plane had been dispatched to the West Coast with a load of critically needed Newell-designed bomb-sight parts. Washington had kept him informed of Tod's movements and when he heard Tod was due to arrive at Mare Island, he grabbed the opportunity to fly along with the shipment.

He made no reference to the telephone conversation between Tod and himself during the time Tod was in the Pearl Harbor hospital. Except for the initial remark, Tod's father seemed genuinely concerned about his son's next tour of duty. He described how the activities at Newell Industries had expanded and how urgently Tod was needed in the administration of its wartime production effort. He pointed out that Tod had fulfilled his patriotic duty. He could now pursue a shore-based civilian career with dignity and honor. He was not asking Tod to make a final decision now. He would be able to give the matter full thought during the two weeks he was assigned to temporary duty at Newell Industries. It was his leave time, of course, but it would give Tod an opportunity to see how urgently he was needed at home.

Tod said he would give the matter his full consideration. In spite of his father's opening remark and the fact that the plane had been going to the coast anyway, he was still deeply affected by the surprising personal welcome. Glancing at his father, he saw the lines of fatigue and the cruel sags of flesh and the dark circles under the eyes, signs of pressure or advancing age he had not noticed before. The old man was aging, even mellowing. Perhaps they could get along this time. He would try, anyway.

They were not alone on the return trip. The passengers included six wounded Army fliers and two nurses to attend them. They had been at Corregidor when the Japanese attacked and had been among the last to escape before surrender. This was their first time out of the combat zone. Their faces were yellow from the Quinacrine they took to combat malaria. The two nurses looked as though they needed as much care as the wounded.

The plane made a refueling stop at Des Moines. The night air was cold. Tod and his father leaned against the wind, crossing the cement strip to a quonset where matronly Red Cross ladies served up coffee and fresh doughnuts. One of them had a son in the Marines. Could the young Navy officer say where he had been? Tod shook his head. Were things really going badly out there? Things were going as well as could be expected, Newell said. Had they heard the news that had just come over the radio? American planes had dropped bombs on Tokyo. Newell shook his head good-humoredly. There were all sorts of unconfirmed action reports, wild as the wind, he said. This was probably one of them. To all of this the elder Newell listened with a father's pride.

They carried back coffee and doughnuts to the wounded fliers and the nurses and chatted with them while they ate.

The flight was smoother east from Des Moines. Everyone slept except Newell. His thoughts still carried the terror of *Gloucester*'s last hours. Night fell. To Newell sleepless, the twinkling lights of inland cities were the constellations upside down. Quite proper in my topsy turvy world, he reflected. The droning motors lulled him to a welcome drowsiness.

In the main compartment one of the wounded fliers moaned. A nurse was quick to comfort him. Her voice in Newell's troubled dream was unfamiliar to him. Nameless and sweet, it filled him with longing and he wished he had a girl like that, waiting for him somewhere.

The plane put down at Newark the next morning. The nurses jumped out and kissed the runway and wept. Three Red Cross ambulances stood by and the corpsmen went in for the wounded. The wind blew cold. Tod waited until they were all out and shook the hand of each man except one who had none. The ambulances rattled off. The rain fell fine and hard, whipping his face like desert sand.

Another limousine, a duplicate of the one in California, awaited them. It whisked them to Manhattan through the Holland Tunnel and swung north up the West Side Highway and the Henry Hudson Parkway into Westchester. The lightness of traffic surprised Tod. It had been a long time since he had been here and he had forgotten about gas rationing. It felt good to see green again that belonged to solid land and was familiar to his eye. The limousine rolled north through stately Millbrook, through the bustling main street of Amenia and across the Connecticut line. Here the countryside roughened to natural fields and patches of wood. He hoped the war had not altered the scenes of his childhood. In Sharon the car followed the wide divided village green past the trim home of Admiral "Tommy" Hart, on to Lakeville past the gates of Hotchkiss School that could not hold young Newell and farther on, the neat clapboard and brick buildings of the village. Then down the Canaan road skirting the twin ponds where the untamed Irish Shanahans still held the land and there, scooping the water from a skiff's bottom, sat Tim Shanahan himself who waved. Tod leaned forward to ask the chauffeur to stop. His father's arm blocked him. "We'll have nothing to do with that drunken Irish scum."

Tod sat stricken. They were past Tim and the frayed summer cottages fringing the pond and the road turned and it was too late.

They were approaching Newell country now. His father pointed to acres of land that Tod remembered as woods and fields through which he once had rambled and daydreamed as a child. Bulldozers had leveled it all. Out of the ugly excavations rose steel skeletons of buildings in every direction he looked. Crews of workers hauled and hammered and sawed. Job bosses clambered and shouted. Lines of trucks dumped gravel and unloaded steel, concrete and lumber. Newell swept his cheviot arm in a grand sweep. "All yours, son." Dust clouds choked the air.

The gates of Newellton at last. The embraces of a tearful mother and assorted proud aunts, uncles, and cousins, alerted by the incomparably efficient Newell family network. Tod finally made it to his room and stretched out to rest before dinner.

He would tell the old man tonight how things were. It would not be easy but it must be done. Would he ever know how close he had come to winning? He had practically won until they had swung past the twin ponds and Tim Shanahan, and the old man had cursed because the land-poor Shanahans for all those years had refused to sell off a square foot. "Going to seed and rot," his father had stormed. "Two hundred acres of wasteland to pasture a few sorry horses and cows. Ten years ago I could have made those drunken micks rich enough to buy all the booze they could drink for the rest of their lazy lives, if they'd have taken my offer. Now they can rot in hell. I've bought all around 'em. Let 'em starve on their stinking land. They know my price. They'll be around on their knees begging me to buy it."

That had done it. That and a minute later seeing what could happen to the good earth in his father's hands.

He was up at dawn. He slipped two pints of Johnny Walker Black into a small bag with some fishing gear and cut across the back fields to the fence that divided Newellton from the Shanahans' land. He found Tim at the landing, grinning widely, readying the boats for the day's hire. "Knew you'd be down," Tim said. In a few minutes they were heading across the pond, Shanahan at the oars. They put over their lines trailing long beaded Davis spinners. Tod broke out a bottle and opened it and passed it to Tim who raised it and winked and drank. He wiped the mouth of the bottle and passed it to Tod who rocked it back.

Like old times, Tod thought, happy for the first time. Here was Tim, fifteen years older than he, a hard-drinking, sweet-talking lover of the land, a misfit by most men's standards, lord of two hundred acres a Shanahan had bought, borrowed, or stolen a hundred and fifty years ago. Or maybe, as he claimed, it had been granted to an Irish hero (descended from Irish kings, me lad!) twenty years after the War for Independence. A matter of records lost or obscured in the town's history. Newells were newcomers by comparison. Tod had grown up forbidden to associate with Shanahans, or any of the local children, but had managed to find opportunities to spend time around the boat landing. Tim had been a strapping youth in his teens who had quit school in disgust, who could quote Byron and Keats, and who helped his father with the rental of skiffs and motors and the sale of live bait. When the old man passed on, Tim and his sisters carried on the seasonal business. They lived in a tangle of sagging shacks surrounding the original homestead and barn in a grove of rusting farm machinery and gutted jalopies. A variety of livestock—cattle, sheep, dogs, and cats came and went. There always seemed to be a horse somewhere with a Shanahan moppet, straw-haired, barefoot, and dirty-faced, astride its broad back. It was a freckled, laughing Shanahan girl who showed Tod at sixteen what a hayloft was for.

Now home again, Tod Newell was reminded of the good times he had shared with Shanahans and the times with Tim were the best by far. Tim would go the carefree way his father had gone— with whisky and talk and an open hand with a dollar. And to preserve it from falling apart and keep it right with God, was the simple and enduring love of the land. A man the equal of Harry Paige, Tod thought, and marveled at the wild abstraction of the idea.

Tod felt the swift strike and reeled in and Tim swept the net under the shining salmon trout. They took three more before the sun was over the pines and a pint of the whisky gone. Tim took up the oars and they headed back. Over the green crest of the low hills Tod saw the gaunt steel framework of the rising factories that soon would forge the tools of war.

"Not pretty, is it, me boy?"

"No, Tim."

"You'll be master of it all, some day."

"Not me, Tim."

"You will. Just the same as you went to the war and you swore to me you hated war."

"I had to prove something."

"Only what a fool you are."

"They would have drafted me."

"I didn't go, me lad."

"That was another war. Now you're too old and too drunk."

"They came for me and I didn't go."

"It's different now. If I refused to go, they'd drag me."

"Better to be dragged to war, than go whistling 'Yankee Doodle.'"

"This is a different war."

"No war's different from any other. If all the lads said no, there'd be no war."

"There'd be no country."

"If all the lads in all the countries said no, there'd be no war."

"You're a dreamer, Tim."

"There aren't dreams enough, lad, to cure war and the world's troubles." He pointed to the rising steel framework of the munitions plants. "That's what you get instead of dreams."

"I've no answer to that, Tim."

"We hear you'll be on hand for a couple of weeks and are getting a medal from the President himself," Tim said.

"I'm leaving in the morning."

"The old man again?"

Tod nodded. "I want you to keep the trout and the other Black Label."

"You've grown into a cocky lad, haven't you?"

"Baptism by fire, Tim. And there's a price goes with the fish and drink."

"The Newell in a man will out. What's the price, Yankee?"

"Don't sell the land."

"So you've heard."

"He's the Evil One, Tim, believe me."

"He's made us a most tempting offer, Tod."

"Don't sell, Tim. I'll take care of it some day."

Tim Shanahan stuck out a big hand. "Never fear, me lad. The land's not for sale and never will be. Newells or not."

21

Joe Allen had no friends in Pasadena. The only friend in the world Joe Allen ever had lay on her scaly side in the ooze on the bottom of Bantam Bay. When Joe left Newell he went into Vallejo and took a swing down Georgia Street. It was the same drunk world of friendly B-girls and horny sailors in and out of uniform. His uniform was wrong now and he could not join them. He took a last unhappy look and caught a cab into San Francisco and boarded the train to Los Angeles. He spent most of the time watching the California landscape fly past the window. Joe Allen had been born and raised in California, part of a sprawl of migratory farm workers, but he had left it for the sea as a kid of seventeen. He had only the dimmest recollection of the animal shapes and folds of her lion-colored hills. All he remembered sharply were harsh words and hunger and the parched land and the jalopy that took them from place to place.

Life aboard *Gloucester* had been heaven. Now it was done. He did not blame Paige for what had happened. Nor did he blame Paige for what was going to happen, the business about duty involving flying. When you came right down to it Paige was only doing his duty and you cannot hate a commanding officer for doing his duty. A war was on and they had been through hell together and he was lucky to be alive and in one piece and not like poor Stick Wilson who would have to drag a piece of furniture with him the rest of his life. It was too bad things were turning out the way they were, but that was the Navy for you. He had all of those good years in *Gloucester* under his belt to think about when he would be feeling sorry for himself about that duty involving flying.

When the train got to Union Station in Los Angeles, he took a cab to Beverly Hills. He got himself a room in the Beverly Hills Hotel because he had heard and read that this was where the big movie stars could always be seen. He hoped to see one and he spent a lot of time cleaning up. He dressed carefully and went down to the bar. Everybody was having the time of his life, but none of them looked like movie stars. Nobody looked twice at Joe Allen and he left. He went out to the pool. It was full of people laughing and splashing and having the time of their lives. Nobody said hello to Joe and he didn't recognize any movie stars so he went through the gate down the side street and crossed Sunset and went into the park.

It was a small park full of nurses and kids and flowers. A huge oval bed was bright with red and yellow cannae in full bloom. The dark moist earth was freshly turned and the air smelled marvelous. It reminded Joe Allen of his first time at sea.

It was *Gloucester*'s shakedown cruise and Joe was a seaman second class and proud of her and himself and really in love with her. She anchored off one of those Caribbean islands and when Joe's section made liberty he toured the island on a rented bicycle.

He hated to leave the ship but as a kid he had never spent time in parks and he had to see what a tropical island was like. When he saw the wild and exotic plants and flowers, it gave him the funniest feeling inside. He wanted to cry. It scared the hell out of him, wanting to cry, but it was so beautiful, he could not help himself. It made Joe Allen wish he had brought someone along to hold on to, someone to share all that beauty, but there was nobody and Joe could not stand it and pedaled back to town and returned the bicycle and ran all the way back to the ship. It had really scared him. He had never cried, that he could remember. He felt safe on the ship and he never got off her again. Not until she sank in Sunda Strait.

Now he sat in this park off Sunset thinking what a shame it was there were no flowers on ships. He watched the nursemaids and the kids and a couple of coiffured poodles on leashes sniffing each other. He wondered where they walked Rin Tin Tin. He had never missed a Rin Tin Tin movie when he was a kid and could afford it.

Everybody having the time of his life, he thought. Even those poodles. Everyone's got someone except me.

After a while he left the park and walked to Wilshire. It was a long walk past the most elegant houses he'd ever seen. No two were alike, except for signs advertising them for sale. One of them looked like a Spanish castle with red tile roofs and arched doorways and its lawns cropped smooth as the green baize cloth in *Gloucester*'s wardroom. He wondered why so many houses were for sale. The war? The depression? People scared? He tried to imagine himself living in a house like a Spanish castle, with a wife in a Chinese brocade housecoat and scrubbed kids in school. Kids like that would have separate rooms, he guessed, in a house as big as that. And any number of servants. If he owned a house like that he'd never sell it. He'd live in it until he died. The way it would have been if *Gloucester* hadn't gone down.

It was dusk when he got to Wilshire. He walked along looking in shop windows at the fancy stuff for sale. He could not believe the prices on some of the things, higher than in Hong Kong. He crossed the street at Beverly Drive and walked back on Wilshire on the other side and turned right and came to Romanoff's. People were getting out of cars, laughing and joking and having the time of their lives. If any were movie stars you couldn't prove it by Joe Allen. They laughed and joked their way right into Romanoff's and without stopping to think why, Joe Allen marched right in behind them.

It was half-dark inside and smelled like the park. Joe Allen was no drinker but he ordered a manhattan. Joe Allen was no smoker but he asked for a pack of Chesterfields. As though it was something he did every day of his life.

He sipped the manhattan and smoked a Chesterfield, not inhaling. Joe tried some of the cheese spread in a silver dish and some of the pâté in another silver dish. The combination was very tasty, he thought. A duck press of chased silver rested on a table in the dining room near the iced buffet. Joe could not keep his eyes off it. He would have asked the bartender what it was but it would take another drink to give Joe the courage and he did not trust himself to take another drink. He toyed with his glass and looked thoughtfully at the duck press and watched the ladies and gentlemen at dinner. Some of the men were in uniform but Joe didn't know any of them. Everybody belongs here but me, he told himself. The only thing I ever belonged to is sixty fathoms deep.

It made him sad and he paid for his drink and the cigarettes and went out. The cigarette had left a taste in his mouth and he would have liked a glass of water. Where do you get a glass of water in Beverly Hills? he wondered. He started back to the hotel.

A woman clacked along ahead of him. She had good legs, slim and straight, and gold slippers and her blond hair glinted softly in the shop window spotlights. She moved along leisurely, studying each display and Joe followed her, a store window away. It's the old game, he thought, a little excited. She glanced back at him and smiled. Why not? Joe asked himself. Why not Joe Allen like everyone else in the world having the time of his life?

He stood next to her in front of a window displaying diamond watches and bracelets. "Funny they don't have any prices," Joe croaked, loud enough for her to hear. She smiled at Joe and said, "It's the old game," and seeing Joe's startled look, she said, "They want you to go inside."

Joe thanked her and tipped his cap and walked along with her. She didn't object. He was surprised to see how much older she looked close up. Forty, at least, he told himself, and wrinkles where the make-up caked. But she had a quick warm smile and chatted away in the friendliest fashion and it made Joe Allen feel good all over. She had a husky voice, kind of sexy, and the way her eyes darted up and down the length of Joe did strange things to him.

She invited him home for a drink and Joe said yes. They walked along a little faster, not looking in any more windows. Her fingers touched his accidentally now and then and it thrilled Joe and he walked very straight.

She lived in an apartment building full of turrets and towers, surrounding a courtyard and a pool. It was imitation French Provincial but to Joe Allen it looked like another Spanish castle. She took Joe inside and the tapestried chairs and towering brass figurines and the tasseled pink lamp shades made him dizzy. He thought of the exotic plants and flowers on that Caribbean island and he could have cried, it was all so beautiful. And right then and there he decided he wanted her, whatever the price.

She had gone directly to a cupboard that turned out to be a bar and she asked Joe what he'd like to drink. A little water, Joe said, if you don't mind, and she came right over to Joe and put her arms around him and said he was the most refreshingly wonderful thing that had come down the pike in ages. Joe said he hadn't come down the pike at all, he had walked over from the Beverly Hills Hotel, and he really meant it about the water, ma'am, he was thirsty.

She got him the water and poured herself three fingers of straight whisky and drank it and refilled her glass and rocked it back again. You can call me Clarabelle, she told him, and threw the empty glass against the artificial logs in the fireplace and sat in his lap. Joe finished the water and was no longer thirsty and turned all his attention to Clarabelle and in no time at all she was begging him to love her.

It was too sudden for slow Joe Allen. He was willing enough and lonesome as hell but it was just too fast and sudden for a slow man like Joe. He kissed her and she began to moan and writhe and push her hips against him and her hands were fondling him in ways that Joe Allen had never dreamed of. He kissed her again, getting into the spirit of it, thinking of those huge red and yellow cannae and the manhattan at Romanoff's and the handsome duck press and the cheese spread and the pâté in their silver dishes. It all had something to do with what was going on. It had been a long time since Joe had experienced such pleasure, a long and lonely time and while he was kissing her and she was pushing herself against him and moaning, he was thinking, It's about time, Joe Allen. Live a little. The old ship is dead and gone.

She was caressing the lobe of his ear with her tongue and delighting him in several ways. She leaned close and said, "Get comfy, honey." She loosened his tie and helped him out of his blue jacket. "Thank you, ma'am," Joe said. She led him to the bedroom and soul-kissed him so his knees trembled and she went into the bathroom throwing kisses with both hands and closed the door.

Joe sat on the bed and started to take off his tie. My God, he thought. Charity ass. His fingers shook so badly, he got out the cigarettes and lighted one and puffed at it. What a fancy lash-up, he told himself. He had never been in such a place in all his life. The gilded mirrors with the painted cupids alone must have cost a year's sea pay. This Clarabelle just had to be some kind of a celebrity, a movie star, Joe told himself, to keep an expensive joint like this one going. How lucky can you get, Joe Allen? Free drinks, free love, what have you got to growl about now?

She came out of the bathroom and Joe got up from the fancy bedspread to admire her. She had put on a filmy peignoir and Joe

could see right through it. He could see she didn't wear another
damned thing except a pint or two of eau de cologne.

Well, Joe thought. Well, well. She stood there brown-nippled and
fragrant, a bit shorter than when Joe had last seen her. Her head
was cocked coyly to one side and the light of a shaded bed lamp
glistened on her lipstick. Closer to fifty, Joe guessed, but what the
hell, Joe Allen, war is war. This is where the world began.

She stood at the other end of the bedroom, stretching her arms
to him. The filmy peignoir parted and Joe Allen took a loving look
as she came toward him. My God, he thought. He stepped aside
and she missed him by inches. He marched right past her out
of the bedroom, picked up his coat and cap without losing a step
and went right out the door.

He stepped along briskly. The night air refreshed him. A moist
breeze blew in from the west and Joe tasted the sea salt and liked it.
He was back at the hotel in twenty minutes. A party was breaking
up in the lobby. A good-looking girl in a low-cut gown was draped
on the arm of her 4-F escort. Everybody having a hell of a time, Joe
thought: I'm the loneliest son of a bitch in the whole world and it's
nobody's fault but my own.

He went to his room and undressed and hung away his uniform
and put shoe trees in his shoes and stuffed his socks and shirt and
skivvies into a laundry bag. He took a soapy lukewarm shower and
eased himself the schoolboy way and brushed his teeth and got into
bed. He lay there with his arms under his head, hearing the bass
beat of jazz from the ballroom, the rustle of dry leaves by his
window, the rush of hasty feet and sexy laughter outside. He wished
he were dead.

It was a dirty trick walking out like that. A cheap dirty trick. He
felt sorry for Clarabelle. She was a sport. She had offered him a
drink and the most precious gift in all the world. The least he could
have done was be decent about it and do what she wanted, make
love to her, given her back a bit of the youth she had lost and
needed now to pull her through the last few miserable years. No,
Joe Allen, it was a dirty lousy thing to do, walking out like that.

He would have stayed, he told himself, but there was no getting
away from it, it would have been rough. It would have been too
much for any man. When she had reached out her arms, the night-
gown had parted and there it was, home, sweet home, but to Joe

Allen it looked like nothing less than a torn peacoat sleeve turned inside out.

That was what had killed it for Joe Allen. It reminded him of the ship, of shipmates dead. He would have tried. He'd swear to God he would have tried, just to please the sorry old broad. But it was no good. It was useless. It was as useless as a busted broom to a drunken witch in a windstorm. Being lonely was no damn good, but it was better than a stab at a memory like that.

He closed his eyes and tried to sleep. She has the cigarettes, he thought. It's better than nothing and nothing's all Joe Allen's got. He hoped Clarabelle would understand that.

Good God, he missed the old ship.

22

Harry Paige finished his brief tour of duty in *Lexington* and was flown back to the States. It was past midnight Washington time and raining when the plane put down at Anacostia. Paige had slept little during the flight cross country, keeping awake with black coffee and whisky until it was gone. He spent much of the time writing notes for the improvement of air defense and flight operations as he had observed them aboard *Lexington*.

He climbed out of the plane and was crossing the cement runway when he heard his name blared twice from the airfield's squawk box. Under the streaky lights in the shelter of the operations building, he identified the vast authoritative bulk of his father-in-law. Good of the old boy to show, Paige thought and went to meet him. They shook hands. Rainwater ran from the gold-encrusted visors.

"Welcome aboard!" Blatchford bellowed and the bulkheads trembled as he pounded Paige's back.

"Where's Felicia?"

The commodore hustled him through the half-deserted building to a Navy station wagon. An oversized bronze star gleamed on its metal tail plate. The driver stood in the rain holding the door until they were in and he stowed Paige's gear in the back and climbed behind the wheel. Blatchford belched.

"Set your course for Georgetown, driver, and damn the torpedoes."

"Aye, sir."

The wipers whined. The white fences of stud farms flashed past in the rain, their low lines and gleaming white sides pleasing to Paige's eye. Homes, he thought. Safe and American. He thought of his childhood home not far from the Brooklyn Navy Yard. His mother had been a Democratic ward worker and assembly district committee woman and it was through her political connections that his appointment to Annapolis had come through. Harry was proud of his tough old mother and her ruthless dedication to his future but it had seemed like a hell of a price to pay, back in those days. He had not seen her in years. Now there was Felicia who was fine and the commodore who wasn't, and maybe there is always a price to pay. And where the hell *was* Felicia?

"How's she look, Rollo?"

"Hell, you know Felicia. Lovely as ever."

"I meant *Shiloh*."

He enjoyed the pain this switch gave Blatchford, the wincing visible and audible. He was aware that the commodore reserved to his Navy cronies the right to be called by his Navy nickname. Blatchford had mentioned this in the past to his son-in-law but Paige, it seemed, had a short memory. At any rate that is where Blatchford decided to leave it. He had not the courage to make an issue of it. So he sulked the rest of the way into Washington. Paige smoked and said nothing. It's his own damned fault, he reflected; after two and a half years, the least he could have done was to see that his spoiled daughter made the effort to get out of the sack she spends half her life in, to meet her homecoming hero of a husband. He was surprised when the commodore suggested a nightcap. A drink, yes, but the sight of Felicia would satisfy a more immediate need.

"We'll be home in fifteen minutes. I'll take a raincheck till then."

"I mean before we get home. There's the curfew, you know, but we could stop by my hotel. I've a bottle of bonded stuff in my quarters there." Blatchford gave instructions to the driver. "Matter of fact, you can stay the night with me, Harrison. Felicia's most likely retired by now."

"I'll handle that department, Rollo. Thanks just the same."

"Bit of Navy business, urgent, as a matter of fact; we can discuss it, and over a nightcap's the ideal way."

Paige let him have his way. The commodore led him through the confusion of the crowded lobby, maneuvering round mountains of luggage, frowning at civilians on cots and snapping orders at the desk clerks. He commandeered a bellhop to handle Paige's gear. He plowed through knots of uniformed men with the imperious authority of an admiral's barge. Had he a sabre he would have used the flat of it. When all details had been arranged to his satisfaction, they arrived in his suite. The last bellhop, untipped, had left. The commodore waved toward the bar and breathing heavily sank into a chair and watched Paige prepare the drinks.

"Careful now. You're pouring too much."

"Slack off, Rollo. At the rate you're winning friends here, this hotel'll go under any minute. So let's drink up."

"That's precious damn bourbon."

"I'll let you know after I taste it. Meanwhile, belay the commands. I'm not one of these hotel flunkies you get so much pleasure pushing around."

"I said a nightcap, not a binge. All I can have is one teeny snort per diem, doctor's orders. Anyway, this is no time to get stinking. We're due at the White House at ten hundred hours." He studied his wrist chronometer. "That's eight hours from now."

Paige handed him a tumbler of whisky and sat on the edge of the bed and sipped the whisky and it was excellent whisky and he winked at Blatchford and drank half the tumbler in two swallows.

"Damn it, Harrison, you'll get cockeyed drunk." He struggled up, alarmed.

"Drink up, Rollo."

"Ten hundred hours, East Portico of the White House, uniform of the day, dress blues, white cover—" He saw the look in Paige's eyes. "What's wrong?"

"Park your butt, Rollo."

"Now damn it, this is no time—"

"Sit down, goddam it, or I'll knock you down!"

Like a stricken balloon settling, Commodore Blatchford lowered himself into the chair. Wincing, he gingerly assisted a leg to rest on the bed. He unlaced the shoe, the effort purpling his jowls. "Might show a full commodore a bit of respect, you know."

"Respect for what? You eat and drink like a pig." Paige sipped at the rest of his whisky. "Look at you."

"Gout," the commodore wheezed, "has nothing to do with diet. Medically proven. Hereditary. My curse is overdeveloped taste buds." He held the whisky to the light. "So I walk a gangplank between diarrhea and colchicine." He unbuttoned his jacket and loosened his belt and his vast belly spilled over. "All right, then." He sipped greedily and settled back with a sigh. "Now you relax, Harrison. Got to be fresh for the morning. I have the gate passes, copies of your orders and the plan of awards. President, Secretary of the Navy, and COMINCH himself'll be on hand. Press corps, some family and assorted dignitaries."

"Felicia?"

"Kind of early in the morning for the girl, don't you think?"

"Why the hell wasn't she at the airport?" The truth struck him suddenly. "Did you let her know I was flying in?"

"Of course I let her know."

"You're lying, Rollo. I know when you lie. Your lips pucker. You never told her a word."

"It's the whisky makes my lips pucker."

"Moose shit. I'll call right now and prove it. You want me to call Felicia now and ask her?"

"It's too late. That was the only reason. Hell, Harrison, the morning's time enough."

Paige set his glass down so hard it chipped. "It's been so long, you've already forgotten what it's like. I've been away, old man, and I want to go home to my wife."

"Relax, m'boy. Your nerves are in rotten shape. Rest and recreation's the order of the day for you. It's my fault. Don't blame Felicia. She's a fragile little thing, Harrison. Best of health, of course, a true Blatchford there, but needs her rest, plenty of sleep, you know. As for standing in the drafty airport waiting for a plane that could've been hours delayed, she's just a bit too delicate for it."

"Delicate my ass. That woman's strong as an ox and tough as nails. Lash her to the deck and cut her in a thousand little pieces and any one of 'em could rise up and destroy you and me both. Trouble is, she's spoiled rotten. By you and that nigger maid Lizzie waiting hand and foot on her day and night."

"Now take it easy, Harrison."

"Easy my ass. She should have met me." He squinted at the bottle, reached for it. "So I'm having one more snort and I'm heading home to my ever-loving wife." He bowed to Blatchford. "Your spoiled but charming daughter."

"She'll be sound asleep, Harry."

"She's not so damned delicate she can't be awakened. And

I know just how. Any other dame'd be sitting around all night for a husband she hasn't seen in two and a half years."

"She's *been* sitting around for two and a half years. That's a long time for a girl to sit."

"She damned well could have come out to Manila when I asked her in '39."

"And leave the house and those precious heirlooms?"

"Precious heirlooms, my ass. A load of junk."

"Five generations of family antiques."

"Is Felicia married to me or those cruddy antiques of yours? Christ! I've been carrying the load for that houseful of junk long enough. Don't look so shocked. You know damned well that's where my allotment goes. Sea pay and combat pay and flight pay and every goddam cent I can lay my hands on, to keep that Blatchford private Smithsonian intact. Between the termites and three mortgages, I'm surprised she hasn't sunk." He splashed whisky in the glass and threw it back and wiped his mouth. "You're thinking why the hell didn't I make it back on leave all that time, aren't you? Try it on a ten-day pass and lousy transportation and no priority because there's no war."

"You had thirty days before taking over command of *Gloucester*. That I know because I arranged it myself with BuPers."

"Thanks for nothing. I wanted a carrier and you damned well knew it. And what leave there was, I spent in flying time so I'd be qualified for carrier duty. And every other damned minute was spent on board while she went through a major overhaul at Cavite."

"They could've spared you for a couple of weeks."

"And leave my ship in the hands of those drydock morons, half of 'em Jap spies, to foul her up from stem to stern? Like hell! I watched every rivet and bolt and cable that went into her."

"Ain't the way I heard it, McGee."

"Meaning what?"

"That Filipino sugar heiress."

"What the hell you talking about?"

"You brought the subject up, not me. Felicia's my daughter, after all."

"She's married to me, Rollo. You're off the hook and I'm paying the freight."

"Some marriage, thousands of miles apart and you carrying on like a stud bull!"

"That's a nasty old man talking."

"It's the gospel truth, isn't it? I've been getting the hot dope on you daily with the guard mail from Manila. Round by round, almost. What's it like with a countess, Hardtack? Tell an old man. Is it true what they say about those South Sea women?"

"Your geography's as screwed up as you are." Paige stood and brushed off his jacket and scowled at himself in the mirror. "Who the hell's been feeding you these lies? Sure, she's a countess, all right. And her name's Ynez. Ynez de Padheco de Novato Bolinas and they used to own half of Marin County, California, and we had a few harmless drinks in the Manila Club. And always with her father. A *real* gentleman, Rollo. A quality you wouldn't recognize."

"Those half-breeds are all alike."

"Spanish aristocracy with ancestors that make your lousy five generations look sick. And your antiques. And right now they're in Nip prison camps because you lard-assed shore-based bureaucrats were too late with too little."

"You still could've made it home to Felicia had you wanted to."

"Okay, Rollo. You win. I tried and didn't make it."

"Amos Flint made it."

"So it was Flint."

"Everybody told us."

"That mealy-mouthed bastard. Okay, Rollo, your point. Now it's off your chest and the cat's out of the bag and you've had your little triumph and your nightcap as well, so I'm bidding you and your gout good night."

"And if I order you to stay?"

"Don't."

Blatchford was silent for a while. "Your funeral. Just be here at 0930, Captain."

"Very well, Commodore. You mentioned another matter. Urgent Navy business."

"Ah yes. That young Newell. One of your junior officers."

"What about him?"

"How did he do?"

"For a tennis bum he did okay. Did fine. Good man."

"You know who he is, of course?"

"You mean do I know who his old man is. I do."

Blatchford's eyes gleamed. "Thomas A. Newell is flying in for the medal ceremony. Said not to tell the boy."

"Did you?"

"Me go against the direct orders of Thomas A. Newell?"

"You outrank him, Rollo."

"Not in do-re-mi. This is the beginning of a beautiful friendship." He winked at Paige. "No accident his boy drew orders to your ship, you know."

"I didn't know and I don't like it."

"Know what the boy's worth, Harrison?"

"I know he came through in the pinch. That should be worth something to the Navy."

"I mean in dollars."

"I don't really care."

"Take a guess."

"Go to hell."

"I'll tell you what his old man, Thomas A. Newell, is worth, net. Five hundred and sixty million. Over half a billion. That's dollars, son. Not marks or rubles or yen. Good old American dollars. Know what it means to you and me that his kid was aboard your ship and you got him off with a whole skin? And a medal to boot? Just in the old man's gratitude alone, know what the market value could be?"

"You're beginning to fascinate me, Rollo."

"Go on. Take a guess."

"You tell me. You seem to enjoy it so much."

"Market value—anything you want. Sky's the limit. You can name it and Thomas A. Newell will cheerfully deliver it."

"Dirty pool, Rollo."

"I don't think so. His only son and heir? It's a fair deal."

"And suppose the boy hates his old man's guts?"

"Why should he? Anyway, no concern of ours. Thomas A. Newell owes us one hell of a big favor and I intend to ask for it when the time comes."

"You're a real sport, Rollo."

"You never knew what it was like after the last war, did you? You were a kid and everything looked rosy, eh? Maybe you don't remember how a uniform was laughed at. What a slob the man was who wore it. I'm not forgetting it. And this war won't go on forever and when it's over, things aren't going to be any different than they were twenty years ago. I'm looking out for me and mine and whether I like it or not, that includes you, Harrison. We're into Mr. Newell for something big and I don't intend to let him forget it. So tomorrow morning when we meet Thomas A. Newell, you just be real sweet to him."

"Yes siree."

"I mean every word, Harrison. Get smart."

"A bath would be nice," Paige said, "but it's late. I'm going home."

Blatchford grabbed his arm. "You on the wrong wave length? Don't you receive me? That's Thomas A. Newell I speak of. *The* Thomas A. Newell. And I'm trying to get it through your thick, punch-drunk skull what it can mean to all of us. You want to be a second-rate slob when this war's over or do you want to sit behind a mahogany desk as big as the battleship *Texas* and advise Thomas A. Newell on military contracts? You so dumb, Harrison, you can't see I put that boy on board your ship to give you the biggest break you ever got in all your born days? What good has that two-bit Olympic boxing crown ever done for you except to twist my poor Felicia's head so she turned to jelly and married you? Best break you ever got till now was marrying a Blatchford and you damned well know it."

"Best break I ever got is *Shiloh*, and no thanks to you, Fatso. I risked my life to get her and damn near my Navy career. You think for a moment it was your lousy name or Newell's money that sent me into Sunda Strait? Like hell it was. So get your fat filthy scheming fingers off my sleeve. I'm going home to screw your daughter."

Blatchford staggered up, a swollen tent of dark flesh, blue serge and pain. "You ungrateful son of a bitch, to say a thing like that to a Navy officer and a gentleman. After all I've done for you, a nobody, a nothing, a bastard son of a cheap two-bit ward-heeling bitch in a Brooklyn slum, to marry *my* daughter! The shame. My God!" He threw the empty glass at Paige's head, a wide miss that fell unbroken, almost gently, on the pillow. The lack of a satisfying crash enraged him further. "Whoremaster!" he shouted. "You disgrace the uniform you wear!"

Paige retrieved the tumbler and placed it on the bedside table. "Rollo, you stink. Your aim stinks. Everything about you is dry rot and decay and if I stepped on you something sticky and yellow would run. The only reason I don't step on you is your daughter whom I happen to love and I am going home to her and I am going to love her hard and good, not only because it's my rightful duty and not only because it is a deep pleasure to me and to her, but because it obviously gives you great torment and pain and this I enjoy."

He moved close to Blatchford who sagged in the chair. "If anyone's a disgrace to his uniform, it's you. You never earned it. You wear it because your old man wore it and his old man before him. You use it for greed, for your own cheap schemes and that's the sad simple difference between us. Sure I'm a bastard but I'm a born bastard, not your kind—self-made. And sure my mother peddled political favors for a living, but it got me where I am and thank God I'm earning my keep and a bit to spare. I sweat blood and bullets for it and maybe I'll die for it. But with honor, Rollo, not like you, a scheming dirty old man."

He capped the bottle and stuffed it into his barracks bag.

"That's my whisky," Blatchford whined.

"It's a risk I'll run."

Blatchford nursed his foot, breathing coarsely. "The driver's dismissed. You can't get home."

"I'll find a taxi."

"You've been damned insulting, Harrison, and I demand an apology."

Paige adjusted his cap and zipped the barracks bag and went to the door.

"You hear me?" Blatchford cried. "An apology!"

"How about a duel, you silly old fahrt?"

"Stand fast! That's an order, Captain! A command! Avast there! You're under hack. I'm you're superior, damn you, and I command you to stand at attention. You hear me? Attention!"

"Drop dead," Paige said.

23

~~~~~~

The way it had always been. A pure sweet joy, he thought, naked and resting. As though he had never gone away. The wonder of it. A cigarette in his fingers glowed in the darkened bedroom. He reached for the Revere porringer on the night table and centered it on his navel and tapped ashes into it. The wonder of love, a simple service bringing such sweet reward.

Smooth Felicia sleeping, a calm to envy, no whimper, no murmur or outcry when he opened the door. Moonlight across the coverlet revealing all he had come for, the outline of her body molded to the sheet, her face in moonlight not beautiful but serene in the fashion that had first captured him. Offbeat loveliness that could melt the marrow of his bones, still there, enhanced by the absent years and him an unexpected voyager in her bedroom at night. She had stretched her slender arms and whispered *My darling Harry, welcome home.* And welcomed him.

It made him want to shout his joy, their love-making effortless and deeply satisfying long after the moment had passed.

The room smelled of fresh violets, the damp bunches he had bought not an hour ago from a ginny Negro who had chanced past driving a rickety pickup in from the Maryland countryside to the market in the square. Paige had badgered the befuddled old man into selling all he would part with while the taxi driver grumbled about his gas running low and no ration coupons and he, Abe

Steinberg, was taking no more guff from no Navy officer so *shikker* he could hardly stand on two legs.

Paige's ID card aided and abetted by a slug of the commodore's bourbon not only mollified Steinberg but changed him from a carping hack-driving Bolshevik to a dedicated hero-worshiper. At the doorstep he refused payment and embraced Paige and blessed him and his children and his children's children and kissed him on both cheeks and drove off honking.

So Felicia had wakened to violets and reached her arms and the violets crushed fell round and on and between and under them and it could have been a wedding night, the woods smell of violets everywhere. Now she slept and in drowsy content he wondered about the others who might have come here between this time and the last. A sour taste of whisky filled his throat and he crushed the cigarette and got out of bed and in the bathroom examined himself in a full-length mirror for the first time in years.

He was wide awake now. He hunted for a razor, opening drawers and cubbyholes and the medicine chest. Whose razor am I really looking for? he wondered. Felicia shaves her legs but in all the years of being married to her I don't recall seeing her razor. Unguents, perfumes, cold creams, bath salts, colognes, deodorants. No razor. Ah yes. One, a Durham Duplex, well hidden in a drawer. The hell with it, he thought, how many men had come here, lain with Felicia, knew me, spoke of me, laughed and shaved. Or had she the decency (or shame?) enough to go elsewhere with them, Rehoboth or Virginia Beach, New York, Palm Beach, Bar Harbor, or a shady hotel for a matinee? My friends are legion, he thought. American Legion. What the unmarried sailors said: Why buy a cow when milk's so cheap? Why the hell would she hide a razor? The shave was impossible.

He showered instead and rubbed dry and found her talcum and patted himself white. He opened a package containing a sterilized toothbrush and squeezed a fat coral worm of paste the length of its bristles and he gargled. I'm Caruso, he gargled, and refreshed went back to her bed.

"Darling Harry."

"Didn't mean to wake you."

"Where were you?"

"Toothbrushing."

"Bless you. You reeked of booze. Now it's Elizabeth Arden."

She turned on her side to face him. Her fingers touched his scars. "You've had a bad time, Harry."

"Scratches."

Their fingers entwined, bodies touching, cool now. "Wild dreams. Straight Freud. Those big waves at Virginia Beach. The roller coaster at Funland. Tunnel of Love. Every symbol of erotic something."

"How about the Washington Monument?"

"Don't brag."

"I don't dig that Freudian crap anyway."

"You're the hundred percent American man and you believe in the American Dream."

"Is that so bad?"

"It's wonderful. I believe in fairy tales, too. I'm a princess. This princess, see, who can't sleep on a hundred mattresses because there's a tiny pea under the bottom one. I'm also Sleeping Beauty."

"Would Sleeping Beauty like a shot of the commodore's bourbon?"

"She'd lap it up."

He poured whisky in two glasses. He lighted two cigarettes and they sat propped against the pillows and sipped the whisky and smoked a cigarette. "Hans Christian Andersen would turn over in his grave if he knew his Sleeping Beauty was drinking and smoking."

"He'd forgive me if he knew I've been sleeping alone for two and a half years." Her lips brushed his. "Did Daddy meet your plane?"

"He did and we may not be speaking for a while."

"Already? You just got back."

"We had words. He forgot to tell you I was coming home."

"Why does he do those things, Harry?"

"He's your father and he's protecting you from evil."

"Nice evil."

"He tells me you are delicate and fragile and must be handled with kid gloves."

"Poor Daddy."

"Poor, my ass. We're the poor ones, trying to keep this white elephant of a house on a captain's pay, just to store his sentimental attachments."

"They're really priceless antiques."

"Then let's unload 'em and pay off some of those priceless mortgages."

"Daddy would die first."

"Don't tempt me."

"Let's not quarrel. Not now."

"As soon as I'm back for good, we're unloading this dump. David'll be gone and we can sell the junk and clear out."

"He won't give up a teaspoon of it while he's alive. You know that."

"I've taken steps."

"What do you mean?"

"I told him to drop dead."

"He would if he saw what you're doing with his Revere porringer." She handed him her glass and he set it on the night table. "I do wonder about him, darling. He so enjoys hating you. And the wild stories! He should have sense enough to know he's hurting himself as well as you."

"Most of them are probably true."

"Don't I know it? And know you, my love? The image of you staying aboard ship reading your Bible and sipping ginger beer doesn't quite come off. But that doesn't excuse Daddy for being, shall we say, an unspeakable cad about it."

"You should have come to Manila."

"I much preferred staying here and risking your infidelities there. Manila, darling. After all."

"He chewed me out for it."

"A contessa, he told me. I'm rather proud of you."

"I'm beginning to see signs of your father in you."

"He wouldn't dare."

"What do you mean?"

"Never mind. Do you know, I'm beginning to feel that little drink?"

"Little, hell. It was a man-sized slug. Want another?"

"Tell me about the contessa."

He poured himself more whisky. "Funny thing, there's nothing to tell, really, except that she was small and lovely and shy and her old man was always with us. They're in San Tomás prison, now. Dead probably."

"What about the others?"

"What others?"

"Women others."

"The Blatchford curiosity verges on the indecent."

"I've a right to know what you were doing while you were away."

"Read the papers."

"A girl likes to know what the competition's like." She took his glass and drained his whisky. Some of it dribbled down her chin. He put the glass aside and wiped her chin and kissed her. "There's never been any competition."

"Just substitutions." She pulled away and sat up. He could see the start of tears. Rotten luck, he thought. "Ah, Harry," she whimpered.

"And you?" he said harshly.

"Not me, Harry."

"You spoke of Virginia Beach a minute ago."

"Twenty years ago! Harry! A dream!"

"I'm not lying about my life, Felicia."

"Harry, darling. Put aside your muscles for a moment. Please? Your war and the blood and guts, for a moment? Just you and me and will you skip the look of Jesus on the cross or I'll get up and out of here so fast—can't you guess what it was like without you? What I went through? Night after night without you? I'd read until I couldn't see the words. I would lie here and listen and there would go Lizzie downstairs grumbling and creaking off to bed and then the house would be quiet. Then the refrigerator would hum and I would lie here and make it into the tunes we used to love, the Gershwin, remember, from *Lady Be Good?* I would think of you, Harry, in all the ways a woman thinks of the man she loves. Until the pain was too much and I had to get up and go into the shower and force myself to stand there until I was so cold and weak I could barely dry myself and crawl shivering back to bed and I would begin praying for something to save me, to do something to keep me from letting go like all the others were letting go. It would get light outside and I would hear the milkman clinking and I still had not slept and I would lie there drained just from thinking and I would thank God for—oh yes, and Neptune and Davy Jones and Ernie King—for pulling me through the night and not succumbing to temptations such as phoning the officers' club, any officers' club, or going out on the town with the other lonely Navy wives or simply asking the butcher pretty please to make his deliveries upstairs. And I would swear I'd kiss the Blatch-ford heirlooms goodbye and get on the first plane or train to join you in Manila. Then Lizzie would bring the mail and breakfast and I would finally sweetly delightfully fall asleep unless Daddy chose the morning to come barging in, his chest covered with more ribbons than a circus tent, puffing and steaming up the stairs, his mouth dripping eggs and snippets of gossip, all the disgusting and nauseating scuttlebutt about cheating wives and switching cou-ples, the terribly private and obscene and dirty little stories he hears, and always in that righteous, fire-and-brimstone style of his, the pious fraud, until I wanted to bury my head under the covers or pour hot wax in my ears to shut out the booming filth he so delights in telling. Yet there was something good about it, something now that I'm telling you about it makes me want to laugh until I cry and it is this, that having Daddy coming here to tell me things so scared and disgusted me, that any urge to dress and go out on the town was squelched. I was safe and protected here and there was no reason to leave and so I never did. And nobody came here, Harry. I would have died first. In all that time, my love, this bed of ours has been a sacred place.

"And people talked and Daddy listened and he would come each day to tell his filthy tales and guzzle your booze like soda water and stuff down Lizzie's chicken pies and popovers like they were peanuts really, to listen to his awful stories and have him bully me about for not getting up and out and socializing now that the Navy was having its day and was on its way and sailing down the field with anchors aweigh. 'You're a Blatchford my child and there's a war on,' he'd say, 'and I've half a mind to fetch you some company, gentle-born and trustworthy, high-ranking flag officers, well placed, of course, and fun-loving lads, every last one of them.' Pimp-ing, darling, I swear to you, my own father pimping for his only child. Soon as he'd go I'd want to leap from the bed into some clothes and get as far away from him as I could, but how and where and with what? It was too much, too much, darling. Even the victory garden I never planted, too much. But here in this sacred place I was safe, where you left me, where I've waited, until I thought I'd die without you. And I would have, I suppose, if you hadn't just come along. I'm no damned good without you, Harry, you see that, don't you? No damned good is how a Navy wife's supposed to be, isn't it?"

Her shaking body rested against his and he comforted her until she calmed down. They lay close together in love in the invisible sea of violets.

Later she said, "He wrote once that God was the father image and the Virgin Mary the mother image—virgin because no man will tolerate the idea of his mother or daughter making love, sexual love, I mean. And it sort of helps explain Daddy, doesn't it? Claiming to do things that help you but which really don't help you, because he hates you for sleeping with me?"

"Who wrote?"

"Freud."

"Nuts. They tried to hand me that line on the ship. My exec cracked up and turned yellow. The ship's surgeon, a hell of a good man, Lefferts, tried to hand me the Freudian routine. Oley needed a psychoanalyst, he said. Just out of respect for Lefferts, I read up on this guy Freud. Junk. Nothing to do with Oley turning yellow and I said so. I didn't buy it then and I don't buy it now."

"It's nothing to get so upset about."

"Then don't hand me this mother image crap. I know your old man like the palm of my hand. Fat, greedy, and selfish, sure, but he's got a hard head and he'd be the first one to agree that Freud's for the birds. That crap I read about mother image and father image and death wish and penis envy—my God, it got so disgusting I heaved the goddam book over the side. You got any of it here, I'll flush it down the drain. And anybody peddling that filth should have his mouth washed out with soap and water."

"People's minds, Harry. You have to understand—"

"I understand what I'm trained to understand. War, ships, sailors, the sea. Anything else gets in my way. I got a job to do and I got to do it better than the next fellow or somebody gets hurt."

"Yes, Harry."

"War is all I need to know. I need to know it better than anybody else in the business. In a couple of hours, the President of the United States is pinning a medal on me. Why? Because I'm neurotic? Because I have a suppressed desire to screw my mother? A hell of a lot of good it would have done me that night in Sunda Strait. Penis envy, sure—if the guy in the next bunk has a bigger one than me."

She reached for the night light and switched it on. "You had better get some sleep. It's almost four o'clock."

"Sleep isn't what I need. Turn the light out."

"Promise you'll try to sleep."

"Will you stand with me when I get that medal?"

"If that's what you want, Harry."

"I'll try to sleep." He settled back. "Rollo said Newell's flying in. Thomas A. Newell himself. Big man. What are you laughing at?"

"I love you. You're a big man and I'm in love with you and we're together and that's why I'm laughing."

She reached for the light and against its mauve rose glow he admired the mound of her breast in splendid isolation. *With hogans like that,* he thought, *who needs the Taj Mahal?* And his rough hand captured it.

Felicia, he thought, proud. Sleep came like a clout in the head as he lay there drained. And he wakened later to milkman sounds, the clinking of bottles strange to his dream of the sea. He shaved with the Durham Duplex and dressed and scribbled a note for Felicia to meet him at the hotel and he set the alarm to allow her enough time to make it. Down the paneled hall of colonial trappings he went and tiptoed down to Lizzie in the kitchen at this ungodly hour in slippers and an ancient housecoat. She stood yawning over the chipped enameled pot she brewed her chicory coffee in, her back to him and not aware of him until he raised her aloft where she squealed in terror until she saw his face and switched to bubbling almost hysterical laughter and prayers of thanks. He drank two cups of Lizzie's formidable coffee, praising her beauty with extravagant lies and commending for loyalty and bravery all the stewards mates and Negro mess attendants whose names he could recall or invent, who had served and died for Paige, God, and country. He solemnly reassured Lizzie they had not died in vain. The doorbell sounded Taps and there was Riley with the station wagon, orders of the commodore. It was time to meet the President.

24

The East Portico. Harrison Paige with the Purple Heart and the Navy Cross on his chest and sweet Felicia on his arm. A clutch of uniforms surrounded by a pride of VIPS. Blatchford resplendent in the May sun in full possession of Thomas A. Newell's hairless pink ear. David in from Annapolis for the big day, young and grave among the seasoned warriors and the bereaved.

A splendid day for heroes, the President said, and for our troubled nation. And grinning shook heroes' hands and waved and was wheeled back to war. Shutters clicked. A Navy quintet in brass thumped a military air. At the near gate a lean picket bore a battered sign demanding an end to imperialism and our boys home by Christmas.

Stick Wilson by a miracle of Navy legerdemain was on hand for the ceremony. He had been flown from Pearl and had arrived in Washington the night before, decked out in dress blues and sporting a crutch to help him about. His clean-shaven face was thinner than his shipmates remembered and his eyes, bloodshot from five thousand miles of airborne drinking, murky with brooding. Paige thought he looked terrible and said so.

"Try sleeping in Union Station with an aluminum gizmo for a leg," Stick muttered, "and see how *you* look in the morning."

Even one-legged and hung over, he had not lost his old steam. He had to know who all the crudlovers were, the brown-nose goldbraid dripping scrambled eggs and chicken guts, the hooligans in gloomy business suits like crows among peacocks, the squaws in churchmouse threads over crooked hems, their gams like slats. He demanded to know and Newell full of sadness told him. Next of kin.

"Who needs them?" Wilson grumbled.

One younger, slim and straight, not red-eyed like the others, circled the admiring throng to Paige. "I'm Mary Olsen, Captain."

"Oley's—wife?" The widow word big in his throat.

"His sister."

"Sorry about Oley." The same eyes, he thought, Norse blue and steady and a bit mad. "Is Mrs. Olsen here?"

"No."

"Too bad."

"Not at all. She left him six months ago. Ran off with an Army colonel."

"Sorry," Paige mumbled.

"I had to come. I'd heard so much about you."

"That's very kind of you, Mary Olsen."

"I had to see what you were really like." Her smile a sword. "The man who crucified my brother."

And slim and straight gone. The sun dazzled his eyes. The Capitol lawn as green as fresh paint and overhead a dome of gold. It was Blatchford to the rescue, the ear of empire filled to overflowing. "We brunch with Tom Newell." Trumpeting loudly enough, Paige thought, to raise brooding Abe Lincoln clean out of his marble chair. "Private party," Blatchford gloated. "His penthouse suite in half an hour. I'm going ahead with my man from Public Relations. You and the others follow his limousine." And sensing Paige's reluctance, muttered, "Now don't muff this one, Harry, for God's sake."

Felicia weeping down the walk to the gate, David holding her arm, tall in his midshipman uniform. What the hell is brunch? Paige wondered. Do you eat it or drink it? A gathering of the curious hemmed the official cars. "Quit bawling and pull yourself together, Felicia," he said, grinning for the crowd, "you're a bloody Blatchford, remember?"

A dumpy, perspiring woman of fifty detached herself from the others and blocked his way. Her ice cream pink suit and picture hat were dyed to mismatch her handbag and pumps. The entire ensemble had the musty air of resurrection from last year's Easter

Sunday. She clutched Paige's hand and raised it to her lips. "I feel as though I've kissed the hand of God," she breathed.

Paige pulled free not gently. Through the crowd he caught a glimpse of Mary Olsen's straight back as she walked to the bus stop. He rubbed the lipstick from the back of his scarred hand and muttered to no one, "I wish to hell they'd make up their goddam minds."

In spite of wartime restrictions, a lavish buffet had been prepared in Thomas A. Newell's hotel penthouse and hard liquor, presumably rationed, flowed freely. Tod Newell observed that this private party, like previous ones he had attended, ran true to form. It offered pleasure for business reasons. He had understood that the reception was to honor the four *Gloucester* survivors, but he and the others were soon swallowed up and forgotten in a noisy sea of trade talk between top-echelon politicians and military brass who had come to pay homage to his powerful father and his black market booze.

Although no one had asked him, Commodore Blatchford assumed the duties of social and military liaison. Assisted by the eager-looking lieutenant from Navy's Office of Public Relations, he directed the flow of traffic to and from the presence of the big man.

When the Paiges arrived, Faygill, the brisk public relations officer, immediately took Paige aside. A Navy photographer hovered in the background, "First, Captain, we want to get some publicity shots of you with the commodore and old man Newell."

"Forget it," Paige said amiably.

"It's the commodore's orders," Faygill said. "Now let's go."

"Take the commodore's picture. He loves that." Paige started to rejoin Felicia and David but Faygill grabbed his arm.

"You don't understand, Captain. I'm Floyd Faygill, Hollywood. I've been assigned to you. The public image, you know? We've got a whopper of a program laid out for you—at home, aboard your new boat, bond rallies, official functions, balls—"

"That's it right there."

"You mean you'll cooperate?"

"I mean balls." He removed Faygill's fingers from his sleeve. "You never lay a hand on a superior officer, Lieutenant Faygill. It's considered bad form. And it's a ship, not a boat."

"I've been officially assigned, I tell you."

"Then carry out your official orders in the prescribed manner and through proper channels. Also, your shoulder boards are on backwards. I'm off duty now and you're standing between me and a much-needed drink. Now shove off."

Commodore Blatchford was preening himself for the interview he had arranged and had missed the exchange. He seated himself in one of the more ample armchairs and was testing the microphone by hissing at it. It hissed back, startling him. He nodded to Faygill's radio engineers that he was ready.

Paige picked up a drink and drained the glass and with another in his hand joined the circle of guests surrounding the commodore and Thomas A. Newell. He stood alongside a small man in an immaculate black suit, a man with the tight unsmiling face and hard eyes of a faro dealer. He half-supported his bleached blonde and bosomy wife who had already had a few too many.

". . . warriors and guns and the gold to fight with," the commodore was saying through a fine film of brandy. "That's war and war is life and we are the chosen few."

"I thought we were the chosen," murmured the bosomy wife and leaned one against Paige and winked. Her husband shrugged and edged closer to the commodore and her free arm engaged Paige's. "I love uniforms but I hate war," she confided.

"Warriors, guns, and gold." Blatchford repeated the words, mouthing them lovingly with the cognac. "'Twas ever thus and always will be. Right, Tom?" And Newell taken by surprise nodded and the commodore dipped the end of a fat green cigar into the crystal inhaler he held. Flash bulbs popped and the commodore lit up like a cheaply gilded Buddha.

"What's he saying," Paige whispered to the bosomy one.

"You better ask Milton my husband. He's the brain. He's in woollens and he knows everything."

"Thank God you're not in woollens," Paige said.

"Me? I'm in nothing. I go along for the ride. I'm just fascinated, you know? Just watching that fat general the way he keeps on dipping that big cigar of his into that glass of whisky and then sticking it into his mouth." She looked up at Paige and recognized him. "My God—you're him. The Navy hero with your picture in the morning paper."

"And you're from New York."

"You mean you can tell?" She seemed pleased. "How?"

"I used to live in Brooklyn once myself."

"Wait, I want Milton should meet you. What was the name again?"

"Dewey. Admiral Dewey. You can call me George."

"You kidding me? Dewey's in New York running for governor."

"Ssh. Your general's making a statement for his vast radio audience."

". . . the happy warrior," Blatchford boomed. "If I may quote the immortal words of another great American, William Wordsworth:

> 'Who, doomed to go in company with Pain,
> And Fear, and Bloodshed, miserable train,
> Turns his necessity to glorious gain.'"

"Hear, hear," cried Thomas A. Newell applauding heartily.

"My sentiments exactly," said Milton in woollens.

David Paige in the circle spoke out in a clear voice. "Soon there won't be warriors, Commodore. Only victims."

The commodore pushed aside the microphone and struggled to rise like a tangled balloon. "Who said that?"

"Man's about to outsmart himself," David continued, "and his old slave Science will soon be his master."

"Please, David," Felicia said.

"Anyway, Wordsworth was British," David said.

"I'm shocked," Blatchford said, "to hear a United States Navy midshipman speak like that. Suppose you just hold your tongue and listen, young man."

"Baloney," David's father said. "He's got as much right as anyone to speak his mind."

"Just what the hell's going on here?" Newell demanded.

"A friendly little family discussion, Tom." And turning to Faygill, Blatchford muttered, "Not a word of this gets out, understand?"

The crowd thinned to fifty in the late afternoon. Exactly at five, Thomas A. Newell excused himself from a circle of goldbraid and fawning sub-contractors and with Blatchford at his heels took Captain Paige aside. "I've run into a small problem, Captain, and Commodore Blatchford here came up with a really brilliant suggestion. Now I'm not one to beat around the bush. It concerns my son over there, with whom you're well acquainted by now. In spite of my busy life with commitments everywhere and a split-second schedule, I took the time out last night and half this morning in an effort to reason with him, to get it through his skull that he's done his bit now for God and country and it's time he served where he's best needed, where he can do the most good, and that of course is right at home with Newell Industries."

"Didn't know you had a tennis team, Mr. Newell."

"Ha, ha. Very good. Now you know, Captain, I'm as patriotic as the next fellow. My contribution to the war effort is a well-established fact. There is no need to reassure you that my wishes in this particular matter are not in any way to be regarded as nepotism since no one knows as much as I do about the needs of our defense plants and the qualifications essential to the key jobs. Naturally, Tod's combat record overseas and his previous business background suit him ideally for the job I have in mind for him in management and liaison. Matter of fact, all it takes is a phone call from me and Tod'd have a set of orders cut and delivered by noon tomorrow."

"You're a real patriot, Mr. Newell."

"We all do our share, don't we? You see, by combining Tod's most useful qualities, we're augmenting the war effort to the nth degree. He's already put in three years with the company in a variety of executive training capacities grooming him for my job some day. It cost me a small fortune to get him a diploma after he bust out of Hotchkiss. I had him all set for Harvard and eventually the Business School. He lasted two weeks at Cambridge and took off on some cockeyed South American tennis tour. He's been chasing rainbows ever since. The boy's got a fine head on his shoulders and if he'd only listen to me, he could make a success out of his life. He'd be a Newell vice-president and director this very minute if he paid some attention to what I tell him. Well, no fair airing the family wash at a time like this. My private plane's waiting for me right now out at the airport and I have got to get back to Connecticut tonight. Tod and I thrashed this out last night. He's still set on this new carrier of yours and damned if I can get him to change his mind."

"Why don't you just pick up the phone like you said and have his orders cut the way you want them?"

"I would, damn it, but he'd sure as hell know and I'd have him back in Newell Industries against his will and bitter and sullen and knowing him—well, Captain, he'd be as uncooperative as hell and nothing but a detriment to the war effort. Now that's where you come in. He's already told me that meeting and serving with you has been the most rewarding event in his life. His very words. That boy worships the ground you walk on, Captain, and I'm frank to say I envy you because it's a hell of a lot more than he would do for me. Now all it takes is a word from you to straighten out his thinking."

"From me?"

"I want that boy back where he belongs, Captain Paige, where he can do the most good for the war effort and for all concerned. Both the commodore and I feel you're the man who can swing it and believe me, Captain Paige, it will be appreciated."

"You listen to what Tom is saying," Blatchford said through a mouthful of food.

"To put it bluntly," Newell continued, "this war won't go on forever. Career men like yourself, heroes right now and all that, just better be thinking about the future. A lot of smart young officers are coming up fast, a cocky breed full of this new electronics stuff. They're bright and well-trained and they're going to give all you older fighting men-of-the-line a run for your money. Believe me when I tell you electronics is the Navy of the future and unless you're in it from the bottom up, the Navy isn't going to want you around."

"I'll take my chances."

"Fortunately, there's no need for that, Captain. Newell Industries will be honored and proud to have you when the time comes. I remember meeting you back in 1932, wasn't it, at the Bath shipyard in Maine. I liked the cut of your jib then and I do now. When this little war blows over, you and I are going to sit down and talk, eh?"

"It doesn't look like a little war to me, Mr. Newell."

"When I say 'little,' Captain, I don't mean easy. It certainly won't be easy. But at Newell Industries we are already blueprinting the weapons of the future and if these electronics boys know what they're talking about, 'little' it is. Well, never mind that. You know what I'm driving at. That boy across the room is my only son and heir, the only child my poor dear wife Martha could have. He's a chip off the old block although I must admit there are moments when I don't quite understand what goes on in that damn fool head of his. Now I have got to get out to the airport and all I want from you is your assurance that you'll tell him what's best for him."

"I'm not the one to do it, Mr. Newell."

"No time for modesty, Harry," Blatchford said.

"Modesty, hell. He's over twenty-one and he should know what's best for himself."

"You're his commanding officer, Captain Paige, and we're at war. It's perfectly all right to bring your influence to bear as you see fit."

"Well—"

"Knew I could count on you," Newell said. He gripped Paige's shoulders. "Let's give Tod the word before I go."

With an arm across the captain's shoulder he crossed the room to a corner where his son stood talking with David Paige, Stick Wilson, and Joe Allen. Blatchford in their wake paused enroute only long enough to race his practiced fingers through a silver dish from which he expertly sifted the cashews from the peanuts.

Thomas A. Newell broke into the conversation. "Captain Paige has a word to say to you, Tod."

"Yes, sir?"

Paige hesitated. David excused himself and moved off. Had the approach to Sunda Strait been any worse than this? Paige wondered. In the silence, Thomas A. Newell's smile stiffened. "Go on, Captain. Tell him."

"Your father's worried about your next tour of duty, Tod."

"Yes, sir. We've already discussed it."

"Well, he and Commodore Blatchford want me to help you make up your mind."

"It's already made up, Captain, he knows that."

"Seems he's not very happy about your decision and feels that as your commanding officer I should exert my influence to get you to see things his way."

"Influence, sir?"

"As your skipper, of course. According to Navy Regulations and in addition to the responsibilities of command of a vessel or station, I also carry certain responsibilities to my officers and men under Chapter 22, section 9, which make it my duty to keep myself informed as to the individual peculiarities, characteristics, and dispositions of the officers and of as many of the men under me as is possible."

"Yes, sir."

"Now suppose a set of orders shows up for one of my officers and these orders involve a change of duty for which I feel he isn't qualified. That means if I endorse those orders I'm endorsing something that isn't in the best interests of the service, The United States then being in a state of war, right? Then I am committing a dereliction of duty, an offense the punishment for which is too horrible to mention in front of all these nice people. Right, Commodore?"

"Right as rain," Blatchford boomed munching.

"And under such circumstances I could hardly be expected to endorse such orders. Right, Mr. Newell?"

"You tell him," Tod's father said.

The color drained from Tod's cheeks. "Are you trying to say I'm not qualified to serve with you, Captain?"

"Not at all. I'm simply pointing out that it is my sworn duty to serve the best interests of the Navy and that is what I intend to do. Now the way I see it, you have a choice of two assignments. Either you serve as assistant gunnery officer on one of Shiloh's five-inch mounts or you take over the antiaircraft batteries in Sky Two aft. Which'll it be?"

Young Newell grinned. "I've grown rather fond of those AA guns, Captain."

"Sky Two it is then. Tomorrow morning at 0800, Newport News shipyard."

It had happened too quickly for the commodore to comprehend, but not for Thomas A. Newell. "What the hell are you pulling off here, Paige?"

"Influence, Mr. Newell. Works like a charm."

"You're a damned fool," Newell said after a stunned hard look. "And that goes for you, son."

"Aw now, Tom," Blatchford began.

"Don't Tom me, you fat fraud." Newell roughly elbowed the commodore aside and pushed through a ring of curious guests. "We leave in two minutes," he snapped at his secretary. "Phone the garage."

Blatchford's martini spilled down the runways of his wrinkled dress whites. He whirled on Paige. "Damn it, Harry, that was a stupid thing to do."

"Up yours, Rollo." He pounded his father-in-law heartily on the back, triggering a salvo of caviar, cashews, bits of smoked salmon and deviled egg.

In exactly two minutes Thomas A. Newell and entourage, complete with briefcases and frowns, departed. The party over, the remaining guests slipped away, sleek and quiet as trained mice. Tod

Newell asked David Paige to remain and join him for dinner, but David declined, explaining that it would be the one evening he would have with his family before his graduation. The Paiges departed with Commodore Blatchford in tow, purple and damp and still muttering. Joe Allen said goodbye to Tod Newell and caught the train south to Florida and flight training.

The resident staff commenced to clean up and Tod, now alone, poured himself a drink and wandered through the French doors to the terrace. Below him the streets were thick with cars and people running. The sight reminded him of his desperate need to share their urgent lives. It did not matter where they were headed—to war, to drink, to love—or what drove them. All that mattered was that he become a part of it. He was the eternal outsider looking in. The loneliness and despair into which it plunged him was often too much to bear.

It was always like this following each confrontation with his father. On the surface their rare meetings seemed casual and friendly. Such admirable reserve was just about what one might expect of a civilized New England father and son. But it had never been easy, he recalled bitterly, and he had invariably come away from these tension-charged dialogues drained of strength and affection. Then would follow a period of doubts mixed with regrets and guilt feelings and the pure hell of knowing he was alone.

Well, he had done it again and it would set in motion the usual routine at Newellton. In the early morning the tearful entreaties from his mother would begin via long distance, begging him to understand and to try to love and respect this dictatorial autocratic corporate prince she had married as a mere slip of an heiress and to whom she had given the best years of her life. Tod felt sorry for her and in loyalty endured his mother but he could not forgive her habit in these crises, of phoning him the moment she awoke, which was usually at dawn. The subsequent barrage of perfumed letters, all air mailed special delivery, was worthy of the least talented of the Brontë sisters at her lowest ebb.

It was his lot, he decided, to keep moving as far and as fast as he could from the sentimental trap of those phone calls and airmail letters and from the clutch of those dictatorial and autocratic fingers that had made such a mess of his early years and now threatened his independence as a man.

What is it the old man wants of me? he wondered. My balls? Am

I threatening him in some cockeyed psychotic way I don't even recognize? I don't want his job or his fame or his bullied, barren wife. *My God what a vile thought!* What a crazy lousy dirty idea to enter the head of a clean-living, well-raised White Anglo-Saxon Protestant 100 percent American lad. Forgive me, Mom, and bake another apple pie.

The hell with all that. It was a treat to see the look on the old man's face when the skipper foxed him. You had to hand it to a sport like Paige, taking on the old man at his own game and playing along, not batting an eyelash, until the shit hit the electric fan. Serves the old man right. He got what he deserved, didn't he? Then what the hell am I crying for? He never loses. I can damn well guess at the fat plum the old man must have offered Paige to make that pitch. There must be a shipload of passed-over four-stripers sweating out their inescapable day of retirement, desperate men who'd leap at an offer like that from Thomas A. Newell. Not Paige, though. Not a salty swashbuckling ballsy pirate like Hardtack Harry Paige.

And you can bet your bottom dollar he knew damned well the price he could have charged for his blackmail and right now he damned well knows the penalty he's going to pay for passing it up. And double for making a chump of the old man. Well, class will tell and it makes no difference if it's tennis or top brass or life and death itself. Either you have it or you don't and the crowd can always tell. Paige has it and the old man does not and that's about the size of it.

Too bad David Paige could not stay for dinner. Tod had sensed a certain rapport, recognizing the familiar reticence of a son in the shadow of a powerful father. When the old man had barged over with Paige and had broken up their conversation, he understood the swift hurt look that had clouded David's face a moment before he excused himself. There was more there, he believed, than met the eye. He hoped there would be more opportunities to know David Paige.

It was a hell of a way for a party to end. A hell of a day of medals and the President and the old man and all, and it called for a celebration. He went inside and flipped through a pile of unopened invitations on the foyer table. He was in no mood for an evening of Washington's gay wartime society or its veddy private parties. Mint juleps, he decided, under the shade trees of the Chevy Chase

Club and a run out to Clara May Downey's Olney Inn for fried chicken.

He went down the corridor to shave and discovered Stick Wilson in the bathroom slumped on the toilet seat. A half-filled pint bottle stuck out of his blouse front. He had rolled up his right trouser leg and removed the artificial limb. His left leg was supported by the rim of the tub. The fitting, a contraption of plastic, metal, laces, and leather, stood on the tile floor in its regulation Navy shoe and black sock. Wilson rubbed the loose flesh of the stump. He looked drunk and ugly.

"You all right, Stick?"

"Goddam foot aches."

Newell gingerly picked up the artificial limb and studied it. "Doesn't it fit right?"

"Ain't the gizmo hurts. It's my goddam *foot*."

"Stick, you don't have a foot."

"Hurts, I tell you. Like a hooker's snatch on Sunday morning."

Newell stared at the place where the leg ended a few inches below the knee. The skin was turned up and neatly sutured. Grayish streaks alternated with red in the mottled flesh but otherwise it was not swollen or infected. He looked up and saw the tears of pain in Wilson's eyes.

"It looks okay to me, Stick. Let me help you get it back on."

"Hurts," Stick said. "Goddam foot."

Newell fitted the artificial leg gently to the stump and began to secure it. "Would a doctor help?"

"Only help I need's a goddam drink."

"That's the old Stick. Soon as you're dressed."

"To think I'd see the day a lousy feather merchant jaygee's got to help me put my shoes on." He looked at the fancy bathroom fittings. "Some head. Your old man must be loaded."

"Comfortable's the word he prefers."

"A regular Daddy Warbucks. That was some party he threw. I mean all that goldbraid."

"Influence, Stick. He likes to push people around."

"I was there when the skipper lowered the boom on him."

"Lovely, wasn't it?"

"How come you let him get away with it?"

"My father?"

"Hell no. The skipper. Pulling that crap on your old man."

"I thought the skipper handled it rather well."

"He signed your death certificate, smart ass."

"I'll risk it, Stick."

"It don't figure, kid. With your dough and your brains. You got a screw loose or something?"

"I got to prove something."

"All you're proving is what a dumb jerk you are letting that accident-happy bastard con you into shipping out again."

"He thinks I can't take it. I've got to show him I can. I've got to show myself I can."

"You think he gives a shit? Really? He's a killer, kid."

"Come on now, Stick."

"He skippered a blood boat, didn't he? You were there. You saw it with your own eyes. He don't give a shit who he kills."

"You're crocked, Stick."

"You don't need him. You're no trade school joe striking for admiral and a chestful of medals. You ship out with Paige again and sure as hell you'll end up buried at sea or a frigging cripple like me. Here your old man comes up with an easy out, no strain, no pain, and what d'you do? You ram it right up and break if off."

"Lay off, Stick."

"Wise up, kid."

"I thought you and Paige were buddies. Old China sailors, shipmates, all that jazz."

"We *were* buddies. I don't have to tell you. But something come over him since Pearl and damned if he's the same man."

"It isn't the peacetime Navy any more, Stick."

"Could be it's that lard-ass commodore got to him or the Navy Cross the President pinned on his chest. He sure as hell ain't the same Harry Paige. It's like he's striking for admiral and don't give a shit no more for his buddies."

"You're peed off because he bust you from chief that last night in Tjilatjap."

"He also give me this store foot. And the deep six to a shipful of men. How's about the exec, Olsen? He sure as hell give Olsen a black name for life when all he needed was maybe a little shoreside duty."

"Commander Olsen needed psychiatric help. I got it from the doctor. The scuttlebutt was, Oley's wife ran off with an Army colonel while he was stuck out there in the middle of the Pacific Ocean with a war on and not a damn thing he could do about it."

"This skipper must've known that. He could've fixed it so Olsen could go stateside and straighten out his old lady."

"We were on the run, remember? He had enough headaches."

"I don't like what's happened to him, is all. And I hate seeing you suckered in, where your old man has got a soft berth all figured out for you."

"It's what I want, Stick."

Wilson was testing the foot. "I gotta get going."

"Hang around. I'm alone and I sure need a friend. Remember the raft?"

"Goddam right I remember the raft. You were a raving maniac on that raft and I was all for dumping you."

"I never saw men die like those men in the water died."

"Better them than us."

"How'd *you* feel, Stick?"

"Mad as hell."

"Why mad?"

"That bastard Krueger went down owing me thirty bucks."

"The captain bleeding and unconscious and Joe Allen bawling. Tears running down his face."

"You'd bawl too, was your ship sinking before your eyes and you a plank owner."

"Plank owner?"

"Anybody's in the first crew of a new ship, they're plank owners. Funny thing is, *Gloucester*'s the only ship Joe ever served in."

"I didn't know that."

"Hell, he come aboard the *Gloucester* a seaman second back in 1930 and she's been home to Joe Allen ever since. Until she went down, of course. Joe's a mustang. Went from seaman second to lieutenant commander. There's the skipper for you again. Here's a sailor like Joe, one of the best, wants a deck command and what happens? He gets orders to aviation school."

"That's just so's the old team can be together."

"Team, my ass. You know damn well it was Joe who pulled us through. The skipper knows it, too, and that's why he wants Joe. Here, hand me that crutch."

He brushed aside Newell's proffered arm and swung up awkwardly. "I got to learn to navigate this gizmo alone."

"What's it like, Stick?"

"Like everything else Navy. You get used to it."

In the living room, Newell poured two drinks. "On the plane coming east there were these wounded Army pilots, nice-looking guys on stretchers. We got pretty friendly and when we got to Newark I went over to say goodbye and shook hands with them, all except one. He had no hands."

"They laughed when he sat down at the piano, but when he began to play—"

"Not funny, Stick."

"I can see it all. He gets shipped home. His old lady opens the front door. He hollers out, 'Look, Mom. No hands.'" Wilson took a long pull at his drink, choked and noisily spit it out. "What the hell you doing? Trying to poison me?"

"That's a vintage brandy, Stick."

"Shove your fancy goldbraid booze up your ass. Don't anybody drink rye whisky in this crumb joint?"

"One rye whisky coming up." He took Wilson's empty glass and filled it. "Any plans, Stick?"

"Who the hell has plans? For me it's Bethesda the next two weeks for walk training. After that—" He kicked the crutch with his good foot. "They give me this frigging crutch because I quit the hospital in Pearl too soon. After Bethesda I dump it." He rubbed his crotch. "Any broads in this hotel?"

"Sure, for three-stripers and up."

"We got to get our ashes hauled."

"You speak words that would endear you to the hearts of Swinburne, Shelley, and Keats. We must indeed get our ashes hauled and the chair is open to suggestions."

"Baltimore."

"That's thirty, forty miles."

"I got some unfinished business in Baltimore."

"There's plenty of stuff right here."

"Baltimore."

"I'm due aboard *Shiloh* at 0800 and I don't want to miss that train to Norfolk."

"You'll make it. Let's head for Baltimore."

"Only if you tell me what's so damned special that you got to go there."

"This broad, see? The Beast. She's there." He drained his glass and held it out for more. "One for the road. Then call us a cab and I'll tell you about The Beast on the way out. Take the bottle. It's a dry ride."

The hotel staff's reaction to the name of Newell dispelled any doubts Tod may have had about getting a taxi in wartime Washington. The bell captain was reassuring and the doorman courteous and solicitous beyond the call of duty. A cab arrived promptly and they got in. Wilson sat with one leg outstretched on the jump seat. The driver wove through the late afternoon traffic headed for the Baltimore road. Wilson drank rye from the bottle.

"The Beast," Newell reminded him.

"I first got to know the Beast in Valley Joe."

"Where's Valley Joe?"

"Shoreside of Mare Island, north of Frisco. There was this chief gunner's mate, see? So god-awful ugly you would puke your guts just looking at him. But son of a bitch if he didn't have a heart of pure gold. Give you the skivvy shirt right off of his back. His booze. His pay. Do anything for a shipmate. We nicknamed him Beauty, being he was so ugly. Beauty and me put in time on the old river gunboats, just like the skipper. When he made chief they transferred him stateside and two years ago he falls for a Georgia Street hooker, a broad who has been plowed by every Asiatic sailor from Shanghai to Dago, a good-looking broad with great knockers and tough as leather. Funny thing is, she goes for Beauty, hook, line, and sinker. In no time they are shacked up together. Maude. That was her name. But the guys right off give her the name of the Beast, but nobody ever tells Beauty what a public piece she once was because he is such a four-oh Joe. I'll say this for her. She never cheated on Beauty and anybody who tried, God help him. They were set to get married last Christmas when his hitch was up. Beauty never made it. He got his Purple Heart at Pearl in the *Arizona*. Posthumous. He's still there."

"What makes you think you'll find her in Baltimore?"

"She wrote me a letter when she got the word about Beauty, said she was heading back east where she come from, which is Baltimore. Couldn't stand the sight of Georgia Street without him. Then I run into this old buddy in the train station last night and he swears she's working this B-joint, The Oriole. What the hell's an oriole?"

"A song bird. The Baltimore oriole. Very pretty. Black with orange."

"I was born and raised in Baltimore and damned if I ever heard of an oriole."

"And you're going to all this trouble to pay a condolence call."

"What the hell is condolence?"

"When somebody dies, you call on the surviving relatives to offer sympathy during the period of mourning."

"I'm seeing The Beast only to find out can a man with one leg still get laid."

"All the way to Baltimore?"

"No hooker'll take on a guy with one gam. The Beast's a buddy and an old pro. So why take a chance with a stranger?"

The taxi crept slowly through the jammed suburbs toward Baltimore. The driver turned to Newell. "Sorry it's taking so long, Lieutenant Newell. The traffic's murder."

"No hurry," Newell said. "How come you know my name?"

"The hotel doorman, Pat, said I got to take good care of you. The name's Maguire."

Wilson cackled. "Can't win, can you?"

They moved north slowly, hemmed in by heavy trucks loaded with military matériel and passenger vehicles carrying the changing shifts of workers to and from the defense plants. Road repairs and detours slowed their progress. Twice they were brought to a dead stop and sat breathing dust and fumes in the stifling heat to give priority to cavalcades of war-painted transports loaded with the fresh tools of battle and sustenance for fighting men.

An air of urgency seemed to hang over everything. Where new construction had not violated the earth, the rolling countryside stretched from the cement highway to woods and farther fields flush with young crops ripening for late summer harvest. Past College Park, deep in a field beyond rows of slender corn, a tall white farmhouse and its outbuildings caught Newell's eye. The dying sun bathed its clapboard sides red, casting angular shadows, cool indigo on the flat green fields. Newell thought of Edward Hopper landscapes and Newellton and the proud Shanahans and once again his need for people possessed him. He touched Stick Wilson's sleeve. "Out there," he said, "look at that set of buildings."

Wilson squinted across the fields, leaning to one side to favor his outstretched leg. "Something wrong with it?"

"It's peaceful, Stick, and when I think of where we've been and what we've seen, just looking at it warms me. To me, it means a lot of good living's left in this cockeyed world."

"But you still want to go back out there."

"That's right."

"You need another drink."

It was growing dark when they reached the outskirts of Baltimore. Fog rolled in from the harbor and the traffic had eased. Wilson directed the driver through a series of complicated turns along dimmed-out store fronts. They cruised past commercial piers and boat slips to a street alive with sailors and their girls making the rounds of the bars and small cafés. Neon shone through the steamy mist. Bail Bonds. Chili. Oasis. Gaiety. Circus Bar. A faint aroma of rotten fish hung in the moist night air.

"Where are we?"

"The Block."

They parked in front of a tattoo parlor. Wilson swung open his door and slid out. The tattoo artist, a bony, bespectacled woman with a sweaty mustache greeted him with a happy curse and shout.

"Home again," Stick crowed and roughly kissed her. He leaned against a lamp post and with the crutch tucked under his arm, struggled with a match and cigarette. "Where the hell's The Oriole, Meg?"

The tattoo artist nodded down the street.

"Pay off the cabbie," he told Newell.

"I tried. He says he's going to wait for us."

The Oriole was new and noisy, not fifty yards from the tattoo parlor where the taxicab was parked.

"Makes the Golden West on Georgia Street look like a funeral parlor," Stick said.

The Oriole was filled with sailors, women, and blue smoke. An invisible jukebox somewhere along the back wall thumped the melody of "Paper Doll." In the din of voices Tod could distinguish little more than the rhythm of the bass section. He sat with Stick at a small table close to the crowded dance floor. The table was wet and littered with glasses and cigarette butts. Wilson stopped a waiter in mid-flight and ordered their drinks. His eyes searched the room until he caught Newell's amused expression and grinned back at him. "Who's worried? She'll show."

Newell did not care too much whether she showed or not. This

was more fun than the Chevy Chase Club. He was having the time
of his life. There wasn't another officer's uniform to be seen.

"Like the joint?"

"I like it, Stick."

"Only way to fight a war."

"I'm beginning to believe it."

He knew it wasn't the only way to fight a war, but maybe this
was why the wars were fought—for kicks, for easy sex and the
glamour of military plumage. He had to admit it felt good, it felt
incredibly good. He was high and he was happy and if he was lucky
he would have his ashes hauled. He hoped all the sailors and the
Marines and the few heroes in Army uniforms who had the guts to
risk the odds against them by entering this one-sided Navy saloon
would all get their ashes hauled. The whole goddam world, he
thought, getting its ashes hauled. Who would have had such golden
ash-hauling opportunities if there had been no war?

Stick was wrong, of course. There was another way to fight a war
and it was out there where the war was. Tomorrow he would be
aboard *Shiloh* and Captain Paige would be there and the lovely
Bofors 40-mm. AA guns would be there and the day would come
when he would prove to that salty son of a bitch that second best
could never be good enough for Todhunter Newell.

Wilson elbowed him. "There she goes."

"Which one?"

"The red dress without sleeves."

She had just come in, a Marine on each arm. They went directly
to the bar and ordered drinks. Newell could see enough woman
through the smoke screen to justify Wilson's determination to drive
all the way to Baltimore. "There isn't much of her that doesn't meet
the eye," he said.

"The biggest goddam forward twin mounts in the U. S. Navy,"
Stick said. "Get her over here."

"She's got company."

Stick finished his drink and wiped his mouth. "You gonna tell
her I'm here or do I chop my way alone through these jokers?"

"I'll get her," Newell said. She had already left the bar and to low
whistles and turning heads twisted her way to the dance floor, a red-
headed Marine partner in tow. Moments later she recognized Stick
Wilson and went to him.

"Stick, baby! What a surprise!"

"Hi, Maude." He stretched for a chair and pushed it under her. Maude sat. Her escort stood bristling, uncertain how to proceed.

"When'd you hit town, Stick?"

"Yesterday. You're looking four-oh, Maude."

Newell thought so. She was no more than thirty, large and handsomely proportioned, her shoulders and throat firm and the flesh delicately marbled where the swell of her splendid breasts was exposed. Her voice, deep and vibrating, excited Newell. Maude had bold snapping eyes. Just now they were feasting on every inch of Stick. "Last time you were wearing chief's stripes, Stick."

He shrugged. "I was robbed. How's about a drink?"

"She's drinking with me," the Marine said.

"Scram," said Maude without turning, "this is an old buddy."

"You owe me the dance, sister."

"You heard what the lady said." Stick moved his crutch a few inches.

"I'll be with you in a sec, Red, honey," Maude said. "Wait at the bar." Red left, walking stiffly. "These kids figure they buy you a few blue moons, they own you."

"What'll it be, Maude?"

"You bring anything?"

"Half a pint of rye is all."

"I'll order the house regular and a couple of set-ups and we'll share. What's with the leg?"

"Gone from the knee down."

"Sweet Jesus." She was quiet for a moment. "So you got my letter about Beauty and come all the way here just to see me. That was sweet of you, Stick. Damn sweet."

"That was one of the reasons. A condo—" He glanced at Newell for help.

"A condolence call."

Maude saw Newell for the first time. "Who the hell is he?"

"That's Lieutenant Newell, Maude."

"You mean he's with you?"

Stick nodded. She stared at him. "You got to be kidding."

"He's okay, Maude. Shipmate from the *Gloucester*."

"A mustang, right? Up from the ranks?"

"Nope," Newell said. "I'm a cheap, lousy, feather merchant son of a bitch of a Navy reserve boot and terribly ashamed of myself."

Maude grinned at Wilson. "At least he knows his place. How long you been in the Navy, mister?"

"Five months."

"Sweet Jesus, the Navy's already got more time in me than you'll ever put in the Navy." She ignored the drink the waiter had brought her and made herself a rye highball. "You said something else brought you here, Stick?"

"It's about the leg."

"What about it?"

"It's healed up in good shape, Maude, but I got to wondering. You know. Like could it change my way of life."

"You sure as hell won't be chasing after any Frisco cable cars."

"That's not what's worrying me."

"Out with it, Stick."

"I got to know once and for all, can I still do it."

"Why the hell not? Or was it more than just the leg you lost?"

"It's all there, Maude. Just not having the leg, well, you know how funny some women are."

"I don't meet the funny ones. Come to think of it, I never did it with anybody didn't have both legs to work with." She sipped her drink thoughtfully. "You know, you got something there, Stick."

"I figured you'd be the one to ask, Maude."

"Could be a problem, couldn't it?"

"That's what I come to find out."

"Could be real interesting. I mean in my line of work."

"Exactly what I was thinking," Stick said.

"There's a war on, see? This kind of situation could come up time and again." She turned to Newell. "You got any ideas, Lieutenant?"

"I'm all for research and education," Newell said, "and for anything that helps the war effort."

"If you will excuse us, then." Maude rose and whistled and a burly man in a tight tuxedo materialized from the haze. "Rico," she said. "I left two Marine pigeons at the bar. They brought me and could be they'd get the wrong idea seeing me leave with Mr. Wilson here, so I want you to keep an eye on them. Mr. Wilson here is an old buddy from the coast and was very close to my dear late husband Beauty who you frequently heard me speak of very often. So I'm taking Mr. Wilson here with me for a couple minutes to give him some precious souvenirs left him by my dear late husband who especially wanted he should have them."

"Glad to meet you, Mr. Wilson," Rico said.

"Likewise," Stick said.

"And this is Lieutenant somebody."

"My pleasure," Newell said.

"Don't worry about those two punks, honey." Rico squeezed her arm, including as much of her ample bosom as his thick fingers could reach. "Just don't stay too long. We're busy as hell."

"Thanks lots, Rico." She helped Wilson to his feet. Newell rose and remained standing while they crossed the room to a hall that led past the rest rooms to a door beyond. When Newell sat again he saw the two Marines at the bar watching him. He smiled pleasantly and raised his drink and toasted them and ordered another. *Noblesse oblige* and all that.

He passed the time in silent and imaginative contemplation of the infinite variations and the wonderful possibilities of nationwide research and education. He could run for President of the United States on a platform like that. He might not make it, but with The Beast for his campaign manager, he could certainly conduct a most provocative and unusual campaign, which the nation would remember and which would give his less imaginative opponents a run for their money.

But my father now, he wondered drunkenly. Would he *allow* me to run for President?

His reverie was interrupted half an hour later by the arrival of Stick Wilson beaming and Maude dewy eyed. Stick's arm encircled her and his fingers were deep in the sweaty paradise between her breasts. "It is obvious to conclude," Newell said as they joined him, "that the experiment has been a smashing success."

"Whee," Maude said.

"Your French is impeccable," Newell said, "and your courage admirable. Will you say a few words to the radio audience?"

"Hello, world," Maude said. "Kiss my mother-fucking ass."

"Thank you, Miss America. And now a word from the next President of the United States, your friend and mine, Stick Wilson."

Wilson clasped his hands overhead in a boxer's salute.

"Thank you, Tony Galento." Newell called to their waiter. "Champagne, garçon, for the wedding party. The best in the house, *s'il vous plaît*."

"Silver plate in this joint?" Maude said. "Fat chance."

Instead of the champagne, Rico arrived. He was followed by the two Marines. "What the hell's going on here?" he demanded of Maude.

"You tell me, Rico."

"These two gentlemen claim you took them for a hundred eighty bucks."

"These two gentlemen are a pair of mother-fucking liars."

"You holding back on us, Maude?"

"Sweet Jesus no. The house gets its cut of the drinks and you get yours, Rico, right off the top. What the hell do you want from us girls? The sweat between our legs?"

"She brings us here and ditches us for these swabbies," said the red-haired Marine.

"I told you to wait," Maude said.

"She promised us a private party, four girls," the one with pimples said. "The other three never showed."

"Never mind," Maude said. "They got their money's worth."

"I don't want trouble, Maude. None of your old tricks." Rico looked at the littered table. "Where are those souvenirs you said you were getting for this guy here?"

"We sent them parcel post special delivery to his dying mother in Pasadena, California, to be placed alongside her in the bronze casket he ordered from Forest Lawn. That's what took so long."

"You been drinking, Maude?"

"This ain't a tearoom, Rico. You don't run a church social here at El Oriole."

He sniffed her drink. "Hitting the hard stuff again, breaking the rules."

She got to her feet swaying. "So what? I'm about ready to puke up twenty gallons of blue moons, so stand aside." Rico backed off. "I'm telling Augie," he said. "You're through, you lush." He pushed through the crowd of dancers.

"Screw him," Maude said. "Let's blow."

"Not with my ninety bucks you don't." The pimply Marine unbuckled his broad leather belt. "C'mon, Red. I had enough of this swabbie shit."

He swung the belt in a vicious arc. Newell ducked and grabbed his ankles and spilled him backward. The Marine fell against the next table. Glasses, sailors, and B-girls went crashing in all directions. The waiter arrived bearing champagne in a bucket of ice. Before he could retreat, Maude lifted the bottle by its throat and smashed it against the table's edge. Drenched in bubbles, she swept it within an inch of Red's ear. Wilson on one leg butted the Marine full in the stomach and fell with him, doubled in pain and gasping, to the floor. A fight broke out at the table that had been dumped. A chair flew and above the hubbub, the waiter bellowed for help. Rico circled cautiously. Maude pointed the jagged edge of the bottle toward him. "Step up, you crummy bastard," she said. "I'm paying off."

Someone blew a whistle. "Get us out of here, Maude," Newell said. He helped Wilson up and they followed her down the path that opened magically before her swinging arm. She led them to the ladies room and locked the door. "Pardon us," she murmured over a pay toilet door. Newell pulled Wilson through the window and turned to help Maude. "Scram," she said. "I'll hold the fort."

"What about Rico?"

"He can drop dead."

"He'll be rough on you."

"Not while Augie's still sweet on me."

The door knob rattled. "Haul ass," Maude said. "That'll be the Shore Patrol." She looked tenderly at Wilson. "It was real nice, Stick."

Newell said thanks and Wilson blew her an obscene kiss. They made their way through the narrow alley to the street. A crowd had gathered at the door of The Oriole and they circled it to reach the taxicab where Maguire stood watching the crowd.

"Getting worried about you," he said. "Get in." They drove off past running Shore Patrol officers. "What happened in there?"

"You won't hardly believe it," Stick said.

"A real lady," Newell said.

"Inside and out," Stick said.

"Like the Statue of Liberty," Newell said, "with a glass shille-lagh."

"Where to?" Maguire wanted to know.

"Any place," Stick said. "I gotta pee."

Maguire turned toward the docks and drove down the length of a broad pier and dimmed his lights. In the darkness Wilson got out, balancing himself, cursing and laughing, fumbling with the many-buttoned opening of his Navy tailor-mades. He stood close to the hull of a large masted vessel. Newell's eyes grew accustomed to the darkness and he saw her name on the gleaming transom. Wilson was cleared for action and taking aim.

"Hold it, Stick."

"You nuts or something?"

"That's the *Constellation*."

"So what?"

"You can't do that to an American shrine, Stick."

"Watch me." Newell stood by helplessly while Wilson as helplessly soiled as much of himself as he did the side of the ancient frigate. Roaring drunk now, he returned to the taxicab and directed Maguire to find a whorehouse in Baltimore. It was out of his territory, Maguire said. He pulled over to the curb and cut the motor while they discussed the matter. Newell invited him to have a drink and the bottle passed among them several times. Maguire explained that he, too, would be in uniform but he had seven children to support and his wife and her mother. "Listen," he said, inspired. "I'll take you home and give you a knockdown to my mother-in-law. She's ready."

"How much?"

"A deuce a pop."

"Any port in a storm," Stick said.

"She's got store teeth and a wooden leg—" Maguire giggled.

"Knock it off, hear?" Stick tilted the bottle and heaved it. The rye was gone. Newell suggested they head back to Washington. Wilson would have none of it. They could go to the Black Bottle on Guilford, or to Corral's on South Broadway for the best spick meal in town. His mood had darkened with the last of the drink and he cursed Maguire under his breath. They settled finally for a round of nightcaps. Maguire cruised until he found a bar in a row of neglected red brick houses. A faded poster curled in its window advertised a day of racing long past at Pimlico. Maguire would not go in with them. He did not care to run the risk of losing his cab, he said. Wilson stood swaying, belching, staring with drunken eyes at the racetrack poster. Newell told Maguire they would be out after they had a nightcap, two at the most. He was concerned about Wilson now and he gave Maguire ten dollars and asked him to pick up a couple of sandwiches and black coffee to help sober up Wilson.

The fat and pale bartender was slouched over the far end of the bar deep in local sports talk with a soldier on a stool. Stick Wilson slapped the bar and demanded service. The bartender looked once at his flyblown clock and came over. "Be closing soon, fellers. What'll it be?"

"Two brandies," Newell said.

"Me too," Stick said and laid his head on the bar. "Two brandies."

"Two brandies," said the bartender.

"What brand do you have?" Newell wanted to know.

"For you guys in uniform, nothing but the best."

"I mean the brand name."

"Look, friend, you can't trust the labels today, anyway, so do you want what I got or don't you?"

He uncorked a bottle and set up two bar glasses.

"Do you have snifters?"

"I tell you there's nothing wrong with this brand, Lieutenant." He poured a scant inch into each glass. "Not many places serving brandy these days. Ain't that much around." He corked the bottle. "You want a chaser? Ginger ale, maybe?"

"You yack too much, Fatty." Stick swallowed his drink. Newell sniffed the raw fumes and shuddered. The bartender was studying his campaign ribbons. "You guys been somewhere?"

"Another shot, Fatty, and quit beating your gums."

"Now look," the bartender said and leaning forward saw the crutch across Wilson's lap. "Sorry, sailor. Just don't call me Fatty."

"Sure, Fatty."

Newell slid a twenty-dollar bill under the man's angry eyes. "Keep the change," he said. "And pour my hero friend another drink. He's got to fill that hollow leg."

The bartender poured another drink. "I know how it is," he said. "Fellow over there. In the Army six months, lost his arm."

"What the hell you run here?" Stick demanded. "A saloon for cripples?"

"Ask him to join us for a nightcap," Newell said.

The soldier came over, a thickly built young man of nineteen or twenty, with a broad Slavic face and close-cropped blond hair. His khaki uniform was neatly pressed and his heavy paratrooper boots well-shined. The left sleeve was flat and pinned to his tunic.

"The lieutenant's buying, Carl."

"Thanks, sir."

"This is Carl," the bartender said. "My name's Jack."

"I'm Tod and my buddy here goes by the name of Stick. Drinks for everybody, Jack." He lighted a match for Carl's cigarette. "What are you drinking, Carl?"

"Mount Vernon and water. Jack knows."

Wilson put his face close to the bar and sipped his brandy without using his hands. Some of it spilled. "Ain't so hard once you get used to it," he said.

"Take it easy, sailor, will you?" said Jack.

"Shut your hole, Fatty. Look, Tod. No hands."

"Can't you order him to behave, Lieutenant? This is a friendly place."

"Behave, Stick. That's an order."

"Fuck you, Lieutenant junior grade Todhunter Newell, United States Navy Reserve."

Newell turned to Carl. "Is the Army like that? Is that what happens when you treat an enlisted man like an equal?" He passed another twenty-dollar bill to Jack. "This is a donation to perpetuate this friendly place for posterity. A sign, Jack, a plaque to go over the bar, telling all who come here 'This is a friendly place.'"

"It is," Jack said. "Everybody says so."

"Jack runs a nice bar," Carl said.

"Who gives a shit?" Wilson swung to face him. "What happened to your arm, dogface?"

"Lay off, Stick," Newell said sharply.

"I don't mind," Carl said. "It was an accident. I never even got to leave the States. I enlisted last November and got trained to be an Army baker. Fort Bragg." He tapped the empty sleeve. "It got caught in the bread mixer." He drank some of his whisky. "Maybe I'm lucky. They tell me my outfit's headed for North Africa."

"A bread mixer. Some war. My aching ass."

"Look, sailor, accidents happen."

"Sometimes they're made to happen."

Carl flushed. "Not this one, sailor. I didn't have to enlist. My brother got his on convoy duty. Lost at sea. I was left sole support of my mother and the two kid sisters."

"What convoy duty?"

"North Atlantic."

"What ship?"

"*Kearny*. A tin can."

"The *Kearny* wasn't sunk."

"Nobody said she was. But she sure as hell took a torpedo last

October 17. We got the War Department papers saying what a hero Joe was. My brother." He angrily pushed his drink aside. "What the hell, Jack. Who needs this? I don't have to prove nothing." He stood up and fished a crumpled dollar from a pocket and threw it on the bar. "Thanks for the drink, Lieutenant."

"Don't mind him, Carl. Finish your drink."

"Drunk or sober, sir, he shouldn't of talked the way he did, to you or nobody else. Who the hell does he think he is? I don't see no Purple Heart on his chest."

"Shit," Stick said. "Any dogface can walk into an Army-Navy store and buy all the goddam campaign ribbons they want."

"It's closing time," Jack said uneasily.

"Fuck you, Fatty. You're a four-eff from the word go. You goddam civilians, you're all alike. Take our pay and lock the doors. This saloon don't close until we give the order, hear? Or we'll close it so tight you'll never in your fucking four-eff life be able to open her again."

Carl's eyes narrowed. He regarded Wilson with an odd, amused smile. "Know something, Jack? I'm beginning to like him, even if he is a swabbie." He studied Wilson's hashmarks. "What's your rate, Stick?"

"Quartermaster first. I been busted from chief more times than you could whistle 'Dixie.' "

"I mean it, you guys. Carl, I got to close up." Jack went to the front door and tugged nervously at the wrinkled green blind. Stick and Carl ignored him. Newell watched them drunkenly, his friends, his buddies, not really caring what might happen to him. Only to them. He no longer felt sorry for himself. If he felt sorry for anyone, it was the bartender, Jack, without a friend in the world.

Jack seemed badly frightened. He tugged repeatedly at the green blind which refused to stay down. Poor abused bastard, Newell thought, with a brace of sorry cripples for customers, both of them trigger-happy enough to tear the joint apart just for kicks. Jack must feel the way he would feel if a Republican midget and a Democrat dwarf came in the day before Election Day. Or a pregnant bearded lady and a cross-eyed shortstop from the House of David. He knew. His father had told him freaks were bad for business. Here at Jack's it was bad for business. It would scare off the regulars and he could understand why it made Jack nervous, the two of them sitting there, limbs chopped like chickens, nothing but trouble in their small talk.

Carl was asking politely about the crutch. Wilson pulled up his trouser leg. "Some piece of machinery," he said proudly. He called for more brandy and a Mount Vernon for Carl. Jack was sweeping behind the bar and did not answer. "You fat four-eff bastard," Stick yelled. "We want another round, hear?"

Jack appealed to Newell. "Tell him we're closed, will you, Lieutenant? One drink after hours and sure as hell I lose my license."

"Let's go, Stick." Newell took Wilson's arm and turned to Carl for help.

"One lousy drink?" Stick whined. "I can't have one lousy drink?"

"It's breaking the law," Jack said. "I don't want no trouble. I don't want to have to call a cop."

Wilson pulled loose from Newell's restraining arm and, standing on his good leg, swung his crutch with both arms and smashed a row of glasses behind the bar.

"Get that crazy bastard out of here," Jack said. "If he had two legs I'd throw him out of here myself."

The crutch whistled through the air. Jack ducked. Another row of glasses smashed in pieces. Jack swung his broom. It caught Stick across the side of his face, staggering him. He lifted himself to the bar and, with one leg dragging, started crawling. Jack ran.

"You fat bastard. I can take you with no feet and one hand tied behind my back. Come on out here and fight like a man, you fat yellow son of a bitch of a four-eff civilian bastard." Jack at the far end of the bar picked up the phone and was dialing. "Go on, call the fucking cops. Call the Shore Patrol and the FBI. I'll take you all."

Newell and Carl took Wilson by his arms and dragged him struggling to the street. His hoarse cries filled the night. "What the hell's the matter with everybody? Forget the goddam foot. Who needs feet?"

The three of them stood in the yellow glare of the street lamp. Stick cursed and threatened and bragged in a steady stream but no longer resisted. Heavy tears coursed down his cheeks.

"Thanks for helping," Newell said to Carl.

"What the hell, sir, I was the same way two-three months ago."

"We had a cab waiting," Newell said. "I don't see him."

"There's an all-night beanery around the corner," Carl said. "He might of went there."

"I'll check. Keep an eye on Stick." He went to find Maguire.

"I'm okay now," Stick said to Carl. He wiped his eyes and his nose and fumbled for his cigarettes. Carl helped him while he lighted their cigarettes. The door lock clicked shut and the lights went out behind the green shade in Jack's saloon. The soldier and the sailor were alone under the yellow light in the darkened canyon of red brick and white stone steps.

Wilson spoke through cracked lips. "Lost my goddam white hat."

"You left it in Jack's."

"I'm going after it."

"Forget it. Jack's closed."

"I'm out of uniform, dogface."

"The lieutenant'll be right back with a cab. Nobody'll know the difference."

"Except me. Slack off, hear? I'm going after my white hat."

"You're waiting for the lieutenant. He gave me an order."

"Don't pull that GI chicken shit on me."

"Why not? You General MacArthur or somebody?"

They stood wordless, breathing hard, hating each other. "You said you lost it in the Java Sea," Carl went on. "But I don't see no Purple Heart. You ashamed of where you were?"

"Hell no."

"What ship, wise guy?"

"The *Gloucester*, in Sunda Strait."

"You're full of crap. She went down with all hands."

"Except me and the lieutenant and Joe Allen and the skipper."

"Sure, I heard where the skipper saved his own skin, but nobody else got out alive. I happen to know. A kid went to school with me, he was aboard the *Gloucester* when she sunk."

"Don't shit me, soldier. You had no buddy on the *Gloucester*. No man I ever shipped with would have a one-armed, chicken-shit dogface Polack baker like you for a buddy."

"His old man swears to God it was the captain's fault, going where he did. Killed more of his own men than the Japs at Pearl Harbor."

"He's the best goddam skipper this Navy ever saw."

"How the hell would you know? You weren't there."

"Out of my way, Polack. I'm kicking down that goddam door."

"What with? You sorry one-legged son of a bitch."

"You Polack prick, put up your hands."

Newell arrived in Maguire's cab a few minutes later. Wilson had already put his artificial foot through the glass door of Jack's saloon and was on the sidewalk locked with Carl. Windows rattled open. A cluster of people watched from a safe distance across the street. A siren wailed.

Newell started out of the cab but Maguire held him. "Forget it, Mr. Newell."

"Stick's my buddy."

"I got orders to get you back in one piece."

"I can't leave him there."

"That's the paddy wagon you're hearing, Mr. Newell. You got to be in Norfolk by morning, right? You start in with this mess and buddy or no buddy, you can kiss Norfolk goodbye."

"They'll kill each other."

"Them two? Fat chance." He slammed the door shut. "Believe me, Mr. Newell, it's not for you."

"Let me go, Mac."

"He's no good, I tell you. You saw him urinate on a national shrine. You call that a buddy? C'mon, Mr. Newell, don't do it. He ain't worth it." He pushed Newell back into the cab.

They began the long run to Washington. Newell sat back sick at heart. Maguire was right. It was not for him. It was too bad about Stick but Stick would heal. The Stick Wilsons of the world bleed easily and heal fast. His own wounds were of a different making, more scalpel than club, the scars invisible. Wounds less likely to heal and impossible to forget. Hurley impaled. Men in the flaming sea. The violence from which he now fled.

He would not forget Carl and Stick Wilson on the sidewalk, the street light reflected a thousand times in bloody shards of shattered glass. He would not forget the short vicious stabs of the Army boot into Wilson's groin. He would not forget the glint of light racing the length of the polished crutch shaft as it fell and fell again across the face and body of one-armed Carl, the soldier who lost it in a bread mixer.

Newell buried his head in his arms.

"You feel okay, Mr. Newell?"

"Okay, Maguire."

"You two guys sure had yourselves a toot."

"I should have stayed."

"Would he do the same for you?"

Newell thought about it for a while. "I hope nothing happens to him."

"A cripple in uniform? They'll be falling all over their selves helping him out."

Newell closed his eyes and leaned back. "Who pays you, Maguire?"

"The front desk."

Newell began to laugh. Tears ran down his face. Maguire watching him in the mirror began to laugh, too. "I knew you'd see it my way."

"It's funny."

"What's funny?"

"He never heard of an oriole and I never got my ashes hauled."

Maguire left him at the hotel. Well-dressed people were asleep in the lobby. Newell went up to the suite. The phone was ringing. He let it ring but they had given him the key at the desk and they knew he was there and kept on ringing. He sprawled in a chair and picked up the phone and wearily closed his eyes.

"Hello, Mother," he said.

25

Paige awoke at dawn, having slept poorly and alone. The family evening had been a disaster. All he wanted now was to get away.

He moved about the bedroom quietly, not wanting to disturb Felicia asleep on a studio couch in the adjoining sewing room. Commodore Blatchford, fallen in battle, had also spent the night and his snores from a guest room down the hall strengthened Paige's determination to clear out as quickly as possible. Only David remained and Paige would deal with him at breakfast.

He devoted ten intensive minutes to a variety of setting-up exercises. Because of the tenderness still in his fingers he omitted the customary fifty push-ups. He showered and shaved, dressed in a new set of khakis purchased for him during his hospital stay at Pearl. He stuffed soiled linen with clean into a canvas barracks bag and lugged it with his bulging briefcase to the head of the stairs. He wakened David and in passing, thumbed his nose at the swollen, rumbling mountain of flesh that was his father-in-law. He carried his gear down the stairs through the half-darkened house and dropped it near the front door.

It was not yet six o'clock. He could hear David moving about in his room above. He phoned the Navy transportation pool and arranged to be picked up at seven. In the kitchen he filled a coffee pot and set out china and silver. He shook a batch of Lizzie's corn muffins from the pan in which they had remained untouched since dinnertime and stacked them on a platter. Bacon and eggs were launched in their traditional ways. He unlocked the kitchen door and retrieved milk and cream and stowed them in the refrigerator. He found an orange and peeled it and stood leaning in the doorway thoughtfully breaking sections of the orange, chewing them and spitting the pulp into Felicia's blooming rose garden.

He had to admit to himself it was indeed a lovely rose garden, its beauty and mystery greatly enhanced in the hazy morning light. The early blooms with a soft almost ghostly coloring reminded him of dawns at sea and he missed the sea and it surprised him that the sight of a rose garden could evoke such a feeling of loneliness and self-pity.

Who the hell knows anything about anything? Felicia turned bitch and a night of tenderness and love so badly needed lost to both of them. Who the hell ever knows?

It had begun in the car enroute from the Newell party. Blatchford, wasting no time, resumed his denouncement of Paige, berating him for his cavalier treatment of Thomas A. Newell. To this he added several choice comments on Paige's stupidity for "not knowing a good thing when he saw it." Paige ignored him. Frustrated by his son-in-law's refusal to engage, and enchanted by the sound of his own words, Blatchford continued with a recital of Paige's previous acts of unofficerlike conduct which included disloyalty, infidelity, and consorting with enlisted personnel. These being largely unverified incidents invented in the rage of the moment, Paige still refused to be baited and Blatchford, now dangerously out of breath, wound up with the announcement that he was through going to bat for such an ungrateful wretch of a son-in-law. He had warned Felicia it was a mistake to marry an ill-bred, clownish brute whose only contributions to the Navy were his two thick fists and it was too damned bad she had chosen him over an officer and a gentleman the calibre of Amos Flint.

In the past Paige had listened to variations of this theme numerous times and endured it this time only because he long ago had promised Felicia he would. Had this not been the case, he would happily have pitched the old curmudgeon out of the moving vehicle into the street and run the car back and forth over his oozing body. In a more tolerant mood, he would have found some sour pleasure in trading insult for insult with the old boy, having in his repertoire certain insults learned on China station that would make the commodore's hair stand on end. And there was also the hope that some ultimate and choice obscenity in plain English would trigger a coronary or at least burst a few blood vessels. In view of the abuse he had submitted to over the years, it was not too much to ask, and the sight of blood pouring from the aristocratic Blatchford nose would do much to even the score.

So he said nothing and the car rolled toward Georgetown and Lizzie's delectable dinner. Paige's one regret was that David, seated alongside the driver, had to hear the old windbag make a jackass of himself. It was at this moment that Felicia, to everyone's astonishment, spoke up. "Daddy's absolutely right," she said.

Paige stared at her. "What the hell's come over you?"

"You see," she went on serenely. "You're crude. Ill-mannered. You shame and embarrass us and I for one have had enough of it."

"Well I'll be damned."

"Oh yes indeed you will. And it's about time." She turned as well as she could in the squeezed tonneau between Paige and Blatchford. "All Daddy was trying to do was help you, help David, help that poor confused Newell boy, and you mucked it all."

"You're drunk, Felicia. Now just shut up."

"You should have done what Daddy wanted you to do. If for no other reason than out of respect for his age and rank. But you had to humiliate him, didn't you? It wasn't enough to humiliate me in front of a thousand people, was it? Daddy too, and David—"

"What the hell are you talking about?"

"That simpering hussy on the White House lawn."

"She grabbed my hand and kissed it. What the hell could I do?"

"And the cheap blonde wife of that New York manufacturer? Who was doing the grabbing there?"

"I was being polite, that's all."

"You couldn't keep your filthy hands off her."

"He's a bounder, Felicia, and a cad. He's no damned good and I've told you so a thousand times." The commodore, no less astonished than Paige and delighted to find an ally, beamed and nodded as his daughter railed on. It was too much for Paige and he lashed back. Three vilely drunk fishwives could not have behaved more badly. Both David and the driver sat through it staring straight ahead all the way home.

Lizzie met them at the door, all smiles and sweet welcome and for a few moments in her innocent presence and with the aromatic promise of her smothered chicken dinner in the air, a truce seemed possible. But the commodore waved her inside and roared for brandy. Paige stopped her in her tracks. This was his home, he said, and he would give the orders. The commodore blustered back. It had been the home of Blatchfords for the past hundred and fifty years and he'd be damned if a cheap, conniving bastard of a Brooklyn thug was going to take it from him. Paige pushed him lightly and the commodore sat heavily on a comb-back Windsor chair too narrow for his buttocks and too fragile for his avoirdupois. It gave beneath him with an antique grace, its four splayed legs yielding equally, and there the commodore sat, unable to rise alone. David and the captain assisted him to his feet and guided him to a more substantial mooring. Lizzie retreated to her quarters and prayer. David turned on his heel and quietly said, "You're all acting like a bunch of silly, spoiled kids," and stalked out being careful not to slam the front door. Felicia called to him but it was too late or he chose not to hear. She raced sobbing up the stairs and this time a door did slam. It shook the commodore from his stuporous state and he rose from the sturdy velvet-covered Phyfe sofa calling her name. Marching grandly across the room to comfort her, he tripped on the rug and once more fell heavily.

Paige was too mad to be amused, too bitter to help the old man once more to his feet. He poured himself some brandy and turned on the radio and listened to the war news. News of the Coral Sea fight was being made known to the public and for several minutes he listened attentively, completely removed from the scene of disaster surrounding him. It was clear to him that the Japanese fleet had been stopped for the first time. His one regret was that he had not been there to deliver a blow.

He snapped off the news and stared unhappily at his father-in-law, now snoring noisily on the ancestral Sarouk. After debating the choices, he lifted the commodore's feet and dragged him to the foot of the stairs. He turned him and took a firm hold under the arms and pulled him up the stairs a step at a time and slung him on the bed in the guest room. He removed his shoes and loosened his collar and left him.

Felicia had locked herself in the sewing room. Paige rattled the knob.

"Open up." He kicked the door and threw his weight against

it. He hammered the panels with his fist and finally he stood there and for a furious minute cursed every Holt and Blatchford he could think of. He delivered a parting kick that twisted his ankle and still cursing he limped down the stairs.

In the dining room he poked a finger in the platterful of chicken. It had turned cold and greasy. He poured himself some brandy and went out to the front of the house and stood on the brick steps in the warm sticky night. Down the street in a parked car a couple stirred, moved apart and watched him reproachfully. He stared hard, hoping it was David, but it was not David and in a few minutes, the car drove off. *The hell with you*, he thought scowling. Least you could do is wait until it's decently dark. He leaned drunkenly against a white column and felt it yield slightly. *Termites*, he thought sourly, *eating away my life*.

He went inside, suddenly drowsy. The day's exertions had been more demanding than he expected and he remembered the doctor's final admonition about taking it easy for a while. Hell with the doctor. Hell with everybody. Felicia certainly had not helped the situation. Nor had David. Nor had any damned person or thing since he had come home. Every bone in his body ached to be at sea. Damn shore duty. Damn the commodore. Damn women. One minute a hero and a bum the next.

He felt the warm glow of the brandy inside him and he got to his room and threw off his clothes. He opened his briefcase and tried to read some of the classified information on recent aircraft carrier operations but the words danced and blurred and he put the manual aside. He closed his eyes. Damn Felicia. What the hell had got into her? Certainly not Hardtack Harry Paige. Not tonight. Big hero. What was it Mary Olsen had called him? He fell asleep trying to remember.

He heard David coming down the stairs and he went into the kitchen and removed the bacon from the skillet and drained it on layers of the *Washington Post*. They avoided looking at each other.

"Good morning, sir."

"Morning, David."

"Smells like real coffee."

"Lizzie's chicory? Hardly." He filled two cups and passed one to David and worried the eggs with a chipped spatula. "There's last night's corn muffins, still virgin." He served the eggs and bacon and watched his son dig in. He still could not reconcile this grave and taciturn midshipman with the image he had carried during the absent years. David when last seen had been about twelve or thirteen, redcheeked and touslehaired, playing John Paul Jones. His father's newly won commander's cap bright with its "scrambled eggs" on the black visor sat halfway over his ears and he had charged down the stairs with Paige's sheathed sword clattering between the balusters, chipping the venerable white paint as he flew by.

Seven years ago? Eight? David now—nineteen? How the hell was he supposed to know? Raising children was a mother's chore and he had too damned much to think about. Twenty? It hardly seemed possible, boy into man, just like that. Where was the in-between and if it was lost to him, wasn't it Felicia's fault, not his? She and her damned roots and the Blatchford-Holt fixation that kept her from him all those years. Certainly he had tried. In spite of the wretched peacetime pay and the strangling red tape, he had made it twice from duty to home. Both times under protest, he remembered, because Felicia had refused to budge. Not to Manila or Pearl and certainly not to that uncivilized frontier called California. Both times he had missed David—the first time because he was out of the country with his grandfather on a Navy mission and the second time at sea during his midshipman summer cruise.

But what he did remember and cherish was a wonderful Sunday morning spent with David at the Washington Zoo. He had been a lieutenant then, home from destroyer duty in the Atlantic, and it was David's fifth birthday. While Felicia slept, he and David fed peanuts to the elephants and made funny faces at the monkeys and stood respectfully before their highnesses, the lions, and saluted them. A fine memory, terribly alone.

Where have my forty-two years gone? And what have I to show for them? A few ribbons and a blow-hot, blow-cold wife and her idiot old man? David sipping coffee and silently hating me? Why the hell did *he* fail me last night? Come on, Paige. You know the answer to that one.

"Drink up," he said in a cracked voice, "and we'll talk."

"About what, sir?" The cup in midair. *Will he throw it? Let us see.*

"Time's running out, son, and before we go our separate ways

I'd like to leave you with a few pearls of salty wisdom. How are you getting to Annapolis this morning?"

"Train."

"A Navy pool car's picking me up at seven. I can run you out to Annapolis and still get to the Anacostia air station for my plane to Norfolk."

"No need for it, sir. Thank you."

"Okay then. Why'd you run out on us last night?"

"Had about all I could take, I guess."

"You're part of this family, David, whether you like it or not. It was a sorry show and I'm sorry it happened. But you're as involved as any of us and you don't solve these things by running away. I was looking forward to the evening with you. When I needed you, you were gone."

David remained silent and Paige drained his coffee and went on. "A mess it was and no fault of yours, but you shouldn't have run out. Maybe what I want to get across to you, David, is that things aren't as fouled up as they look. In spite of the bickering and occasional blasts, all really goes well with us Paiges. I want you to understand that."

"Yes, sir. Sorry I took off."

"I felt everyone had deserted me, everyone was against me. When the smoke cleared, the commodore had passed out, Mother was barricaded in the sewing room, you had shoved off." He grinned. "I was ready to scuttle the ship."

"I saw no sense in hanging around, sir. In another minute the commodore was going to blast me for my rank insubordination at the Newell party and I had no stomach for it. So I went back to the hotel and tried to reach Tod Newell. He'd asked me to dinner, you see, sir? But he had gone off and I settled for a hamburger at the canteen and came home."

"No booze? No broads?"

"I just came home, sir."

"I hardly know you, David."

"What's there to know?"

"The kind of guy you are—what you're like."

"I'm twenty. I weigh a hundred and fifty-eight. My eyes are blue."

"David, for Chri'sake—"

"What do you care what I'm like? Suppose I told you I write

poetry and Ellington's *Mood Indigo* makes me sad and every time I hear *Anchors Aweigh* I'm sick to my stomach. Is that what you want to know, Captain?"

"Yes, damn it, that's exactly what I want to know. If that's the way you are. But you don't need to be so damned hostile about it."

"Well, sir, now you know." He pushed back his chair. "I'm shoving off."

"Sit down."

"And that's an order, I suppose?"

"Sit down, David." He ran his hands wearily over his eyes. "No, it's not an order." David sat slowly and for a moment their eyes searched each other's. "Okay. I asked for it. It's what I deserve. Now do me the courtesy of staying a while longer and I'll get what I have to say off my chest. Sure. The years we could have had together are lost, but I swear to you they haven't been wasted. One way or another, you've grown up. You're a man and I'm proud, looking at you, hearing you speak out. And you couldn't have come of age at a timelier moment in your life."

"What do you mean, sir?"

Paige winced and gently said, "This 'sir,' David. Is it because I outrank you?"

"Are you serious?"

"You know damned well I'm serious."

"Then you must have forgotten. When I was a kid, it was one of the house rules."

"I don't remember any house rules."

"It was the commodore's rules. I just assumed they were yours as well."

"They're not and never have been. So knock it off."

"Yes, sir."

"Try 'Dad.' See how that works."

"Very well."

"Go on. Try it."

"Dad." He looked directly at his father. "Sound okay?"

"Sounds damned good. A hell of a lot better than 'sir.' That's the Blatchford-Holt fixation in you."

"Give me a little time. Maybe we'll both get used to it." His face broke into a warm smile so rare and genuine that Paige could have reached across the table and embraced him. Instead, he glanced

at his watch and rose and began to clear the dishes. "You asked
what I meant by a timely moment. It's simple. Here you are
cutting your eyeteeth on one hell of a war—a sea war. Most
career officers go through a lifetime without a war in which to
prove themselves. They're lost from sight like the rings in the
trunk of a tree. How many peacetime admirals can you name since
Sims? Or generals since Pershing? I mean big names that have
gone down in history. We know a few because it happens to be
our profession, but the average man in the street wouldn't know
a peacetime admiral from the doorman at the Ritz. And a four-
striper like me—a big man in my business? I'm no different than a
bus driver in the eyes of the average man. Without a war, David,
we're out of work. So lucky for both of us, we've got us a war
and it couldn't have happened at a better time. Me with a hot
carrier command and you ripe and ready for the business you've
been trained for."

"You call that lucky?"

"It's what we're here for."

"I don't think I'm lucky stepping into a war."

"Oh come on, David. It's the chance of a lifetime."

"For you, perhaps, but not for me."

"Then what the hell are you doing in the Naval Academy?"

"What's expected of me, I suppose." He moved restlessly. "Look,
you have got to get to your new command and I'm due back
at Annapolis. You don't want to get into this hassle now, do
you?"

"Get into it? Get into what hassle? All I want to know is what's
going on in that strange mind of yours."

"Well. You're not going to like what I have to say. All I ask
is that you hear it. That way you'll know how things stand. How
I feel."

"Fair enough."

"You just spoke of the Blatchford-Holt fixation. You didn't mention the new Paige cult. You're a big hero. Your picture's everywhere. And don't think I'm not proud of it—of you. Always have
been, Dad. But you weren't around to see it. Anyway, all I've
ever heard all my life is Navy this and Navy that until it came
out of my ears. I never cared for the idea and I've never had the
guts to say so. I've gone along with it because it was what was
expected of me. If I had a free choice, I'd quit today."

"And do what? Get drafted? Or join the Army?"

"I don't really know, except that I would be doing what I felt was right. Don't you see, it's *feelings* I'm talking about—not family tradition or patriotic duty. Feelings. What I would do if I weren't the product of what I am. No one ever asked me what I wanted to be. It was taken for granted. I was born with the anchor already tattooed on my behind." He stood up and carried the rest of the dishes to the sink. "This is no passing mood, Dad. This is how I've felt for years, through Severn, through the Academy. Who was I supposed to talk to? The commodore? He'd have me shot, most likely, or hung from the yardarm of *Old Ironsides.* Mother? She's in a dream world full of her antiques and her roses. She's terrified the commodore's going to ruin you and I'm hardly the one to snap her out of it. And you were always in Manila or Hawaii or Hong Kong. FPO San Francisco was as close as I could get. Not that I'm blaming you. Just that you should know how things were."

"I wrote you—"

"I know. I have a collection of picture postcards to prove it and a stamp album that died four years ago." He spoke now with new confidence. "You never got to read the letters I sent you, starting about four or five months ago."

"I haven't seen a letter from you in almost a year, son."

"Right after Pearl Harbor. You never saw them because I'd write 'em and tear 'em up. I had to unload my true feelings—somehow—put down exactly how I felt about everything—you, Mother, war—but then I'd ask myself, how the hell can I do this to the guy? The Navy's his whole life. There's something I better say right off, anyway. I admire you tremendously and would rather die than hurt you. I have the deepest respect for the way you've come up, really from nothing. You're a hell of a man, Dad, and the Navy and the whole world knows it. What you said about the rings of a tree will never apply to you because you're the tree itself. I wish I could be the son you want me to be. But I can only be what I am."

"And what are you, David?"

"Dad—I've shunned violence as far back in my life as I can remember. Kids fighting in a school yard used to make me sick. If I had to fight, I'd stand fast and take it but I would not cry. And now—" He stood up. "I better get going."

"There's still time, David." Paige rubbed his jaw. "Mother know about this?"

"She suspects something. Instinct, I suppose."

"Your grandfather?"

"I couldn't care less."

"That's encouraging."

"He's a tiresome, pompous bore and I avoid him. He rubs people the wrong way. He pushes little people around. He lives in a dream world of swords, sailing ships, and—I'm sorry."

"Oh no. Go right ahead."

"I suppose it was wrong to bait him yesterday, but somebody had to talk up."

"You sure as hell surprised him. Me, too."

"He's already notified me of his displeasure. I'll hear about it when I get back."

"Are you this outspoken around the Academy?"

"I say what I think. I always did." He smiled. "I think a bit before I say it, though."

"You speak out about the service, war, violence, so forth?"

"Mostly in bull sessions with the guys. Why not?"

"They'll lower the boom on you."

"They haven't yet. Is it because of the name?"

"Not mine, certainly. Blatchford or Holt, possibly. Hell, I don't know, maybe things have changed since my days. Just try to stay clear of the commodore."

"Dad, since I was a kid he's been ordering me around like I was his own personal boot. The times I've stood by at attention while he and Amos Flint sipped port and ran down the lists of their Navy ancestors, the brigs and frigates they commanded and the number of guns and the glorious maimed and dead and lost at sea until I could puke. I did, once."

"When was Flint here?"

"Lots of times. Mostly when he was at the War College; the last few times when he was attached to Operations and he had just made admiral. I came in from Annapolis once after the Army game in Philly, I remember we had a big party here."

"Like him?"

"A dressy type. Makes an impression, all right."

"A good tactician but no in-fighter, no guts. Lots of fancy footwork but a slow puncher. Sweet on your mother, you know, and not what you would call a Paige fan, since Mother picked me. Your grandfather hasn't recovered or forgiven me, either. As you've heard."

"That why he picks on me?"

"He's proud of you, David, and I'm sure he wants to see you make admiral and carry on the glorious Blatchford tradition. Wish to hell I'd known your feelings a long time ago. We should have talked and spent time together like ordinary fathers and sons. I should have been on hand, that's all. Now it's all down the drain. Let's face up to the situation as it exists. You sure you haven't spoken to anyone at the Academy or in the service about your feelings?"

"I've kept it to myself. And don't get me wrong. I'm doing my job. I'm in the top quarter of my class."

"I was at the tail end of mine."

"I know. But since the word is out on Sunda Strait, I'm suddenly a target. Newspaper interviews—all declined. But the attention from the old-timers would make you laugh. Hardtack Harry's boy, aren't you? Well, well, well. Knew your old man in old DesRonBat Div Whoozis back in Ought Three. We served under Old Charley Noble and believe me, I knew then that Ol' Hardtack was a winner. You know, Dad? That kind of stuff, day in, day out."

"Does it bother you?"

"I love it. Listen, all these years I've loved you. Remember the time we went to the Zoo?"

"I was thinking about it this morning."

"You make sense. You do exactly what you believe in. When you read off old man Newell yesterday, I could have hugged you. It was a cheap trick, asking you to intercede for Tod. He heard. He knew what was coming. Maybe that was why I walked out last night. I couldn't face Mother and the commodore after what they did to you."

"Thanks for that, David."

"But I'm no chip off the old block, am I?"

"You speak your mind. Right now, it worries me."

"I'd have sworn you'd hit the ceiling when you heard what I had to say. Cuss me out, threaten me, maybe issue a few orders and demand a few salutes."

"Look, David, I'm going to level with you. I will do everything I can to help you, but you're sure as hell heading for trouble and it scares me. What happens next? You graduate and get a combat assignment and what do you do? What kind of line officer can you be, torn between your feelings and your duty? I sure as hell wouldn't want a junior officer like that in my command."

"Don't you believe there are men with deep beliefs—deep enough to be contrary to the work they do, who go through the motions just the same because it has to be done?"

"Why the hell should they?"

"For all sorts of reasons. Thoreau says 'Most men lead lives of quiet desperation.' It's just that there can be other considerations that for practical purposes outweigh the deep beliefs."

"Then they're not deep beliefs, son, they're delusions. If you believe in something deeply enough, you honor it. You stand ready to die for it. You don't betray it."

"You know what you're saying?"

"I'm telling you that if you feel the way you do deeply enough, you should resign from the Academy. You can't honor both your deepest feelings and your duty. It's one or the other."

"You're really asking for trouble."

"I'm asking only that you be honest with yourself."

"I couldn't do that to you."

"The hell with me. I can take care of myself."

"Do you know what they'd do to you? What a field day it would give that friend of the family, Amos Flint—how much mileage would he get out of that choice scandal?"

"The hell with Flint and the rest of the goldbraid politicians. They're no skin off my ass. I've been trained all my life to do a job and I've learned to do it well and they know it. I like to think I learned it a little better than the next fellow, picked up a few extra tricks here and there to keep me alive a little longer. My work is war. I don't hate it and I don't love it. I didn't invent it and I don't preach it, but somebody has got to take care of it when it comes along."

"You happen to be damn good at it."

"Thanks, son. When it comes right down to it, most men are lily-livered and gutless and too slow to protect themselves. So they feel perfectly justified in hiring professionals to do the nasty job for them. Obviously, it's a task that goes against your grain and I respect you for speaking out about it. But speaking out isn't enough. You've got to go all the way. Don't expect it to change a single thing, though. Man's murdered man since Cain killed Abel. You expect him to stop now?"

"Funny, you should say that."

"Why not? There's always a war someplace in the world and if there isn't, it's just a breathing spell before the next one."

"And that's the world I'm stepping into."

"Why should it be otherwise? It's man's nature to fight and if it isn't why doesn't God strike us all dead? What's He waiting for —Hitler to do the job? Why doesn't he strike Hitler dead? And if there's no God to strike Hitler dead, who's around to do the job?"

"I don't know. You're confusing me."

"I'll be the first to retire when the honest answer to war comes along, David. I swear it. Meanwhile, millions are dying in Nazi concentration camps and more millions are being trampled to death by the Jap and I'm damned happy to be on hand to stop it, to kill those who kill without reason. In this day and age, it's an honorable calling."

"I say we're better off dead. Why go on?"

"Because there's more to life than war and death."

"I've yet to see it in my time."

"I'm not about to argue philosophies with you, David. It's not my line. I don't care if you give up the Navy. It's your life to live. All I say as a father is, find some kind of life for yourself that is fulfilling. I've found mine and while it's no bed of roses, it's what I like best. Find out what's best for you and fight like hell to have it. Life's too damn short. If we can't make it a happy one, maybe you're right. Maybe we're all better off dead."

"You missed your calling. You'd have made an awfully good chaplain."

"That's also part of my job. Now what about it, David?"

"What do you recommend?"

"Resign."

"It'll raise all kinds of hell."

"Mother can take it. If we're lucky, the commodore might catch permanent heartburn."

"It's you I care about, Dad."

Paige went to him knowing in that moment how much he loved the boy. He put an arm across David's shoulder. "Nobody's going to hurt me, not you, or Mother or the Blatchfords and

Flints and Newells or the whole cockeyed world." He held up his two fists. "That's what I live by, David. Here, at sea, anywhere. They're all I need."

"You're strong. I envy you."

"You're strong too, David. You can prove it."

"I can. I will. There's nothing to stop me now."

two
U.S.S. SHILOH

26

The duty Marine officer at the shipyard's security gate checked Paige's orders and saluted and waved the jeep driver in. The word was passed by phone to *Shiloh*'s quarterdeck. In moments, a signalman stood by the flag bags with the crisp new halyards in his fist, ready to lower the commanding officer's absentee pennant for the first time. Informed of the captain's arrival, the executive officer in his cabin breathed a prayer of thanks, smoothed his wrinkled khakis and made his way to the quarterdeck. The word passed through the ship like swift fire.

Paige's jeep threaded its way through the maze of streets past warehouses piled with crates and cartons, past wire-fenced acres of anchors and buoys, past stacked life rafts painted the dark blue-gray of winter seas. Giant gantry cranes on tracks swung steel plates mast high and lowered them to gloved hands gently. Noise was king. Sparks flung themselves in cascading showers and died. At each turn public address speakers blared raucous messages. Paige thought he caught the word *Shiloh* and his heart leaped. Men toiled. Women in slacks pedaled past on urgent bicycles. No children were to be seen. The racket of tools and steam, machines and shouts, filled Paige with wonder and joy. He rammed the driver in the ribs. "What's taking so long?"

"We're almost there, Captain."

And round one corner and another, there she was. *Shiloh*.

Paige grabbed the top of the windshield and stared up, up. *My God*, he thought, *how do you conn a big bastard like that?*

"Stop here," he said.

"The gangway's just ahead, Captain."

"Deliver my gear to the officer of the deck. I'll go aboard in a few minutes."

"Aye, sir."

Paige climbed from the jeep and watched it head toward the gangway two hundred yards distant. Decks and dockside were scenes of enormous activity. Cargo nets swung stores to the hangar bays from barges that hemmed *Shiloh*'s outboard side. A nearby working party, naked to the waist, handpassed five-inch ammunition to the open hoists where it was struck below. Paige took shelter from the sun in the cavernous doorway of a maintenance building smelling sweetly of steel shavings and lubricating oil. He removed his cap and wiped the damp sweatband.

Here at last. The giant flesh and bones, the steel skin and teeth of her. He knew he might never see her again like this and he stood silent and tense for a few moments, drinking it in. *One minute alone is not asking too much*, he told himself.

Not fifty yards away, *Shiloh*'s bow swept upward with the simple deadly grace of a scimitar. At its apex in the shadow of the flight deck's overhang it flared into a circular steel enclosure housing two mounts of quadruple Bofors 40-millimeter antiaircraft guns. Eight black flash guard muzzles aimed skyward. A crew in dungarees and khaki clambered about, squinting through optical instruments and shouting "Stand by!" and "Mark!" emphasized by obscenities appropriate to the delicate and exacting task of aligning and boresighting complicated weapons in a summer's forenoon sun.

Following the ship's lines aft, Paige's eye took in the bristling array of more Bofors 40s on the gallery decks between rows of 20-millimeter Swiss Oerlikons and the powerful dual purpose five-inch guns. On the island structure, a duty signalman stood by the absentee pennant at the dip, and high above, in a jungle of radar antennae at the peak of the mainmast, a yard technician calmly went about his business.

She was all the ship he ever wanted. *How the hell can I lose?* he wondered and set his cap at a jaunty angle and without another glance upward, strode to the gangway.

Seen from aloft by the radar technician, he was an insignificant figure like hundreds of others, dwarfed by the hugeness of everything around him.

Paige sat with his executive officer in his spotless captain's cabin and listened to the verbal report of *Shiloh*'s readiness for sea. The exec was a gray-eyed Texan named Lobo Logan. He had a bony face with weathered cheeks and a broad thin line for a mouth. His eyes were red-rimmed with fatigue and Paige decided he would do something about leave for Logan before he did anything else.

Logan had a wife from Brownsville, Texas, now in a rundown room at Virginia Beach—a freckled blonde who golfed in the low eighties, who never drank, who was as barren as a stone. Paige would never know about it. Logan was a taciturn man, all business.

He delivered his report with a marked absence of small talk and with enough quiet authority to assure Paige that in his absence, his command duties had been performed as though he had been aboard himself. Paige had heard from the commodore that Logan had been hand-picked by Admiral Nickelby to serve as his second in command in *Shiloh*. Checking the record, he learned that Logan had been transferred to *Shiloh* in April from duty as air group commander in *Wasp* when she had been made available to the British in the defense of Malta. Logan had then been assigned to temporary duty at Quonset Point, Rhode Island, in charge of the precommissioning training of the ship's company, then being assembled. He acted in Paige's capacity through the daily business of division organization and the assignment of duties to the various departments. He had stood in for Paige during the commissioning ceremonies two weeks ago and just now was bringing him up to date on the personnel situation. He handed Paige a copy of the mimeographed roster of officers, and kept one himself.

"Heads of departments are aboard with the exception of two— Commander Miller LeClair, the air officer, and the navigator, Commander Joe Allen. LeClair's with the air group at Patuxent and Allen's taking the observer's course at Pensacola and won't report for two weeks. These other department heads have been working with yard personnel and BuShips on armament, power, hull, and so forth and holding general drills daily for the entire crew. You've got Fillmore in Gunnery; Meserve, Engineering; Vaughn, Communications; Thornton, Hull; Duntley, Supply. All three-stripers.

The ship's medical officer is Commander Moore. The flight surgeon's off with the air group at Patuxent. I don't have his name and the air group roster isn't complete yet."

"When do we get 'em?"

"They fly aboard when we shove off for shakedown. The scuttlebutt is, we go to Trinidad."

He indicated two piles of papers on Paige's desk. "The left-hand file is copies of dispatches I signed in your absence plus other official and semiofficial stuff. The big pile is personal mail, nothing to do with the ship's business that I could see. Anything I was sure was outright junk, I gave the deep six. Could be you'll put me under hack for it, but, Captain, you never in your life saw such a waste of Navy time, manpower, and money. And with each sack of mail we take aboard, it multiplies quicker 'n jack-rabbits."

He consulted his notes. "There's a few odds and ends and more'n likely I'll be thinking of things from time to time. The yard supervisor and his people have been damn cooperative, trying to get us out of here. Everybody's under a lot of pressure with tempers rubbed raw and I try to stay out of things not rightly our responsibility and let the technical fellows handle it. Anything looks fishy and I go to the commandant. Intelligence and the FBI and the yard police are in and out, sniffing for trouble and there's all kinds of goldbraid wanting visiting privileges for their kids and out-of-town guests. On a weekend you'd think it was a carnival show we were running and not a fighting ship. And there's the usual, drunks, jailbirds, and a few over the hill."

"Any real problems?"

"Captain Paige, sir, I'm keeping my fingers crossed. The dock trials and inspection teams have been over her from stem to stern with a fine tooth comb and the changes they been recommending seem nothing more than nit-picking. From what I hear, the boys at BuShips are happy as clams. The fire-control people are still working on the cut-out and limit-of-fire stops on those new forties and twenties but they should finish up before the week's out. No, sir, far as I can judge, there are no real problems."

"I took a look around from the dock and there's enough AA stuff topside to shoot the sky down."

"We sure can use it, sir. The old stuff on the *Wasp* didn't have power enough, excuse me, to push a sick whore off of a bed pan.

And the dual five-inch are checked out and ready to go. If there's a trouble spot, I reckon it'll be the catapults. They been having the worse run of luck, all kinds of production and delivery snags and as of 0800 this morning, we still have no catapults."

"I saw the port catapult track on the flight deck and a crew installing the starboard one."

"It's the below decks machinery that's fouling us up. Without it the flight deck tracks are as useless as a piss-hole in a snowbank. Meanwhile, COMINCH has been hollering for your progress and readiness report and I worked up a rough draft to date, ready for you to look over." He handed Paige a thick folder. "The heads of departments all worked with me on it and after you check it out, sir, we'll put the yeoman on it for typing."

"How's the crew size up?"

"Green, but not too bad. Looks like we go to sea with maybe seventy percent enlisted reserves. And out of that, maybe fifty percent with no previous sea duty."

"And what about officers?"

"Runs about the same. We're short qualified deck officers to stand even the in-port top watches. Just this morning a jaygee off of your old command *Gloucester* reported aboard and right off I assigned him to stand a top watch. But I hated to do it."

"Newell? Won't hurt him."

"With all the newspaper publicity and such, I thought you might want him elsewhere."

"That's your first mistake." Paige grinned. "I was beginning to think you weren't human, you're so damned efficient. Hell no. Newell's like everybody else on board. He has a job to do and he damn well better do it. You, too. Me, too."

"Suits me fine, Captain. I reckon that about covers the situation to date, except to say how glad I am personally to see you on board."

"Thank you, Commander. Now here's my first order to you. You're to take forty-eight hours rest and recreation commencing tomorrow morning immediately after muster on the flight deck."

"Thank you kindly, Captain. I don't think I had ought to do it, though. The way things stand right now."

"It's an order, Commander. You're bushed. You been holding down double duty long enough. Get out to the beach and chase a few broads and swig a few drinks."

"I do that, Captain, and Mrs. Logan'd skin me alive." He seemed confused for a moment. "There was a Lieutenant Commander Faygill called this morning from Public Relations. Said it was urgent, he had to see you this morning without fail."

"Lieutenant Commander Faygill's business isn't urgent and he'll be taken care of in due time. Anything else?"

"No, sir, unless you want to reconsider that forty-eight hour rest and recreation."

"Hell no. You've earned it." He flipped a few pages of Logan's report, reading at random. "How'd you find the time to put this all together?"

"Bits and pieces. There's no shut-eye on board with the yard crews working around the clock. And I figure *you* earned it, Captain. You been having no ball where you were."

"I've had all the rest and recreation I can take. Set up a meeting with the heads of departments for eight tonight."

"Some of 'em have requested permission to leave ship tonight and I granted it."

"Cancel it. All I need is forty minutes to say my piece and take a turn through the ship. Now give me a few hours to plow through the mail, the dispatches, and your report. Don't I have a steward?"

"He's ashore after supplies, Captain."

"Any good?"

"A Chamorro from Guam name of Valdez. Gold hashmarks to his chin. I'd say damned good."

"What's he weigh?"

"Weigh, sir?"

"Bantam, welter, lightweight?"

"Maybe one-thirty, soaking wet."

"I'll fatten him up. Thank the orderly for stowing my gear. I'm short a lot of stuff and I'll have Valdez pick some things up at ship's service. Who's the orderly?"

"Marine private first class, name of Shane. The detachment commander, Captain Bonelli, hand-picked him. Your chief yeoman in the office is a salty Jewboy name of Marcus. They tell me he is so good he can type with both feet. He was with me in the old *Langley* and he knows carrier command routine from Able to Zebra."

"Keep the pack off my heels until I'm through this report. Just bring me up to date so I can relieve you."

"Very well. We're moored portside to Pier Eight in the James River. Ship's in Condition Three, no guns manned, all departments conducting general drills. Boilers two, four, and eight are on the line in standby condition. Yard crews are aboard, working parties are loading ammunition forward and stores aft. Smoking lamp is out and—let's see—the captain's on board and in his cabin."

Paige grinned. "One question, Commander. If all hell broke loose like it did at Pearl, how do we stand?"

"We could cut all lines, dump yard workers, and shove off in two hours. Give a damn good account of ourselves, too."

"Very well. And well done." Paige saluted. "You're relieved."

Logan sagged ever so slightly and saluted back. "Welcome aboard, Captain. And I mean *welcome*."

Paige sat behind the shut door of his cabin, struggling with the readiness report for COMINCH. He had met with Valdez who was disappointingly small and frail. Paige outlined his preference for simple food well cooked and the instant availability of hot coffee, strong and black, round the clock.

Marcus arrived shortly after Valdez had been sent below for clothing to replace what Paige had lost in Sunda Strait. Marcus was everything Logan had said and Paige liked him at once. In stern language he made it clear to Marcus that his duties as chief yeoman depended not alone on his ability to type with both feet, but also on his ingenuity in procuring from the various shore establishments a continuing supply of lox, cream cheese, bagels, halvah, and occasional windfalls of skinless boneless sardines. "I'm a Brooklyn boy myself," Paige told him. "So I happen to know all about these things."

"I have a cousin in Flatbush," Marcus said with a puzzled shrug. "But I was born in Buffalo."

Paige went back to the report. The flow of air through the overhead ducts annoyed him and did little to cool the room. A metalsmith and a pipefitter came in response to his complaint and after a few minutes of tinkering and saluting, they left, promising immediate results. The results were more than Paige had bargained for. With a whining screech, a blast of air with wind-tunnel force sent his papers flying. He ordered the ventilation system to his cabin shut down and he turned back to his work.

He sat naked and worked sullenly for the next three hours. He drank iced coffee from a tall glass stamped with the same blue Navy anchor insignia tattooed on his arm. When he drank, the coffee dripped, trailing crooked rivulets in the matted hair of his chest. He read and corrected and scribbled and sipped and thought, what a fine war it would be without the goddam paper work. He gnawed the pencil tip, frustrated but with growing admiration for the job Logan had done. He tried not to think of Oley Olsen.

Power tools pounded and chattered on the decks about and below. The bulkheads shook. Several times he heard Shane politely and firmly turn visitors from his door. His phone did not ring and he knew Logan had given the order. At noontime he waved off Valdez's tray and called for a fresh towel. When he had the report done to his satisfaction, he tackled the dispatch file and finally the stack of personal mail.

The bulk of it had been forwarded from BuPers and dated back to the earliest mention of his name in newspaper reports of the action in Sunda Strait. He was surprised to see how much of it came from people he did not know and had never met. He read some of the letters. A few were fervent with praise. Several were openly ardent. Some were vicious and others obscene. He stopped opening them and shoveled the pile—envelopes, letters, news clippings, proposals of marriage, tinted photos—into the wastebasket.

He had put one letter aside, a special delivery postmarked Brooklyn the day before, addressed to him in his mother's spiky unmistakable scrawl. He tore it open.

Dearest Son Harrison I see where our beloved Democrat President Franklin Delano Roosevelt may God preserve him gave you this great Honor on the front page of the Journal American news clipping inclosed and I am writing to say it hurt me something terrible you not inviting me to the Affair or any word about it after all Im still your Mother your own flesh and blood no matter what is come between us since you married that Washington DC society snob she never once answered a word I wrote her and no thank you for the wedding present the pair of solid silver miniture cuspidors with both

your initials intwined which I had to pay extra in all those
years Well just the same Im proud of your great success son
it comes as no surprise you were made for great things
born in a caul under the sign of Aries by nature fiery hot and
dry and the diurnal House of Mars how could you miss Well
Son Harrison it would do my heart good to see you I am
not well since we lost out to this crazy Mayor and Brooklyn
politics gone to H—— pardon the expression But what can you
expect from a Mayor hes part wop part sheeny a lunatic so
Im stuck in this ward till things change for the better please
God At least Im still alive which reminds me your face is
terribly skinny in that newspaper picture I hope and pray you
are taking good care of yourself and eating nourishing food
where you are and once in a while drop your old Mother
a penny postal and let me know how your getting along The
allotment check comes regular you are a good Son from Your
Ever Loving Mother

Rose Maloney Paige

PS They were meant to be used for ash trays Maybe she is too
dumb to know it but I forgive her being she is your wife

The old girl's gone soft around the edges, he thought. He leaned
back and closed his eyes and there she was, a portly, wheezing
fortress of corsets and stays, through whose primary defense of
pearl gray bombazine and pink silk, he could always detect the
unabashed presence of huge and familiar nipples. He could hear
the deep hacking cough trapped in phlegm and taste the odd sweet
mixture of cologne and gin that marked her presence. For a few
moments he yielded himself to a euphoric nostalgia, strangely gratifying in the midst of the tools and thunder of a wartime shipyard.

Downtown Brooklyn in those days had been an adventuresome
place for a boy who liked to roam. The Paige apartment occupied
the first-floor front of a brownstone in the borough's tenderloin,
and Rose's parlor a gathering place for its top cream politicians. Rose
Maloney had been born there and as Rose Maloney Paige, she
had the run of the ward. The house brimmed over with beefy
Irish aldermen in hard derbies who, in their cups, would tearfully
uselessly plead with Rose to give up her renegade shame and
come back to the Church. The boy would never forget the softness

of the picture-hatted, ripe-bosomed ladies with perfumed Pekingese
in their arms. They cuddled him and whispered words that made
him blush and touched him naughtily until he squirmed away confused and strangely excited.

She took him wherever they went and no one minded. Supper
parties at Lundy's and Rector's. Down Ocean Parkway in an
open carriage, young Harry snuggled under bearskins among the
tangle of beefy silken legs. Later, poorer, she still took him along.
Rides to Coney Island on the elevated Culver Line, returning under
summer stars past dank scary verdant Greenwood Cemetery. Swims
in Gravesend Bay at Captain's Pier, the Goldman Band concerts
in Prospect Park. And growing up, poorer still, his mother a fierce
and loving presence until he finished high school. Then pick-up
jobs, the clink of money in his pockets, saloons and toughs near
Borough Hall, the Sand Street cribs, the *DeWitt Clinton* of the
Hudson River Day Line to Bear Mountain, his first amateur fight
at Bushwick Oval and his picture in the *Brooklyn Daily Eagle*.
The glow of triumph in her eyes when she waved his hard-bought
Annapolis appointment under his nose.

And always the mystery of Paige.

He wiped his eyes and glared at the dead blower system. He
tore her letter to bits and got up and stared at his face in the
mirror. Skinny hell. The old girl's bats. For the next few minutes
he danced about the cabin shadowboxing briskly, pausing from time
to time to make a brief inspection of a new fitting or detail. He
wound the bulkhead chronometer and tested phone circuits to various parts of the ship. The cabin continued to delight him. The
Waldorf-Astoria, he told himself, compared to *Gloucester*.

He tried a locked door alongside the bedroom on the after bulkhead and wondered what it was for. None of his keys fitted the lock.
He made a note to ask Logan about it. Valdez came in to set
the table for dinner and in his trips to and from the pantry, Paige
still appraised him hopefully as a substitute sparring partner for Lee
Chin.

He polished off Valdez's dinner in minutes and spent the remainder of the time reading over the revised report. At ten of eight
Vaughn, the communications officer, appeared and introduced himself. He apologized for being early but explained that it seemed
a good time to get the late dispatches out of the way. One in

particular seemed important enough to warrant the captain's immediate attention.

The message in code had originated at the office of the Chief of Naval Operations in Washington. It stated that Admiral Maury Nickelby, CINCPAC, with members of his staff, planned to visit *Shiloh* for a brief inspection the following noon. The visit would be informal and unofficial. It was requested that the customary honors and etiquette attendant on an admiral's visit be eliminated this time. The absence of CINCPAC from the Pacific area was top secret information.

Paige initialed the dispatch and invited Vaughn to a seat and coffee. Commander Logan arrived followed by the other heads of departments. Introductions were made and Paige quickly got down to business. He expressed his regrets for not being aboard during the commissioning ceremony. He complimented them on their conscientious devotion to their duties, the preparedness of their crews and equipment, and the ship's apparent degree of readiness for sea. He reported the executive officer's estimate of two hours to get the ship under way and in fighting trim. He hoped there would be no emergencies to test that estimate and pending his inspection, he saw no reason not to accept it.

He would give each of them a free hand in running his department. One thing, however, must be made clear: *Shiloh* would be the best fighting ship in the fleet. There must be no compromise, no alibis, no excuses. To achieve this goal must be the aim of every officer and enlisted man on board, and the prime and direct responsibility for it lay with the heads of departments. This was an order. He was aware that *Shiloh* was the prototype, the name ship of her class and there was bound to be error and even tragedy before she would be the perfect fighting machine he wanted her to be.

"There are many unpredictables, gentlemen, and we're the guinea pigs for the other carriers now on the ways. We're larger and heavier than the *Enterprise*, smaller and lighter than the *Sara*. Until we get the hang of her, we can expect problems in ship handling, seamanship, the use of the flight deck and propulsion machinery, all the fancy new radar and fire-control equipment, and so forth. I expect there will be errors but not the same error twice. Is that clear?"

He studied their intent expressions. "I don't know what you've heard about me as a skipper. I'm informing you for the record that I'm a strict one and I try to be a fair one. I believe in a taut ship and a happy one. Too often that term 'happy ship' is a sad excuse for a sloppy ship, loosely run, its readiness uncertain and the invitation to accident and sudden death wide open. If I had to choose between a taut ship and a happy one, I'd take the taut ship every time. Every taut ship I've served in has been a happy one. To make the point—this morning I observed a working party shirtless. In the future, all hands will wear the required uniform of the day. Any questions?"

There were none. He relaxed slightly. "I'll let you in on a secret. It's no accident each one of you is here. I know a bit more about you than you may suspect. Take Thornton here. Damage control officer aboard the *West Virginia* at Pearl on December seventh last. He's the guy you read about, whose quick thinking and fast orders to counter flood allowed the old *Weavie* to settle up-right on the bottom. Saved hundreds of lives, right, Commander? That's Herb Fillmore over there, our gunnery officer. Skippered a 'bird' class minesweeper last Christmas in Sulu Bay and fought off three separate air attacks with nothing but a couple of 50-calibre machine guns. Shot down three, wasn't it, Guns?"

"It was a Negro mess attendant, Benjamin by name, who had the eagle eye, Captain. I had headaches enough at the wheel, chasing the bomb splashes."

"Commander Meserve, chief engineer, is a Maine Yankee and just a month ago was mere Lieutenant Commander Meserve in the *Lex*'s black gang in the Coral Sea. What I'm telling you about the Coral Sea is still restricted information and no word of it leaves this cabin, but Meserve was able to turn up twenty-five knots in spite of torpedo hits, three boilers out, and internal explosions. I might add that the same modest gentleman canceled his well-earned shore leave for a billet here. I'm not going to embarrass any more of you with praise, but I want you to know how things stand. Our navigator isn't aboard yet. His name's Joe Allen, he's a mustang who was with me when we lost *Gloucester*. Air officer's with the air group which we'll pick up during shakedown. He's Miller LeClair off *Yorktown*. He skippered a bomber group and was one of the guys responsible for sinking a Jap light carrier and raising hell with a couple of their big ones. We still don't have the final word on that Coral Sea action.

"So you're pretty special to me, gentlemen. When I was laid up in Pearl I went through more than two hundred record jackets to find the kind of men I wanted to serve with me. I got what I wanted and, in some cases, it was grand larceny. Now let's get on with that inspection. It'll give me firsthand information for the progress and readiness report and expedite our shoving off. I don't enjoy shipyard life any more than you. That's it for now. Let's have a look at the old girl."

They started below decks, led by a gravel-voiced master-at-arms. They went through the power plant and engineering spaces, the crew's living quarters, supply and damage control areas, the ammunition storage and the air and gunnery nerve centers. Paige opened hatch covers, peered into workshops, tested watertight doors, asked endless questions. He visited sick bay, chief's quarters and the library, where he called the chaplain "padre" and chatted with a few enlisted men. Occasionally he muttered a few words to Logan who jotted them down.

On the hangar deck, the forward elevator had been lowered and a basketball game was in progress. About fifty men sat above, on the flight deck, watching the game through the opening created by the lowered elevator. "I like that," Paige said. "Keeps the men in shape and happy. What about volleyball? You've got all the room in the world here for athletics."

Logan made notes. The party moved aft where air crewmen were still working.

Paige stood by while the port side deck edge elevator was raised and lowered and he timed it with a stop watch. He carefully studied the location of the spare aircraft fuselages and parts triced overhead to the supporting members of the flight deck.

His quick eye seemed to miss nothing. The promised forty minutes became an hour and a half. It was almost ten o'clock before Paige relented and dismissed the inspection party. He retired with Logan to his cabin and called Valdez for iced coffee. He indicated the locked door alongside his bedroom. "Any idea what's in there, Commander?"

"No, Captain."

"Everything here checks out with the blueprints except that damned door. None of the keys you gave me fits it."

"Wasn't any, sir. I'll have the metal shop turn out one in the morning."

"You're shoving off in the morning. I'll take care of it. It's damned odd not having it in the ship's plans. Who's next senior officer?"

"Fillmore, Captain."

"He'll be acting exec, then, and I'll let him worry about it." He swallowed his drink thirstily and picked up Logan's notes and studied them. "A few things bother me, but we can talk about them when you're back aboard. Heads of departments look four-oh. See that the uniform of the day ruling is carried out. We've got to look smart. And pretty soon somebody's going to catch hell about this lousy blower system. It just doesn't work. That's about it, Lobo. Maybe I'll stretch my legs and hike over to the officers' club."

"We got us a jeep and driver assigned to you, Captain."

"I can use the exercise. I'll be back before midnight. Leave the plan of the day on my desk. See that Marcus types up these notes. After 0800 tomorrow morning, Lobo, I don't want to see hide nor hair of you for forty-eight hours."

Logan drained his iced drink and reached for the phone to notify the quarterdeck. Paige put on his cap and straightened his tie. Going out, he stared once again at the locked door. "Beats me," he muttered.

They went through the passageway and up the ladder, Paige leading. He paused at the hangar deck level. "You hit it damn close when you estimated two hours, Lobo. I think maybe we can trim that figure to an hour and a half." He shoved out his hand. "I'm a lucky skipper having you on board."

Logan could do little more than mumble his thanks. His grip made Paige wince.

It was bright as day under the floodlights topside. Quarterdeck personnel snapped to attention. The captain was pleased to see that Tod Newell was OOD and had managed to muster four sideboys for his departure. "Looks like we're winning the custody battle, eh, Mr. Newell?"

"My father doesn't give up that easily, Captain."

"Maybe he thinks that Navy 'E' he won gives him equal privileges with admirals."

"I wouldn't know, Captain."

"In any event, you're here and it's his move. Welcome aboard, Commander Logan knows where I can be reached."

"Aye, Captain."

Newell watched Paige descend the gangway. The quarterdeck resumed its usual routine, distracted only by the yard crews changing shifts and the shouts of the basketball players. He reviewed the luckless day.

He had reported aboard that morning with a hangover and feelings of guilt. He could not shake the conviction that he had deserted Stick Wilson in a time of need. He brooded uneasily on his father's next course of action. The shipboard confusion dismayed him and the jarring din of pneumatic tools did little to help his jittery nerves. He needed things to do to keep his mind occupied and he welcomed the executive officer's announcement that he would be standing the evening watch.

His living quarters were on the starboard side, third deck forward. After stowing his gear, he consulted the ship's organization and the watch, quarter and station bills. He had been assigned duties as the sixth division officer. His watch station was on the bridge as an officer of the deck and his battle station was Sky One in command of the ship's antiaircraft guns. During the noon meal, he met the junior officer assigned to the sixth division, an ensign named Rowe. Rowe was a Princeton graduate, a chubby, red-headed extrovert. Newell liked him at once.

Rowe had proceeded from midshipman school to the precommissioning detail at Quonset Point and was well-acquainted with the enlisted men in the division. They went below and Rowe introduced Newell to the division's chief petty officer. After an inspection of the division's living and cleaning spaces, Rowe and Newell went topside to Sky One.

They climbed the ladders of the island structure to the exposed deck above the navigation bridge. Newell swung himself over the splinter shield and took a look about. The scene of shipyard activity stretched as far as he could see, a jungle of steel masts and cables, steam, clouds, and sky. A Navy tug nosed a stripped cruiser hull into the stream. Newell looked down at *Shiloh*'s flight deck, big as three football fields. Men in dungarees were painting lines in different colors. Marine gunners were running through drills on the gallery deck alongside, loading and unloading dummy clips of twenty-millimeter ammunition. He looked aft and just below Sky Two a team of fire controlmen were making last-minute adjustments to the Mark XIV sights on the new forty-millimeter gun directors.

The sun bore down and Newell, discussing phone circuits with

Rowe, felt curiously dizzy and removed his cap. He stared upward where the radar technician leaned dangerously from the swaying bosun's chair to tighten the fittings of a bedspring-shaped antenna. Newell's heart began to pound and the swaying figure aloft dazzled his eyes. I have been here before, he thought, startled, and in the heat of the day the yard clamor became the screams of maimed shipmates and the chatter of their tools gunfire from enemy torpedo boats. Horrified, he saw the radar technician plummet headlong like Hurley in his death dive during *Gloucester's* last moments. Newell covered his eyes and reeled against the bulkhead. His knees buckled and he sank to the deck. His fingers gripped the edge of the shield and he clung to it until his head cleared.

Rowe bent over him, badly frightened and unwilling to touch him. "You all right, sir?"

Newell nodded slowly, not trusting his voice. His mouth was sour with bile and he wiped his chin. His body was drenched with perspiration. He could feel the thin fabric of his uniform clinging to his skin.

"I'm okay now." He got to his feet and looked aloft where the radar technician was still at work. Newell put on his cap. "The damned heat," he said. Rowe still stared at him and Newell grinned feebly. "Too much booze last night and no sleep." *That should do it*, he thought. A language familiar to the boys at Princeton, a language everyone understands.

"You sure handed me a scare," Rowe said.

Newell made it very steadily to the ladder. "I'll sack out for a while. Get me some shut-eye. That'll do the trick." They parted on the hangar deck and he said, "I'd be grateful, Rowe, if you wouldn't mention this to anyone."

Alone, he began to tremble. He went below and lay on his bunk thinking it was going to take more than rest to do the trick. His heart still pounded and he undressed and went down the passageway and showered and this time when he got back on his bunk, he slept. He slept through mealtime and was still asleep when the officer of the deck's messenger awakened him for the evening watch. He dressed and went to the quarterdeck feeling much refreshed.

Shortly after Captain Paige left the ship, the basketball game broke up. The ship quieted down and Newell in the glare of the floodlights was grateful for a brief respite from men's shouts and the deafening dialogue of steel with steel. It gave him time to think. The occurrence in Sky One troubled him and he tried to analyze the phenomenon of *deja vu* that had triggered it. He was sensible enough to know that he had been through an experience aboard *Gloucester* nerve-shattering enough to destroy men of lesser resource than his own. He had never doubted (until now) his own strength of mind. It must have been sheer coincidence that he had identified a man aloft with the image of Hurley lodged in his memory. Those quirks of the mind you read about, he told himself. It could have been sheer fatigue and lack of sleep. It could have been a mild sunstroke. He had sweated out any number of tennis matches in worse shape than this, with less sleep and more booze, under hotter suns, and his knees had not quit and his vision had not blurred. His last medical checkup had been fine and he was in better shape right now than he had ever been, his mind clear, his legs and wrists strong, his belly flat and hard.

What had happened then? Had his problems ganged up on him? Certainly, his relationship with his father was not conducive to great peace of mind but he had lived with that ulcer too long to let it throw him now.

It was too bad it had happened and it was not exactly what the Navy would recommend to inspire trust and confidence in one's junior officer. He would straighten Rowe out once they were at sea. That was what he needed most, to get back to sea again, free of parental pressure and the claptrap of civilians, back to the clean, uncluttered sea routine.

He looked about him at the wild confusion of tools and mechanical gadgetry and all the light and heavy machinery alien to the honest running of a ship and it occurred to him that in its seeming harmlessness, in the well-meaning hands of these yardworkers (many of them half-trained or not at all) these innocent objects could be instant death and in that moment under the pitiless floodlights he saw clearly that the twisted coils of brightly colored wire and cables were the shiny insides of torn men.

He turned away sharply and walked to the gangway and stared at the murky reflections between the dock and the ship's side. The quarterdeck crew seemed to watch him curiously and with a great effort he turned and faced them. He knew now there was trouble ahead. He knew as long as there was no night, there was no place to run and no place to hide and he must learn to stand where he was and do what was asked of him. It could be bad but it would be a hell of a lot better than Sunda Strait and Sunda Strait had been a hell of a lot better than Newellton.

And what had happened at Sky One must not happen again.

27

Paige had ordered his second highball and was considering a conciliatory call to Felicia when the club steward told him there had been a phone call. "It's the yard commandant, Captain. He asked that you call him at home as soon as it's convenient."

"It's convenient now." He followed the steward across the wood-paneled room reserved for high-ranking officers, through the crowded noisy bar to a small office. Its walls were hung frame to frame with photographs of Navy ships and officers. To Paige it had an air of needless adulation, reminding him of bars he knew that featured signed photographs of long-forgotten celebrities.

He dialed the number and wondered what was in the wind. "Captain Paige," he said, "returning the commandant's call."

"One minute, please." Subdued voices in the background and, a moment later, a familiar and surprising one in his ear. "Harry? Maury Nickelby here."

"We weren't expecting you until noon tomorrow, Admiral."

"Plans change. You know that. Where are you?"

"The officers' club. Can you join me?"

"I'm shoving off in the morning, Harry. I'd like a quick look at you and your new command. I'll pick you up. Be out front in ten minutes."

"Aye, sir."

"Harry?"

"Sir?"

"Informal and unofficial. No pomp and ceremony, please."

Paige finished his drink quickly and went outside and stood on the broad steps. The evening had cooled. In spite of the night-time yard activity, a softness touched the raw surroundings. The silhouettes of ships were limned against a sky of stars, hard shapes of steel made gentle by the night. Blinker signals flashed across the water; distant lights cast moving shadows. Somewhere close by a jazz band played Chicago blues. The moody melody rose and melted in the soft air. Paige felt the second highball now. He had drunk it too quickly. He was sorry he had not got through to Felicia and he cursed his bones that ached for female company.

The admiral's car drove up and Paige got in and Nickelby shook his hand. "I know," he said. "Don't say it. A hell of a way to run a war."

"Delighted you're here, sir."

"You used to call me Nick."

"It's that new star. Congratulations."

"Thanks, Harry. Isn't this a hell of a yard? I can't tell you what the sight of so much activity does for my morale."

"Why rush off?"

"Got to. But I had to have a look at *Shiloh*—the first of the litter."

They arrived at the quarterdeck as the midwatch came on. Ignoring the confusion, they went below and settled down in Paige's cabin.

"How do you like her, Harry?"

"My first day on board, Nick? Give me time."

"I hoped you'd have something to report."

"I do. It's being typed first thing in the morning. I can shoot you a copy before noon. Things are shaping up damned well. A few problems to iron out. One's the ventilation system, as you can tell. Care to take a look around?"

"Maybe later. Right now I've a few things to get off my mind. How do you feel?"

"Four-oh."

"The hands?"

"You shook one. It works."

"You look fit. You looked lousy in Pearl, but that was ages ago. You know we lost *Lex*. A costly blow, Harry. I think she might have been saved. The late reports are in now on the Coral Sea clambake and we didn't do as well as we thought."

"The scuttlebutt is, we clobbered them."

"Somebody's got to get it through the skulls of our over-optimistic aviators, there's a difference from the air between a carrier and a tin can. What the hell's the matter with their eyes? And their recognition training? And near misses aren't sinkings. If anything, Coral Sea results give the enemy a bit of an edge. Tactically, anyway. They lost more men and planes than we did. They lost *Shoho*, a measly twelve-thousand-ton carrier, against our thirty-thousand-ton *Lex*. They also lost a can and some patrol craft, but they sunk our tanker *Neosho* and the destroyer *Sims*. It's the first time two carrier forces had a chance to slug it out and I tell you, it was a battle of blunders, some funny, some sad."

"Tell me a funny one."

"The Jap planes from Rabaul bombed our cruiser-destroyer force and are claiming a sunk battleship and a cruiser. Actually there was no damage whatever—not even from an attack by our own Army B-26s from Australia."

"With friends like that, who needs enemies?"

"It's not all bad. Strategically, we're ahead. We've finally checked a Jap invasion, Harry. They've had to withdraw the Port Moresby landing plan with the objective not attained. They've also had two of their big carriers out of commission. A kind of side benefit is that attention was diverted from the surrender of Corregidor which happened at the same time. No telling where the nation's morale would have been if not for Coral Sea. Incidentally, we have reliable reports that over three hundred and seventy of your *Gloucester* survivors were picked up by the Jap."

"Is that good or bad?"

"They're alive, damn it."

"If you call a Jap prison being alive." He got up quickly. "How about a drink? An extra star and a new carrier should rate a drink."

"No thanks, Harry. Not on board."

"Not even a shot of my esteemed father-in-law's private stock?"

"Thank you, Harry, and please thank Rollo. But no. Anyway, I'm not one of his favorite admirals right now and he might resent my drinking his precious corn likker. One reason I was in Washington was to settle the silly battleship versus carrier controversy. Coral Sea did it. I left Washington with assurance of full support, top priority, and a stepped-up carrier building program. Certain hulls designated for battlewagons are being redesigned to carriers. It doesn't make Rollo or any of the other ship navy boys very happy, but until we find a more effective arm of sea power, it's the course we're taking. Maybe history'll prove us wrong, but I doubt it."

"He's sure put up a fight for a battleship navy."

"Don't sell Rollo short. He was one of the first to point out risks and disadvantages inherent in carrier warfare. Low volume of fire, especially at long ranges. The time it takes to organize, launch, and arm an attack group, the time it takes to reach the enemy target, and the time to return, refuel, and rearm. Compared to sixteen-inch rifles loaded and fired, it doesn't look too good, does it? And weather can keep planes out of the air but it won't stop a ship's main batteries. Night effectiveness of air attacks is almost nil. Carriers have to turn into the wind to launch and recover planes and it's our tough luck the wind in the South Pacific is always from the east. And finally, a carrier's a fat target loaded with high-octane fuel."

"You think maybe Rollo's right?"

"You know who's right, Harry. If you didn't before Pearl Harbor, you sure as hell should now. One thing the battleship boys can't change. Bombing a fixed military base is like mailing a letter. You know the address. A carrier force has no address."

"I've been telling that to Blatchford for years."

"Rollo's been doing what he's best suited for—coordinating personnel and public relations. Which brings me to my visit here. This morning out of the clear blue, I was handed a confidential memorandum over the commodore's signature. Subject: Captain Harrison Paige. It sets forth a series of grievances, very official-sounding, and winds up with a recommendation for an investigation and at least an official reprimand."

"What grievances?"

"Refusal to cooperate with shore establishments carrying out their official business. Conduct unbecoming a Navy officer. Activities detrimental to the war effort. Care to see the full memo?"

"He's lost his marbles, Nick. He's pissed off because I don't bow and scrape before his six generations of blue-blood admirals."

"His father was one of the best, Harry. I knew the old boy. Rollo just never lived up to the family expectations. But he means well. Why can't you get along with him?"

"He doesn't really give a damn about the war. He's already scheming for the future. He says it's the big break he's been waiting for and he's moving right in."

"I don't follow you."

"He's been after me to make public appearances and speeches to service clubs and bond rallies."

"What's wrong with that?"

"His real interest is to get chummy with important people so he can tap them for top executive jobs when the war's over."

"If he hates your guts, why should he bother?"

"It's the Blatchford name he's thinking of. My boy, David, is half Blatchford and Rollo figures that's about the best he can manage for himself and the family name. If it stops there, he's sunk." Paige grinned. "Rollo's big tragedy was having a daughter instead of a son. You can damn well bet when David marries, Rollo will see to it personally that it's a boy and his name will be Blatchford Holt Paige."

"I don't buy that."

"You don't know Rollo."

"Rollo is slick as a smelt. He may have selfish ambitions but that doesn't change one simple truth. You happen to be the Navy's number-one hero. The public's been starving for something or somebody to cheer about. Whether you like it or not, you're it." He waved at the pile of mail on Paige's desk. "Peanuts. You haven't seen the sacks of mail addressed to you at the White House, the Navy Department, the Chief of Naval Operations. I've seen envelopes with only 'Hardtack Harry, U. S. Navy' for an address. You call that a scheme cooked up by Rollo Blatchford?"

"I just resent his using me to further his own ends."

"Get one thing clear, Harry. I'm not interested in your personal vendetta with your father-in-law. He may not be the brightest Navy officer the Academy's turned out, but I've yet to see any honest reason to question his integrity. I don't want to hear another word from you disparaging a superior or even a fellow officer, related or not. Is that clear?"

"Yes, sir."

"I've got problems a hell of a lot more world-shaking than a Navy family feud. For your information, Rollo happens to be right on the ball. If you're not getting along with your father-in-law, that's your problem, but the Navy's not about to let it stand in the way of raising a couple of billion dollars to pay for this war. I've stuck my two cents into your personal mess for one reason. I damn well need you out there—not sidetracked by petty politics into some obscure billet in the Southeast Atlantic Command, measuring bananas. I've got a stake in you. I've gone way out on a limb for you, and I'll be damned if I'm going to lose you."

"Why should you? I've got my ship—"

"Harry, what I heard around the Department, just in one day, could put enough teeth in Rollo's report to keep you in a shore billet the rest of your Navy career."

"What the hell's going on, anyway?"

"Somebody high up's been asking a lot of sharp questions. Your record, your reliability, your judgment in Sunda Strait. God knows what else. When the Chief started asking, I smelled a rat. I said I'd look into it. I made a few personal phone calls and dug up a few clues. You know who Thomas A. Newell is, don't you?"

"Christ!"

"Not yet, but he's striking for it. Thomas A. Newell doesn't like you. If he had his way, you'd be up before a Navy Board of Inquiry quicker'n you can say 'treason.'"

"That tears it. Treason?"

"The way I got it over the phone, Harry, it could be. It could also be dereliction of duty, drunkenness, desertion, even impersonating an officer. Anything Mr. Newell fancies. Murder and rape were not mentioned and of course, we don't fancy Mr. Newell. But he is a taxpayer and has certain inalienable rights. Anything to say in your defense?"

Paige threw up his hands. "It's all true. Obviously, you were sent here to chew me out and you're doing a splendid job. You think the commodore's dead right in lowering the boom and you're scared stiff of Newell. Do you want my sword and epaulets now, or would you prefer to do it in style, in front of the entire ship's company?"

"No need to blow your stack, Harry. I'm here to help you. Newell's a meddler but he's a powerful meddler. When those big shots decide to put a finger on us, damned if I know what we can do except our duty as we see it. I looked into it and that's what you've done, Harry. Your duty. We're behind you all the way."

"Thanks, Nick."

"If I may make a small recommendation, it's that you cooperate with Rollo's public relations fellows all you can. They're trying to do a job, just like us. It makes sense, Harry, and it means dollars."

"I'll try."

"Newell was after your scalp. It was that dirty business about a special deal for his son. You knew that?"

Paige nodded.

"I don't stomach Navy politics or politicians any more than you, Harry. But they work fast. It went to the White House this morning, to the Chief at noon, who passed it to me at lunch. This is the same incredible American combination of gall and efficiency that builds fortunes and smashes competition. It even wins wars. Some day it will run the world. Or try."

"They'll still need us."

"Only until they find a way to buy and sell us. Like any other business, Harry, the Navy gets all kinds, good and bad. The incompetents, the schemers, the boozers. Believe me, for each one of those, there's a hundred men good and true who toe the line, who'd lay down their lives without question for their country."

"I think right off of Tully, Rogers, Gallant, Lindsey—"

"Hundreds, Harry. Never mind names. Any Navy officer worth his salt walks a thin line between duty and his own human nature. Failing, craving, weakness, call it what you will, it's a tough line to walk in this kind of world and he can't favor one without damaging the other. We've become a terribly materialistic nation, Harry. Our commitments and our objectives today are quite different from the idealistic ones that motivated the founding fathers. Civilian interests influence our military strategy a hell of a lot more than ever before. I'm not about to say I'm for or against it. In a democracy, I suppose, that's the way things should be. So far we've been pretty lucky with the politicians elected to high office and I trust enough in God, Ernie King, and the American people to believe it will ever be thus. The alternative isn't pleasant to contemplate, is it? Civilian influence on military strategy is all right as long as it's intelligent, informed, and humane, and not motivated by selfish interests. If it lacks any of these it can only lead to disaster."

"I still don't believe a nation can survive without its military establishment."

"Not until the peace planners figure out what causes the war disease and do something about it. Clemenceau said that war was too important to be left in the hands of the generals. The Old

Tiger had the hard head of a businessman. Thomas A. Newell's a businessman, too. Right now he's playing a penny-ante game with his power, but who knows? He may be flexing his muscles for bigger things. I would hate to see the day when you or I could not tell him to go fly a kite, and get away with it.

"Now to the clean business of war. From the bits and pieces Intelligence has been putting together, it looks like the Jap is building up a tremendous push in the Central Pacific, probably for Midway. Nothing that happened in the Coral Sea seems to have altered this plan. He's also got the cockeyed idea that *Tarrytown*'s sunk, along with *Lex*. She was hit all right and lost sixty-six men, but we repaired her in Pearl in forty-eight hours and right now she's back with the task force. In peacetime, Harry, that repair job would have taken ninety days."

"A man moves fast with a bullet up his ass."

"The Jap also sighted *Enterprise* and *Hornet* in the South Pacific and figures that gives him an unopposed sweep and a crack at Midway. He's gathered together one hell of a big invasion force to swing it. He's got a lot going for him, but not enough. For one thing, we know when and where he plans to attack and he doesn't know we know. And we picked up a few clues to his tactics during the Coral Sea scrap. All this will be spelled out for you in detail when you receive your battle orders.

"We're going to need every carrier and plane we can lay hands on, and fast. I met with the yard supervisor, the dock trials boss, and the commandant here, and I have a pretty accurate picture of *Shiloh*'s readiness. I'm aware of the missing catapults and the volume of uncompleted hull work. Also, she was designed to include cruising turbines as part of the main drive turbine installation and they're hung up because of production difficulties. What I want from you, Harry, is some approximation of her capabilities right now."

"Put an air group on board and give me a few days' shakedown and I'll tell you."

"No time for that. How does she look to you?"

"Very good."

"Heads of departments?"

"Four-oh."

"The exec—Logan?"

"An ace. Thank you for that."

"Ship's company?"

"Green, but they'll ripen. The feel is good. You know, Nick. You can *feel* when a ship's right."

"How much notice to get under way?"

"Forty-eight hours would be nice. It would give us a chance to get liberty and leave personnel back on board and the yard crews and gear over the side. Given an air attack—ninety minutes."

"Very well. Here's the situation. Your orders are already encoded and your ship communications should be receiving it about now. Cancel all leaves and liberty commencing 0800. Expedite all yard work and see that no commitments are made for additional work. Keep yourself in standby condition to get under way on twenty-four hours' notice. Advise heads of departments only, of this immediacy. Several sets of orders have been prepared and depending on the situation, you will be notified which set to open and operate under.

"Shakedown will consist of the run from here to the Canal and from the Pacific side to the West Coast. On the basis of your recommendations enroute, preparations will be made for limited alterations and repairs at San Diego. If it means critical parts, try to give them enough notice so the parts can be shipped from here in time to get to you there. You'll probably have yard and production technicians on board during the Atlantic run and, if necessary, through the Canal to the Coast. The single important fact to keep in mind, Harry, is to get this ship out there where we need it, in time for it to be useful."

"Understood."

"I've got to clear out of here. I'm due in Jacksonville in the morning to help graduate a class of aviators and then to Pensacola to do it again. Then back to Pearl." He leaned back and closed his eyes. Paige saw the grayness in the hollow cheeks and the faint stubble of beard.

"Chief gave me strict orders," Nickelby sighed. "Take a Florida vacation, he told me. Nobody'll miss you. Can you imagine that? Me working my fingers to the bone to save America and he says nobody'll miss me. Sometimes I wonder why I got into this racket in the first place."

"You look like you could use a little rest, Nick."

"I should relax and let the western world go to hell, eh? Come to think of it, I've got some fishing gear laying around and I just might get a line wet before I leave Florida. It's the time of year for small tarpon on light tackle. That would make me happy indeed."

"Do you good, Nick."

"You ever fish, Harry?"

"Sure. When I was a kid. In the Gowanus Canal."

"Where the hell's that?"

"Brooklyn."

"Reminds me. If you get the chance, Harry, take a run up to the Brooklyn Navy Yard. They're trying a new ventilation system on a couple of the carriers now on the ways. Maybe you could pick up some ideas in case there's time to do the job on the West Coast."

"I can also visit my mother."

"Mother?"

"In Brooklyn. She's alive and kicking and pushing eighty."

"Funny thing about you, Harry. I never thought of you having a mother."

"What the hell did you think? I was won in a crap game?" He got to his feet, scowling. "You want that inspection tour now?"

"Skip it." Nickelby remained seated, smiling easily. "It breaks my heart, Harry. You with all these new gizmos to play with, and me sweating it out behind a desk in Pearl."

"I'll give you a visitor's pass when we get to Pearl."

"If you make it."

"And why the hell shouldn't I make it?"

"She's a lot of ship to handle."

"Why don't you get one of your desk captains to take her across then?"

"You'll make it, Harry. I'm not worried." He got to his feet and walked casually around the cabin, inspecting fittings and furniture. His sarcasm had nettled Paige. Paige wished he would go, but sensed that something was detaining the admiral.

"Mighty fancy digs, Harry."

"They'll do."

"I mean, fancy for an ex-pug."

"Damn it, Nick, you're picking on me."

"That door, Harry. What's it for?"

"It's just a damned locked door without a key and it's not in the plans."

Nickelby reached in his pocket. "Try this." He tossed a key and

Paige caught it and unlocked the door. It was a fitted closet about
two feet deep. It contained bar bells, a punching bag with a circular
board, and a set of boxing gloves. A small brass plate bolted dead
center read:

Harrison Paige, Captain, USN
Last skipper, USS Gloucester
First Skipper, USS Shiloh
with pride
from the men who build them
to the man who fights them
Newport News Shipbuilding & Drydock
1942

Paige took down a pair of the gloves and ran his hand gently
over the leather. He loosened the laces and pulled them on and
without looking at the admiral, he said, "Care to go a round, Nick?"

"Not with you, thanks just the same."

"Sixteen ounces. Couldn't hurt a baby."

"Rank has its privileges." He watched Paige pull off the gloves
and hang them away. "Damn it all," he said frowning, "I've had
my little surprise party and you've got your damned dumbbells.
Let's get out of here before I bust out crying."

"I'm at a loss for words."

"No need for words. Just stay in shape and on your toes. You'll
need to, out there." He paused. "One thing, Harry. The booze. Ease
off. You can't fight two wars at one time. I'll say no more."

"Thank you, Nick."

"Stay clear of Rollo Blatchford and Old Man Newell."

"They sure make it a sad sack world."

"Who knows how the world will go? I'm a sad old party myself,
Harry. I spent the juiciest years of my life playing at war, but
never got around to a real blood-spilling. Now it comes along and
I find myself still playing games. For keeps, this time, but still
playing. You hit it just right, you lucky stiff. You're out there where
you belong and for you, it's a lovely break."

"It would be a hell of a lot less lovely without you there to
call the shots."

"Know something? I rather like it my way. I don't believe I
could stand the sight of blood and wreckage for long, and I'm
one of those impossibly romantic idiots who would insist on going

down with his ship. Now lead me from this tempting shell. I'm going fishing."

At his car, he handed Paige a thick envelope from his briefcase. "Rollo's report and my notes on Newell's request. Read and destroy. Maybe they'll catch up with us in some Navy veteran's retirement home years from now, when we've swallowed the anchor. Knowing channels, that's about how long it will take. Meanwhile, good luck."

"Thanks, Nick."

"You'll need it. You're a hero and there's no peace for heroes."

28

Next day, Paige flew north in a Navy J2F amphibian and taxied from La Guardia to the Navy Yard in Brooklyn. The scene of activity was no different from the Virginia yard—a noisy convulsive shaping of the tools of war. He paid his respects to the yard commandant and described the purpose of his visit. He was turned over to a talkative three-striper who praised briefly Paige's boldness in Sunda Strait and spent the rest of the tour in a self-pitying diatribe on the unsung sacrifices of shore-based officers. Paige finally made it to a telephone and dialed his mother's number. It rang a long time. He hoped she was all right. And what to say after twenty years? Hello, Mom?

"Hello?"

"This is Harry. I got your letter."

"What number do you want?"

"You're Rose Maloney Paige, aren't you?"

"Of course I am. Who'd you say is calling?"

"Your son. Harrison."

"Harrison? Praise the Lord. Where are you, Harrison?"

"The Brooklyn Navy Yard. I'm coming over to see you."

"My own son Harrison after all these years." She was weeping and he was having difficulty himself in keeping his voice even.

"Can I bring you something?"

"Yourself, my son. Just yourself. So you got my letter. Imagine,

I just wrote it the other day but I gave it to the cleaning woman to mail and you never know. I don't get around like I used to, is why it takes so long just to answer the phone. It's in the kitchen and I don't budge a step from the house."

"Your letter worried me a little, Mom."

"I didn't mean it to worry you, son."

"It sounded—kind of depressed."

"When a person stops living, you start dying."

"You feel all right?"

"Thank God."

"Still as beautiful as ever?"

"Knock wood." Her pleased laughter splintered into a violent and prolonged coughing spell webbed in phlegm. He had forgotten about her coughing—a chronic ailment she blamed on Brooklyn's factory air.

"You sure I can't bring anything?"

"Cigarettes, maybe. Some gin. I ran out yesterday and there's nobody around here I can trust. And listen, Harrison?"

"Yes?"

"Be careful on Sand Street. It's full of drunken bums and bad women."

Cigarettes. Gin. He would find roses. She had always claimed the Lord had invented roses especially for her. He remembered her cigarette brand, the green pack with the red circle in the center. He could do her a real favor, he thought. He could forget the cigarettes and bring her a carton of Luden's cough drops. And be careful crossing Sand Street.

The green cigarette package with the red center was white now and Paige bought a carton before he left the yard.

He bought a dozen roses in an ominous flower shop next door to a funeral parlor and found a retail liquor store and purchased the gin. The clerk admired the campaign ribbons and agreed to sell Paige a bottle of vermouth ". . . on'y because you been out there, Captain. There just ain't no more of that imported stuff around."

The old neighborhood had changed. His grammar school on the corner looked gritty and severe behind its high iron fence and a new wing of ugly yellow brick had been added. It was hemmed in by cheap-looking store fronts. An oil-smeared service station occupied the corner that had once been green lawn and flagpole.

Children in the cemented playground ran to the barrier and gripped the posts and stared at his uniform. From the dark insides of the classroom building, seen through its open doors, his mind recaptured the smell of dried ink in the inkwell of his scarred desk. Dipped pigtails, he thought.

The Paige house in its row of brownstones seemed shrunken and seedier. It was flanked now by the narrow basement shops of Mme. Eleanor, Beautician à la Mode, and a tailor named A. DiBiasi, Prop. The empty lot across the street where he had played Prisoner's Base and Johnny Ride the Pony now was occupied by an Italian delicatessen, its surrealist window festooned with a phallic assemblage of sausage and provolone.

He mounted the stone-chipped steps and pushed the brass doorbell and was startled by the heartiness of his mother's shouted welcome. He hung his cap in the foyer on the mirrored coat stand. Its frame of golden oak was crowned with a familiar antlered deer's head. The stand had a bench seat under whose lid he used to store his overshoes and baseball junk. He raised the lid. His Spalding baseball mitt was still there, the leather rotting and the rawhide lacing shredded under a quarter-inch of velvet dust. It's going to be one hell of a weepy afternoon, he told himself and went into the parlor.

His mother sat framed in a dozen multicolored cushions, a life-size aging Kewpie doll in shiny black moire taffeta. An assortment of keys on a coarse gold chain rested in the deep wrinkled swell of her bosom. Her swollen legs were supported by a faded tapestry footstool across which she had thrown a bright-paneled afghan. Religious books, astrology charts and pamphlets, cluttered an oval marble-top table on which an ashtray dripped cigarette butts and tiny ants explored an open box of melting chocolate-covered cherries.

She had been more than pretty once, the finely turned features still clearly evident in the sags and folds of veined flesh. Tears made shiny tracks down the talcum of her cheeks. She held out her arms.

Paige embraced her, confused because he, too, wept—a hardened man inside and out and he had not expected to. He had not wept for anyone or anything in thirty years. They clung to each other for several moments. Quite abruptly, she pushed him away and dabbed at her eyes. "A fine son," she sniffed. "You ought to be ashamed of yourself. Roses." She looked fondly at him and blew her nose, and coughed. "How is she? What's her name?"

"Felicia. She's fine."

"There are some people in this world. Not even a thank you. Well, never mind, you're here and healthy and the Lord is good to me, except for the arthritis."

"Do you see a doctor?"

"What can a doctor do? They give you pills and take your money and I'm still in pain."

"Can you get around all right?"

"I use the cane. And where would I go? Who wants me? I sit here thinking of the good old days, Jimmy Walker, the Tammany crowd. Now all of us just sitting, waiting for that fat little fireman in City Hall to drop dead." She handed him the roses. "Before they die, Harrison. You'll find a cut-glass vase on the windowsill in the kitchen."

"Ready for a drink?"

"There's a tray of cubes in the icebox. You'll use the top ones, Harrison. They're fresher."

In the kitchen he filled the vase with water and roses and brought it into the parlor and set it down near the window. She gave him the key to a glass cabinet and he unlocked it and took a glass mixer and two long-stemmed glasses into the kitchen and mixed a batch of martinis and brought them in.

"Here's looking at you."

"Drink hearty." She sipped and while she lighted a cigarette, she coughed.

"You should knock off those coffin nails, Mom."

"It's not the cigarettes," she wheezed. "It's the dirty Brooklyn air." She began to reminisce, reminding Paige of the good times they had shared. He had been an obedient boy, she said, a handsome muscular little devil, and the girls were crazy about him. He remembered nothing like that but he did remind her of her Irish anger when he had got himself mixed up in a free-for-all in Fort Greene Park. It had taken all her pull with the local police to hush it up and straighten him out. She recalled the Election Day block party in her honor when they swept the assembly district at the polls from top to bottom. And hadn't Mayor John F. Hylan himself come out to thank her personally?

The hours slipped past, the afternoon of misty-eyed memories punctuated by frequent trips to the kitchen to refill the gin pitcher. By late afternoon they were stiff with drink and sloppy with sentiment. For Paige it was as though he had never left home.

Now's the time, he told himself. "What about my father?"

"Ah him." She rocked herself gently. "Passed on. Didn't you know?"

"That was thirty years ago, Mom. You told me once you'd tell me about him."

"Jack Paige was a gentleman to the core."

"What did he do for a living?"

"A seafaring man like yourself, and in that uniform with all the braid and ribbons, you're his spit and image."

"Last time he was an international banker. London, Paris, Rome, that sort of thing."

"In banking, yes. Traveled the high seas, always on the go was Jack Paige. A model of a man, your father. Too bad he drank. He drank too much, you know. He died of drink, in that hotel in Egypt, is it? You know, you read about it all the time, society people always running into each other there."

"Shepheard's. But you're cockeyed drunk, because—" He saw the tears gathering and he stopped and said, "Go on, Mom, tell me all about him."

"He retired, you know. Settled down to get his health back. Consumption. Just sat around and drank himself to death. Rotted from the inside out. Wasn't worth the price to ship him home, they told me. I mean to hold together all the little pieces. It gets very hot in Egypt."

"Is there a picture of him? Any letters, or the marriage papers, birth certificate—?"

"Burned. Every scrap of it, in the fire."

"What fire?"

"When you were gone, that fire. Didn't I write you? You were, I don't know, Annapolis or Hong Kong, married to that snob, she never wrote a thank you for those solid silver cuspidors. Initials. What a time I had here, a widow, alone, no friend to help me, nearly burned to death. I never heard from you, not once, except once long-distance and a letter after the wedding and that dirty picture postal from the Orient."

"The house looks just the same. You'd never know there'd been a fire here."

"Not here. The vault, where we always kept the family things. My valuables. Those letters he wrote. Tender, sweet. Surprising in a sporting gentleman. He always wore a solid gold watch chain with an ivory tooth, and a diamond ring as big as an egg."

He stood at the window and stared at the Italian delicatessen across the street. "I've a right to know," he muttered.

She began to weep and rock herself. "What do you want of my life? I raised you a clean and honest Christian, worked my fingers to the bone. And got you the Annapolis appointment, didn't I? What more do you want of me? Jack Paige, your father, was a gentleman, a fine and loving picture of a man and now he's dead and buried and you're jumping on his grave."

He went to her and wiped her tears and refilled her glass. "It would help a lot to know, Mom. That's all. Now drink up, like a real sweet girl."

"You're not mad at me?"

"Hell no. I love you."

She looked at him with shining eyes. "You're handsome and I'm proud of you. A Navy captain and your picture in the papers with the great FDR, our President. The whole neighborhood knows it. And I don't let 'em forget it, what an honor it is, you born right here in this room. Some day they'll stick up a bronze plaque out front, you mark my words."

"What'll it say, Mom?"

"It'll say this is where Admiral Harrison Paige, United States Navy hero, was born. You're going to make admiral, Harrison. The good Lord will see to it."

"Maury Nickelby might have a hand in it, I figure."

"It's the will of the Lord, son."

"How come a renegade Catholic like you is so hopped up on the Lord?"

"Every time I pray to him, He answers my prayers."

"Moose shit, Mom."

"That's a sacrilege, Harrison! I'm ashamed of you and the Lord'll punish you for saying filthy words like that."

"Okay, He'll punish me. Or try. So will Tojo and the Commodore and Amos Flint and all those other jealous bastards. The hell with them. I'm in the punishment business. I can take it."

"You shouldn't blaspheme the Lord. He's up there to protect us all."

"Where the hell was He that night in Sunda Strait? I lost a ship and over seven hundred men."

"He saved you, didn't He?"

Paige grinned. "Like I was His own Son."

"He hears my prayers. He's on the side of seafaring men."

"Hallelujah!"

"He loves admirals and he protects them on land and on sea."

"Ay-men!"

"They are His precious messengers, His pets, His angels, riding the waves of world love. Your life is entrusted to His sacred hands and no harm will ever befall you." She was pawing through one of the pamphlets. "Just listen to this: 'Come gather for the great Supper of God, to eat the flesh of kings, the flesh of captains, the flesh of mighty men—' "

"Hell, I'm a captain!"

"It refers only to army captains, son. '—the flesh of horses and their riders, the flesh of all men both free and slave, both small and great.' "

"That's just about everybody."

"It doesn't say a word about admirals."

"Then I just better the hell make admiral fast or get eaten alive, right? Finish your drink. This is the last batch coming up."

"And the boy?" she asked. "My grandson?"

"His name's David. Didn't we send you a card or something?"

"That was twenty years ago. What's he like now?"

"Quiet. Kind of deep, you might say."

"Who does he take after?"

Paige was thoughtful a moment. "Damned if I know, unless it's your good friend and mine, Jack Paige." He went to her and kissed her brow. It smelled of stale cologne. "Ever hear from your old crowd? The precinct cops and Irish politicians and all the fine-smelling ladies with the big behinds?"

"All gone. Dead or moved or done in by the Fusion Party." She dabbed at her eyes. "A fancy lot, may they rest in peace. I miss them something terrible."

"You're still around, Mom, and that's what counts." He poured the last of the batch into her glass. "To the good old days. To those lovely ladies with the big behinds." He raised his glass, spilling some of the drink. "Wish I knew then what I know now."

"Lord love 'em. Those poor dear girls."

"Honi soit qui Noilly Prat."

"Never heard of them."

"Who?"

"Honey Swatt and Nelly Pratt. There was a Phoebe, though, and Black Tim Callaghan's sweetheart, Birdie Molloy—"

"To Birdie and Phoebe. Down the hatch and up the snatch."

They drained their glasses. Rose Maloney glowed. "We used to sing the sweetest songs. Today nobody sings. Not even the birds."

"You always sang a mighty rich soprano, Mom."

They put their drunken heads together and tried the refrain from *Moonlight and Roses.* Her voice was raspy as a file and she coughed a lot. She did better on *Silver Threads Among the Gold.* When they came to *Break the News to Mother,* it was too much for Rose Maloney and after dissolving into tears, she quietly passed out. A smile of beatific repose shaped her cupid bow lips. She began to snore. He kissed her nose and left.

He spent the night at the Brooklyn Navy Yard in bachelor officers' quarters and flew south at dawn. Visibility was excellent and he handled the controls with the virtuosity of Jesse Crawford at the console of the Paramount Theatre's mighty Wurlitzer organ. All the way back he bawled out the old-time songs at the top of his lungs. Bastard or not, he told himself, I never felt better in my life.

Logan met him at the quarterdeck.

"I told you forty-eight hours, Lobo."

"You did, Captain. But I got the word this morning to report back on the double and here I am."

"What's up?"

"We got us some orders, Captain."

"Like what?"

Logan's Texan eyes glowed. "Like maybe this is it."

Nickelby stood on a bank of stiff Florida grass, a lank night figure anonymous in faded jeans and sneakers. An old cotton fishing hat was pulled well over his eyes. At the approach to the bridge where he stood, an overhead light shone on the copper tackle box he had cleaned that day. It gleamed like a burnished helmet. He bent and opened the lid and wiped away the last vestige of green mold embedded in the riveting.

The inside of the box was brilliant with color. Red feathers curled like battle plumes. A hank of yellow bucktails hung together like dried strands of Hun hair. A curved spoon shone like a scalpel.

One of the lures had a slim white body with a red head and a gleaming blade of metal clamped between its blood-red wooden lips. It was the admiral's favorite. He studied its beady yellow eyes and fondly recalled the times it had served him. It possessed a dangerous grace, could dart and dive, could run deep and silent. He admired it because it was lethal as well as beautiful, and most of all because it was obedient to his command. Without the guidance of his firm skilled hand, it remained a lifeless thing of wood, metal, and paint. The thought made him smile. It meant so many things and the smile meant so many things.

He closed the lid and took up the box and the limber rod and the good reel anointed in oil and carried them to a secluded place where the water coursed swiftly beneath a stone bridge. He set down the copper box and secured the lure to the hook at the end of the wire leader and descended the bank and studied the swift current as it spilled past on the changing tide.

Schools of small fish appeared and swam in graceful arcs, smooth and live as *corps de ballet*. They came and went and except for the pull of the tide past his eyes, they were all that moved. The admiral remained motionless, watching them with mixed delight and melancholy. He had seen this classic doomed ballet before. He had seen it many times.

From the depths without warning, a silvery body rose swiftly in a faultless charge and slashed cruelly into them. The surface exploded in an angry shower of phosphorescence. The lucky ones escaped. A few that remained thrashed feebly near the surface and were soon devoured. The water, peaceful again, rushed on.

The admiral sighed, a mournful sound in the still night. He had witnessed savagery, pure and primitive and forever lost to man. He thought: True battle, warrior's battle, is gone for all men for all time. Man is civilized now and cunningly invents his complex machines of violent death. The hunt—the purest sport—is dead.

Nickelby waited until the last tremor of emotion left him, every sense honed sharp. All he felt was the single instinct for the clean kill, the ancient joy of the true warrior.

Once more the swift bodies flashed in the luminous water and he cast his bright lure among them.

Tod Newell took his search for peace of mind to the city of Norfolk. The wartime seaport was strained to its limits. Each arriving draft of sailors posed a threat to the virgin daughters, drained the city's resources, and crowded the local residents out of their accustomed public haunts. Norfolk had seen and suffered this before in the war to end all wars. Now they did not hesitate to make the best of it. They sold their beer at whisky prices and turned their proper backs on open vice. They locked their doors against the homesick kids from Terre Haute and Dallas, Lewiston, Toledo, and Dubuque, and made no bones about depriving the suckers of every cent of sea pay they could lay their hands on.

The sailors, lonesome for gentler sounds and homely faces, were dismayed by the reception the townsfolk gave them. They roamed the stores and sidewalks buying useless souvenirs and cursing every crooked inch of blistered pavement. They had been fed a bellyful of hate and fear and loneliness. They brawled and drank and whored and called the place the asshole of the universe and sullenly sweated out the war.

Newell bought a pair of swim trunks and a bus ticket to Virginia Beach. He sat next to a woman in a formidable straw hat. She was thin-lipped, about forty, and tightly clutched a soiled white mesh bag in her lap. The bus left the confusion of the station and followed a maze of hot cobbled streets to Olney Road. At each stop, passengers got on, but few left the bus. It seemed to Newell everyone must be going to the beach.

The bus rattled past endless rows of unpainted houses leaning one against the other. Negroes sat listlessly in the shadows of warped porches, dark silent people on rockers, slack in backless chairs. Spiky-legged children sprawled along the weathered railings. Newell watched, fascinated, until the woman in the window seat turned a long hard look on him and flustered, he turned away.

Out Park Street now. The sun a hanging cauldron of flame, the air choked with flannel dust and the bus a creaking trap of mortals, each contemplating his cool and private destination at the seashore.

The city snarl uncoiled to flat and open countryside. Cool wind fanned the open windows, the promise of holiday on each breath. Passengers stood restlessly in the aisle, whites forward, Negroes toward the rear. Conversation became more animated now and laughter easy on the passengers' lips. The driver whistled a tune and the bus seemed to stretch itself toward the cool distant beach and sea.

It slowed past a bone-dry service station now abandoned, stripped of paint and chrome and gleaming pumps. The driver stopped the bus and turned his head and called out "Pungo." On his lips it could have been an obscenity. Through the window Newell watched two young women, one pregnant, leave the desolate untidy Negro settlement and board the bus. Heat fumed through narrow spaces mixed with gasoline smells and the odor of stewing bodies. The doors swung shut. The two young women undertook a slow difficult passage to the rear. They got as far as Newell's seat and could move no farther. The pregnant one was twisted helplessly over him, her face inches away. Her eyes were wide and yellow, filled with a desperate look, a mixture of apology and fear. Pain dragged down the corners of her full-lipped mouth. He squirmed up and aside and helped her into his seat.

The woman at the window glared at Newell in absolute disbelief and turned on the girl. "Get back where you belong."

She was terrified and eager to oblige but Newell stood firm over her.

"It's okay. Stay," he said.

The other girl alongside Newell, in a low excited voice, said, "You stay right there, Willie Mae, like the officer tell you."

"Go on," the woman said. "Get out."

"It's my seat," Newell said. "She stays."

Conversation in the bus died slowly. The girl wept softly, a crumpled yellow handkerchief in her fingers. Newell saw the USN embroidered in bright blue on a corner and it gave him strength. The woman at the window stood, lips bristling, and in a voice a thousand years old called out, "Driver, come put this nigger in the back where she belongs, hear?"

The driver's cheerful whistling had stopped moments ago. The bus slowed and swung to the side of the road and stopped. He opened the door and turned half-round in his seat and said to the people nearest him in the aisle, "'Bout ten of you folks kindly move on out, please. That's right. Down the steps an' out."

They stared at him, annoyed in the still hot place, unwilling to move. They stared back sullenly into the bus where the girl sat bent and troubled.

"This bus don't move an inch without you folks step down and we get us squared away back there." The driver's voice was full of calm authority. The people began to move without complaint, trusting him. He watched until an even ten stood outside, looking somewhat forlorn. With an easy swing to his wiry body he left his seat and went to Newell who stood above the cowering girl. "She can go back now. There's room."

His tone was respectful and he did not look at the tight-lipped woman in the window seat behind him. Newell heard angry whispers from the rear. He studied the driver's lean and bony country face.

"You can see her condition," Newell said. "She has to have a seat."

"We got us a state law in Virginia, mister. I don't make it no more do you make the Navy regulations." He leaned past Newell and took the girl's arm easily and led her back and made a place for her in the wide last row. Passengers climbed back aboard, jamming the aisle once more. The bus began to roll. A warm blast of air filled the aisle again and conversations resumed.

Newell's seat remained empty. The woman was talking to herself, shabby triumph brightly kindled in her eyes. He caught occasional disjointed phrases. None of them seemed to make sense. The words clicked along like the faulty mechanism of a rusty shrill machine. The passengers heard and turned to watch her. Streaks of hair slipped loosely and awry beneath her battered straw. Her bosom heaved and spittle gathered in gray bubbles at the corners of her mouth. Her bony fingers clutched the dirty white mesh bag in her lap. The bus lurched toward the beach.

The driver was whistling again, a tune the people liked. Some of them hummed along. Newell stood over the empty seat, sick at heart, trying desperately to hear only the cheerful tune the driver whistled. All he heard was the gibberish of the woman at the window. Everyone watched the road ahead, searching for the beach and soothing breeze, its sweet escape.

Newell could not know that for him there was nothing of the kind ahead. No escape. What hope remained and what sanity had managed to survive in Sunda Strait, began to die inch by inch in that bus to Virginia Beach.

Commander Joe Allen did well in the ground school at Pensacola. In no time at all, he knew everything he had to know about plane engines, radio, gunnery, bombs and torpedoes, and aerial navigation.

It was in the air that Allen met his Waterloo. Flying a dual instruction SNJ for the first time, he froze on the controls just thirty seconds after take-off. Before the startled instructor could regain control, the plane spun into a sickening dive and crashed on the beach at the edge of the Gulf of Mexico.

Lonesome Joe Allen died with his smashed head buried seven inches in Florida's clean white sand, in a place he did not choose to be, in the performance of a duty that terrified him. He was a good man and an honorable officer. This could be his epitaph:

He had one love—Gloucester.
He had one duty—to serve.

In his thirty-two years, Joe Allen made love to few women and to none whose last name he knew. But you would not put that on an epitaph.

29

Paige read the orders.

Shiloh must get under way on a night tide within forty-eight hours for the West Coast and further orders. All activity and information relative to her departure must be treated as "Most Secret." Two new destroyers of the *Bristol* class, *Avery* and *Kline*, were being detached from the Atlantic Sea Command and would serve as escort to *Shiloh*, with plane guard and anti-submarine duties.

The small group would rendezvous enroute with *Shiloh*'s air group sortieing from Patuxent. The run south and then west, because of the emergency nature of the orders, would serve as the shakedown cruise for *Shiloh*. She was to make best possible speed, allowing for hazards to navigation and the maneuvers necessary to carry out normal flight and gunnery exercises. Tactical command would be in *Shiloh*. Extreme caution was to be exercised during the Atlantic run. Enemy submarines were known to have entered the Panama Sea Frontier.

At nine o'clock that morning, Paige issued his orders to the department heads. A Shore Patrol party rounded up stragglers from the hotels and bars, the dance halls and jails. Commander LeClair flew down from Patuxent to get things going in the air department. A replacement for dead Joe Allen was hard to come by on such short notice, and it was decided that the assistant navigator, a lieutenant commander named Newman, would serve as acting navigator until *Shiloh* arrived in San Diego.

The men moved about their duties quietly and efficiently. The air seemed charged with the tension created by the unexpected orders and Logan's crackling presence everywhere. By evening chow time every shipyard worker had been checked out and had left the ship. Quarters were arranged for civilian and military personnel involved in inspection and installation work, whose duties would keep them on board.

Special sea details were set at 2330 hours and all lines were cast off promptly at midnight. *Shiloh* nosed into Hampton Roads with the tide, exactly fifteen hours after Paige had issued his first order. She stood south and east for Panama.

Minutes before departure, though burdened with last-minute details, Paige had gone down the gangway to a dock telephone and put in a call to Felicia. The commodore answered the phone. Felicia was sleeping, he said.

"Put her on, please, I've got to talk to her."

"Damned if I'm waking her for you, Harry, or for anyone else. You know what time it is?"

"Please just put her on."

"I will like hell. You've got some nerve, calling at midnight out of the clear blue, never a word all week long. You're drunk, aren't you? I can tell. Out somewhere in a cheap saloon with one of those Norfolk floozies, is that it? And you feel guilty and you think you can just pick up the phone and smooth-talk this poor confused girl of mine into whatever it is on your filthy mind. Well, you listen to me, Captain. She's not here. She's out with *her* kind of people, enjoying the decent things in life you never were around to provide for her. And when she comes in—"

Paige hung up. There was no sense in hearing any more of it. He hung up quietly, which surprised him because every instinct urged him to slam the receiver on its hook. Because Felicia slept? Or did she? Was she even there?

It really did not matter now. It would have been unwise to let the commodore know why he was calling. It was just the sort of business the crafty old rascal would embroider into an offense against the national security, an act of treason or any one of a dozen heinous crimes he could dredge up for a Naval Court of Inquiry. Well, the hell with him.

A rage of frustration pounded his temples. There were countless things to do before shoving off and a ship to conn and he had better the hell have his wits about him. He was bone-weary and ready to drop but he was getting a carrier under way at last, his own command. It was a hell of a wonderful moment in his life and no fathead of a father-in-law was going to spoil it. Just the same, it would have been nice to hear the sound of Felicia's voice before he left.

He was too wound up to sleep. He sat on the darkened bridge while the deck watch changed at 0400. He was pleased to see that Newell was the relieving officer of the deck. The watch standers settled down to the early morning routine. The sea was calm and the night moonless, cloud-black without stars. Only the green-lighted radar repeater showed the positions of the escorting destroyers. The acting navigator had been understandably nervous, once they cleared the familiar landmarks. He was unable to take a star sight and kept plotting and replotting the ship's course until Paige took him aside and told him to relax and forget about it and steer the son of a bitch south and east until morning. Then they would shoot the sun for a position and set a course from there.

Newell came over to report the tin cans on station and all secure throughout the ship.

"How do you feel now, Mr. Newell?"

"Fine, Captain."

"Like old times, isn't it?"

"Not quite, sir, without Commander Allen."

"Terrible shock, losing Joe. A damned good navigator and too bad he had to go."

"He didn't want to go, Captain."

"I didn't mean it that way, Mr. Newell. What I meant was, it's a shame to lose a good officer like that. A senseless crash."

"Yes, sir." Newell was silent for a few moments, weighing what he was about to say. "That leaves the two of us."

"That's right. So it does." Paige yawned and stretched to hide his irritation. "Everything's under control, I see."

"Yes, sir. Tin cans on station, we're steady on course one-seven-zero, making twenty-five knots."

"Very well. General quarters at one hour before dawn. We ren-

dezvous with the air group at 0730. I'll be in my sea cabin if
you need me."

"Good night, Captain."

Paige lay on his bunk without undressing. Just the two of them.
Funny, he had never thought of that. A hell of a way to look at
it, he reflected. Like looking down the wrong end of a telescope.
It worried him having an officer who looked at things in a strange
way like that.

In the morning, following dawn general quarters, all hands not
on watch were mustered on the flight deck. Paige spoke to them
through the bull horn in flight control. His voice was relayed on the
intercom's squawk boxes located throughout the ship.

"Men, this is your captain speaking. What I have to say will
be short and sweet. The whole world has its eyes on *Shiloh*.
Everybody wants to know how good a fighting ship she is. Well,
we're going to show 'em. We'll show 'em we can launch and
recover planes faster, move through the sea faster, fire our guns
faster than any ship in any navy before us." A few men cheered
and he held up a hand. "That's not all. Before we're through, we'll
have sunk more enemy ships, splashed more enemy planes, bombed
more enemy bases than any single ship in the history of the world."

This time the men cheered in unison and continued lustily until
Paige, grinning, held up both hands. "That isn't only my promise
to *you*. It's your promise to *me*. We're in this together, men. We're
going to work together. Work hard. There'll be times without sleep,
without a hot meal, times of pain and tragedy. Each of us must
believe in what we're doing and in each other. Okay now. We'll
be taking our air group aboard within the hour. The moment that
last plane is on board, we're a full team. We're one ship—a taut
ship, a fighting ship, a happy ship. From the bottom of my heart,
I welcome each and every one of you aboard. God bless you."

They cheered until their division officers dismissed them. They
moved to their duties highly charged by the captain's words. The
first planes of the air group were sighted and flight quarters were
sounded. Signal hoists flapped in the wind. The destroyers turned
and raced with foaming wakes to their stations. *Shiloh* turned into
the wind. Minutes later the first plane moved into position astern
and, on the flight deck officer's landing signal, came to rest with
its tail hook cleanly engaged by the arresting cable. The others

followed until the entire air group was aboard. Paige gave orders to resume base course, sent *Avery* and *Kline* a "Well done" and went to his cabin for coffee. He sent for the gunnery, engineering, and air officers, called Logan, and lit a cigarette. He sat back with the coffee cup in his lap, quite pleased with the way the morning had gone.

Fillmore, Meserve, and LeClair showed up a few minutes later and Paige waved them to seats. "We're off to a good start, gentlemen. I have a hunch we're going to keep it up. You all heard what I said to the men this morning. I want to reassure you, I meant every word of it. *Shiloh*'s got to be the best. What I'm going to say now, I'm saying in confidence. If, after I'm finished, any of you feels it's your duty to speak elsewhere about what I'm proposing, there's little I can do to stop you. Now here it is." He pointed a finger at Fillmore. "Guns. I want you to take another look at the limit stops, the point where each gun's fire cuts out when the line of fire approaches a portion of the ship's superstructure. This safety margin may be six inches or a foot or whatever way ordnance regulations has set it up. I want you to cut that safety margin in half."

"That would be going directly against BuOrd orders, Captain."

Paige nodded. "And if something's a bit out of whack or wears down too quickly, we might direct gunfire into the superstructure, cause damage, possibly injure or kill a shipmate. I know that. But I also know we're going to need every added second of firing time to bear on a fast-moving target and believe me, the Jap planes are fast-moving targets. Those few inches can make the difference between a kill and a miss."

"We could do it," Fillmore said slowly. "I've a couple of fire-control chiefs worth their weight in gold."

"Any of the yard ordnance people on board?"

"No, sir. We left the last of them in Norfolk."

"Good. Now Meserve."

"Sir?"

"With the present safety valve set-up, I understand that the boilers are capable of delivering thirty-three knots. I want thirty-six knots. Can I get it?"

"Not without risking boiler damage failure and explosion, and the possibility of serious injury to below decks personnel."

"But by reducing the safety factor, you can give me thirty-six knots, right?"

"Yes, sir."

"Reduce it. That leaves you, LeClair. Any ideas how we can cut to the bone the time it takes to launch aircraft?"

"It's a goal we're always working toward, Captain. We might cut time launching prop to tailfin."

"You mean a plane in motion before the one ahead has cleared the forward ramp?"

LeClair nodded. "Takes a raunchy launching officer, split-second timing, and lots of prayer. The risks are obvious. A deck collision, even an air collision over the bow. Any one of a number of contingencies could cause a hell of a mess. Which is why certain standards and safety regulations were adopted by BuAir."

"Understood. Greater risk. But it would give us more planes in the air faster, right? Which we need, having no catapults."

"Yes, sir."

"So we agree that by taking a hell of a lot more risk than the regulations allow, your three departments can increase the fighting efficiency of this ship and make its attack factor a big plus over that of other carriers now operating. Okay. Now I have got to go to the head for a minute and brush my teeth. You men are free to discuss your feelings among yourselves. Commander Logan here, as second in command, is also free to speak his mind. I'll be back in a minute."

He returned in exactly sixty seconds. They still sat where he had left them. Logan was grinning. "You didn't have to leave, Captain. You never give any of us the chance to say we're with you all the way."

"Thank you, gentlemen," Paige said. "When we arrive in Dago, we strip ship. Every piece of excess crap, personal, official or otherwise—over the side. I want this ship down to bare bones for maximum fighting efficiency. Pass the word to all divisions heads. That's it. Dismissed." He stood. They saluted and filed out briskly.

He drove them hard all the way. The men of *Shiloh* drilled from dawn to dark and swore and drilled again. The flight and gunnery crews sweated through their exercises, stood fast while Paige commended them and called for even greater efforts. The gunnery crews fired at sleeves towed by their own planes; the dive bombers hurtled from the sky to drop their dummy loads on yellow sleds streamed astern. Below decks, the damage control crews drilled themselves against disaster; the "snipes" in the engineering spaces schemed to deliver the speed their captain demanded.

Paige stood each day with a stop watch over Commander Le-Clair's shoulder, timing the intervals between launchings, counting the seconds it took to free a plane from its arresting cable and taxi it below. Time and again he blessed the deck edge elevator amidships on the port side. Its "down" position did not create a gaping hold on the flight deck, as did the center line elevators fore and aft. Its "up" position provided additional parking space outside normal contours of the flight deck. He cursed the absence of the catapults and trained his crews to deliver full load launchings just the same.

The weather remained clear and hot and with the faulty ventilation system, the men assigned to below decks spaces stewed in their own juices. Off watch they dragged their mattresses to topside spaces and slept in areas normally restricted to such use. Between drills they sat stupefied with exhaustion. Paige never let up. Men growled. Some wondered after the first week, if all the sweat was worth it. Some talked of jumping ship in San Diego. Others, in the silent way of sailors, nursed like some exotic plant a growing hate for Captain Paige. Mostly, the men of *Shiloh* took the orders without question and did their duty as sailors should.

And slowly, his passion for perfection began to show results. Seconds slipped away between launchings and recoveries. Towed sleeves were torn from the air by forty-millimeter and five-inch gunfire; the twenties ripped the target balloons to shreds.

By the time they skirted the southern tip of Baja California, Paige had fashioned a smooth and effective fighting machine. There were areas of loose performance, but he knew that time and practice and the pride men took in work well done, would bring the deck and air crews as close to perfect performance as human tolerances allow. He had also learned the mechanical defects in his command and prepared a comprehensive estimate of the adjustments and repairs needed.

The faulty ventilation system was his highest priority. It was impossible for men to work below deck, he wrote, in confined spaces, without fresh air to breathe. His report pointed out that the ship would probably be operating in climates hotter than those where she had been built, and without correction of the system, the crew's efficiency would be critically reduced and the men's lives endangered.

He requested time for installation of at least one catapult, pointing out its necessity in the event of a deck crash or foul weather, both of which would impede the normal deck launchings.

His final recommendation had to do with the ship's trash burner. Considering its shortcomings, Paige wrote with commendable restraint.

> It does not burn trash. It burns people. It is located in the very heart of the ship's office spaces. At the present rate, we are considering a change in menu, from toasted foreskins to toasted yeomen. I would have a mutiny on my hands, were not the victims too weak to rebel.
>
> There is no provision for storage of trash waiting to be burned. Narrow passageways are cluttered with men attempting to reach the burner with loads of trash blocking the way. As to the trash burner's design, a blind, armless Rube Goldberg could have done better. Its design, however, is superior when compared to its construction. Following a sharp turn in Mexican waters, only a week out of Norfolk, it practically came apart. Its door fell off the hinges. Bricks flew and struck a chief yeoman who is presently in sick bay, already weakened by the foul air of the ventilation system, and he has requested information regarding his eligibility for the Purple Heart. The added heat generated by this infernal machine which undoubtedly was designed, constructed, and placed in its present location by saboteurs, has prostrated enough of our yeoman staff to require this petition to be written in long hand by the commanding officer himself.

He touched on details of lesser importance and requested the work be done in San Diego if time permitted. Lighting was inadequate in many passageways and compartments and in the topside system of anchor, running and signal lights. The forward masthead light needed relocation. The forward range light presently cast illumination on the deck below, an open invitation to enemy sighting, and should be redesigned or relocated. It was also necessary to raise the after masthead light which presently interfered with gunnery orbits. He did not explain that this circumstance had come about

after the unauthorized change by shipboard personnel in the safety
limits of that particular gun mount.

The arrival welcome in San Diego included a Navy brass band.
The crew stood by divisions on the flight deck and heard the
cheers and the thumping military airs and they felt seasoned and
proud, as though they had come back from where they were yet
to go.

30

Among the first visitors to step aboard *Shiloh* in San Diego was the ubiquitous public relations officer, Floyd Faygill. He had flown west from Washington after meeting with his superiors and Admiral Nickelby. He fidgeted impatiently in the passageway outside Paige's cabin under the coldly impersonal eye of Marine private Shane. Faygill was waiting until the yard officials who were in conference with Paige, completed their trivial business so that he could take up the urgent matter of Paige's public image. Faygill was a dapper man in his mid-thirties. His tight-fitting khaki uniform, tailored of a specially faded tropical worsted, seemed to glisten as though embedded with crushed sequins. His campaign ribbons, had he worn any, would have carried the stripes of Hollywood and Vine and battle stars won along Sunset Strip.

He smelled of anise. Tiny beads of perspiration clung to his pale forehead. He gasped from time to time like a small fish out of water, which he was. The Navy was not for Floyd Faygill and he almost believed it. It had been the lesser of two evils that had brought him here. He was a clever Hollywood agent but not clever enough to placate his draft board officials. In spite of a seltzer bottle deliberately dropped on his foot and his efforts to win them over with the promise of favors from his lesser known starlet clients, he was given twenty-four hours to choose a service or be drafted. A minor studio executive engaged in the preparation of

Navy training films paved the way to an appointment in Washington and the rest, of course, made brief history in the Hollywood trade papers.

The public image of Harry Paige was Faygill's first assignment. It rankled that he had been handled badly at the Newell reception in Washington, and he said so.

Commodore Blatchford, wise in the labyrinthine ways of the Navy, went directly to the man who mattered and who happened to be in Washington at the time. The interview with Admiral Nickelby was one Faygill would not forget for the rest of his days.

"Not a chance," Nickelby said flatly. "Captain Paige is a sailor, not an actor."

"He's a hero, Admiral. The Navy's first. The American public deserves a look at a real hero."

"Sorry. We need Captain Paige elsewhere."

This is no different, Faygill thought quickly, from negotiating with studio heads. The unfamiliarity with uniforms had thrown him off. He smiled the smile that had tied the fabulous Mona Warren to a ten-year contract. "Then Captain Paige is indispensable to the war effort. Is that it, sir?"

"No one's indispensable." Nickelby frowned. Why did he allow those shore-based knuckleheads and paper-shufflers to get him into this? "He just isn't available and, in the present situation, cannot be spared."

"It would be good for the morale of the folks at home to see the hero of Sunda Strait in the flesh, Admiral. More than that, it would reflect the generosity of the Navy and help the Navy image." He warmed to the sound of his own voice. "You were the man who released the news of that victory to the American people. A generous gesture, believe me, and the American people are grateful, and the way they can show their gratitude is with dollars and those dollars, billions of them, will come from the pockets of the people who attend these bond rallies. Bond rallies, Admiral, in my humble opinion, are as essential to the war effort as battleships and—I beg your pardon?"

"I said shut your hole. You talk too damn fast and too much. Don't tell me about battleships. You've never seen the inside of one." He rubbed his jaw and his eyes raked Faygill who seemed to shrivel before their icy blueness. His shoulders slumped. The animated expression in his eyes faded. Nickelby could not know this identical ploy before the crowned heads of Magna Coronet studios had won Faygill's male star client, Toby Tremont, the lead over Gable and Tracy in the 1939 epic, *Flames of Fortune*.

Nickelby's tone softened. "I'm running out of time, young man. I know you have a job to do. So have I. You're quite right. The public interest *is* important to the war effort. Paige will be out on the Coast in about ten days. You can have him for twenty-four hours, no more." He consulted a desk calendar. "Two weeks from this coming Sunday. He'll be skippering the new carrier *Shiloh* and he'll have his hands full. I'll have Captain Miehle cut the orders at once."

Faygill straightened. His eyes were moist, a trick Mona Warren had taught him. "How can I thank you, Admiral."

"By just shoving off. I've got work to do."

"How's about a tinted photograph of my client, Mona Warren, personally autographed by her?"

"Mona Warren? You're a real con man, Faygill." Nickelby almost blushed. "I'd be delighted."

"Listen, so will Mona. An admiral, no less." He zipped his briefcase closed, all crisp business again. "Anything I can do for you, Admiral, just return the courtesy."

"Thank you." He gravely waved Faygill to the door. Faygill paused. "Ever think of a movie career, Nick? You'd make a hell of a Lincoln, that big head, dignity, suffering. It comes across. You project it. What's Massey got you ain't got? When this war bit's over, you give me a ring, we'll get together."

He waved goodbye to Captain Miehle who stood at the open door, and was gone.

"Come in and close the door," Nickelby said smiling.

"If I hadn't heard it with my own ears," Miehle said.

"Mona Warren, no less. Not a bad way to fight a war." He stared at Miehle for a long moment. "Tell me the truth, Charley, do *you* think I could play Lincoln? I mean really?"

The yard officials left and Paige waved Faygill into the cabin. He was not exactly delighted to see Faygill but Nickelby's advice lingered in his mind. "Welcome aboard, Lieutenant." He repressed a smile. "I'm pleased to see your shoulder boards properly attached."

"Live and learn, Captain."

"It's permissible to remove your cap, Mr. Faygill. In fact it's obligatory."

Faygill obliged. He clutched his slim leather briefcase to his breast. "You know, Captain, you're harder to see than Sam Goldwyn."

"Sam who?"

"Ha, ha! That's one for Skolsky. Sam who! You Navy guys kill me. Like Nicky last week in Washington?"

"Nicky?"

"That admiral, Nicholas? Nixon? To me he's Nicky. He's the one got the approval for the bond rally you're gonna be at. So anyways—"

"What bond rally?"

"Hollywood Bowl. Salute to the Stars. You're the big star, the war hero, along with Mona Warren of the silver screen."

"When's all this?"

"Sunday. Day after tomorrow."

"What makes you so cocksure I'll be here?"

"These orders." He tapped his elegant briefcase.

"Show me."

Faygill unzipped the briefcase and handed a thick official envelope to Paige. "You told me to go through channels. In Washington, remember? Obeyed your orders to the letter, Captain."

Paige read the orders. Faygill was quite right. They had more endorsements than the Declaration of Independence.

"How come I didn't get a set of these orders?"

"You were at sea. The Bureau decided I'd be authority enough in person."

"Looks like we'll be around here at least forty-eight hours, anyway."

"You'll have time to do this rally and still get the necessary repair work done. Kill two birds with one stone. That's what Nicky said. What a character. Wants to be an actor when the war's over. Wants to do Lincoln."

"Admiral Nickelby?"

"None other. Okay. You're a busy man. I'll give it to you fast. Everything's set for Sunday. It's all there in that envelope. Meet you at the airport and we roll to the Bowl. There's a big money raising affair that night at Chickie Dee's, you remember, the child actress? Now she's no child any more and she never was an actress. But she's big in charity work now. Big in other places, too. Hahaha."

Now how long you gonna be around? After the Bowl bit, there's all kinds of deals we can swing."

"Just the one, Lieutenant. We're not going to be around too long."

"Sunday then. And we'll knock 'em dead. There's a billion dollars riding you, Captain."

"And you get ten percent."

"Hey! You're on the ball! Listen—"

"I won't play Lincoln. Or Washington or Jefferson. That's all, Lieutenant. See you on Sunday."

He turned back to the estimates of yard work that could be accomplished within forty-eight hours. Not too bad, he mused. He called Lobo Logan. "We've got forty-eight hours. They'll be tearing out sections of the ventilation system all over the ship, Lobo. I'm due in Los Angeles on Sunday and rather than live through the ruckus here, I'm checking into a hotel in town. Here are the job orders. They can't touch the catapults, damn it, but just about everything else is in the works. Highest priority is the vent system. They're relocating and completely rebuilding the trash burner and if it's not ready before we shove, we'll complete it at sea. Lighting's no problem, they tell me. So it's all yours, Lobo. I'll check with you by phone from L.A." He pulled out a suitcase and began to throw some clothes into it. "There's time for one port and starboard liberty. See that the men get it. And you can tell 'em for me, Lobo, they've earned it. They're doing one hell of a fine job."

31

~~~~~~

Los Angeles in 1942 was still untroubled by air pollution. But the
end of May, smog or no smog, is a time of year even the most
chauvinistic of Southern Californians will not brag about. Spirits
sag and tempers rub raw easily. A dry invisible gloom hangs over
the city; it looks and feels like rain but it never rains. Yet the
Hollywood Bowl was packed. Floyd Faygill had done his work
well and the common people had come for a firsthand look at
the hero of Sunda Strait. He could not miss. Had Faygill arranged
for Paige to stand on a flag-bedecked enchilada anchored off the
Santa Monica pier, they would have marched into the sea to cheer
him.

For three hours, dull speeches echoed back and forth across the
Hollywood hills. The people listened to the mayor, two governors,
a minister, a rabbi, a priest, the Commandant of the 12th Naval
District, an American Legion commander, three film stars (one male,
one female, one neuter—all of whom detested each other), the president of the Gold Star Mother-in-Laws of America, and the United
States Navy Band. There were others eyeing the microphone long-
ingly, but the crowd began chanting Paige's name and the sound
swelled and the mayor shrugged and conferred and finally took
Paige by the arm to the center of the stage. The crowd went wild.
Here was a war hero in the flesh, first run, a world première. They
stood and cheered him for three minutes. The mayor's words were

lost in the roar of their voices and it was too bad because the mayor had spent many hours with his speech writers, polishing phrases like "unscathed from the fiery cauldron of combat" and "salty, seagoing saviour of Sunda Strait."

Cameras rolled and the band blared *Anchors Aweigh*. Paige was reminded for a startled moment of David. He stood very straight, not smiling, wishing they would shut up and let him say what he had come to say so that he could go back where he belonged. When they finally quieted down, he spoke and what he said quite simply was this: He was deeply moved by their ovation. It was too bad the men who died or who were taken prisoner at Sunda Strait were not on hand to hear it. The war was still a losing war and warriors were not necessarily the men in uniform alone but every American everywhere who believed in the ideals of our great nation. Unless each and every one of them did his part, it would continue to be a losing war. But with the help of every one, the war would be won. He was going back out there again. All he wanted from them was the promise of their support—moral, physical, and financial. It would assure him that, when he returned to the men at war, there would be a heartening story to tell them. And he thanked them very much.

Men wept. Strong women fainted. Hats, bags, flags, bottles, purses, cushions, and two small children were flung in the air. A spunky pacifist sandwiched between two protesting statements was squeezed to unconsciousness when he tried to mount the stage. He was flung into the pool and upon being revived was rushed to the County Jail. Pickpockets and sex deviates had a field day and three sorority sisters from UCLA zipped out of their summer dresses and marched arm in arm clad only in one red, one white, and one blue rayon slip.

Ushers who had passed out pledge cards and war bond blanks, were besieged. One made off with a tidy sun of unreported cash. Nobody was killed or died of a heart attack. A colored baby boy, born in the ladies' rest room, was christened Instant Harrison Jones.

It was five-thirty when Faygill brought Captain Paige to Chickie Dee's Sunset Boulevard home. The party had already begun. Attendants dressed in white shirts and red bow ties, and looking remarkably fit for 4-Fs, met the arriving guests at the huge stone entrance gates. One of them took over the wheel and maneuvered the official Navy sedan up the curving drive, tires squealing, to the broad steps where a reception group of hardfaced kids with auto-graphs waited for them. The books were thrust at Paige. It was a new experience and he looked at Faygill for guidance.

"Five," Faygill said. "We're already late."

Paige scrawled his name, rank, and serial number five times, and followed Faygill up the steps and into a moving wall of news reporters and photographers.

"Two minutes, boys," Faygill ordained.

"How's it feel being America's first Navy hero?"

"The name's Paige, not John Paul Jones."

"Did you get bawled out in Washington for risking the multi-millionaire's son's life?"

Paige looked at Faygill who shrugged and said, "Newell's kid. The tennis player."

"What about Newell?"

"Faygill here—"

"Faygill wasn't there. Nobody got bawled out for anything. We were lucky to get off together."

"Why aren't the other survivors with you?"

"Weren't invited, I guess. This looks like a pretty snooty party."

"Don't print that," Faygill squealed.

Someone shoved a newspaper under Paige's nose. It showed Thomas A. Newell, sleeves rolled up, at work in his munitions plant. A three-column headline read: TYCOON BLASTS NAVY SKIPPER HERO. "ENDANGERED MY BOY'S LIFE," SAYS NEWELL.

"Care to comment, Captain?"

"Two minutes are up." Faygill grabbed Paige's arm and pushed through the crowd.

"How's about a few group shots inside, Floyd?"

"You guys nuts or something?" He led Paige through the open door past a bowing butler, grumbling, "That's all we need is pictures inside of this here Roman orgy." He moved ahead of Paige like a scenting hound. Paige followed, his eyes focused on the non-regulation mat of black oily hair that glistened at the nape of Faygill's neck.

"I'd have liked to answer that Newell lie."

"You kidding? No matter what you said, they'd cockalize you."

"They ought to know the truth."

"Let's get one thing straight, Harry boy. You kill Japs. I do the talking. Okey doke?"

Paige contained his anger. Thanks to Faygill, he had not had a drink all day, or a free moment, or a chance to defend himself against a published lie. Now Faygill's jaunty disrespect was the last straw. Chickie Dee's effusive welcome interrupted his thoughts. She took both his hands in hers and embarked on a garrulous eulogy. She had been there and wept with the others at the Hollywood Bowl, she said. Her eyes were dewy and kept blinking away the mascara. She was not yet thirty and trussed in her four-way-stretch armor, she looked rather desperate, he thought.

"The captain's all mine now, Floydsie." She pulled Paige's head down and delivered a moist and gin-soaked kiss some where near the bridge of his nose. Blind, too, Paige thought and resigned himself.

"He's all yours, Chickie darling."

She clamped her arm around Paige's sleeve and led him off.

"He can have that drink now," Faygill whispered and winked at Chickie Dee.

"What's the damn joke?" Paige demanded.

"Come along, you great big hero man, and meet these darling people."

He met them in all sizes, shapes, and colors. Men in dinner jackets ranging from desert white to midnight blue, with small lapels and wide lapels and no lapels, in materials of silk and cashmere and iridescent alpaca. The ladies were consistent only in the low altitude of their décolletage. Except for Faygill, no other Navy officers were present. There were several Army officers in dress uniforms. Chickie introduced them as directors, writers, or producers, rattling off their names and screen credits in the same breath. Paige had not heard of any of them, and had never heard films called credits.

They greeted him with studied deference. A real privilege, they said. An *honor*, and when he left, they examined their soft hands for bloodstains.

He was fed two watered drinks before dinner. They got him nowhere except closer to Chickie Dee, who announced that dinner was served. There were four places at a small café table and he sat down to dinner with a hundred others on a lavishly landscaped terrace.

It was hot and he was thirsty and he drank a lot of wine. He sat between Mona Warren and an actress whose long blonde

hair half-hid her face. The half Paige saw and the rest of her,
looked fine. Her name was Joyce Something and she spoke in a
low voice trained to sound breathless and sexy. She was sexy all
right, Paige decided. Driving to Chickie's earlier, Faygill had touted
Mona Warren as the hottest Hollywood property since Harlow.
The concept of any well-stacked female as "property" intrigued
Paige. Joyce Something, however, made Mona Warren look like
something the cat dragged in.

He had also observed that after a brief nod, the two women
had nothing to say to each other. The fourth place at the table
was reserved for Faygill. After a token stab at his cracked crab
and a gulp of wine, he had flown off like a nervous sparrow, hopping
from table to table. That was fine with Paige. He chose to concentrate on Joyce but to his surprise, Mona Warren would have
none of it. She demanded his full attention, firing questions at
him and barely waiting for his answers. She had an oddly rasping
voice that dredged up memories of tarts in the Sand Street beer
joints. Her words seemed loose and carelessly strung together and
her hands were never still. She had long soft auburn hair which
she constantly pushed back from her face. She wanted to know
everything. She wanted to know it right now. Wild as a hawk,
Paige guessed, and just as cuddly.

Sunda Strait, she demanded. What's the color of the water? The
hills? Why? Was anything omitted from the newspaper accounts
that she should know? That he could tell her? She wanted it
straight from the horse's mouth, she said. Newspapers are too
damned vague and they're censored something awful, aren't they? She
began to interest him. In male defense he moved his thigh until it
touched Joyce's, an unyielding and indifferent contact. Her back was
lovely and Paige yearned to stroke it. Mona wanted to know in a
strident voice if he had ever tried Javanese women. How big is an
eight-inch shell? In everyday inches, she insisted, because she had
seen pictures of them and they looked a hell of a lot longer than
eight inches. She was wide-eyed and her lips were provocatively
moist and he did not miss the curious line her questions had taken.
He wondered how she'd react to the sausage and provolone in the
Italian delicatessen store window in Brooklyn.

He removed the empty magnum from the ice bucket and wiped
it with a cloth and held it up and explained that this was about
half the size of an eight-inch shell and the diameter of the base is

what usually determined the calibre designation. Mona was delighted and took the magnum and stroked it and hefted it and measured Paige and they laughed together and he removed his thigh from Joyce who could not have cared less.

The waiter brought a fresh magnum and Paige settled down for a long run. It's been a hard day at the office, he told himself. I need this little pick-me-up. Before I know it I'll be out there where they're throwing hot steel for real and all this gash and bash will be nothing but a wistful memory.

Mona rattled on. Why is a ship called "she"? Is it because the sailors ride her? Is it true, she asked, all innocence, the salty ones bugger the younger ones at sea? An old warrant officer, retired now, had told her that. On she went, all business, witty and sharp. Paige found himself entranced. She was direct and not phony and he began to respect her. She was talking now about the rat race Hollywood was. Dog eat dog and a knife in every back. He glanced once more at Joyce, lovely as a Dresden doll, and he thought of all the things these star-struck kids must do to get anywhere. He could see at once why Mona could make it and Joyce never would. Balls, he thought. Even on women. What I have, he told himself surprised, and a hell of a lot of other men don't.

A man named Sherm joined them. Sherm was Mona's business manager, he announced proudly. A short, broad-beamed man with a cast in his right eye, he wore a white dinner jacket with white satin lapels and a red velvet cummerbund. He had to see how Mona was making it with a real-life hero, he explained while his arm snaked round her to touch the side of her breast. Paige sat through two minutes of trade talk laced with free feels and low level *double entendre*. Snide innuendo was Sherm's sole stock in trade and Paige was relieved when Faygill signaled him to come over. It was time for the "shpiel," Faygill said, the pitch, if the good captain would be so kindly.

The orchestra struck up *Hail, the Conquering Hero Comes*, and Captain Harrison Paige, U.S.N., was introduced to the assembled guests by Chickie Dee, who had to be propped up and prompted.

Paige said just about what he had said that afternoon at the Bowl. He told them the war was being fought right here in Chickie Dee's pool garden just as much as it was being fought out there in the blue Pacific. The only difference was, you didn't get hit in the same places. Here you got hit in the pocketbook, but that didn't mean it didn't hurt as much.

After the applause died, he looked but could not find Faygill. He went back to the table and both girls were gone. An actor who was passing out pledge cards for funds handed one to Paige and he handed it back. He wandered toward the high prickly hedge that shut the view of Sunset Boulevard and stood there in the shadows listening to the purr of traffic. One of the guests came over and began talking. He was J. J. Blodgett, he said, and he wanted Captain Paige to know how much he had enjoyed his speech. Paige thanked him but there was more than thanks on J. J. Blodgett's mind. Did Paige know he was the J. J. Blodgett of Galveston and he had just pledged twenty-five thousand dollars to the war effort? He had read that stinking piece Old Man Newell had stuck in one of his newspapers and it was a goddam unpatriotic shame and somebody had ought to take after that traitor with a rope and a six-shooter. Yessiree, J. J. Blodgett of Galveston and he didn't make it in oil and cattle like all the others, he made it in scrap iron. Yessiree.

"I got to thinking, hearing you talking nice and quiet and straight from the shoulder and I tol' myself, Ol' J.J., there's your brand of hombre, and I got to thinking, what's a hombre like that got waiting for him when the war's over but peacetime nothing. I said to myself, Ol' J.J., you going to do that hombre a good turn, and Captain, here it is. Comes the day the war's over, there's going to be a mess of ol' battleships setting on their rusty ol' bottoms, nobody wanting them. And all you got to do is you come work for Ol' J.J. and rustle up them surplus bottoms and we bust them down for scrap and make us a pile."

He's too small to hit, Paige thought, and too greasy. And I'm the guest of honor and I'm in the uniform of a commissioned officer of the United States Navy and pledged to die rather than bring shame or dishonor on it. He pushed J. J. Blodgett of Galveston gently into the prickly hedge and wedged him there.

He avoided the guests dancing and feeding on the terrace and circled to the side of the house. He went through the vast kitchens to a billiard room where he was surprised to find a bar set up with a bartender in attendance and no drinkers. He ordered a double bourbon and tasted it and put it down. "Tell me something," he said to the bartender. "How come a wealthy dame like this Chickie Dee waters her booze?"

The man looked embarrassed. "She don't, Captain."

"Well if this is Old Grandad, I'm the King of Siam. It's nine-tenths water and you know it." He started to leave.

"Captain Paige, sir. I'm only following orders. I was told to serve you watered-down drinks."

"Whose orders?"

"That Navy lieutenant commander brought you here. Was it up to me you could have it straight by the case." He grinned. "I was in the Armed Guard on the Atlantic convoys in World War I, sir."

"Well, pour me an honest drink, damn it. I've some catching up to do."

"Aye, sir."

Paige drank two, deep and straight, and he rode it all the way to the bottom. He turned on his heel and marched straight out into the arms of Floyd Faygill who grabbed him.

"You won't believe this, Harry. It's already over a hundred eighty thousand smackers." He stared at Paige closely. "You hear what I said?" And sniffed and shrank back. "You been boozing behind my back. Let go my arm. Hey!"

Paige stood him against the shadows of the pool machinery shed. "You ordered my whisky watered, didn't you?"

"Just at the start, Harry ol' boy. Protect you so you could make that pitch with dignity, pride, reflect honor on the service—ow! C'mon, willya?" His voice rose shrilly. "You're hurting my arm."

"I ought to break it, you cheap crumb. I'll put up with your bond rallies and teas and rummy kid actresses, but you so much as touch a glass of my whisky again, Faygill, and I'll bust every bone in your chicken shit body." He rammed Faygill once against the shed so hard, his teeth rattled. "Now get me out of here and back where I belong."

"We can't go now. The party's just beginning."

"For you, Faygill. I got work to do."

"We need you for the final drawing, Harry baby. The door prize."

"I'll be in the bar." He released Faygill who sagged to the grass. Paige stalked into the bar and moodily drank another bourbon while the bartender recalled the hardships of the Armed Guard in 1918. Paige escaped to the garden where the tables were being cleared and some of the guests were dancing. Chickie Dee had passed out and had been carried to her boudoir. Her current lover, a fake flamenco dancer called Paco, was instructing Mona Warren in a rumba. A small party of guests watched an exhibition of the Lambeth Walk. On the tennis court, ignored, a stunning young blonde with a long pageboy bob was draped over the net, throwing up.

Faygill came out of the house trying to look as though nothing had happened. He carried two brandy snifters and handed one to Paige. "A hundred ninety one thousand, Harry. How you like them potatoes?"

"When do we go?"

"Two hundred grand's the goal. That doll Mona Warren raised sixty grand alone."

"At how much a throw?"

Faygill spilled some of his drink, laughing. "Got to tell Mona. She'll split a gut. Where's my gal, Mona?"

"Rubbing bellies on the dance floor with Chickie's wetback."

Faygill weaved onto the dance floor and Paige looked for Joyce. She was deep in conversation with a uniformed producer whose hands fondled her abstractedly while she talked. Paige wondered what his credits were. None of them showed. He walked by the pool, full of drink, sick of small talk, his head whirling. He was bored stiff with people who could buy a battle with a checkbook. He thought of the scared Dutch resident in Tjilatjap with his acres of ruined tea and his German *Frau* and his pathetic efforts to save his skin with a few bottles of gin.

He was sorry he allowed them to talk him into this. It was the last time he would be suckered into the hero crap routine. He wished Faygill would get his two hundred grand fast so they could clear the hell out. He wandered into the house again avoiding the loquacious 1918 hazard to navigation behind the bar. He found a wood-paneled library in a remote wing of the house. The bookshelves were cluttered with a senseless collection of bric-a-brac. A set of tall volumes in leather bindings caught his eye. He took one down and opened the crisp vellum pages. It contained a script of a film Chickie Dee had starred in fifteen years ago. Stills from the film and several hand-tinted closeups revealed what a healthy and detestable child she must have been. The frontispiece was inscribed by the scenario writer. *To America's Darling, the heroine of this, my first book.* It was signed with flourishes under the title *Alice in Wonderland.*

Paige settled down in a satin-covered love seat to wait for Faygill. The fabric felt cold and slithery against the back of his neck. He put his feet on a carved coffee table and sipped the good bourbon.

A glittering statuette on the table near the toe of his shoe was a miniature replica of Chickie Dee in a juvenile role that had made her fortune. It stood a foot high on an onyx base, gold with an ivory halo over her rigid curls. He was nudging it with his shoe when Mona Warren came in.

"I've been looking for you, Captain."

Mona Warren, he thought. Looking for me. And closing the door, by God. "Here I am, Miss Warren."

She crossed the room and he liked the way she moved, swingy as a cat. She stood over him across the coffee table and he decided he was too drunk to risk standing. He motioned to the seat alongside. She did not move. "Floyd just told me what you said."

"What'd I say?"

"And he had the unmitigated gall to repeat your cruel remark in front of God knows how many people. I could have died."

"That would be a great loss."

"And they try to tell me about officers and gentlemen."

"What did I say? I don't remember anything I said."

"About the money I personally raised in pledges. 'How much a throw?' you said. Did you or did you not say it? Or is that son of a bitch Floyd lying again?"

Direct and to the point. You had to admire a broad like that. Paige got to his feet not ungracefully, all considered. He bowed. "I said it. It was unkind. I should have known better than to expect Faygill to keep his stupid mouth shut."

"Do you think I'm a whore, Captain? A prostitute? Running around dropping my drawers for a fee? That was a loathsome and uncalled-for remark and I trust you're gentleman enough to do what's expected of you under the circumstances."

"I'd marry you, Miss Warren, and make you an honest girl. But I'm already married."

"You could offer an apology."

"I'm sorry."

"Thank you." She smiled and it was a lovely sight. "It was a very funny remark. Do you have a cigarette?"

He found one in a leather box on the table and looked for a match. She picked up the statuette and pressed Chickie Dee's halo and a tongue of flame licked out of her golden lips. Paige held it while Mona lighted her cigarette. She took his wrist and her fingers were firm and cool. They sat and she examined him critically. "They tell me you're a tough character. *Mucho hombre.*"

He thought of J. J. Blodgett. "I can be tough when I have to."

She touched his nose. "How'd you do that?"

"Boxing."

"My nose has been broken three times."

"Never know it. It's a perfect nose."

"That's why it was broken. To make it perfect. People get the idea being in pictures is a cinch. You're as good as your plastic surgeon, your wardrobe designer, your director, your cameraman, and your agent. It's a rat race."

"Why do you do it?"

"Why do you do what *you* do?"

He grinned. "Okay. We're two of a kind."

"I had that feeling, too." She seemed amused. "You kind of dug that Joyce, didn't you?"

"She's a very lovely-looking girl."

"You'd never get to first base."

"She never gave me a chance."

"She didn't dare."

"Why not?"

"She belongs to the horniest bull dyke west of Denver."

"What a waste."

"Oh, she'd like a fellow, but she has no choice. The old bull is hard as nails and rich as Rockefeller. Joyce is cute, I'll admit that, but she can't act worth a damn. Her dyke friend runs her life, gets her bit parts, lines up the producers and directors for her and picks up all the tabs."

"She here tonight?"

"I didn't see her, but she keeps a private eye on Joyce twenty-four hours round the clock. She'd have you mugged if she thought you wanted a piece of Joyce."

"Even the small piece I might want?"

"Especially that."

"Thanks for the tip."

"Believe me, Captain, Sunda Strait was easier."

He really liked her now. "Can I get you a drink?"

"Never touch it."

"Good for the soul, sometimes."

"I like my soul the way it is."

"Lucky girl."

"Oh, I've got problems. Whisky won't solve them, though."

Someone knocked. "Bust down the door," Mona yelled. It was Paco. "You slipped away, *guapa*," he said. "They playing the rumba. Come on." His teeth shone and his soft brown eyes watched Paige uneasily.

"Too tired, darling."

"But you love the rumba." He executed a few steps. "Eh? You remember?"

"Some other time, Paco."

"The best time, right now—"

"Vamoose, will you?"

"You heard the lady," Paige said. "And close the door."

"Sorry, Admiral." Paco closed the door behind him.

"I hate cheats and phonies," Mona said. "Ye gods." She kicked off her shoes and stretched.

"Nice man. Called me admiral."

"You like that?"

"Feels good inside."

"I was queen of a Navy hop once. Nineteen thirty-five. My date was the top of his class. Real cute. Crewcut. Had a sword and all that golden stuff on his shoulder—what'd he call it?"

"Chicken guts."

"Right. Chicken guts. Ugh. Was I dumb. Seventeen. Did anything then for publicity. Wonder whatever became of him?"

"What was his name?"

"All I remember, he was from the Midwest. How can a Navy man come from the Midwest?"

"Ernie King's from Ohio."

"Who's Ernie King?"

"My studio boss."

The door opened and Sherm stuck his round bald head into the room. Mona jumped to her feet. "Sherm, you dumb jerk, I've told you a hundred times never to walk in on me without knocking."

"Sorry, baby. Excuse, please, *mon capitain?* Mona, for Chri'sake, everybody wants to know where the hell you are."

"So tell 'em."

"You're supposed to be seen, baby—"

"I'm being seen right now by the United States Navy and next time you knock, or you're minus one client and ten percent."

"Sorry, I swear. Now c'mon."

"What do you want me to do?"

"I want you should mingle."

"I'm mingling with Captain Paige. Paco sent you, didn't he? You go back and tell that two-timing grease ball to keep his nose where it belongs, which is right up his alcoholic girl friend's crotch."

Sherm left hurriedly. "I get so mad," Mona said in a small voice.

"You should drink," Paige said. "Works wonders."

"Let's just blow this crummy joint. I've had it. And I like you. You've got something I haven't seen for a long time." She kissed him and before he could respond, she reached for her shoes and slipped them on and was across the room. "Meet you out front. Tell the boys to bring up my Caddy. Mingle. For a bloodsucker like that Sherm. Can you imagine?"

He picked up his cap in the entrance hall and went out to the broad steps and asked for Miss Warren's car and when they brought it he sat in it in the shadow of tall eucalyptus trees. Their spicy smell and the beige shagginess of their peeling skins relaxed him. The top was down and the leather glove-soft and he felt very good alone, waiting for the celebrated Mona Warren who was a plain everyday girl like a hundred others he had known. Cars were parked bumper to bumper in the driveway and along the shaded street off Sunset. He could hear traffic below, over the big expanse of shrubbery and a lawn planted with what seemed to be cabbages but which he knew were some exotic growth. Nobody in Beverly Hills would plant a lawn with cabbages. It was a clean place except for the people. He liked the look and the feel of it and he thought it might be good to live in California after the war, to drag his lovely Felicia by the roots of her hair if necessary, out of that termite-ridden tomb of Navy memorabilia and away from the cruddy commodore and the tight dry world of military ritual to the sunny warmth and open spaces, and own a piece of God's earth that wasn't a Navy hand-me-down. And what was taking Mona Warren so long?

She came along the side of the house trailing a fur coat and he could not understand why anyone would want a fur coat in the hot weather of Southern California. There were so many things he did not understand about the place, he decided to skip it. The boy held the door and she was in and they were off.

"They'll be mad as hell," she said. "We have car pools now and I brought three others with me."

"Let 'em walk." He thought of Faygill. "I can have Faygill take them home."

"Forget it. I want no favors from Faygill. Costs too much in the end."

"I thought everybody loved him."

"He's a stinker, but he's the smartest flack on the Strip."

She turned off Sunset into the hills. The road twisted and climbed past arty villas half-obscured by shrubbery planted to the road's edge. Mona raced on the turns, skidding dangerously and keeping her foot hard on the pedal. The dimout made the edge of the road difficult to see. Neither of them spoke. The way she drove occupied both of them. He was relieved when they finally got there.

32

She lived on the summit. She led Paige to the living room and excused herself and he went out to the railed terrace and looked down two thousand feet to the floor of a canyon. The lights in the distant valley flickered like votive lamps. He had been aloft in the foretops of ships rolling in heavy seas that had alarmed him less than this. He went inside and Mona was there waiting. "You're the first man I've ever known who did not say a word about the way I drive."

"I was too scared."

"You weren't scared." This time she kissed him and stayed there and he knew everything was going to be all right.

There was a small fireplace and he got a fire going while Mona fetched ice and drinks from the kitchen. Bookshelves lined two walls. Crane. London. Turgenev. Conrad. Gogol. Kipling. Crazy, he thought. The bottom shelf held nothing but books about the mind. Psychoanalysis, science and sanity, psychology and in a curious collection apart—Rama, the fables of Panchatantra, the Surangama Sutra. How does a healthy dame like this get trapped into a cruddy mess like that? He remembered what she had said about problems whisky wouldn't solve.

Mona came in with ginger ale for herself and a tall bourbon over ice for Paige. "How'd you know it was bourbon I wanted?"

"Smell."

"Smell?"

"I learned young. My father was a drunk." She kicked off her shoes and sat next to him, close to the fireplace. "Beats Chickie Dee's a mile."

"Cheers." He needed this one, he reassured himself. "When do you find time to read all those books?"

"They're mostly my husband's."

"You didn't tell me you had a husband."

"You didn't ask. And you told me you have a wife and I couldn't care less. Anyway my husband and I are separated. He went back to New York a year ago June."

"And left all his books."

"And his clothes. Papers. Everything. Fed up with Hollywood. With me, too, I guess." She laughed, a dry sound. "Some old two-bit actress once told me Jews make the best husbands. She should know. She tried all kinds and she's on her fifth and he's Jewish. Strong for family, she said, good providers, love their children, good in bed. So I married one. Oi! He wanted no family, he detests kids, he couldn't provide beans and he was lousy in bed. He didn't even like Jews. Know what he had the gall once to tell me? This'll kill you, Captain. 'You *shiksas*,' he said, 'you're great for the short haul, the party, the booze, the roll in the hay. For the long haul give me a Jew broad any day.'"

"What's a *shiksa?*"

"A gentile girl. Which I happen to be. He used to say it was our Puritan heritage that makes us lousy lays. Our conscience bothers us and we need liquor as an excuse and that kind of malarkey. He really sold me a bill of goods with his Jewish superiority and all of a sudden one day I woke up and realized here I am supporting this lazy intellectual snob, waiting on him hand and foot and all I get is the snotty holier-than-thou routine."

"So you separated."

"It was his idea, finally. He was sweet in a way. He'd bring me coffee in bed once a week. Recite poetry I didn't understand."

"Is he in the service?"

"He'd cut off a leg first."

"A slacker."

"You'd see it that way, of course."

"Why not? You got him outgunned in the love department so he's probably half queer. And he thinks defending his country is beneath his dignity. You call that a man? How come you fell for a slob like that?"

"We met in New York, you know, actors, and we lived on the west side in this one-room tenement over near Death Avenue and once in a while we'd get a bit part, a walk-on. Then I hit it three years ago in *Fare Thee Well*, my big break. It ran almost a year and Metro gave me a contract and we moved out here and the studio started this big buildup, see? Well, it galled Kent, my husband. Kent Collier, but he was Kenny Cohen when I married him. Anyway, he couldn't take it, me making the money, and he began to drink but on him it didn't look good and he said the studio was breaking up our marriage and my God how I tried to keep it going. So anyway, one day he got mad at Floyd and knocked him down, pushed him, really, and he walked out. Didn't you know? Don't you read Winchell?"

"Do I look like I read Winchell?"

"So because of religious reasons and studio reasons, we're still married, but I go to bed with Zen."

"You still love him?"

"Love! Some day they'll pass a law against that word and it'll cut the divorce rate ninety percent and people'll be happy."

"How long are you married?"

"Five, almost six years."

"Any children?"

"What would I want with kids?"

"A home . . ." He thought of home. "I don't know. Hearing you talk, I got the idea you liked kids."

"I do, damn it."

"Then have a half-dozen."

"I can't. That screwball husband of mine made me take care of that little thing a long time ago."

"What do you mean?"

"There's nothing there but the box it came in."

"Get a divorce. Adopt a few kids."

"I thought of that. The studio's against it. The publicity. A mess." She brushed the hair from her face. "Hell, I'd marry again and it'd go on the rocks again."

"Maybe you don't like men."

"I love men. It's marriage that fouls me up. When I was fifteen I eloped with a man twice my age. A mechanic, very muscular.

The judge annulled it fast and Rex, that was his name, got in all kinds of trouble because I was a minor. I like men all right. But I'm beginning to think no actress should ever get married. The two don't mix."

"Lots of actresses marry and have careers."

"It takes too much out of their acting. You can't do justice to both. It takes real guts to stick to a career. You got to be peaches and cream on the outside, and a tough, scheming bitch on the inside. You know damned well any woman like that's going to marry a man weaker than herself. So I become a machine. No sentiment, no softness. I do a job."

"Join the Navy. We can use machines built like this."

"I steer clear of love and read my books. The bottom shelf. Those are my books."

"The Chink stuff?"

"Don't knock it. It's a big help to me."

"How long you been on it?"

"I quit high school after two years to go on Broadway and one of the boys in the chorus, a fairy but you know, not dirty or anything, he got me started on the stuff. Hinduism, Zen, the works. I get a bang out of it. You should try reading some of it. I mean with all that time on a boat. Being you're a Navy officer, for instance, you should read Motse on war."

"You mean Mahan."

"Motse. He was an ancient Chinese religious teacher. He shows how stupid war is and he uses plain everyday language. Translated of course from the Chinese."

"I don't think I'd learn anything about war from an old Chink dead a few hundred years."

"Must you use that ugly word?"

"What word?"

"Chink."

"You lived with them as much as I did, you'd call 'em worse names than that." He reached for her. "You didn't bring me here to talk about dead Chinks, did you?"

"You also say dago, kike, and spick, I suppose."

"If that's what they are, sure."

"You military bastards. Race snobs. You're all alike."

"So are civilians who treat us like bus drivers or hotel doormen.

Until a war comes along and scares the hell out of them. Then we're heroes."

She pushed him away and went to the record player and switched it on. "Did you know Confucius was a hypocrite? Motse points it out."

"Moxey. He had an army. Marched on Washington."

"You could be sweet if you weren't so damned sarcastic. I'm trying desperately to educate myself and you make fun. My hairdresser, she's English, she says I should read Henry James. Or is it James Henry?"

"O. Henry?"

"Hemingway. She says I should read him, too; all about bull fights, not those Mexican phonies from Tia Juana but the real Spanish McCoy from Spain. Sherm is all the time telling me to brush up on current events. Current events are very important today. I'm always trying to improve myself. Just the other day you'll never guess who I bunked into in the studio commissary. This Southern writer from Mississippi by the name of Faulkner. A perfect gentleman, soft-spoken and so polite at first I thought he was soused. You could have knocked me over with a feather when they told me later who he was. I could sit and listen to that Southern accent all day long. That's the one thing I'm good at, the studio says. Mimicking accents. In *Fare Thee Well*, I was from Canarsie, Brooklyn, and I rolled them in the aisles. Why not? I spent three weeks in Canarsie listening. Even Sherm, who's from the Boro Park section of Brooklyn would have sworn I was from Canarsie, my own business manager. Even now I'm taking elocution and diction. Voice teachers. All last week I spent learning how to cry. It's a real art."

"Talk Brooklyn for me."

"So listen, I could sit here all night waiting for an invite you should dance with me?"

"That's very good." He got up carefully. "I'm inviting."

"I'm dancing."

They came together in the semidark, moving, not quite dancing. "The newspapers call you Hardtack. Why?"

"A Navy nickname."

"I like it. From now on I'm calling you Hardtack. Hi, Hardtack."

"Hi. All engines ahead full."

"Watch out for the lamp."

"All engines stop."

"You know we're going to make love, don't you, Hardtacksie?"

"We are?"

"Indeedsie."

"If that's the policy of the house, ma'am, I've no choice but to go along with it."

"It's not the customary policy. It's just that the management, due to wartime conditions, is willing to make an exception."

"I admire a well-run shore establishment, ma'am."

The phone rang and Paige jumped. "Ignore it," Mona said.

"Man your battle stations," Paige said.

The phone continued to ring and she removed it from its cradle. A male voice squeaked. Mona put Paige's arms around her.

"You could hang up and cut off the damned squeaking," he said.

"I like it. Sounds like a mouse with a leg caught in a trap."

"Sweet girl."

"It's an unlisted number. There's nobody that has the number that I care to talk with right now. Anyway, it's probably Sherm checking up." Her lips brushed his ear. "I do not care to be interrupted in my war effort." The squeaking clicked abruptly into a dail tone and Mona returned the phone to its cradle. "Where were we?"

"I was stepping on your feet and bumping into things."

"Dancing. Yes."

"What I need's a breath of fresh air."

She helped him out to the terrace. He sucked in the clean night air. In the distance along the hazy curve of coastline dimmed headlights of cars moved north and south. Somewhere beyond that, he thought drunkenly the war is waiting. He reached for Mona and they kissed and still kissing, moved against each other.

"Feel better, Hardsie?"

"Best."

"No more to drink for you."

"Says who?"

"You're enough man without it. Ye gods, the creeps I meet day in, day out, pawing like I'm a bargain mink in Macy's basement."

"I'm pawing."

"I like it." Her hands ran over him. "You're solid rock."

He took her in his arms and it was everything it should have been. She pulled away, breathing hard. "One more like that and over the railing I go."

"I need a drink."

"Can't you love me without a drink?"

"Has nothing to do with it."

"The hell it doesn't. Kent was right. *Shiksas, shaygitzes*, it's all the same. Son of a bitch. Goddam puritans. I'm going inside."

He followed her, stumbling. "Where d'you keep the booze?"

"It's your wife, isn't it? You haven't the guts to cheat on her. Right?" She shook him angrily. "I knew it. What's she like?"

"You crazy or something?"

"Fat and ugly with pus sores and an ass full of tattoos. Don't tell me. I know Navy wives."

"She's twice the woman you are. In all departments."

"I'll bet."

"Beautiful. Wealthy. A hothouse orchid."

"Get Sherm to give her a contract. I'm going to bed, Captain. Good night. Where the hell are my cigarettes?" She sat by the fire, trembling.

"Where's my drink?"

"Get your own goddam drink. I hate the stink of alcohol."

He brought her a cigarette and lighted it and poured himself a drink. End of the line, he told himself. Down the hatch and goodbye snatch. Mona reached for him. "You bastard, I got a real letch for you." She pulled him down until his head rested in her lap. "She loves you, doesn't she?"

"She barely puts up with me."

"A hero like you?"

"No man's a hero to his wife."

"Why the hell not?" She pounded the rug with her fist. "What's with these Navy wives? Don't they know what they've got?"

"Not much with the war on."

"I just bet. Oh those poor little old neglected hot-pants Navy wives. Don't tell me, Hardsie. I've seen 'em with my own eyes. In Tia Juana, drunk as slobs, playing grabass with the greasy gigolos. In the El Cortez and the Del Mar lapping it up like there's no tomorrow. And everything on the house or paid for by Uncle Sam. You don't suppose your ever-loving wife is sitting home right now by the fireside knitting mittens for you—"

He caught her across the side of her face with his open hand. She inched closer, her teeth bared. "You think any of these free and easy allotment bitches know what hard work is? What it's like to be on the set in full make-up at dawn and stand till your nipples freeze while a rundown has-been of a Hungarian director spits all over you in broken English because his Swedish Lesbian of a wife turned a cold ass to him the night before? You think hitting me hurts?" She spit at him. He slapped her again. "Go on," she said. "I can take all you got. I sweat and bleed for pricks like you twenty-four hours a day to stay ahead in this rat race. You think your lily-white wife could stand up to it? The knives and the lies and the crap and the ten percent of everything torn right out of your flesh?"

He took her in his arms and they kissed hard. She bit him.

"The hell with that," he said.

She clung to him. "No, no. I like it."

"Who needs it?"

"You. Me."

"Let's get comfortable."

She slipped from his arms and scrambled to her feet. "Don't try to run my life, damn it. Every son of a bitch who comes along tries to run my life." She threw her cigarette into the fire. "Go on. Go home. I'm going to kill myself."

Their eyes met. "I know," he said. "Greta Garbo in *Camille*." She began to laugh and their arms went round each other. He laughed hard and he could not stop and the tears ran from his eyes and he could not remember the last time he had laughed so hard or had been so happy. Mona Warren, exotic star of the silver screen is Greta Garbo, is a wise tough kid from the wrong side of the tracks. He held her tenderly.

"Stay right there forever," she whispered. "You're so damned good for me. So much like me, it scares me." She took his hand. "One difference. Here," she said, surprising him. "Only here."

"Thank God for the difference."

"Magnum," she said. "Jereboam. What's next?"

"Paige," he said.

Her body was smooth and warm and her bared breasts marvelous to his touch. "I'll make you so happy, darling," she whispered.

Outside tires crunched on stone.

"Christ!" Mona sat up. "Sherm the bloodhound. Right on schedule."

"Get rid of him."

"He's like a leech."

"I'll get rid of him. Fast."

She pulled on her bra. "The damned studio's got a morals clause in my contract and Sherm's scared stiff he'll lose his ten percent." The door chime sounded. "Nobody home," Mona yelled.

"C'mon, Mona. Open up!" The doorknob rattled.

She leaned over and kissed Paige slowly and deeply. "You're sweet," she murmured, a child now. "Protect me, my prince."

"Mona, for Chri'sake, open the door!"

"Why can't those filthy bastards ever leave me alone?" She ran wailing from the room. The bedroom door slammed shut. The lock clicked.

I'm back in Georgetown, Paige thought sourly and zipped up his trousers. He went to the front door and opened it and Sherm pushed past him with Floyd Faygill at his heels.

"Where is she?" Sherm leaned against the bedroom door and began to argue violently with Mona.

"What's the matter with you guys?" Paige demanded.

"You, mister," Sherm snarled.

"Clear out before I throw you out."

Faygill puffed up his bird breast. "Know what the papers'll make of this if it leaks out?"

"You're the only leak," Paige said. "You drip."

"Okay, hero. Into your uniform and back your plane. Those reporters are hot on our tail."

"Who the hell you think you're talking to?"

"Look, Harry boy. You're plastered. On heroes it don't look good. So let's get going."

"Don't make me pull rank on you, Faygill. Shove off and take your fat friend with you."

"You outta your mind, Harry? You got a wife and a kid. You wanna *yentz* away your good name and your career?" He picked up Paige's coat and cap. Paige swept them to the floor. He grabbed Faygill by the collar and the seat of his pants and hustled him to the terrace. Sherm left Mona's locked door and circled cautiously, his face putty gray with fear.

"What're you doing to him?"

"I'm going to hang this little squirt."

Mona came running. "What a marvelous idea." She clapped her hands. Faygill wriggled and Paige slapped his face several times. Sherm fell into a chair and pressed his soft hands to his heart.

"Stop him, Mona, for God's sake, before somebody gets killed."

"Me, Sherm? A slip of a girl? Stop the hero of Sunda Strait?"

"Mona! Sherm!" Faygill's voice echoed hollowly across the canyon. "Call the police."

"I'm having a heart attack," Sherm announced calmly.

"Mona," Paige said, "I'm going to swing this guy from the yardarm. Stand by."

She turned to Sherm. "Do I have a yardarm?"

Paige held Faygill with a knee and one arm. He reached in his pocket for his clasp knife and opened it with his teeth and cut the stout awning cord from its cleat. He wound several lengths round Faygill's right leg and tied the other end to the railing. "You're a Navy officer of the line, Faygill. What knots have I used?"

"Harry boy, for God's sake, let me go!"

"Captain Paige to you. Read your Bluejacket's Manual lately? Okay, sailor. I'm giving you a fighting chance before I heave you over the side. A running bowline? Half hitch? Sheepshank? Cat's paw? How about it, Faygill?"

"Please, Captain. I beg of you."

"I'm busting you to seaman second, Faygill."

Sherm crawled to the terrace. "Captain. I beg of you. You had your little joke? So quit now already?"

"Save your breath and learn the ropes, Sherm. You're next."

Sherm ran to Mona. Paige lifted Faygill and lowered him until the line was taut. He doubled it and took several turns round the railing and secured the ends to the cleat. Faygill's body swung in the night, suspended by a thin ankle. Mona cheered. Paige turned toward Sherm who bolted for the front door. Mona got there first and slid the chain lock in place.

"Out of my way, Mona."

"This is war, Sherm. Remember Pearl Harbor."

Paige cut down the other awning line. He glanced over the railing and checked the lines. "Stand by for your buddy, Faygill."

"We're leaving," Sherm screamed. "I swear to God may I drop dead on this spot we're leaving." He clawed at Mona. "Tell him, darling. My word's as good as gold."

"Make him walk the plank, Hardsie. Sherm the worm. He's crooked as a snake."

Sherm dashed for the bathroom and locked the door. Mona slid to the floor, weak with laughter. Paige came in swinging the awning line like a lariat. "Where's that little kike gone?"

"Damn it, don't *say* things like that!" Mona began to sob.

Paige grinned. "This is a real party." He went out to the terrace and leaned over the rail. "Faygill, can you hear me?"

"Yes, sir."

"Will you leave quietly and not come back?"

"Yes, sir." There was a pause. "You mean by the door, I hope."

"By the door and with your fat friend Sherm. Swear?"

"I swear."

Paige hoisted him to the terrace where he collapsed whimpering. Paige stirred him with his foot. "Tell Sherm it's safe to come out now, and shove off." Faygill began to throw up.

When they had gone, Paige coiled the lines neatly and spliced them and restored them to their cleats. "I'll have that drink now," he said to Mona.

"Aye aye, sir, my captain," Mona said meekly.

They were naked in bed.

"The secret," Mona was saying, "is to know control. This I learned from the *guru*. He's the spiritual teacher, see? Before him I had no control, no *samyama*. I was a pushover. Now with *samyama* I choose the partner, the time, the place, the exact moment. It's like *swayamvara*, where the bride selects the husband she wants from all the other suitors."

"All this on straight ginger ale," Paige said.

"You liked the last position?"

"Astonishing."

"Now I'll show you the pelvic pose. *Supta Vajrasana*. Took me a week just to learn how to pronounce it."

He watched her flex and sway like a cobra and wondered when he would get it. He had to get back to his plane at the airport and time was running out. He sipped some whisky and put the glass back on the night table.

"Watch this closely," she said. She kneeled and leaned back stretching her arms over her head until the scarlet tips of her fingers touched the sheets. She arched her belly upward with sinuous grace.

"And that one's—what?"

"*Supta Vajrasana.*"

"Hold it." He dribbled a few drops of bourbon into the hollow of her navel and lapped it.

"That tickles," she said.

"You could make a fortune in Panama with a trick like that." She began to sag. "It's easier on the floor. More support."

"Okay, Mona. Now let's knock off the fancy Oriental acrobatics and get down to some old-fashioned screwing."

She twisted with surprising swiftness and knocked him flat and pinned his shoulders. Her nipples grazed his chest. "Know something, Hardsie? It's eight months since I've had a piece. Know what that would do to most healthy women? Drive them nuts. Not me. I'm different. Control. *Samyama.* If you have control, you have everything."

"You're a crazy bitch, Mona."

"And we're going to make love. I'm going to pleasure you like you've never been pleasured before. Know why?"

"Quit beating your gums, will you? My God, you're either shooting off your mouth or twisting and turning like a double-jointed monkey."

"You're hurting my feelings."

"You're hurting my you-know-what. Get off me and let's go."

"I want you to know why I chose you to make love to, after eight months of celibacy. Simple Oriental wisdom. You see, if I make love to you, in a sense I'm making love to a million men. How? By association. I close my eyes and when you are in me I say to myself he's not alone. With him are thousands of young lovers who have wanted me but who are dead now—"

"For Chri'sake, Mona!"

"—the black and white and brown men. The yellow men. All the poor darling lovers trapped in a fool's game by selfish old men who send them to their deaths."

"Goddam you." He pushed her away.

"Now," she said suddenly. "*Now!*"

Her arms encircled him and their mouths came together open and searching and she moved not with grace or love but with raw need. He struggled to match the intensity of her passion. She overwhelmed him. They clung in sweat, writhing. Minutes passed.

"What's wrong?" she moaned. "Don't for Jesus sake stop now."

He rolled free, his body heaving. "Sorry," he said thickly.

She sat up. "You fake. You goddam cheating tin hero of a fake."

He climbed over her slack body and found the bourbon bottle in the kitchen. Hottest thing since Harlow. Moose shit. He went through the living room with the bottle and stood naked on the terrace and had a drink. The night air brushed softly on the cold sweat of his body. He went into the bedroom. Mona had a cigarette in her shaking fingers. Tears coursed down her cheeks. Last week's homework, he thought.

"Light my cigarette, please." She did not look at him.

"Light it yourself."

"I talk too much, don't I?"

"Yes."

"I just tried to make everything beautiful."

"Too many dead men in one bed isn't beautiful."

"Will you stay, anyway? I'm so alone."

"I'm due back in San Diego." He began to dress. "I don't have to come here to see dead men, Mona. I don't need a woman to remind me of what they look and smell like." He laced his shoes and put his tie in his pocket. "Give me your car keys."

"I'll drive you," she said.

"I'd rather go alone. I'll leave the car at the airport."

"I don't understand what happened. We were getting on so divinely." She wiped her eyes. "It was so funny. Sherm and Floyd."

"I could die laughing. The keys, please?"

"No."

"Why not?"

"You're in no condition to drive."

"I'm stone sober."

"The keys are in the ignition." She threw away the cigarette and went to him. "Please stay?"

"You're all mixed up, Mona. Go back to bed and wait another eight months."

"Harry? Please?"

"Get in that sack and close your eyes and count all the little white crosses until you fall asleep. When I'm back in Washington, I'll give your regards to Arlington Cemetery."

"You bastard."

He went through the kitchen to the garage and started the car and backed it out. The roadway was narrow and the big convertible barely made it. He drove carefully down the mountain, very sure of himself and not squealing the tires the way Mona had done. It had been a long time since he had driven a car. The throb of power beneath the hood returned to him his sense of strength and command. He felt relaxed and the burden of too much drink had left him.

Mona was wrong, he decided. No woman could function as faultlessly as a machine. Not even Mona Warren with all her control and her spirit and her toughness. A hell of a shame, he thought. All that meat and no potatoes and no good for the long haul. She had been right there with him, though, when Faygill was swinging by a leg over the canyon. She never batted an eyelash. It was too bad things hadn't worked out and there was no one to blame but Mona herself with all that blabber about the dead. What the hell do people expect? To live forever? Everybody's got to die at least once. So damn her to hell. Damn them all. What do they want from him? Mercy? Last rites? What the hell got into her to bring on the dead? Was that what the sight of him brought to her mind?

The more he thought about it, the angrier he became. Mercy? Mercy was damned well what she had plucked from him. The sly conniving bitch. The cunning cockteaser.

He slowed the car and swung into a steep driveway, scraping bushes. He slammed the gears into reverse, turned the car and raced back up the hill. This time the tires squealed.

She was crouched by the bookshelf on her knees and she had been reading from one of the Oriental philosophies. She wore a short transparent gown and huge black-rimmed glasses which she quickly removed when he came in. She smiled.

"You came back. I knew you would."

Without a word he took the book and scaled it flapping through the open terrace doors. "Damn you," she said, "that's an autographed copy." He lifted her bodily and carried her to the bedroom and threw her on the bed. She fought him hard, scratching and kicking. "I'll scream bloody murder," she panted, "so help me God."

"Your friend Faygill screamed," Paige said. "A hell of a lot of good it did him."

She pleaded and cursed and threatened but she did not cry out.

It made no difference. She never had a chance. He took her like a dog in the street. When he was finished, she lay drained of strength, looking more dead than alive. He left without a word. All the way to the airport he had the radio volume turned on full, blaring jazz.

How right she was. There was nothing there but the box it came in. Dry as an old sea biscuit and he had plowed better in the filthiest cribs of Panama and Manila.

The hell with her. She had it coming. She had begged for it. No two bit movie tramp was going to lecture him on mercy and when it came to control, he could give her cards and spades.

He dabbed at the scratches on his face and began to laugh. The sly bitch. She still won. For a moment back there he had almost let up, shocked by what he was about to do. But an expression in Mona's eyes, a look of rapture at once lust and evil, betrayed her and he had plunged ahead. She had loved every inch of it. All he had done was to give her exactly what she wanted.

33

The clerk at the hotel desk in San Diego had a message for the captain. Mrs. Paige had arrived and had waited up for him until two in the morning.

Paige stared at the man stupidly. "My wife?" He could not believe it. A mistake. A joke of some kind.

The clerk shrugged. "She's somewhere on the mezzanine. We're full up, you know."

"She could have gone to the room."

"You left no word, Captain." He smiled demurely. "There's a war on and we can't be too careful, can we?"

"Who the hell do you think she is? Mata Hari?" He went to the mezzanine. Felicia slept curled up in a cavernous red velvet armchair with her overnight bag in her arms. He shook her gently. "Felicia."

She opened her eyes for a moment and closed them. "Dear Harry. At last."

He bent and kissed her cheek. It was wet. "You should have called and let me know you were coming."

"I did. I called the ship. Hollywood Bowl. The Commandant of the 12th Naval District. Everywhere except Travelers' Aid." He helped her up and took the bag. Her eyes were red and her cheeks streaked with soot. "I was in San Francisco, you see. With David."

"What the hell's David doing in San Francisco?"

"Shall we go to your room, dear? I'm filthy from the train and not well and terribly tired."

Paige ordered coffee with Otard brandy and drank it while Felicia bathed. Felicia out of bed and Georgetown and actually here. He wished he had not drunk so much. He wished several things had not happened. He wondered how a simple life could become so complicated.

He phoned the ship and requested the quarterdeck to advise Commander Logan that he would return aboard at 0800 as planned and he could be reached at the hotel if needed. The officer of the deck acknowledged and told Paige there had been several calls from Mrs. Paige and she would wait for him at his hotel. Paige thanked him and hung up.

Felicia came out of the bathroom wearing Paige's bathrobe. She looked woefully small and bedraggled. He lifted her in his arms and settled her in bed and she pulled the covers to her chin.

"Your face is full of scratches," she said.

"Tell me about David."

"David. Yes." She sighed deeply. "It began with a phone call from a friend of Daddy's at the Academy. It seems David had put in a surprise resignation immediately after graduation exercises and it caused quite a furor and so they called Daddy and of course he rushed right down there. Exactly what happened I don't know. Everyone seemed intent on shielding me from what was going on and of course my only concern was for David. The poor boy. He's always been rather withdrawn—"

"What the hell *happened*, Felicia?"

"Well, they came home and there were some words and next thing I knew, Daddy had orders cut for David to ship out at once. I flew with him to San Francisco and he's on his way to war right now."

"What ship?"

"David couldn't say and there was a dreadful hurry. A destroyer was taking him out there. I went with him as far as the Navy Pier. I was really too upset to ask more. It happened so quickly. And then David—well, he was so strange, Harry. Very tight-lipped. You know? Polite and all that and he kissed me goodbye very sweetly, I thought. But he was remote, Harry, and cold. So very very cold." She reached into her handbag. "Did you know David writes poems? He left these with me at the Navy Pier. I copied them down for you, waiting on that dreary mezzanine. It seems so odd, a son of Harry Paige writing poems."

"He's your son, too, Felicia."

"One never thinks of that."

"How did his orders read?"

"All I know is, Daddy sent him to Amos Flint for some assignment on his staff as a flag secretary or something."

"Flint's flag is in *Tarrytown*. My God, David's just a green ensign. Hasn't got his sea legs yet."

"It's your Navy, Harry."

"The kid knew what he wanted. It's none of the commodore's damned business."

"Daddy was furious. He put the blame squarely on you for what happened."

"Moose shit. David's got a mind of his own and a damned good one. And a lot more sense than your fat-headed old man." He punched the headboard. "I just can't get over him shanghaiing the kid like that. Didn't David fight back?"

"Oh, yes. It was quite a scene. Daddy threatened a court-martial and David told him to go right ahead and then Daddy backtracked, but he said he was only protecting you. David laughed right in his face and that infuriated Daddy and I was afraid he'd have a stroke or they'd start hitting each other and so I told David he had better do as he was told."

"And what did David say to that?"

"He gave me the strangest look. It sent chills up and down my spine. As though he was seeing me for the first time in his life. 'Is that what you really want, Mother?' he said and I said it seemed best. After all he was in the Navy and there *was* a war on. After that, he was meek as a lamb. Agreed to everything except, he would not shake hands with Daddy even though Daddy told him he was doing it for his own good." She looked at him plaintively. "It is for his own good, isn't it?"

"Who the hell knows. It's done now. If he's been ordered to Flint's staff, I'll probably see him soon. I'll talk to him. I'll let you know how things are."

"I tried, really, to get word to you when it happened. You're restricted information, did you know that? Even Daddy wouldn't help me."

"I phoned you the night we shoved off from Norfolk. He answered the phone. Said you were out on the town."

"He never told me."

"Were you?"

"Harry."

"Sorry, darling." He began to undress. She watched him.

"Those scratches on your face, Harry."

"Courtesy of Mona Warren."

"The movie queen? How nice! And what did you do to provoke her highness?"

"Damned if I know. After the bond rally, there was one of those Hollywood parties you read about. To raise more money. This was at Chickie Dee's shore establishment."

"But she's only a child, isn't she?"

"Anyway, I was the star and I guess it made this Mona Warren jealous and she was plastered anyway and that's it."

"Let's hope those are the only souvenirs you brought back from Mona Warren."

"Now that's a hell of a thing to say."

"I was hoping she didn't break your heart, dear. That was all." He had put on his pajamas and got into bed. She stroked his cut face. "Is she beautiful?"

"No woman who's drunk is beautiful."

"I read somewhere she doesn't drink."

"She's got a smart press agent. Look, honey. The ship's due to shove off tomorrow night. That's tonight, isn't it? I've got to be aboard at 0800 to see how the yard work progressed and then get squared away for departure. Why don't you come on out for the day? You can stay on board, take it easy in my cabin, and we'll have a little farewell dinner, just the two of us."

"I don't think so, Harry."

"It's our last night."

"I know, Harry."

"You're angry with me."

"It's not you, Harry. It's the ship."

"You've never been aboard a ship of mine. *Shiloh*'s a beauty. You'll love her."

"I'll hate her. I hate ships. I hate the sea." She turned to him and very slowly said, "In all my life I never hated anything. Now I hate. I hate with such passion I can hardly believe it's me, Felicia

Blatchford, a sweet little child I used to know." He began to interrupt and she stopped him, almost serene. "Your sea and your ships have robbed me of everything I love, everything dear to me. I don't want to see your ship, Harry. Ever. It's you I came to see. If not for David and you, I'd never have had the courage to set foot out of Georgetown."

"But you have and it's a brave thing you've done, Felicia. You're here, we're together. Let's make it wonderful. California isn't that bad. After the war, we'll find us a place and settle down here. La Jolla is lovely, Felicia. And Laguna Beach. Up north there's Santa Barbara and Monterey—" He saw that it was hopeless.

"I love you, Harrison Paige. You will never know how much. Or how it was without you all those years."

"Please stay, Felicia."

"I'll stay with you tonight, what's left of it. Tomorrow I'm going home."

He helped her out of the bulky robe. "One way or the other, there'll be no sleep tonight."

"Why not, my dear? There's not much else we can do."

He kissed her, very tender about it.

"You smell of another woman," she said.

He left at seven. Felicia slept. He left, not touching her, feeling unclean and not worthy. He loved her with all his heart and he loved his son, David, and he hoped the day would come when he could be both the husband and the father he truly wanted to be. It was a late time to start and he knew it would not come easy. It was something you learned by working hard at it. Like being a skipper, a damned good skipper, the best. It was a serious business and it took a long time and you could not expect to do it well just some of the time.

34

A day out of Pearl Harbor, a single incident marred *Shiloh*'s smooth and uneventful passage west from San Diego. The usual basketball game was being played on the hangar deck. The forward elevator had been lowered and about a hundred men sat close together under the guard rail at the flight deck opening. It was a hot morning and the captain had given permission for the crew to strip and sunbathe when not on watch.

The ball glanced off the rim of the basket on a long shot and spun against the bulkhead switch that controlled the raising and the lowering of the guard rail and the elevator. The ball tripped the guard rail switch and the warning buzzer sounded. No one moved quickly enough to reset the switch and the spectators topside scrambled clear of the lowering rail.

One man did not make it. He was a pipefitter, second class, who was called Skinny, because he was so fat. He struggled to get clear but he was too slow and too thick through the middle and the guard rail caught him across the back of the neck and jackknifed him. He died of a broken neck in sick bay an hour later.

It was a freak accident and in wartime there are all kinds of accidents not related to battle. It was *Shiloh*'s first fatality and because she was only one day away from the war zone, some of the old-timers regarded it as a bad omen. Most of the men just put it down to a fat man's hard luck and tried to forget about it. The pipefitter's body was placed in the chaplain's custody for burial at Pearl or shipment back home and *Shiloh* plowed on to war.

There was another incident, unknown to the others aboard *Shiloh*. Tod Newell had witnessed the accident and that night came on deck for the midwatch slightly before midnight. The captain had left his night orders and had retired early. A zigzag plan was in effect. A change of course had just been executed and Newell stepped out to the open bridge to observe how the destroyers took station. It was a clear calm night with a full moon. A faint breeze swept the starboard wing as *Shiloh* turned and Newell stood for several moments expecting its cool touch across his face. Instead, the air was strangely warm and oppressive. His heart began to pound. He was startled to hear the sound of music and peering over the splinter shield, he discerned the shapes of three sailors, sprawled atop the twin five-inch mount below. He recognized them at once. They were characters out of a book of sea legends he had read and loved as a boy.

One of them, Shem, held a concertina and worked it with a loving grace. It was an old and battered instrument and Newell could see its fittings reflected in moonlight. They shone like beaten gold. The other two sailors, Bones and Pape, seemed absorbed in the aimless melody Shem played. It was an undulant and peculiar air and much of it was lost in the wind. Their voices echoed hollowly.

Pape said, "I remember a score of triremes off Naxos and a bold captain named Arius and a thousand amphorae of Macedonian wine."

"A pure man could part the sea in those days," Shem said.

"The Bible lied," said Pape.

"The bibulous one did not," Shem said.

"He knows," said Bones who was black. "His old man told him so. Number one."

"Noah?"

"Yes, sir."

"And what of this one?" Meaning Paige, Newell knew at once.

"He might could," Bones said. "He's also Number one."

"What think you, Shem?"

Shem thought a moment. "Olympus the hard way."

Pape nodded. Bones stared off at the moon-speckled sea. "Play us a hot tropic tune on that squeeze box. Hear, Shem?"

Shem obliged with *Kol Nidre.*

Newell could contain his delight no longer. "Shem!" he shouted. "Pape!"

The bosun's mate of the watch came running out of the pilot house. "Something out there, sir?"

Newell, after a moment, said very steadily, "Whales, I guess, or porpoise. The cans are on station. When's the next zigzag change?"

"In two minutes, sir. Left, to course two-one-zero."

"Very well." He went into the pilot house and checked the chronometer and the zigzag plan. At thirty seconds before the change he said to the helmsman, "Stand by." Precisely on time, he gave the word to execute the order and stepped out on the open bridge. The destroyers raced to their new stations. Newell looked down at the five-inch gun mount.

No one was there.

35

"Time's running out, gentlemen," Admiral Nickelby said. "This briefing will be short and sweet." He paused. "Perhaps not so sweet." He nodded at his operations officer. "Charley, take over."

Captain Miehle, carrying a pointer, went to the large chart of the Central Pacific area. "That's Midway," he said. "It's eleven hundred and thirty-six miles west northwest of Pearl at the end of the Hawaiian chain. The whole damn thing is six miles in diameter, smaller than Wake. Pan American's used it as a base since 1935 and it's been a naval air station since last August when we put in a Marine garrison and some AA stuff. It consists of two islands surrounded by a reef. The big island, Sand, is maybe two miles long; the other one's called Eastern Island and our runways are there and she's barely a mile long.

"We've been doing what we can to beef up Midway and her present air strength is up to what her facilities can handle, which is damned little. There are thirty PBYs for reconnaissance, six new TBFs, a mixed bag of Marine Corps fighters and scout bombers, cast-offs from some of our carriers. There's also a couple of dozen Air Force B-17s. The beaches and surrounding waters are mined and you will find these charts in your operations plan portfolios."

He went on. The assembled task group commanders and warship skippers riffled through their portfolios. Paige sat back, enjoying the air-conditioned conference room and the fact that he had got here in time. Through the window he could see the hospital where he had convalesced from his Sunda Strait injuries. Barely three months ago. It seemed a century.

He knew most of the officers present, either by sight or name. Several were Academy classmates. It was a simple matter to identify the skippers afloat. They were the weathered-looking ones compared to the tired-eyed staff officers whose work, no matter how inglorious, was equally as important. On the other side of the locked conference doors, he heard the muted counterpoint to Miehle's words—the steady chatter of telegraph keys, the click of women's heels in the corridor, female laughter. He felt confident and fit and primed for battle.

Nickelby took over. "Not sweet, I said, gentlemen. Here are the facts. We lost *Lex* in the Coral Sea. *Sara*'s still in San Diego. Her repairs are completed but we've been unable to scrape together an escort and a qualified air group for her and it's doubtful she'll make it here in time. We've brought *Tarrytown* up from the South Pacific and in three days completed repairs that would ordinarily take three months. *Shiloh*'s tied up here this morning after cutting an astonishing thirty hours from our most optimistic estimate of her time of arrival.

"We learned a few lessons in the Coral Sea and we also learned how the enemy thinks and operates. A dangerous and costly mistake we've both made is the wildly inaccurate reporting of hits and sinkings. Get this through to your pilots and let's save ourselves the risk and embarrassment and the downright danger of wild goose chases after cripples that don't exist.

"The Coral Sea fight was the first time in history two sea forces fought a battle without ever seeing each other. The outcome for us, and I'm sure it's the same for the Jap Imperial Command, was totally indecisive. It proved nothing. The Jap is still sore because he missed our carriers when he hit here last December, and he's probably kicking himself for not going after them while he had us on the ropes. He has got to make a fast all-out effort to cripple us, move in, take over. He knows damned well we've got the industrial power, the resources, and the labor force to lick him and all we need is time. From Midway, he can pound away by air and sea and take Pearl. If our carriers don't stop him. He's trying to make sure we don't. He has put together a combined fleet which by our last estimate, numbers over a hun-

dred and sixty ships-of-the-line and auxiliaries. We have less—a
task force built around the two carriers, *Tarrytown* and *Shiloh*,
and that's it, gentlemen.

"We have a few pluses and we need 'em. We know the enemy's
objective, the approximate composition of his forces, the direction
of approach and the approximate date of attack. We have radar
and he does not. That's about all we have going for us.

"You are designated for communications purposes as Task Force
Alpha. You will operate in two carrier groups—Beta under Rear
Admiral Tully in *Tarrytown*, and Gamma under Vice Admiral Flint
with his flag in *Shiloh*. Admiral Flint will be in tactical command
of the combined force. Code names are to be used and strict radio
silence observed at all times and only your TBS circuits employed
for short range talk between ships. Your task group commanders
have additional operational information which will be passed on to
you once you are under way.

"I should like Admirals Tully and Flint in my office after the
others have gone." He paused. "Captain Paige, too, if you please.
That is all, gentlemen. Good luck."

Nickelby waved the three officers to leather chairs and passed
a box of cigars. Tully took several, grinning. Nickelby put his feet
up on the desk. "Sorry to spring a last-minute change on you, Amos,
from *Tarrytown* to *Shiloh*, but we had a quick look at *Shiloh*'s deck
log less than an hour ago. Her running time's incredible and her
flight-deck performance the best we've ever seen. You're in tactical
command and you'll want a fast hull under you and a hot air
group. *Shiloh*'s got Miller LeClair's boys and you won't find any
better."

"I don't exactly relish a change on such short notice, Maury."

"The flag accommodations are the finest. Like the *Queen Mary*,
first class. Hot and cold running stewards' mates."

"Thank you, Maury. I wasn't thinking of myself. The switch
creates a small problem. Captain Paige's son, David, reported
aboard yesterday, attached to my staff."

Nickelby looked from Flint to Paige. "Kind of sudden, isn't it?"

"Not really," Flint said quickly. "Rollo Blatchford's wanted it
that way ever since the boy entered the Academy."

"He just graduated, right? He's only an ensign."

"He's a bright youngster," Flint said smoothly. "I'm pleased to
be the one to break him in. I think in view of the critical need

of good officers, his low rank can be ignored for the present. Point is, Maury, what's policy on having him aboard his father's command?"

"Policy?" Nickelby shrugged. "We just try to avoid multiple risk in one family. It's not against Navy regs, certainly." He turned to Paige. "What's your feeling, Harry?"

"He'll be in my ship but not under my command. As for the risk—" He saw David's clean unsmiling face. What was it Felicia had said? Tight-lipped? Remote? "Who knows? It could hit anyone, anywhere."

"Hell's fire," Tully said, puffing his cigar. "I got me two-three brother teams in my group. Helps build *esprit de corps.*"

"Would you swap if Amos wanted to?" Nickelby asked.

"Sure. Why not?"

"I'd like to keep young Paige," Flint said. "A last-minute change might bother him."

Paige sat up. "Why should it bother him?"

"He just reported for duty. He's settled in. He was ordered here on short notice and he might get the idea he's not wanted or not up to snuff."

"Anyone asked David what he wants?"

"Of course not," Flint snapped. "Orders are orders. You're his father. Have you asked him?"

"Haven't seen him yet. But I agree. He should stay where he is."

"I've no objections," Nickelby said. "Amos?"

"Honored to have a Blatchford aboard," said Flint.

You bastard, Paige thought.

"Settled. Now how much time do you need to transfer your flag to *Shiloh?*"

"We're under way in four hours, right? Two should do it and I'd like the word passed at once to my chief of staff."

"Very well." Nickelby buzzed the intercom and passed along Flint's instructions to be forwarded. He leaned back and clasped his hands behind his head. "May as well stick around, Harry. Amos'll give you a lift back to the ship. Incidentally, what the hell were you using for fuel? Croton oil?"

Paige grinned. "Just wanted to get here, Admiral."

"Get the work done she needed?"

"Everything except the catapults."

"Good enough. I've detached Kitty Catlin from my staff and assigned him to duty as *Shiloh*'s navigating officer. He knows the operational plans, Harry. He also knows these waters like the palm of his hand. He was born here on Kauai—one of the big families. I'll miss him but I know you can use him and he begged for the assignment."

"Thank you, Admiral."

"Now then. I wish I could have been less gloomy in the briefing session, but the boys had to know the truth. I did not care to dwell on the odds, either, but you men are savvy enough to know what we're up against. From the decrypting bits and pieces we've put together, we're certain the Imperial Command is throwing the whole damned Jap fleet into the Midway operation. They're scared as hell of our new construction program. They want us to come out and get smashed before our new ships are built. They think we're afraid to do it and they're hoping to force us into it by occupying Midway.

"The breakdown of those one hundred and sixty ships is impressive. They are operating in five completely separate groups. An advance force consisting of probably fifteen submarines; a striking force built around four carriers; and a five thousand man occupation force in a dozen transports to take over Midway. Backing this up is the powerful main force built around seven battleships with Yoshihara himself in one of their new *Yamoto* battleships behind eighteen-inch guns. 'Jiro' Kaizuka is the carrier force commander. He's the brain who ran the Pearl Harbor show, a gentle soul, a deadly enemy. There's a northern group, partly diversionary, headed for the Aleutians with a couple of light carriers. Yoshihara's intention is to bomb Dutch Harbor and probably occupy Attu, Adak, and Kiska. The enemy's strategy there is to confuse us as to his prime objective and we are stationing some of our available force to handle that eventuality, should it get serious. But we are not weakening or in any way compromising our striking power against the Midway attack.

"He has also set up plans to station two picket lines of submarines north and west of here, hoping to hit us as we sortie from Pearl. It would also serve him with advance notice of our movements." He grinned. "Their rendezvous date is twenty-four hours from tomorrow morning. That's why we're shoving off tonight."

"Do you have those subs' positions?"

"It's spelled out in your operations orders. One group's five hundred miles west of Oahu, the other cuts a line exactly halfway between Pearl and Midway. You'll find all sorts of detailed intelligence in those plans. The hell of it is, even though we know his intention, there's damned little we can do to stop it. It's wishful thinking, believing we can stop it. But we can try, and I've a hunch we've got a sneaking inside chance. The Jap's a tricky enemy and a damned clever one, but he's become arrogant with victory and dangerously overconfident. The element of surprise is always valuable in a military operation and from what we've learned, the Jap is basing this operation entirely on surprise. My guess is, it's a mistake and it may prove a costly one.

"First of all, he doesn't need surprise. He's got us outgunned and outwinged coming and going and all he has to do is concentrate his forces and steam in and grind us down by sheer weight of numbers. But he's spreading himself over two oceans, with a variety of objectives and no opportunity for coordinated action and mutual support. Above all, he's made no provision for the possibility of *no* surprise at all—and there is no surprise. We know what his present intention is and we're ready and waiting.

"So you've got a thin but good chance to deal the enemy a mighty blow." He picked up a sheet of paper. "As stated in the orders:

> "Your mission is to inflict maximum damage with forceful air strikes directed against the enemy's major ships. Govern yourself by the principle of calculated risk. Avoid exposure of your force to attack by superior enemy forces unless there exists the good prospect of inflicting greater damage on the enemy than you would receive."

He put aside the sheet. "Any comments?"

Spike Tully blew a cloud of smoke toward the ceiling. "Maury," he said, "you don't need admirals. You need magicians. You're asking us to go out after this gang five times our size, be careful so we don't get hurt, and knock the stuffing out of them."

"Of course," Nickelby said. "Is that anything new?"

"I'm not complaining," Tully said grinning. "I'm just gonna need a new silk hat and a rabbit."

Paige rode with Admiral Flint back to *Shiloh*. Conversation did not come easily. Both sensed that Nickelby had set it up to break the ice between them. Flint stared ahead, tapping his immaculate fingertips on the polished surface of his briefcase. Paige sat straight and attentive as an outranked officer should. He waited for his superior to lead, but his mind probed dark channels seeking ways to bait his old rival. The wrong war, Paige thought, but it passed the time. Flint finally spoke.

"David's caught on very nicely," he said with an effort.

"David Blatchford, sir?"

Flint sat mildly frowning, thrown off by the unexpected riposte and the "sir." He decided to ignore it. "Your father-in-law took me by surprise. I hadn't planned on having David with me for another six months."

"You could have said so, sir."

"To whom? Rollo? Nick? Hardly. Do David good, anyway. He's with a seasoned staff and he'll have to step smartly." And abruptly he said, "You've seen Felicia, I presume?"

"In San Diego, yes, sir."

"And how is she?"

"Compared to whom, sir?"

Flint looked stricken. "Haven't changed, have you? Same loud-mouthed wise guy from Brooklyn."

Paige shrugged. "I'm what I am, sir."

"Indeed you are. A discredit to the uniform you wear. Let me tell you something. I've been wanting to get this off my chest for a long time. I made my feelings quite clear to Maury last March when he jumped you over a dozen or more officers senior to you and in my opinion eminently more qualified for carrier command."

"Thank you, sir."

"Never mind the sarcasm, Captain. It reflects your typically contemptible and unofficerlike attitude and I can do without it, thank you. My concern, as always, is for the good of the service and not prompted by any personal feelings I may have in the matter."

"Of course, Admiral."

"Whether you like it or not, we're going to be out there together. I suspect Maury effected the transfer of my flag to *Shiloh* so you'd be where someone responsible can keep an eye on you. I'm making my position clear right now. I am in tactical command. I will expect absolute obedience to my fleet orders. Understood?"

"Understood, Admiral. And of course, as captain of my vessel, I will remain responsible for her command."

"And accountable, Captain. None of your cheap tricks. No bids for personal glory or individual honors. No grabbing of the spotlight for yourself. Understood?"

"Understood, Admiral."

"Wipe that ludicrous grin off your face. There's nothing funny in what I'm saying. My carrier skippers work as a team. I've spent years putting this teamwork concept in action. I've forged a fighting machine out here and I'm not about to have you or anyone else throw a monkey wrench into it."

"I read the newspaper accounts, Admiral, where your task force is called Flint's Falcons—"

"Over my repeated protests."

"A clever publicity stunt, I thought."

"I warned those newspaper boys. Matter of fact, I ordered them to keep my name out of it. But the ship's crews themselves unanimously adopted it and insist on using it. Rather than destroy such spirit, I just go along with it. Never mind," he said sharply. "You're new to the group and I'll be watching you closely. Don't you forget it."

The admiral's jeep had come alongside Shiloh's gangway. Paige jumped out and saluted. "Thank you for the lift, Admiral. Thank you very much."

"My staff's already making the transfer," Flint said coldly. "See that your ship's company gives them all the assistance they need."

"Aye, sir!" Paige shouted. The jeep began to move away and Paige ran alongside, saluting crisply many times while the driver and admiral and gangway sentries stared. "Aye, sir! Hail Flint's Falcons! Heil Hitler!" The jeep roared away with the admiral in an agony of rage and embarrassment. Paige mounted the gangway grinning insanely.

The executive officer met him at the quarterdeck and told him David had come aboard with the first load of Admiral Flint's staff material. Paige hurried to the flag bridge. David was unloading cartons and stuffing folders into file cabinets.

He shook his father's hand and then impulsively embraced him. Paige thought he looked fine and said so. David flushed and gave credit to the sea air. Paige told him he had ridden over in the admiral's jeep and Flint had praised David. David looked embarrassed and went back to the files. Paige told him he had seen Felicia in San Diego and she had told him the whole story. How did he feel about it now? David said he had no complaints, now that he was here and Paige asked him what he meant by that.

"Well," David said, "it was rather grim all the way to San Francisco and then I got aboard this tin can and something happened to me. Here were a few hundred young people, officers and men, like myself, all headed out to sea and maybe never coming back. Some were Annapolis and a lot weren't and it didn't seem to make much difference. I got the feeling none of them particularly loved what they were doing yet felt it had to be done. But that wasn't what really got to me. It was the ship itself. *Bradbury*'s her name. She's one of these new *Fletcher* class destroyers, a thing of beauty, truly, and we had been briefed on them in the last few weeks at the Academy and getting on board was a really exciting experience. I don't know why. Because it was just a ship. Maybe some of your saltiness and Grandpa's and all the others rubbed off on me in spite of myself."

"It's possible."

"Anyway, the tin can skipper knew all about you and took a personal interest in me. I stood regular junior officer watches on the bridge and on the last day I qualified to stand top deck watches under way."

"So you liked it."

"Couldn't help myself. That *Bradbury*'s a dream. Fast and rugged and she turns on a dime. We racked up a twenty-five knot average from Frisco to Pearl."

"Hell, we did that in *Shiloh* and launched and recovered planes."

"Well, I see from the admiral's operational orders that *Bradbury*'s assigned to the Gamma group, so you're in good company."

"You're sure as hell not the same David Paige I left in Washington." He felt happy and relieved and proud. "Think you can swallow this man's Navy?"

"Not so fast. It's just that I had a taste of the real thing. Gives a man an immense sense of power, doesn't it?"

"How would I know?" He grinned. "Don't get the idea it's all fun, David. Compared to what's ahead, conning a tin can is child's play."

"I'm not losing my perspective."

"Getting along with Flint?"

"It's not as bad as I expected. He's a very organized admiral."

"Any regrets?"

"Being here? I guess not." He was thoughtful for a moment. "Odd, isn't it, it had to be Mother to point out there was a war on and that was why I belonged here. Everyone else who worked over me—Grandpa, the commandant, all those stuffy cronies of his —had nothing but selfish and personal reasons behind their demands. The tradition of the service. Their good names. Not a word about a citizen's duty."

"And my advice to you?"

"The best of all, Dad. I won't forget it. But it was Mother who got me here."

"Your mother is a remarkable woman." Hs clapped David's shoulder. "Now get to work. We'll be seeing a lot of each other. I'm proud, David, really proud."

"That works both ways, Captain."

Paige climbed to the bridge, humming. He spent the next hour in the chart room with Commander Catlin, the new navigating officer. Catlin was a soft, large man with frank blue eyes under thick brows, an Academy man but no graduate. Somewhere around thirty-five, Paige judged, and from the way he took over, he seemed to know his business. Together they studied the sortie plan and the times and places of the rendezvous with the oilers and Beta. Catlin plotted the courses and speeds in accordance with the operational orders and explained the stages to Paige.

"Beta gets under way an hour before us. Her orders, just in case the enemy has broken our code, are to set a course due north of Oahu and innocently conduct target practice, commencing at dawn, both for her gunnery and air departments. Then at dark tomorrow in strict radio silence she commences a high-speed run to rendezvous with the fueling force at a point we're calling Oasis, about three hundred miles due east of Midway. Gamma—that's us—departs at twenty hundred hours tonight. Our course is generally northwest to a point called Bearskin about sixty miles north of French Frigate Shoals. Our orders, in case the Japs spot us, are also to conduct target practice and flight exercises. There's been no other written or spoken word of our actual purpose or destination except these orders here, and unless the enemy had somebody sitting in Admiral Nickelby's conference room, our whereabouts for the next seventy hours will be an absolute secret and, we earnestly hope, a surprise to the Imperial Fleet."

"It's true, then, that Yoshihara's under the impression we don't have a carrier within a thousand miles of Midway?"

"Roger. On the other hand, we've no idea where this damn fleet of theirs is. Not up to half an hour ago, anyway, when we last heard from our search planes out of Midway. If we don't locate those ships soon, they can sneak into plane-launching range and pull another Pearl Harbor on us at Midway. They know the weather conditions out here as well or better than we do. I know damn well they're moving somewhere under heavy cloud cover. And visibility for our search planes is limited."

"What's the patrol boat search plan?"

"We're flying twenty or so PBY Catalinas out of Midway daily, searching the sector between south southwest to north northeast, seven hundred miles out. One of the Catalinas flies the graveyard watch to cover the expected launching position of the enemy carriers each dawn. We're also flying a few PBYs out of French Frigate Shoals, using it as a seaplane fueling base for our anti-sub operations in that area. The two seaplane tenders, *Berkeley* and *Cambridge* are anchored there and it could help discourage enemy flying boat reconnaissance of our activities here at Pearl by denying them the Shoals as a base for their fueling submarines."

"Let's get back to Gamma."

"Roger. We arrive north of French Frigate Shoals after a day of gunnery and flight exercises. Depends on how long we conduct these exercises, but in any event it'll be darkness or damn close to it when we make Point Bearskin. We hope to avoid detection by any Jap subs in the area. Then we change course due north and make a high speed run to the tanker rendezvous at Oasis and then join up at Point Alamo with the Beta group. Any contact our PBYs or subs make with the Jap force will of course call for an immediate change of plans."

"Where's this Point Alamo?"

"Right here—latitude 32 degrees North, longitude 173 degrees West. Puts us just about three hundred and twenty-five miles northeast of Midway." Catlin put down the dividers and rubbed his eyes. "I've been all over these waters, Captain. Used to sail my own ketch. As a kid, I spent weeks on end cruising these islands, fishing and exploring with my grandfather. I know damned well the weather and intelligence reports we've been getting are reliable.

"The Japs are rendezvousing seven hundred miles west of Midway. The weather boys indicate there's an extended weak front about three hundred miles west and northwest of Midway. With the high pressure areas east of it, they've got perfect cloud cover. That's why our search planes haven't picked 'em up yet. I've seen that fog so thick you couldn't make out the bow of your own boat. If that's where they are, I'll bet dollars to doughnuts they can't keep visual contact with each other. They should be zigzagging and that'll keep 'em on their toes because they don't have radar. Sooner or later, with any unscheduled course changes needed, they just might break radio silence rather than risk collision. If we're on the ball, we can get a fix on their position."

"Goddam game of hide-and-seek. And the area between here and French Frigate Shoals is probably lousy with enemy subs. Our own zigzag plans provided for?"

"Everything's set to be incorporated in your night orders once we're under way."

"Very good, Commander. Welcome aboard."

"It'll be a change," Catlin said, "cruising the islands with guns instead of fish bait."

In officer country below, David Paige looked into Tod Newell's cabin to see if he was ready for the evening meal. Tod was at his desk, writing. He invited David in. "Can't go right now," he said. "I'm trying to finish this will so I can get it ashore before we shove off. Then I've got to see the exec."

"A will, you say?"

"It was suggested in the plan of the day for all hands to prepare some sort of last will and testament. Makes sense. That way nobody fights over your remains, effects and estate."

"No strain here. I don't own a thing."

"I do. There's a huge hunk of Connecticut lakeside and woodlands in my name. If I don't spell out exactly what I want done with it, it will sure as hell end up a suburban slum."

"Your father wouldn't let that happen, would he?"

"He's just the boy who would. The one guy who won't is a

neighbor named Tim Shanahan, a boozy, daydreaming country Irishman. I'm leaving it all to him."

"That's a hell of a legacy."

"He respects God's country. He always will." Tod signed his name and began to address an envelope. "Sure you don't want to leave something to somebody?"

"No," David said. "There's nothing to leave."

"You must own something of value, David."

"Just myself."

Newell sealed the envelope and left David at the wardroom ladder and went to Commander Logan's stateroom. It had taken considerable self-examination before he was able to muster the courage to approach the executive officer with his problem. Now in his presence, he felt a wild urge to mutter some alibi or excuse and keep the whole crazy business locked inside.

Commander Logan was holding out a package of cigarettes. Newell took one, feeling foolish because he never smoked. "I know you're busy, Commander," he muttered, "perhaps another time."

Logan waved him to a chair. "Get it off your chest, Lieutenant."

"It's about the OOD watch, sir."

"What about it?"

"I think perhaps I should be taken off the list of qualified watch standers."

"You're qualified, aren't you?"

"Yes, sir."

"What's bothering you?" The steady blue eyes, oddly, gave Newell strength.

"I'm in some kind of trouble." Logan was calmly lighting his cigarette and Newell tried to find the words. "I'm having trouble keeping my mind on the job, sir."

"Doping off?"

"Not sleepy. Nothing like that. It's just—well, off thoughts, things, run through my head and distract me."

"Like what?"

"Last night on the midwatch, sir, I stepped out on the open bridge and for a moment thought I heard voices."

"It could have been voices, couldn't it?"

"I saw figures, or thought I did. Then they were gone." He described in detail exactly what had happened. Logan studied him. "You want a light for that cigarette?"

"No, thank you." He laid the cigarette carefully on the edge of Logan's desk. "It took an effort to mention this to you, Commander. If I thought it was trivial or just a passing fancy, I'd have forgotten about it. But it worried me. It worries me very much."

"Last night the first time?"

Newell nodded. He did not think just then of the incident in Sky One.

"You were with Captain Paige when the *Gloucester* was lost, weren't you?"

"Yes, sir."

"Think that might have anything to do with it?"

"I don't know, Commander."

"Well, we sure as hell don't want any of our ODs doping off. And we're short as hell on qualified men to stand the top watch under way. Have you checked with the ship's doctor?"

"No, sir. I really feel fine. I have no temperature or disease or mental blocks or whatever. I just thought I had better let somebody know that for sixty seconds or so I wasn't myself."

Logan nodded. Newell was surprised at his lack of concern. "You're the Tod Newell who's the tennis champ, right?"

"Hardly champ, Commander. I've played some tournament tennis, is all."

"You're being modest, Newell. I'm no tennis fan yet I sure as hell have heard about you. I'm no damn doctor, either, but you look fit and your reflexes seem okay. When's your next watch?"

"Second dog watch coming up. It's still light then and I think I'll be okay—" He stopped, remembering the radar repairman aloft.

"Something wrong?"

"No, sir. We're standing one-in-four, so my next night watch will be the eight-to-twelve tomorrow night."

"Get yourself some shut-eye tonight. We'll have the doc check you out first chance he has, but we sure as hell need all you qualified ODs on the bridge. They're damned few and we're headed for Jap sub country, you may as well know it, and could be the whole damn Jap fleet. You feel rocky later on, you let me hear pronto, and I'll arrange a relief."

"Thank you, Commander."

"I'll be talking to the skipper—"

"Does he have to know, sir?"

"Routine, Mr. Newell, but he sure has got to know. He'll probably cuss and tell you to get more exercise." He grinned. "Maybe we'll rig a tennis court on the hangar deck, same as basketball—"

They both thought of dead Skinny and the guard rail that killed him. Their eyes met and Newell laughed nervously. Logan shuffled the papers on his desk. "That'll be all, Mr. Newell. Let me know how it goes, hear?"

36

That night the ships of Gamma in line cleared the channel and nets. Past Kauai they formed up and ran for the open sea north and west in moonlight. The men on watch and off sensed danger and were tense, spoiling for battle. Lookouts aloft had been doubled. In *Shiloh*, Captain Paige had ordered extra hands stationed with binoculars forward in the eyes of the ship.

Before standing his night watch in flag plot, David Paige climbed to the bridge and spent a few minutes on the starboard wing with his father. It was a clear night, the sea smooth and the sky flecked with many stars. The shapes of screening vessels and *Shiloh*'s gentle throbbing as she knifed through the sea was all there was except sky and stars and the two of them. Being together and sharing a common purpose made it a curiously moving moment, serene and brotherly. Both men felt it. Neither spoke until it was time for David to go on watch.

"It's nice out here, Dad."

"It's the only place," Paige said.

That was all. David left. His father's simple words rang in his ears. The only place. It had not been more than two or three minutes they shared. Yet it bonded them and each of them knew he would never forget it.

At dawn, search and combat planes were launched, thundering along the flight deck and aloft, dipping, angling to starboard to clear the ship's path if they crashed. During daylight, the group's base course altered only for the turns into the wind to launch and recover each flight and to conform to zigzag plan. The flight deck crews moved swiftly in their appointed tasks, gaudy as circus clowns, graceful as dancers.

Admiral Flint on the portside catwalk of the flag bridge observed each routine operation with a sharp and calculating eye. His comments to his chief of staff and duty officers were brief and caustic. But he could not complain and Paige, a deck above in flight control with Miller LeClair, knew it. The performance was immaculate, the timing perfect. The returning planes circled and with metronome timing, swept in on the landing signal officers' cut, and raced over the fantail to be caught and stopped and moved to clear the deck for the next one. The single casualty in the day's operations was an F4F fighter whose pilot could not get his tail hook down. After four wave-offs he screeched aboard, brakes burning, and crashed into the barrier at eighty knots. The tail flipped up. Huge splinters ripped from *Shiloh*'s deck as the churning prop dug in. The pilot climbed out, white-faced and unhurt.

That was all. The deck was cleared in seconds and the landing signal officer brought the rest of the flight aboard without incident. Flint went to supper. He had never seen the like of it. His admiration was grudging but sincere. He was a shrewd as well as dedicated officer and what he had observed he knew would add lustre to his own image as well as the much-needed muscle to the fighting body he commanded.

In this first test, he told himself, Paige had handled his ship and his flight crews in a manner that left nothing to be desired. He would praise Paige when the time came, but he would not soon forgive the madcap prank of yesterday, the utterly uncalled-for insanity of heiling Hitler. It was this dangerous unpredictability that he feared most in Paige. The man must be watched like a hawk. And just let him make one error of judgment or indulge in some facetious dereliction of duty! Just one. That was all it would take to lower the boom on the cocky Brooklyn bastard. Flint feasted for a moment on the savory image. For all his qualities as a celebrated sea commander and leader of men, he was as vulnerable as anyone to the corroding foibles of human nature.

The flight deck was respotted. Each plane was held secure against the wind and the ship's motion by tie-down cables lashed from the underside of the wings to steel cleats set flush in the wooden deck. The word was passed to darken ship. The men drifted into the chow lines that snaked from the feeding stations below to the hangar deck and topside along the island structure bulkhead. The air in confined spaces was filled with the hot smells of well-cooked meat in gravy and the good Navy bread.

The ship's radar had picked up French Frigate Shoals four points off the port bow. David Paige, just relieved of the watch and not hungry, felt the need for fresh air. He stepped out of flag plot to the port catwalk and watched the indistinct land mass take form. The peak of La Perousse Pinnacle against a salmon sunset sky shaped up like a gaunt Yankee frigate under sail. He thought of the old prints and family portraits that lined the walls of the Georgetown house where he had been born and where he had spent his childhood years. The stateliness at the horizon recalled ships-of-the-line commanded by these stern-eyed Holts and Blatch-fords, whose faces over stiff-collared dress blues were as familiar to him as his own.

A proud company of heroes, he reflected. If you dig heroes. It's expected of me, as the good admiral and the good commodore have often pointed out, that I join them. And what must I do to join them? And will I do it?

He would not dwell on that. Not in these precious moments of solitude. He chose instead to recall his first exciting days of active duty, an excitement sparked by the run west from San Francisco to Pearl in the spanking new *Bradbury*. He clung to that memory. It was all that remained of joy, all that could compensate for his being here.

Beauty in motion, he told himself, akin to whatever it was that sent the Blatchfords and Holts of other days to the fighting sloops and frigates of America's history. The call of the sea seemed different here. Except for the sleek grace of a *Bradbury*, the modern contraptions of steel and steam with their intricate insides of wires and cables were ugly leviathans designed for mechanized death.

He knew finally and irrevocably and in spite of his deep involvement, that what was here was not for him. The contemplation of this as a way of life produced in him a feeling of utter despair made worse by the sure knowledge that, because of his heritage, there could be no honorable escape.

His thoughts were interrupted by a flurry of activity in flag plot, seen from the corner of his eye. The duty staff officer beckoned and in a moment thrust a dispatch in David's hand. "Get this to the admiral, David. On the double!"

The swift change from reverie to reality made David's cheeks burn. Suppose I tell him to shove it? he thought. Or tear it to bits because I really do not care? But he was on his way to the ladder before he knew it, obedient to orders, reading the message as he went.

A Midway-based PBY, on the final leg of its search, had spotted a portion of the Japanese invasion force through a hole in the heavy overcast. The pilot reported the group to be six hundred miles west of Midway, proceeding at eighteen knots on a north-easterly course. The group consisted of eleven ships, including transports with escorting cruisers and destroyers.

Admiral Amos Flint had loosened his support belt and was swallowing a mouthful of red Jell-o when David was announced. Flint strapped up quickly and wiped his mouth on a linen napkin and instructed the orderly to show Ensign Paige in.

The admiral read the dispatch with what David felt was a spurious calm. Flint affably waved David to a chair and picked up the phone and spoke for a minute or two to his chief of staff. He hung up and signaled for his Filipino steward. "A dish of Jell-o for Ensign Paige, César." He seemed to relish David's uneasiness. "Good for you, David. Not fattening. And you've brought me exciting news. Relax. Get used to it. You'll be occupying quarters just like these some day."

The steward brought the dessert and David ate cautiously. He did not mind Jell-o but he did not like being ordered to eat it. After two token spoonfuls, he excused himself and rose. "I had better get back to the bridge, Admiral. Things seem to be popping."

"They are, they are. You may very well see history made in the next forty-eight hours, my boy." He walked with an arm around David to the door. "History. Yes. Tell me, did you watch flight operations today?"

"Some of it. Yes, sir."

"Your father handled things remarkably well, I must say. If he behaves as well under fire, when the chips are down, David, you'll have much to be proud of."

"Only then, Admiral?"

"What do you mean?"

"I'm proud of him now."

"Of course you are." Flint's voice rose, oddly petulant. "Being his son, it's expected of you. But there have been times, as you well know, when a good word for Harry Paige was hard to come by."

"For you, Admiral. Never for me."

David was past the Marine orderly and halfway to the flag bridge before his rage subsided and his mind cleared enough to gain control of himself. On the open catwalk he plunged through the bright-colored flag hoists the signalmen in the waning light had readied at the dip for Gamma's information. The duty officer counted the seconds, his eyes glued to the bulkhead chronometer. "Stand by!" Five seconds of tense silence. "Execute!" The signal hoists swept upward to the yardarm, two-blocked. Blinker signals click-clacked to the screen of ships. In flag plot the raspy TBS exchanged rogers and wilcos as Admiral Flint's emergency changes in operational orders went out.

Flag plot was a bundle of nerves. Radio messengers came and left, bristling with fresh dispatches. Lights blinked yellow, red, green. A constant litany of voices, sometimes garbled, rose and fell through the speaking tubes to and from the pilot house and throughout the ship. A Pandora's box of delicate instruments fed surface, air and depth intelligence to the crowded company of perspiring men intent only on knowing more and passing the word when they did.

David found a used mug and filled it with hot coffee. He snaked his way to a quiet corner near the starboard catwalk. Too many, he thought, in too small a world. Too hasty a way to prepare for a lifetime of death.

Shiloh responded now to the orders from the helm, heeling to port in her starboard turn and seeming to leap forward like a whippet as the RPMs turned up. Deck gear rattled. Pencils slid from the plotting board and the chief quartermaster cursed softly as he retrieved them. "Skipper think he's got a tin can up there?" he growled and caught David's disapproving eye and shrugged.

The steel covers in flag plot had been dogged down on the six port holes against the gathering darkness. The light-lock doors and curtains were pulled shut to leave the interim space between lighted inside and darkness outside a limbo of security against detection. *Seal one*, the rules read, *before opening the other*. The air in flag plot grew heavy and smelled sourly of stale coffee and men.

Typewriters clacked and sailors with earphones relayed orders and the TBS speaker crackled acknowledgments. Officers with dividers and parallel rulers plotted and planned and two decks below, the admiral finished his Jell-o.

David with binoculars watched the screen of ships take station. He focused on *Bradbury*, broad on the starboard beam. He felt a small burst of pride. The last light of day shone on her superstructure and the leading edge of her raked stacks. Spume flew past her forecastle deck and, fantail awash, the clean sweet sight of her made him want to shout for joy. Abruptly, he turned away. He racked the binoculars and started below. The duty officer caught his elbow.

"Stick around, David."

"I've been relieved." His voice seemed tense, angry.

"Admiral's called a staff meeting"—the duty officer glanced at his watch—"in ten minutes."

"I'll stay then."

"Grab yourself a cup of joe."

"I'll be right back," David said.

He was suddenly afraid of what was happening to him. He had to speak with his father. Now.

He mounted the ladder to the navigation bridge at the moment the ship's p.a. speakers rasped on. David retreated to the shadows and watched his father. Paige was dancing a little on his toes and crouching slightly. He moved close to the squawk box. The men on watch stood by respectfully. The skipper cleared his throat.

"All hands, this is your captain speaking. . . . One of our PBYs out of Midway has finally located a portion of the Jap fleet. It's still a hell of a long way from here, so relax. But it necessitates an emergency change of plans. We are not going to rendezvous with our tanker fleet as planned. We are, instead, joining up with the other task group, Beta, at a point northeast of Midway, code name Alamo. It is from that point, barring no incidents enroute, that we will launch our strikes against the enemy. We estimate that, within forty-eight hours, things should be happening.

"We are not going to wait forty-eight hours to prepare ourselves. This is already 'bogey' country. All topside personnel will treat unidentified planes as enemy until positively recognized as ours. We can expect attack on the surface, from the air, or from below at any time. All hands topside, whether on watch or not, are here and now ordered to be on the alert for such contacts.

"We will continue to fly our search and combat air patrol planes during the daylight hours. That does not mean we're not vulnerable to enemy attack just the same. Therefore, all lookouts will be on the alert at all times, not only to spot the enemy planes but to identify them by type as quickly as possible. Study those silhouette cards. Know those lines by heart.

"Take care of yourselves. You have protective clothing. Use it. Each of you has a steel helmet. Wear it. If you don't own one, draw one immediately. Gas masks have been issued. Carry yours to your battle station or you may never get there. Life jackets will be worn during general quarters. So will helmets, flashproof clothing, a belt knife, a flashlight, a whistle. Don't let me hear any growls that this is for Boy Scouts only. It's no joke. It's to save lives. We need every damned one of you. It's as plain and simple as that and there's nothing funny about it.

"The time for fun and jokes is over, men. From here on out we are knocking off the athletics and the sunbathing, the card games and crap shooting. I want every man jack of you at the ready every minute of every hour, on watch and off. If you're sacked out, be ready to go at a moment's notice. I repeat, the fun is over. This is a serious and deadly business.

"Out there somewhere is the biggest fleet in the world run by a navy that has never lost a sea war in its long history. Now one of our PBYs has picked her up and they have lost face. We've spoiled their big surprise and they know we know they're out there. They'll be fighting mad and take it from me, I have seen personally what they can do. They are tough and experienced. They have a single target—us. They have one purpose—to smash us to bits. They regard it as the highest honor to die for their emperor and will do so gladly to achieve victory. They have us outgunned and outmanned, but I say to you, they do not have us licked. And we won't be licked, not until each and every one of us has given his last ounce of strength to kill every last one of them. Kill Japs, I say! *Are you with me?*"

A roar went up, a full-throated, savage swelling of voices that echoed deep in the bowels of the ship and rose through compartments and passageways where men clustered listening. It ricocheted off the bulkheads of the hangar deck and superstructure and like a steel shaft it lodged in David's heart.

He looked hard and with love once more at his father's highly-charged, shining face and turned away.

"That's it!" Harry Paige shouted. "That's what I wanted to hear! We're as ready to die for our country as they are, but not as fanatics, men. As warriors! Patriots! And not unless we damned well have no other honorable choice. All I ask is that each of you do his job to the best of his ability. Follow instructions. Obey orders. Stay alert. Keep your wits about you.

"Now beginning an hour before dawn as usual, we'll have general quarters and we'll launch aircraft. When we secure from general quarters, all air defense stations will remain manned and ready. I've just had a message handed me—the chaplains will hold a religious service tonight between eight-thirty and nine on the hangar deck. All hands, regardless of denomination, are urged to attend. Thank you, padres. That's all men. Good luck and God bless you."

Someone must act, protest, speak out against it, David thought. *My God in Heaven, we cannot go on and on forever, killing each other.* He yearned to speak, but saw the beatific glow on his father's face and the words would not come. He moved quietly in the roar of cheering to the catwalk. He was trembling. A flag orderly met him at the foot of the ladder. "Just looking for you, Ensign Paige. Better hurry. The admiral's already started the meeting." He hesitated. "You feeling okay, sir?"

"I'm all right."

For fifteen minutes with head bowed, David listened to a recap of flight and battle plans, emergency procedures, estimated times of rendezvous and the freshest decoded intelligence on the disposition and makeup of the enemy force. The urgent words rattled like stones in his head. He was nearest the portside door when the admiral dismissed them. He was the first to go.

He parted the blackout curtains and undogged the light-lock door and descended in darkness to the flight deck level. He passed through another set of security curtains and doors and emerged on the flight deck itself. The clean night wind caressed his cheek. He began to walk. He must have seen the planes clearly. The deck hands of half a dozen fighters and bombers, sprawled under the wings, later swore they saw him step carefully over the tie-down cables. He crossed to the edge of the Number Two elevator and without faltering went over the side.

A sharp-eyed Marine gunner saw him go. He was standing his watch on one of the twenty-millimeter guns on the gallery deck fifty feet abaft the elevator. He reported Man Overboard to the gunnery control officer who notified the bridge at once.

Tod Newell had the deck. He activated the switch that released a lighted Franklin buoy automatically in the ship's wake to mark the spot. The captain heard the report and leaped from his high swivel stool to the TBS and sent a terse message in plain language, alerting the rest of Gamma group. Acknowledgments poured back. The quartermaster-of-the-watch noted the time and logged the mishap. The navigator checked the plot of the ship's course and marked the exact position with the point of a sharp red pencil. The quartermaster entered the latitude and longitude in the log where he had left a blank space.

A barrage of reports and inquiries jammed the phone circuits throughout the ship. The flag duty officer asked through the speaking tube for an immediate report. Paige coolly advised the flag bridge that normal Man Overboard procedure was being followed. Division officers sent word to the leading division petty officers for a quick and accurate personnel count.

Admiral Flint dispatched one of the destroyers to search the area in the vicinity of the Franklin buoy which would drift as a man afloat would. Long minutes passed. A great uneasiness settled over *Shiloh* as she raced with her screening vessels through the night sea. Thirty minutes passed before Admiral Flint asked Captain Paige to report to the flag bridge.

Paige found Flint at the after end of admiral country, that tiny and almost sacred domain on the starboard side of the inner flag bridge where one approaches by invitation only. Flint was alone, standing, his face in the shadows. Paige observed that the duty watch had been stripped to bare essentials and each man seemed painfully intent on his duty. He saluted the admiral warily.

"Anything to report, Harry?" Flint's voice was agitated and hearing the awkward sound of his name for the first time on those thin straight lips, Paige knew that something was terribly wrong.

"All divisions report all hands present and accounted for, Admiral."

"We're short a man in staff, Harry. It's David." He waited. There was no sound from Paige. No movement. "He still may show. But the boys in some of the plane crews saw it happen."

"Saw what happen?"

"David. He left my meeting here. Probably didn't allow enough time for his eyes to adjust to the dark. Lost his sense of direction and before anyone could warn him, he walked off the edge of the Number Two elevator."

Oh David!

"I've detached *Bradbury* to search until dawn—" Flint's voice broke. "Poor Felicia!" He could not speak for several moments, then he said, "Impossible to do any more than I've done, Harry. We can't turn back. You know that. My God, this is a terrible thing for you—"

"For you. And for Rollo Blatchford."

"For all of us. Anything to suggest?"

"Continue with normal Man Overboard routine."

"Of course, Harry. A terrible thing! My God, poor David! There's a good chance the destroyer'll pick him up, you know. Surely by daybreak. David's a strong swimmer. He's got a good head on his shoulders. I just hope and pray—"

Paige had gone. He climbed slowly to the bridge, bent like an old man full of pain. It irked him that Amos Flint knew David was a strong swimmer and he did not. He felt a dull ache everywhere inside him. Did it really matter any more, knowing anything about David? He knew too much already, the regrets, the grief to come settling like a fever in his bones. That would matter. It would matter for a sorry lifetime.

He moved among the silent men of the bridge watch, feeling the pitying eyes he could not see. He closed the door of his sea cabin quietly and leaned against it. For the first time in his life, he was helpless. His fists and guns were useless and there were no words. A nameless terror struck his heart and all that had held tight inside him through the years let go and he wept like a child.

Paige grieved and Flint prayed and *Bradbury* searched the night sea. It made no difference one way or the other. David had made sure of that.

As he plunged toward the sea, his mind flashed to the final page of *Martin Eden* wherein Eden, in a tropic sea much like this, defied the instinctive will to live by diving deeply past the point of no return.

David chose a swifter end. The moment his body struck the sea, he arched toward the ship's side and was caught and tossed into the racing phosphorescent foam. In a matter of seconds he was sucked into *Shiloh*'s churning screws, his last blinding image the beating wings of a million gulls screaming.

37

∿∿∿∿∿∿∿∿∿∿∿∿∿∿∿∿∿∿∿∿∿∿∿∿∿∿∿∿∿∿∿∿

The ships of Beta and Gamma joined forces at Alamo in the next day's twilight and readied for the morning's battle. *Bradbury* had ceased her futile search at sunrise and raced northwest at flank speed to rejoin before dawn and resume her station in the destroyer screen.

The ship's crews stood at a modified version of general quarters—watch on, watch off, round the clock. Visual signals between ships continued to the final moment before darkness. Radio silence was mandatory except for the use of the limited range TBS. All security measures went into effect. Steel watertight doors were dogged down. Men moved to their stations through narrow passageways complicated by the bulky life jackets they wore. In the recognition rooms, pilots sprawled about, some in flight gear just in case, and studied the swiftly flashing silhouettes of the enemy's planes and ships. On the flight and hangar decks, in damage control, everywhere, men tinkered and sweated and swore.

The scuttlebutt ran true to form. Because the fueling rendezvous had been canceled and the tin cans were low, the fleet would run dry in the heat of battle. The high-level bombing attack by the Midway-based B-17s had sunk three enemy ships. Or no enemy ships. Or had been shot out of the air. Nobody really knew and it really did not matter. It was another way to ease the tension throughout the ship. Like the skipper's son. Walked off the flight deck, they said. No accident at all.

Paige sat on his high stool in *Shiloh* and rechecked his night orders for the bridge watch. On the strength of the information at hand, Flint felt reasonably certain that the presence of his force was still unknown to the enemy. He had thereupon changed course to the southwest to arrive at dawn two hundred miles north of Midway—a logical position from which to launch his own surprise attack against Admiral Kaizuka's striking force of carriers. He designated the strike groups of *Shiloh* to be oddly numbered and those of *Tarrytown*, even.

Paige initialed the orders and handed them to the chief quartermaster. Early that day he had also initialed a copy of *Bradbury's* negative search report and acknowledged the sympathy of her commanding officer. Sympathy faced him wherever he turned and he had had his fill of it. It could not bring back David.

He had shut it from his mind and in an odd way was satisfied. A calm possessed him, an eerie peace of mind almost sinister in its serenity. He had returned like a nautilus to its shell. He was in full command of his ship and himself, honed fine, grim and wary in his world of tight control.

The long day of ship maneuvers and flight operations had been conducted with his customary driving style—swift, expert, inspiring. Logan stood by and said little, ready to help if his skipper cracked. He mentioned no word of it but he shared the captain's loss with the curious understanding of the childless.

Amos Flint avoided Paige and found reasons enough to justify it in the swiftly changing events that pressed him toward battle. Paige was grateful. He did not believe he could survive another scene of mawkish sentimentality, no matter how well-intentioned, and certainly not from Flint.

Morning will come, he reassured himself. Morning will come and the flight deck will rumble with the thunder of engines and I will have that moment I have waited for all these years—the enemy out there and in range of my planes; his planes aloft and winging this way; my guns at the ready to defend my ship. And each of us thinking, *This is no drill! This is no drill!* All these years waiting for such a morning to come.

The chief quartermaster nudged the bosun's mate-of-the-watch. "Take a look at that Hardtack Harry, would you?" His awed whisper was a tribute of admiration. "That's what makes heroes, sailor. Ice water in the veins."

He could not see what Paige saw—David's face larger than life, blurry with a father's grief.

To the west of Midway, in the heart of the most powerful armada yet assembled by man, a courtly soul named Yoshiro Kaizuka sat before his evening meal and sulked. He could not eat. He did not like the smell of things.

Vice Admiral Kaizuka, Commander Carrier Striking Force, was a nobleman and a sea fighter in the highest tradition of his ancient country. He had led the ships of his carrier force with distinction since the first sortie from Tankan Bay in the Kurile Islands in late November last. The record spoke. Pearl Harbor in December. Rabaul and Kavieng in January. Java in March. The Easter raid on Ceylon. Tulagi was taken. Port Moresby, like an overripe fruit, was ready to fall. A glorious string of victories. He groaned, thinking of it.

Why this melancholy? He could not be sure. The sixth sense of a sailor told him trouble lay ahead. He felt it in his bones. His fliers had been driven hard through these months. Occasional rest and recreation did little to assuage their fatigue. They drank too much. They whored. An abstainer himself, and a respectable father, he did not approve, but there was little to be done about the drinkers. Even now he could hear their laughter in the wardroom where they hung around with nothing to do until they manned their planes. Somewhere topside a group of jubilant sailors were lustily shouting war songs. He groaned again and ordered the food removed from his sight.

In the passageways, men in undress whites and green work uniforms drifted like ghosts past his cabin as the watch changed. Their voices dismayed him. Too much talk everywhere. Arrogance and overconfidence, even among his top-ranking colleagues. It could only lead to a dangerous loosening of security.

He was troubled because the Imperial High Command did not seem overly disturbed by the stalemate in the Coral Sea a month ago. It relied instead on the unconfirmed reports of heavy American losses inflicted and reported by his own exuberant pilots. Two major carriers sunk and innumerable planes destroyed in the air by our splendid Zeros. . . .

He sniffed. As far as he could estimate at this early date, the only results of the Coral Sea fight were unfortunate results. Only because it was the first carrier-versus-carrier naval battle fought without either side sighting a surface enemy, would it possibly be remembered.

Both sides had suffered painful losses. It was neither victory nor defeat. Nothing was decided. And what would Midway prove? Obviously, the enemy was stiffening his resistance. Imagine his impudence in bombing Tokyo! His mighty industrial resources would soon launch armadas to put this one to shame. Time was getting short, he reflected morosely.

Yoshiro Kaizuka knew the American fighting spirit well, almost as well as his country's own. He had served a six-month tour of duty in the '30s as a naval attaché in Washington. He had met and still admired his good friend, Maury Nickelby, the amiable fly rod fisherman, who called him by his nickname "Jiro." Kaizuka recalled this with a guilty flush of pleasure.

He stiffened. Midway then. My calling card and a deep bow to my gentle friend Nickelby. A Japanese base on Midway will extend our lines eastward to fueling and strike range for Hawaii. It will force the United States Pacific Fleet to a showdown that will determine the final outcome of the war in the Pacific.

So here I am, Kaizuka reflected, and in the morning, Midway. I will strike fast and hard for the Emperor. And when the United States Fleet recovers from our surprise attack and shows itself—and show itself it must or lose Midway—then my planes will smash to bits what we missed at Pearl Harbor.

He recalled the bitter battleship-carrier controversy that had preceded the bombing of Pearl Harbor. He regretted the Imperial high command's inability to act quickly on matters so coldly clear to the Naval General Staff. It was painful to know they had vacillated so long on the Midway attack. Or was it the fault of the Combined Fleet Headquarters? Or was it the Naval General Staff after all?

He stirred uneasily, reluctant to lose the brightening mood he was beginning to enjoy. But it was true. The bickering of official military brass confused and embarrassed him. He was a sea fighter, one of the best, but in matters of politics and power, he was an innocent lamb. He was content to leave these distasteful campaigns to his brilliant and hardheaded commander-in-chief, just now some two hundred miles astern of the Striking Force and safe behind

Yamoto's eighteen-inch guns and the thick protective steel of his flag bridge.

A slow smile creased his brown cheeks. The "Hashirajima Fleet," his cocky pilots derisively called it. Until now, both the First Fleet and Battle Division One had remained in the safe anchorage of Hashirajima behind the camouflaged antiaircraft batteries since the outbreak of the war six months ago.

He felt much better now. True, there had been much to make him melancholy. The cursedly strict radio silence deprived him of any intelligence about the latest enemy movements. The lack of radar represented an advantage enjoyed by the inferior enemy. The thick fog protected him from detection yet blinded his ships to each other's movements. And there was his curious sixth sense that stirred the uneasy suspicion that Fate no longer smiled on the Imperial Fleet.

All this was true but who would deny that Japan's tactical advantage still prevailed? The Coral Sea fight had proved beyond any doubt the skill of his seasoned pilots and the superiority of the Zero fighter over the F4F Wildcat in speed, maneuverability and rate of climb. The enemy's torpedo bombers were clumsy and vulnerable and his dive bombers slower than the Aichi-99 "Val."

Tomorrow he would add another Pearl to his glorious string of victories. In a few hours, his carrier decks would tremble with the fervor of the predawn take-off to battle. He had set the zero hour for launching the strike against Midway at forty minutes before sunrise from a position two hundred and forty miles northwest of the atoll. He had firm assurances from his weather officer of clear skies and ideal attack conditions over Midway.

Morning would tell. His melancholy returned. He knew precisely where Midway was. But where were the enemy carriers?

Between the two sea forces poised for battle lay Midway, packed in haste like an ancient muzzleloader with the fuse about to be touched off. Her island commanders had worked furiously to prepare her. The atoll was ringed with every coastal defense weapon they could muster. The muzzles and barrels of antiaircraft guns bristled like swords pointed toward the sky. Mines and underwater obstacles lurked in the deep turquoise shadows of the reefs and beaches. A mixed bag of aircraft had been assembled—lumbering Catalinas, Flying Forts, Wildcats, Marauders, Vindicators, Avengers,

Buffaloes—tangy American names to bolster the courage of men who knew the odds were stacked against them. They stood shivering in the early gloom with these barnyard tools of war and prepared to repel boarders. All they could do was remember Wake and wait.

It had been one of these Catalinas that made the first contact that had alerted Task Force Alpha. From Midway, nine Flying Forts winged south and west, found the transport group under clear skies and executed three high-level bombing runs with no hits. Four Catalinas followed and in early morning moonlight scored in a low level attack with an aerial torpedo on a tanker's bow. Twenty-three Japanese sailors were either killed or wounded but the material damage was slight and the stolid *maru* maintained her station in the column.

Far to the north, with no radio communication and in dense fog and melancholy, Admiral Kaizuka knew none of this. But the battle was on.

38

Admiral Kaizuka with wind and weather and weight of numbers favoring him launched his first strike against Midway. Six squadrons of torpedo and dive bombers with fighter escorts swept from the decks of the four carriers and headed for the island targets two hundred and forty miles to the southeast.

Minutes later, seven float-type search planes were launched from the screening Jap cruisers' catapults and vectored east and south, each to search a three-hundred mile leg for enemy ships to confirm the assumption that none were present.

The delay in launching search planes did not overly concern the admiral. Imperial Navy strategy supported the primary importance of attack and the Japanese naval pilots were trained and organized to conform to this concept. Search and reconnaissance training and tactics were unwisely underrated. Ten percent of total strength was all that policy would permit for search missions. Treated as an afterthought, the conduct of these operations could be woefully hit-or-miss.

An eighth search plane took to the air an hour after the others. It was a newly converted dive bomber, a type called *Suisei*, redesigned for carrier-based reconnaissance and armed with one light bomb. She was undergoing the first test of her capabilities. She had been detained by a faulty catapult and her pilot, Lieutenant Minoru Oto, fretted in the cockpit until the repair was completed.

Kaizuka watched the tail of Oto's plane diminish in the faint morning light. Ninety more planes in standby condition graced his carriers, armed and ready to follow the first wave. It would be gratifying, Kaizuka reflected, to order them over Midway behind the others and soften up the island in style. But he was still vaguely troubled by the absence of reliable information about enemy surface forces. As a precaution he had armed this reserve group with torpedoes useless against land installations but ideally suited for low level attack against warships. Perhaps his search planes would discover them. Or the American carriers, hearing of his attack over Midway, might close to defend it and make their presence known. Meanwhile, he believed, he was prepared for anything. Soon the reports would be radioed back from the first planes over Midway.

His force steamed eastward, boldly confident of victory, its admiral still unaware of the bombing attack on the Midway-bound transports to the south.

Like Kaizuka, his opposite number, Admiral Flint had ordered search planes launched from *Tarrytown* in predawn darkness. Ten SBD Dauntless scoutbombers sped in a spreading arc to the northwest, each on a hundred-mile radius to protect the group from possible detection by planes from any enemy surface group Commander Task Force Alpha might not know about. The decks of *Shiloh* and *Tarrytown* were spotted to launch air strikes. All hands stood at battle stations.

In *Shiloh*'s cramped pilot house the navigator Catlin conned the ship's course and moved with notable grace for so large a man in tight quarters. From time to time he studied the sweeping green beam of the radar repeater to monitor the stationkeeping of the screening vessels.

Paige stood braced on the outer bridge catwalk near flight control. Like the others he wore the recommended battle gear from steel helmet to whistle. Above him were the heavens strewn with stars; on the flight deck below, the blurred shapes of planes like cattle huddled in windbreaks before a storm. His leg ached and he cursed Sunda Strait. Stick Wilson on the wheel and Joe Allen steady over the charts was all he missed. His tongue sucked the bitter aftertaste of too much black coffee. He stood cold and remote and ready to kill.

Miller LeClair alongside with a bullhorn in his hand spoke easily to the flight deck crews. The pilots had manned their planes. The first to go would be Blaesing, the air group commander. Blue exhaust flame spurted as a cranky engine warmed up. Small beams of red and green light acknowledged the air officer's instructions and pilot and plane responded like sensitive jockeys and their mounts in a starting gate. The crewmen pampered their charges, weaving delicately among spinning props like men stepping on eggs.

The buckled and harnessed pilots in their snug cockpits sweated out the minutes, irked by the delays, faintly uneasy. Plotting board, pencil, pistol, butts in the knee pocket. Check, double check and check again. Twice before dawn they had been briefed and left the ready rooms to man their planes. Each time the admiral had ordered them back. Their nerves were frayed and they cursed the arming and the fueling and the servicing and the goddam pampering and all they wanted now was to roar off the roof of this seagoing garage into the open sky where they belonged.

The minutes dragged. Paige stalked his quarterdeck, his growing impatience barely contained. The ship's radio officer appeared with a sheaf of the morning dispatches. Paige flipped through them —mostly the dull routine of CINCPAC's official business. "Any word from Midway?"

"Negative, Captain. Their search planes are looking."

"Those damn carriers have got to be someplace. What's the matter with those guys?" He savagely initialed the blue sheets. "You're monitoring everything out of Midway, right?"

"Receiving only, sir. Not sending."

"Okay. Those Jap carrier planes are probably on their way right now to hit the island. Radar will pick 'em up on the way in, and search and attack planes are bound to intercept. I want to know it the second it happens and I want the exact position."

"Yes, sir. Of course the flag'll be getting that dope—"

"That's all, Lieutenant."

Paige motioned Catlin to the chart room and sent for the air officer. Together they bent over the plotting board. "This delay is killing me, so let's play war games. Cat, the moment we get a contact report on the enemy strike, I want you and Miller here to take that position and plot a course and speed, and give me a launch point from where we can take off and clobber them." He tapped the chart, his finger on Midway. "We sure as hell are going to hear howls when those bombs start dropping and we'll know when the Jap bombers start back to their carriers, and by that time we should also know where those carriers are, and just about when they take the returning strike aboard. That's when I want to hit 'em. When they're refueling and rearming and the flight and hangar decks are loaded with planes and men and the hi-octane fuel is flowing. Can do?"

"No strain," Catlin said, "once we pinpoint the carriers."

LeClair pointed his thumb down at the deck, indicating the flag bridge below. "What about them?"

"I'm sure the admiral's got it figured the same way. And we're only playing a game, right?" A slow grin spread, the first since David. It warmed the men to see it. "We're only human, you know? The admiral might have a heart attack all of a sudden and maybe the chief of staff'll come down with the diarrhea and be caught with his pants down. I just want to be prepared is all."

"You old Boy Scout, you," LeClair said.

"On our present course," Catlin said, "we need less and less flight time to reach them. Of course we're increasing the possibility of detection at the same time."

"It's an hour and a half past sunrise, Cat, and they haven't found us yet. Their search pilots must be wearing blindfolds—"

The radio officer burst into the chart room and shoved the dispatch under Paige's nose. At the same time Paige heard the flag bridge below come to life with terse orders.

Midway's search radar had picked up the first wave of enemy planes ninety miles west of the atoll. Everything on the island that might stop them had been launched.

Flint's staff worked feverishly on a counterattack plan and the men throughout the ship tensed and waited for orders. In *Shiloh*'s chart house, Catlin plotted the enemy planes' position and waited for word of their carriers.

Kaizuka's death messengers were closing fast. Thirty miles west of Midway a handful of spunky Marine pilots in outmoded fighter planes mixed with the escorting Zeros and were shot out of the sky. The Japanese bombers droned on unscathed. In a few minutes their bombs rained down on Midway. Oil tanks, hangars, hospital, store-houses, erupted in flames.

The island's torpedo bombers had cleared the runways before the holocaust and found the enemy carriers. The planes inflicted no damage and were shot down or badly damaged and few returned to Midway, but not before the striking force's position was made known to Admiral Flint. The time was 0650.

Signals flapped at the flag bridge halyards. The TBS came alive with orders and Harry Paige on *Shiloh*'s bridge finally read Flint's counterattack plan and swore aloud.

FROM: COMTASKFOR ALPHA
TO: TASK GROUPS BETA AND GAMMA
SUBJ: OPERATION ALAMO:

1. SHILOH PROCEED ON COURSE 240 AT 25 KNOTS AND LAUNCH AIRCRAFT AGAINST ENEMY CARRIERS AT 0900.
2. TARRYTOWN MAINTAIN RENDEZVOUS TO RECOVER SEARCH PLANES THEN PROCEED SAME AS SHILOH AND AWAIT ORDERS TO LAUNCH AIRCRAFT.
3. ALL SCREENING VESSELS CONFORM TO CARRIER MOVEMENTS AND CARRY OUT AIR DEFENSE, PLANE GUARD AND ANTI-SUBMARINE DUTIES.
4. ACKNOWLEDGE WHEN UNDERSTOOD. EXECUTE ON SIGNAL.

Paige thrust the dispatch at Catlin. His face was livid. "Nine o'clock! We could all be dead by nine o'clock! Hold up the course and speed change and get LeClair back in here."

He went into the chart room and pored over the plotting board. In the surrounding screen of ships, the signal hoists were at the dip awaiting the admiral's word to execute. A signalman stuck his head into the chart room. "Flag bridge is yacking about the delay in acknowledging the course and speed change, Captain."

"Let 'em yack."

There was a ghostly rumble from the speaking tube. "Bridge. This is Flag Plot. Admiral Flint requests immediate acknowledgment of his last dispatch."

Paige stuck his mouth over the tube. "Dispatch received." Catlin and LeClair had come in and Paige wasted no time. "I don't like this two-hour delay. Those carriers are northwest of Midway and just about abeam of us. The fastest way to 'em is due west on two-seven-oh. Check me if I'm wrong. It's just about seven now. Radio shack says the Nip bombers are heading back to their carriers right now. I want to catch those babies on deck, Miller, like I said. When should we launch?"

LeClair worked on the problem with Catlin over his shoulder.

Paige looked haggard. LeClair glanced at his watch and at the chronometer. "You've got twelve, maybe fifteen minutes to commence launching. After that—" He shrugged.

"Cat?"

"Jibes with my figures within a minute. Miller knows his planes, though. I don't. Two-six-eight might be a shade better course."

"Close enough. They're spread out. But you agree with me, the two-hour delay is real trouble?"

They nodded. He went to the speaking tube. "Flag bridge from Captain Paige."

"Flag bridge, aye."

"Request permission to launch aircraft immediately." He winked at Catlin and LeClair.

There was a shocked silence. The word he expected came back sharply. "Permission denied."

"Request permission to speak with Admiral Flint on a most urgent matter." This time there was no delay from the flag bridge. Permission was not granted. Furthermore, the speaker said, Admiral Flint demanded to know at once what was holding up *Shiloh*'s course-and-speed flag hoist.

Paige was already on the way below. He found Flint drinking coffee with members of his staff. They stared at him. Some seemed amused. Others bore hostile expressions. Flint turned red. "I thought you were just informed, Captain—"

"This is an emergency, Admiral. Life and death. I request permission to speak immediately with you and Captain Leverton alone."

"This is most unusual, Captain. As a matter of fact—"

"In ten minutes, Admiral, it'll be too late to talk and you'll live to regret the delay the rest of your life." He moved toward flag plot and held the door open. "Gentlemen?"

Leverton looked to his superior for guidance. He was a shrewd gray fox of a man, older than the other two, with years of the sea in his face and the guilt mark of Pearl Harbor alongside his name in the records. Flint shrugged and set aside his cup and saucer. The duty staff cleared out of plot and pushed forward to the bridge. Flint closed the door.

"Now damn it, Harry! What sort of conduct is this for a ship's captain! You're playing a dangerous game, man!"

Paige had placed a tracing sheet over the chart table and spoke rapidly while he roughed out his plan. "Here's where we are. If we launch immediately—say ten minutes from now—and fly due west, our boys can hit their carriers while the planes that just bombed Midway are on deck rearming and fueling for the second strike. And *Tarrytown*'s planes should follow up and hit 'em again. On the other hand, delay two hours and they'll be ready and waiting for us in the air." He pretended not to hear Flint's snort of disgust and watched Leverton's cold gray eyes. He remembered Leverton's reputation. An old poker hand. One of the Navy's best. "So I'm requesting permission to cancel the present order and launch a strike at once."

"Not granted."

"May I know your reasons?"

"Yes, damn it, you may know my reasons! I'm in tactical command here. And the matter of your impudence, your questioning of authority, your dereliction of duty, will be taken up in due time. However painful, Captain, a little naval education can't hurt you. By 0900, there will only be a hundred miles of ocean between us and the Japanese carriers. A safer distance for our fliers to fly. A safe balance of fuel to return on. Launch now and you run the risk of empty fuel tanks, loss of planes, loss of pilots. We face a superior force. We must preserve our planes and protect our pilots' lives."

"Preserve and protect for what? The Navy Museum? Damn it, Admiral, this is war. Death is a detail. It's just because we *are* outnumbered that we've got to take risks. We take risks or die anyway. They sure as hell can knock us out of the air. Their planes are faster and better-built and that's precisely why I say, get to them now with everything we've got—full loads from both our carriers—and catch their planes on deck with bombs and fuel everywhere. That's the way to clobber them." He grabbed Flint's arm. "Time's running out, Admiral. How about it?"

Flint stared at Paige's hand until Paige withdrew it. Stiffly he said, "You may return to your duties."

"You're throwing away our only chance!"

"Ridiculous. It's gambling with men's lives and any naval tactician will tell you so. What you are recommending is cold murder." His smile was cruel. "Don't you agree, John?"

"No," Leverton said thoughtfully, "quite frankly I don't."

Flint's smile froze. "You had better explain that, John, and fast."

Leverton sighed. "Until Harry spoke up, I agreed with you, of course. We planned the counterattack together and I believed, all things considered, we were pursuing the best course. Caution— because they have us outnumbered two to one. They've got the wind before them and we have to turn each time to launch and recover. I could go on and on with the reasons why we should play it safe. But with all respect to you, Admiral, I believe he's made his point. There's a lot at stake and it calls for a gamble. I for one am willing to change my mind."

"Have you both gone stark raving mad? You know damned well our torpedo bombers have a combat range one way of only a hundred and seventy-five miles. Launching from here, their chance of dropping bombloads and making it back to a rendezvous is almost nil."

"It's the calculated risk," Leverton said gravely. "If I may respectfully remind you of CINCPAC's special letter of instruction, Admiral, it said in essence that we should indeed avoid exposure to the enemy's superior forces *unless* we had good prospect of inflicting greater damage on them than we might receive. Harry's plan to launch now seems to offer that prospect."

"It's throwing those boys' lives away, John. I don't do business that way."

"It's our only chance, as Harry said. Audacious, yes. Risky, true. But if we don't smash those planes on deck, they're coming back and they will smash us. They can't miss. Midway will go down with us. And we damn well know where the Jap will go from there."

Flint turned to the chart table. For long seconds Paige and Leverton in silence contemplated his tailored rear. Once Paige caught Leverton's eye and nodded his gratitude. No muscle moved in Leverton's face. His expressionless eyes looked through Paige as though he were not there.

Flint's voice was barely audible. "You may launch aircraft, Captain Paige." He did not turn from the chart table and it did not matter. Paige was halfway to the bridge by then.

"Fox at the dip."

The flight deck roared to life as *Shiloh* prepared to launch aircraft. The Fox flag at the halyards snapped, awaiting the two-block order that would trigger the planes aloft. The carrier had turned east into the wind and her bow split the sea cleanly as she raced to gather thirty knots of combined speed and wind across the flight deck.

Plane guard destroyers maneuvered to stations. On the flight deck, wheel chocks were cleared and the deck crews pressed against the safety of the island. LeClair nodded to Captain Paige.

"*Two-block Fox.*"

The white-and-red flag fluttered swiftly to the yardarm. The bull-horn roared. Blaesing's plane revved to earsplitting intensity. The launching officer whipped his arm downward and the plane took off. Paige joined LeClair on the catwalk and together they watched plane after plane thunder down the deck and sweep into the sky.

The last TBD Devastator cleared the deck and Paige ordered the course change westward again. He watched the sections of fighters and bombers rendezvous above. The trim formations disappeared from his sight and he sighed. Done, he thought. Now kill. Kill.

LeClair prodded him with the butt of the bullhorn. "Wishing you were up there with them, Captain?"

Paige regarded him strangely for a moment. "Just wondering *where* I belong, Miller. I've laid my career on the line and Amos Flint knows it."

"No regrets, I hope."

"It's done, isn't it? I'd have launched those damn planes no matter what Flint would have decided. And Flint knows it. It was smart of Leverton to cover for him. I know damn well we're doing what Leverton himself must have tried to do and failed. He's lost faith in his own judgment and it's sad to see. He was tapped once for great things." He stared off at the distant horizon where *Tarrytown* was turning into the wind to launch her planes. "I know Flint too well, Miller. He's not letting me get away with this one."

"Hell, he should pin a medal on you. You were right and he knows it and so does old John Leverton."

"In this man's Navy you don't cross an admiral like Flint and get away with it. He'll throw the book at me the first chance he gets."

"And Nickelby'll catch it and heave it back." LeClair racked the bullhorn. "We've better than two hours before we'll be hearing from the boys, sir. Good chance to catch some rest."

"No rest for me, Miller." He looked at LeClair's likable face, young and full of life. "But join me in a cup of joe. I feel the need for company."

They headed for Paige's sea cabin. The talker told them that radar had just reported an unidentified plane to the north about twenty-five miles, closing. "One of *Tarrytown*'s search planes," Paige guessed. "But keep me informed."

Lieutenant Minoru Oto had faithfully flown the search course assigned him to the north and west. Now he was at the end of the three-hundred-mile radius. In spite of excellent visibility and the favoring cumulus cover, he had sighted nothing but the orange glaze of a porcelain sea and a sky festooned with fluffs of the large white clouds. He was sorely disappointed. He had encountered no signs of enemy ships. His failure in this regard made him feel unworthy of the distinction given him—the first pilot to fly the new carrier reconnaissance *Suisei*. He had wanted most desperately to prove himself and perform honorably in the name of the Emperor.

He banked the plane gracefully for the sixty-mile dog-leg, ran it and swung into a course for home. His eyes ached and he was grateful that the sun now would be behind him. He fought drowsiness and stretched his small wiry body as well as he could in the cramped cockpit. To gather strength he thought of home in northern Kyushu and the faces of his dear parents and his sweet and fragile sister Eiko. These thoughts made him dreamily peaceful and he almost missed the tiny specks in formation at the horizon thirty miles to the south.

Almost, but not quite. His trembling fingers checked the switch of his radio transmitter and the first contact message went beaming to Admiral Kaizuka. Oto circled cautiously for a closer look. Five cruisers and five destroyers, he estimated tentatively. He reported their speed at about twenty knots and their course south and west. Growing bolder he hopscotched through clouds to discover and report twenty minutes later one carrier in the group.

Pleased now, he turned once more for home but Minoru Oto had tarried too long for his Emperor. Alerted by *Tarrytown*'s radar, four Wildcat fighters streaked after him. Oto took to the clouds.

Climbing, diving, altering course, he managed to elude them. Twice they swept past, guns blazing. Oto raced like a fox from the thin edge of one cloud to another, untouched. Instruments alone guided him through their turbulence but he was grateful for such sanctuary. They came looking for him high. He dove low. He came out of cover a scant hundred feet above the sea. To his astonishment he saw dead ahead and fifteen miles distant a second force, the carrier silhouette unmistakably that of the new American *Shiloh* class. Undetected in these precious moments, Oto radioed his report of the contact and raced for the nearest cloud in a burst of machine-gun fire from above.

The bullets whined and smashed through the cockpit and ricocheted with a sickening wildness, splintering wood and metal and much of Oto. Pain tore through his middle and he fought to control the crazily rocking plane. The engine coughed. He sat drenched in blood and sweat, resigned to the knowledge that his time had come.

He steadied the plane through thinning wisps of white and in the clearness ahead found the tail of a Wildcat flush in his sights. His bloody fingers squeezed a painful burst and with grim pleasure he watched black smoke erupt and trail across his windscreen. He forced the stick back and climbed with the Wildcats in pursuit. Four more had joined the chase from *Shiloh*'s combat air patrol. Long bursts at staggered levels raked Oto's last cloud. It thinned to vapor and three miles ahead and below he spied the broad beam of the new American carrier.

Swooping Wildcats closed to kill. In seconds the *Suisei* was afire. She never wavered in her whistling screaming dive. It was what she was made for. Wind keened through Oto's shattered canopy. From four thousand feet she sang her death song to the accompaniment of every weapon the ships of Gamma could bring to bear. The flaming plane broad on *Shiloh*'s port beam plunged over the empty flight deck and smashed against the island just below the flag bridge. Minoru Oto joined his ancestors in radiance.

Steel flew. Skewered men screamed. Bodies flung high fell like split sacks. Rank and rate, the living tangled with the dead. Flames leaped, blistering new paint. Oto's small bomb skittered from its rack and was swept up instantly from the deck by the bomb-disposal officer. Cradling it like a baby in his long gloved arms he coolly walked to the deck edge and heaved it clear of the ship. It exploded in the water.

Paige on the bridge snapped crisp orders and conned the ship to keep the flames from spreading. The fires died. Hot smoking wreckage of the *Suisei* fused to what remained of brave Oto, was dragged to the amidships elevator and dumped into the sea.

Flag country was a shambles of charred bodies and chunks of twisted steel and wood splinters sharp as swords. Among a jumble of torn instruments and scorched books, John Leverton lay dying, a shapeless patchwork of flesh, cloth, and pride once a man. Three other staff officers had been killed and the admiral's Marine orderly with his legs blown off did not care whether he lived or died.

On the flight deck four enlisted men and the fighter squadron's control officer were trapped in the path of the *Suisei* and had caught its full impact. They were nowhere to be seen. Corpsmen moved among the wounded and carried them in stretchers to sick bay. The dead were shoved aside and covered.

Amos Flint was shaken but unscratched. Like Paige and LeClair a deck above, he had been on the starboard side when Oto's plane hit. He surveyed the damage to flag bridge and plot and assessed his situation. There was little choice and time was precious. He uncapped the starboard speaking tube. "Bridge from Flag."

"Bridge, aye."

"Captain Paige, please. Harry? We're in bad shape here, Harry. How about you?"

"Everything functioning, sir. No casualties reported except where the plane hit. A few buckled plates in the deck here. I'm waiting for a final damage-control report on the flight deck situation."

"Most of the equipment's shot here. Transmitters and receivers, radar gear, nav instruments. Looks pretty hopeless. Casualties are light, considering, but John Leverton—" He hesitated because two corpsmen had just pushed past to the starboard ladder carrying a stretcher with a blanket over Leverton and the words would not come. "I'm shifting my flag to *Lewiston*, Harry. Expedite the necessary preparations. The enemy knows we're here and he'll be coming to get us."

"Aye, Admiral." He almost said Amos. He could have. He wanted to. But he turned to Catlin. "Get on the TBS, Cat, and get the chief bosun and let's get the flag bunch transferred to *Lewiston*."

Within the hour the flag staff transfer was completed. Paige stood on the fantail and saluted and some of the men cheered. Wildcat fighter planes kept a patrol overhead, vigilant against attack at so vulnerable a time. Paige felt an odd sense of envy as Flint, unruffled and trim in his uniform, was ferried from *Shiloh*'s fantail to flush-decked *Lewiston*, the newest cruiser in the group.

Have to hand it to the man, Paige thought grudgingly. He moves with style. He could scarcely conceal his relief when the last line let go and he knew that Flint was off his back.

It was nine o'clock. His planes were almost there. He spent ten minutes with Thornton, the first lieutenant, sizing up the damage and getting an estimate of the time involved in making the necessary repairs.

Flag bridge was a burnt-out loss. The portside of the island from the flag bridge catwalk to the flight deck was crumpled like tinfoil. Passageways, ladders and the small compartments where the deck crews and air officers took cover from the weather were smoke-blackened ruins. The flight deck itself was scorched close aboard the island. Two sections of steel cleat strips ripped from the wood were already being restored. There was no hangar deck damage and the five-inch antiaircraft mounts just forward of the crash area were intact.

He could still launch and recover planes and that was all that mattered. He slapped Thornton's back and sent him off.

He joined LeClair who looked sad and only then did he remember that eight enlisted men and officers were dead and thirteen wounded lay in sick bay. He could afford to feel sorry about John Leverton and the other members of the flag staff. Their loss in no way would effect the operation of his command. For the others, the members of ship's company, he had only one thought: When would they be back on the job? He needed every damned one of them.

Ten miles abeam on a parallel course, Admiral Tully in *Tarrytown* muttered a few Gaelic prayers for Harry Paige. His own search planes were on board and his first strike followed *Shiloh*'s by five minutes. Tough Tully was not a religious man but he had observed Oto's crash dive almost an hour ago. Add to that the news he had heard about David Paige and he could do no more than guess at the strain his old friend was under.

Tully knew. He had caught his share of it in the Coral Sea in May. An 800-pounder dropped in a dive-bombing attack went through the flight deck and exploded four decks below, killing and wounding sixty-six men. Oh yes, Tully knew. He had lost his two sons in just as many weeks—an ensign at Pearl and a Marine sergeant on Wake. Nobody had to tell him what it was like with

Hardtack Harry Paige. The luck of the Irish? He wondered what the hell they meant by that.

Like Paige he waited for word from the striking planes. The first wave—*Shiloh*'s torpedo bombers—should be boring in just about now.

The time was 0915.

The Japanese search planes had returned to their cruisers with no surface contacts reported. Although Admiral Kaizuka now felt reasonably certain no enemy carrier groups were within striking range, ninety planes armed with torpedoes were still on his hangar decks just in case. All he wanted now were the results of the high-level and dive-bombing attacks over Midway.

When he received his air group commander's radioed report, he was concerned. They had found no planes on the airfields. Since the primary objective of this strike was to cripple Midway's air strength and destroy its runways, Kaizuka knew he must launch a second attack.

He still felt confident. The Americans on Midway had thrown every plane they could fly against him and his carrier force had either blown them out of the sky or sent them limping back to their island base. He would launch against the island at once and destroy what remained of Midway's aircraft power and blast the runways as well.

Kaizuka ordered the torpedoes removed from the reserve planes and rearmed with 800-kilogram bombs. The armament crews worked feverishly, sending the rearmed planes to the flight decks to be spotted forward for the launch after the Midway planes were recovered. They had completed about half of the changeover when Lieutenant Oto's first sighting was reported.

The admiral with his staff intelligence officer hurriedly plotted the reported position and radioed back for a more detailed description. Two hundred miles separated the two surface forces. If there were enemy carriers present, Kaizuka knew he could be in trouble.

Five cruisers and five destroyers, reported Oto. Kaizuka smiled and his staff officers looked relieved. Sitting ducks.

His four carriers were preparing to take aboard the returned strike from Midway when Oto's startling report of an American carrier was received. It was followed almost immediately by reports from his outlying reconnaissance planes. Many enemy carrier aircraft were approaching from the east and they were engaging them.

Precious minutes passed as Kaizuka debated the choices. He could not stop the recovery of the Midway attack planes. There were wounded fliers in some of them and considerable damage had been done to their planes by the spirited antiaircraft batteries on Midway. Most of the fighter escorts were low on fuel and an added delay would risk the need to ditch them. He was impatient to seek out and destroy the enemy carrier. Two of his own carriers were ready with thirty-six dive bombers. The other two, including his own flagship, had half her torpedo bombers at the ready, but they were armed with the 800-kilogram bombs less effective than torpedoes against surface targets. All his Zero fighters were aloft on patrol against further attacks from Midway's planes. Kaizuka dared not send his loaded bombers out without fighter escort. They would be cut to bits by the lighter, swifter Wildcats of the American combat air patrol.

He respectfully listened to the mixed opinions from his staff and that of the division leader in the other carrier group. His own mind was made up. He would strike his bombers below once more, arm the torpedo bombers with their original loads, and recover both the Midway strike planes and enough Zeros from the combat air patrol to fuel and furnish fighter cover for the attack on the enemy carrier group.

The order was given to clear the decks for the recovery of aircraft. The exhausted flight and hangar deck crews turned for the third time to obey the order. The returning planes commenced coming aboard with record-breaking speed and precision. The re-arming of the torpedo planes on two hangar decks proceeded at an almost superhuman clip, the bombs piled anywhere. The outer screen of destroyers reported visual sighting of the enemy planes and signs of air battle where the Japanese combat patrol engaged them.

The reported number of approaching planes troubled Kaizuka. So many from one carrier? As he puzzled over it, the next blow fell. Lieutenant Oto's sighting of the second carrier force came in, and with it, news of the new *Shiloh* in her midst.

The faces of his staff officers were pathetically long and Kaizuka knew he had to reach out and smash that carrier. It would be a symbolic and glorious blow for the Emperor.

The last plane had settled aboard and taxied clear. At 0905 Kaizuka executed the last phase of his plan. He ordered the Striking Force to change course northward to throw off the approaching bombers. He stood proudly on the wing of his bridge. His four carriers turned into the wind to launch their deckloads and that was how the first wave of *Shiloh*'s planes found them.

Blaesing led. This was the *Shiloh* air group's first taste of combat and he had already shot down two of the intercepting Zeros. He felt like a kid in a candy store. Now he maneuvered into the cloud bank, grateful for its cover. The first plane had just been launched from Kaizuka's flagship and Blaesing swooped down. He let go two quick bursts as the Nakajima 97 veered to clear the ship's path. She faltered and he touched off another blast and she burst in black and orange surprise and smashed into the sea.

He came back on the stick hard and zoomed skyward. "A cad, ain't I?" muttered Blaesing, an opera buff from Jersey City. "Worse than Cho-Cho-San's Lieutenant, B. F. Pinkerton." His quick eyes searched everywhere. He climbed out of savage ship's fire to sweet cloud and above the cloud bank leveled off. He called over the intercom, snapping instructions to his dogfighting Wildcats. He had lost his wingman to a Zero's guns at the first approach, when the tight formation in which he had led the attack was scrambled at the outer perimeter of the enemy air patrol zone.

He searched for the low-flying Devastators and found them five miles distant, skimming in low over the water in single column, according to plan. They came from both sides of Kaizuka's flagship in the face of blistering machine-gun fire from swarms of Zeros and the screening cruisers and destroyers.

The SBDs were nowhere to be seen. Blaesing feared they had vectored too far south and would miss Kaizuka's carriers now headed north. His Wildcat fighters were everywhere he looked, streaking like crazy comets across thirty miles of clouds and sky. The top deck was clean of enemy Zeros. He knew that if he could guide the waves of SBDs, as yet undetected, to a peel-off point, the target carriers could be had. He was drenched with sweat and charged with the emotional aftermath of his three kills. He belted out a few off-key notes from *Madame Butterfly*. He was close enough to see the lead carrier's flight deck choked with planes. Other pilots had reported three more carriers in the same state. He wished to hell those SBDs would show.

The Devastators at wave-top level were valiant but doomed. One by one they were hit. They exploded and burst into flames and smashed into the sea. Some pressed on to meet their gory end moments after dropping the fourteen-foot torpedo into its run. Stick back, the pilots lifted over the carrier deck into sheets of deadly AA gunfire at point-blank range.

Blaesing had almost given up hope when he spotted the first wave of the SBDs. He had guessed right. Their course had taken them too far south. He pressed his mike button and directed the group leaders to a rendezvous point and rallied what fighters he could to join up. All joy of killing had left him. He had witnessed the slaughter of the TBDs below. He resumed battle, poised for a moment in time at twenty thousand feet with his lethal load of SBDs on hand, a calculating machine of death again, the way he had to be, the way they had made him. A joyless machine of death that just happened to dig Puccini.

Spirits soared once more on Kaizuka's flag bridge. They had tallied thirty-two enemy torpedo bombers in the attack. No more than five had got away and, damaged, probably would not make it back to their carriers' decks. Kaizuka hastened to the business of his counterattack.

His carriers, taking evasive action against the torpedoes, had maneuvered independently and with their screening ships were scattered for miles in all directions. They laid on knots to resume formation. The admiral's word went out. "Prepare at once to launch aircraft!" The lean destroyers raced to stations. The mighty Striking Force, still unscathed, commenced to launch their deckloads of impatient planes.

The SBDs came screaming out of the clouds. Lookouts shouted and pointed. Antiaircraft guns swung skyward. The Dauntlesses plummeted in from twenty thousand feet, flaps open, targets lined up in the telescopic sights. At 2500 feet the bombs let go.

Kaizuka, surprised, knew that his melancholy fears of early morning were realized. He stormed for action but his Zero fighters still flew low where they had blasted the Devastators into oblivion. They could not climb in time to meet this new and swift disaster. The first bomb struck the flagship one minute after she had maneuvered to avoid the last torpedo bomber. The bomb exploded at the after end of the flight deck in the midst of planes that just had been refueled and serviced. Two more struck—amidships on the elevator and forward of the bridge, the last one slanting into the hangar deck below.

The bombs and torpedoes had not been lowered to the magazines. The hangar deck erupted in a deafening blast. Again and again she was racked by explosions. Fuel and ammunition tore her insides. Flames crackled and hissed as damage control fought them. Except for that—silent guns now and the enemy gone.

Kaizuka on his flag bridge was stunned by the swift reversal. Five minutes! He would not question Heaven's will but this was bitter tea indeed. The reports, both visual and radio-transmitted, indicated his other carriers had undergone similar attacks. Columns of smoke mushroomed skyward. The sea around him was glazed with oil and burning debris and the bodies of men. He knew in time the sea would be the clean blue sea again but his heart was filled with a desolate grief.

The flagship's tearful captain had a humble request to make. Accompanied by a deep bow and in most respectful tones he begged his Excellency to give consideration to shifting his flag to another vessel. Engine rooms were flooded. Steering and fire control were lost. Communications were gone. As his Excellency could plainly see, flames enveloped the bridge and were threatening his life. It was evident that the ship must be abandoned as soon as possible.

The admiral demurred. His staff implored, pointing out that tactical command could be directed from another ship. His carriers though damaged were still afloat. As soon as communications could be resumed and the damage evaluated, the situation might prove to be less hopeless than it appeared.

Kaizuka gravely accepted this reasoning and the transfer was made with much gloom via destroyer. Its most precious cargo in the brief passage to the cruiser was the flagship's sacred portrait of the beloved Emperor.

The attackers from *Shiloh* and *Tarrytown* headed home high in spirit and low in ammunition and fuel. Most of them whooped and chattered about their kills. A few were silent with their thoughts. They were shepherded by their indefatigable air group commander, Blaesing. Filled with thoughts of divine mission and lacking twelve trumpets and a bass clarinet, he passed the time bellowing "The Motive of Warning" from *Lohengrin*, alternating with a whistled rendition of the shepherd's melancholy tune from the last act of *Tristan und Isolde*. Both were appropriate and they helped him forget that the price of the matinee had come high. Less than half the good men who had sortied with him were returning.

39

Kaizuka realized when the reports were in that his force had been grievously hit. His carrier flagship was a drifting hulk engulfed in flames. He knew that he must sink her by destroyer fire if she were still afloat by dusk and incapable of restoring her own power.

Carrier Two's entire bridge command had been wiped out by the first bomb hit. With the next three hits, planes on deck became funeral pyres. The superstructure was a smoldering ruin and a series of deep explosions belowdecks finally did her in. Those who could, abandoned her. She erupted in a hideous sheet of flame and bubbled to the bottom. Those were *Shiloh*'s targets.

Carrier Three had been the first of *Tarrytown*'s two targets. Tully's boys pitched down in three waves from starboard bow, starboard quarter, and port quarter. Three bombs did the trick, thousand-pounders, one from each wave. The flight deck split open like a melon. Flames, bodies, and blasted planes spewed from the breach. She sank in twenty minutes with her stocky skipper roaring his *banzais* from the bridge.

Carrier Four was the Japanese admiral's Sunday punch. She had maneuvered skillfully and with luck had suffered near misses and no direct hits. She was north of the scene of the carnage with her screen of two battleships, three cruisers, and four destroyers.

Kaizuka ordered her to launch her planes at once, to prepare to receive the planes from the other carriers, and to ready a second strike against the enemy. He radioed to the fleet's commander-in-chief in *Yamoto* his present situation and his determination to seek out and destroy the enemy carriers that had inflicted the damage.

He watched impassively as the strike planes took off from the last carrier's deck. The time was 1105.

Amos Flint wisely put plenty of sea between his two groups and waited tensely for the counterattack. *Shiloh* and *Tarrytown* steamed on diverging courses with their fighter combat umbrella overhead, heading generally southwest from the original Point Option where the strikes had been launched that morning.

Point Option is no fixed point at all. It is a moving ship's position at any given time along a course prearranged between a pilot and his ship. The pilot, knowing the ship's course and speed, his own position and the time elapsed, can set a course that will bring him to the rendezvous. The returning planes had made this rendezvous and now were circling preparatory to being taken aboard. The time was noon.

The Japanese planes showed as tiny specks in the sky to the northwest and *Shiloh*'s fighters streaked to engage them. Paige ordered LeClair to wave off Blaesing's bomber planes and keep them out of the area. The fighters with fuel enough prepared to join the attack.

Tod Newell, in Sky One alongside Fillmore the gun boss, worked with his radar spotters and called range, elevation and bearing readings to his gun director crews. The twin five-inch mounts tracked the incoming planes. When Fillmore gave the word, they opened fire. Their blasts were deafening. The distant sky filled with black and yellow bursts. The fighters closed and Newell through his glasses watched enemy planes fall flaming into the sea. The others came on, very high now, and pushed over and thundered through the sheets of tracer fire, the forties thumping, the twenties chattering. Behind the clamor, the shouts of men were dwarfed by the din and below them the ship's insides groaned and pounded against the violent turns of wheel and rudder.

Planes dove, swooped and climbed, streaking bullets, bits of fuselage and flame. The bombs fell everywhere. Paige stood on the

bridge with his legs thrust apart and a black scowling face barely
visible under the steel helmet. He conned his ship with a sorcerer's
cunning through the geysers of near misses. His guns, freed of
limit stops, sometimes tore away bits of ship's structure to splash
planes they might not otherwise have hit. Startled men at battle
stations ducked and cursed. Altered by sharp-eyed lookouts aloft
and stationed on bow and fantail, Paige called for emergency hard
rudders that heeled the ship in turns that would shame a racing
destroyer.

The last bomb had dropped and no enemy planes remained in
the sky. Fighters almost bone-dry of fuel, begged to come aboard
and Paige ordered LeClair to gather his chickens. With *Shiloh*
headed into the wind, he sent a report over the TBS to advise
the flag of his condition. He closed by saying he would stand
by to launch aircraft against the enemy carriers still afloat, as
soon as ready. He waited for an acknowledgment while Catlin at
the conn checked with damage control for its report.

Flint's acknowledgment was terse. "Your message received. Dispatch will follow. Over and out." Paige called LeClair. "How fast
can we get another strike off?"

"We need time to take 'em aboard, fuel and rearm and service
'em. Say, three and a half hours—"

"Do it in three."

"I don't have a TBD fit to fly."

"Send SBDs with thousand-pounders. Just get 'em there. Three
hours, Miller. I'm going after those two Nip flattops that are still
afloat and I need daylight to do it. Flint won't dare to say no
to this one. Get Blaesing up here soon as he's aboard. The group
skippers, too. I want their reports fast." He had turned and was
gone with Thornton, the first lieutenant, to inspect the damage to
the hull.

Not bad, he thought with relief. Some buckled plates below the
waterline amidships, a ruptured steam line now undergoing repair,
and a thousand broken dishes in the wardroom. "We'll get more in
Tokyo," he told Thornton and took the starboard ladder topside.
Smoke billowed skyward at the horizon. The TBS was bleating
an urgent report to all ships. Beta group was under attack by
enemy carrier planes.

Kaizuka's second wave struck over *Tarrytown* at 1330 hours. She was an older carrier than *Shiloh* by five years and had been hastily repaired at Pearl following the Coral Sea action to have her ready for the defense of Midway. She did not have the extra advantages of Paige's unauthorized modifications and it would not have made much difference anyway. She fought back valiantly but she was no match for the fanatic intensity of the counterattack thrown against her. Her skipper and gun crews and the weary pilots of her fighter group met the avengers with everything they could muster, but *Tarrytown*'s number was up.

A flight deck hit tore through the forward elevator and smashed men, planes, and the bulkheads of the hangar deck. An Aichi-99 aflame let go its bomb and it coursed through the air into the carrier's stack and blasted the boiler room uptakes. Belowdecks men struggled waist-deep in oil and sea water to keep their ship alive. An hour after the attack, her list was being corrected by counterflooding and it began to seem hopeful that she could get under way again. Four boilers were back on the line.

At 1430 the enemy torpedo bombers came. They came in fast and low at masthead height with escort Zeros to guarantee that they made it all the way. With his ship's steering crippled, *Tarrytown*'s skipper could not use evasive tactics. The bombers fanned out and barreled in from four angles. Beta's heavy cruisers raised curtains of solid water with salvos of eight-inch shells fired into the sea in the path of the bombers. Four planes got through. Two torpedoes found *Tarrytown*'s middle and sealed her fate. She lay dead in the water, listing badly.

Tully leaned over the high side of the flag bridge splinter shield. A deck below, *Tarrytown*'s commanding officer wiped his shiny head with a blood-stained towel. Wounded men moaned in the shadows of the crippled pilot house.

"What do you think, Buck?" Tully's voice was gentle.

"It's hopeless, Admiral."

"Let's go, then. We've got two thousand shipmates to move."

The destroyers came alongside and the transfer of the men got under way. Spike Tully was the first to leave. The wounded were next, morphined and lashed in wire litters. He stood on the destroyer's bridge watching the orderly abandonment. He hated to see *Tarrytown* go. He had been through a lot of hell with her and she had known a lot of good times. She was a gallant old girl and it hurt to see her die. He would have been proud to go with her all of the way.

Paige and LeClair with the group intelligence officer had briefed Blaesing and the squadron skippers and sent them to the ready rooms to rest up. No time to change, they were told. Stand by for flight quarters. Blaesing slumped in his dank flight gear, wiping away sweat where he could reach it. He was dog-tired and all he wanted was a shower and a snootful of applejack and some chow. Playing hero aloft was all right but he was no Siegfried and he had had it for this day. Tomorrow was another day and he hoped that the skipper and LeClair remembered that.

Paige in nav plot watched Catlin work out a new course to the enemy's lone-functioning carrier, based on a scout plane's report just received. He wondered what was taking Flint so long to say no and racked his brain for a counter proposal. He sent for LeClair. "How's it going?"

"Thirty minutes," LeClair said.

"I'm making no bones about this morning's performance, Miller. Your boys were great. I'm seeing to it personally they get all the Air Medals and Flying Crosses and whatever else kind of Navy hardware tickles their fancy. They earned it. But there are still two flattops out there and I want my name on 'em. One's a cripple and the other they'll find full of piss and vinegar. If they find her, she'll be a juicy one. She'll have all those planes on deck from the strike that just hit *Tarrytown*."

"I'm as hot for it as you, Captain. But it's a hell of a risk and the boys aren't too happy about it, frankly."

"I'll take their goddam medals away. For Christ sake, Miller. This may be our only chance."

"The boys sunk two of them, Captain."

"Okay. A grade of fifty percent. They missed the other two. Let 'em go back and get 'em."

Miller LeClair's eyes were very blue and steady and when he said "Aye, sir" they had a cold long look they had never had before. He saluted and turned away.

The messenger arrived from the radio shack two decks below. He was breathing hard. Paige grabbed the dispatch board from his fingers.

FROM: COMTASKFOR ALPHA
  TO: CO SHILOH
SUBJ: OPERATION MOP-UP

1. REFER YOUR LAST TBS SUBJECT REQUEST. PER-
   MISSION GRANTED IF ABLE TO LAUNCH IMMEDIATELY
   AND RETURN IN DAYLIGHT HOURS.
2. ALTERNATIVE RETIRE NORTHEAST FOR FURTHER ORDERS.
3. MAINTAIN RADIO SILENCE AND ALERTNESS. ENEMY
   SURFACE FORCE BBS, CAS, CLS, DDS LIKELY IN
   AREA.
4. ACKNOWLEDGE.

He called back LeClair. "We launch immediately."

"The planes aren't fully gassed up yet, Captain."

"Bombs loaded?"

"Just about. But we have got to have another half hour for fueling."

"How many can get there?"

"There and back is what I hope you mean, sir. Two-thirds. Say eight Wildcats and twelve SBDs. The Wildcats carry belly tanks and they'll make it, no strain. But the SBDs are old and bomb-heavy and they eat gas. Even with fully loaded tanks it's going to be close."

"The wind's shifted to the southwest, Miller. They'll have a quartering wind coming back. We'll close the range fast so they don't have too much air distance to cover and take 'em aboard without turning."

"You're sticking your nose awful close to Tojo's fist."

"I wouldn't mind a crack at him at close range. But not tonight. Now launch 'em, damn it, before Flint changes his mind." He turned to Catlin. "Hoist flag signals for our course and speed into the wind, Cat. Point Option is course two-seven-zero, speed twenty knots. Get the word to flight control. All set? Fox at the dip." He nudged the bosun's mate-of-the-watch. "Sound flight quarters."

The radio messenger saluted. "Will you acknowledge the admiral's dispatch, Captain?"

Paige pointed to the flag hoists fluttering at the halyards. "He can read, can't he?"

Blaesing in the lead plane first sighted the smoke of Kaizuka's flagship hull down below the southwest horizon. He double-checked his chartboard, noting distance and bearing and reassured himself it was the second deckload's target—not his. He wigwagged his wings and pointed and called it out over the intercom to the other planes. He radioed the ship giving the position of the sighting and strained his eyes sunward, north and west for a sign of the other flattop, the cripple—his target.

He flew with his fighters at three levels protecting the bombers between them. He had settled on 170 knots as a practical cruising speed that would conserve fuel and get them there and home before pitch darkness. He was bone-weary and sweaty-crotched and he cursed the colossal stupidity of a war that relied on non-heroes like himself. The Academy had been a mistake. He had been the class odd-ball, the classical music lover, for four years. He knocked around after that, mostly in small charter plane jobs. Yet when Pearl Harbor happened, he was one of the first back in the Navy blue and, with his private flying know-how, heartily welcome. Stateside duty had its rewards, he remembered, but this combat crap was for the birds. He loved flying and he knew it cold but this was getting worse than the East Side-West Side shuttle in Grand Central.

It's the goddam skipper, he told himself. Off his rocker since his kid took a dive over the side. Not that I blame the old man and the kid seemed like a nice kid, but why is he taking it out on us? The crazy son of a bitch thinks kill kill kill around the clock like there's no tomorrow. Christ, we sunk two of the Jap carriers this morning. What the hell does he want in a day's work? The whole damn Imperial Fleet?

Well, it's a job with pay, Blaesing thought. That's a sight better than flying charter out of Newark Airport with no gas rations around Newark, Hoboken, and Vicinity, New Joisey.

He wiped his steamy goggles and rechecked the chartboard and his course and speed. Christ, those SBDs must be sopping up the gas and that damned flattop had better the hell be where the search plane had said it would be or he would seek out that scout pilot when he got back and grab him by the tail and pull him inside out.

When he got back. *If* he got back.

He had reached the point on his chart where the enemy carrier should have been and he craned his neck searching in all directions. The setting sun glared off his port wing, a blinding disc of bronze gold. Every low cloud set his heart pounding until he made certain it was a cloud and not a ship. The seven other fighter pilots jabbered over the intercom and the SBD boys were talking worriedly about their low fuel gauges and asking for action. Blaesing knew that SBDs have four fuel tanks and some of them were low on their second and they had not yet started to fight. They had plenty of reason to worry, hadn't they? If it was any consolation, he was a damned sight happier to have SBDs along rather than the slow, vulnerable TBDs. He remembered the morning's slaughter. But the SBDs were okay and the pilots were a cocky lot after their morning's performance.

Got to bring 'em home, Blaesing vowed, especially Tail End Charley. Tail End Charley was the last man to be launched, a gunner, ARM2C, who rode backward in a SBD, a bright nineteen-year-old music major who had quit Juilliard to join the Navy. He livened Blaesing's non-flying hours with blistering tirades against Blaesing's preference for the classical operas when there were modern works to be heard by geniuses like Brecht and Weill and a couple of unknowns named Britten and Menotti whose work, though unproduced, bore watching.

From force of habit, Blaesing began to hum and stopped suddenly. His eye had caught a slight movement in a distant cloud and it vanished swiftly. He had seen enough. The words went instantly into his mike. "Bogey at three o'clock level. Just ducked into those clouds."

Six Zekes in two tight formations swept out of the cover, eight miles distant. Blaesing slammed the rudder hard over, gunned for power and rammed the stick into his middle in a steep climb. He wanted altitude. If Zeros were around, so was the flattop, and he had to know where before he started to tangle. Beyond the cloud bank he leveled and more Zekes swarmed and below them through the open sky he saw the target carrier and its formidable screen of firepower turning, their wakes curling like plumes.

He put out the word and watched the SBDs start climbing for their dive point and satisfied, he raced for the lead Zero head on.

They passed with guns blazing not ten feet apart. Blaesing pulled up and hung for a sickening second and with the stick way over plunged whistling in a dive and caught the Zeke in his gunsight. His tracers streaked away and black smoke streamed past his canopy as he banked and the Zeke spiraled below, past, gone.

The second Zero section had swept in on the tails of two *Shiloh*

Wildcats otherwise engaged and shot them flaming out of the sky with three deadly no-deflection bursts. Blaesing swung in a turn so tight he swore he heard rivets go. He shook a trailing Zero and caught the tail-end of the trio broadside and squeezed the firing button and held it. The Zero simply flew apart. Its fuselage in a single black section plummeted toward the sea. Jagged pieces of the wing fell gracefully, like leaves. The pilot tumbled like a clown.

A bullet had torn Blaesing's left sleeve. He had no time to look. He heard a shouted warning on the intercom, snap-rolled and caught another in his sight and stitched him with tracer fire and raced away to breathe. Blood spread a slow stain where the sleeve was torn. He swerved in short, sharp course changes to throw off pursuit. The air was filled with planes and shouted oaths and fiery death. Too many, he thought, and we have got to get the hell away from here.

The SBDs were ready at the push-over point, bomb sights set. Down they ripped from sunlight to the carrier in the gathering dusk below.

Antiaircraft fire reached for them, a thousand fiery Roman candles. The planes shook crazily but never faltered. Down they raced through muzzle flame and tracer fire into fragment bursts and the deadly shower of thermite bits. Down, down, twelve thousand to the nine thousand release point and let go. Another thousand and the stick jerked back and prayers mixed with bile on a man's lips.

Some left the charred junk of their flying machines and their own remains. The lucky ones flew free. They had all done what they were sent to do. Carrier Four was a dying ship black with smoke so thick the men in the sky could not see her final agony.

Blaesing looked at his watch. Only twenty-one minutes since the first Zeke. He called the others. It was time to go. Five fighters joined him, brushing off the savage passes of the last few Zekes with fuel and guts enough to persist. Looking back, Blaesing saw in the sea below two chutes in the spreading green of the dye markers. Five hundred yards separated them. Neither knows the other's there, he reflected, and it'll be a long time until our cans get back to help them.

His arm had stopped bleeding. It throbbed with a dulled pain. He had worked out the course to Point Option and checked over the intercom with the others and no one disagreed. Too damn bushed to care, he guessed. He made a terse report to *Shiloh. Tar-*

get flattop hit and sinking. Possible hits on one heavy cruiser and one destroyer. That was enough. Very businesslike, he thought.

He guessed those last two hits were accidents, but no one had to know that.

The divisions were forming up as best they could. There were holes where planes should have been. Two fighters gone, three bombers. Not bad at all, yet it made his heart heavy. He looked around at his band of weary warriors, feeling love and pity for the poor bastards who weren't going to make it. Warriors? Kids! The lucky with the cripples, strung out across somebody's sky like the raggedy tail of a kite.

Halfway home they were joined by the returning flight that had been vectored to Kaizuka's flagship. They had finished it off and all planes were intact. The flight leader gave Blaesing the count—four Wildcats and nine SBDs. They had also sunk the cruiser that had taken her in tow, he added proudly.

Nobody cheered. The intercom, only that morning jammed with pilots' rejoicing, was strangely quiet.

Sick of killing, Blaesing thought bitterly. And we've just begun. The first time's the last time. It's not like in the movies at all. This is blood, not ketchup. It's guys I know, not Cagney and Bogart and Gable. *It's me.* War is for Wagner on a stage with loud music and fake spears. For Wagner yes. For Blaesing no. Fuck war.

He'd drink to that. He'd find his ship and come barreling in on the cut without so much as a by-your-leave. He'd head for his locker and his private fifth of Kinderhook and he'd slug it away for the war to end wars.

He loved his mother and he loved his father and he loved his country and he loved all of these things so loving much he'd make goddam sure if he ever got back no kid of his would ever have to go to war.

A voice in the earphones interrupted his thoughts. "I'm out of gas, fellows. I'm ditching."

The words tore at him. Over his starboard wing he watched the glide of the plane's tiny port light. It dropped away. He could see no splash. It had become too dark to see anything except the wing lights of the other planes. He checked his fuel gauge. Enough there to make him feel guilty. He heard another pilot ready to ditch check gallons with his wingman. They both went in together. This time it did not hurt Blaesing as much as the first time.

They heard all of it in Gamma group. They crowded round the receivers in the radio shack and flag plot and where it was piped into the intercom on *Shiloh*'s bridge and below decks. LeClair was openly nervous. "What about a couple of tin cans to pick up those boys in the water?"

"The flag'll handle it, Miller."

"None of these boys have ever landed a plane at night on a carrier deck, Captain."

"They'll have to try. Relax, Miller."

"Can we give 'em searchlights on the flight deck? Once they're inside the screen?"

"Forget it."

"I want to get those kids aboard, Captain."

"They know where we are." Paige moved away. LeClair was getting on his nerves. He knew damned well there were some who would never get aboard, tin cans or no tin cans. There was too much sea between here and there. He'd do what had to be done when the others were in the landing circle and not before. And they had better the hell show soon. Midway's radar had reported a large number of unidentified ships headed east eighty miles due west of the atoll. Obviously, the Nip wasn't ready to give up yet and Midway was tensing for a surface attack. And *Shiloh* had been steaming on a westerly course and was presently some fifty miles north of Midway. Her recovery course was going to head her straight the hell toward the Jap fleet. Too damn close for comfort. The last thing in the world he wanted was a night engagement with battlewagons and heavy cruisers. He'd be *sukiyaki* by dawn.

The first word came from the picket destroyer northwest of the group. It had picked up the returning planes on its radar screen. They were dead on the beam and coming in.

Paige slapped LeClair's shoulder. "Prepare to recover aircraft." To Catlin he snapped, "Present course?"

"Two-seven-zero, Captain."

"What's the wind?"

"Two-four-zero; force, five knots."

Thirty degrees to port at twenty-five knots and straight into Tojo's arms. "Our recovery course is two-four-zero. Ring up enough speed to give us thirty knots across the deck. Get on the TBS. Our present intention is to recover aircraft. Execute when they acknowledge. All hands to battle stations."

"General quarters, Captain?"

"All hands." He heard the alarm and the surprised men clattering to their stations. He walked out on the starboard wing. The night was cloudy with no moon and only a star or two. He listened for the hum of plane motors. All he heard was the racing wake along the ship's side. The seconds dragged. Catlin gave the helm and engine room orders and *Shiloh* heeled into her new course. Paige felt the throb of added speed in his fingertips. His spine tingled. He sure as hell didn't enjoy where they were headed and any moment now Flint would be on the TBS asking questions, wanting to know what crazy Harry Paige was up to now. Well, he had to get those planes aboard, didn't he? There was still a margin of safety but those Japs flew night searches and that margin of safety was dropping away with each added knot they made to the southwest.

Catlin joined him. Sure enough. "The flag wants to know how long you'll be on present course?"

"Long enough to recover planes."

"Aye, Captain."

How the hell could he know how long it would take? That admiral was jumpier than a cat. What he needed was a drink. Just as soon as the last plane was aboard. And the first one could be the last.

Blaesing could not see the ships but he knew they were there. He had picked up the homing signal and headed in on the beam with the others following his lead. His eyes ached in the blackness and he fought to keep a balance of plane and mind. His side felt numb where the blood had glued itself to his khaki shirt and side and to the hairs of arm and body in a congealing glob. Two more SBDs had ditched minutes apart and he hoped their pilots and gunners had got free of the cockpits and into their rafts. He wondered who was next. He watched the needle of his fuel gauge pushing toward empty. He felt sick and abused and tried to think of the poor Jews in Germany and the starving Armenians and how damned lucky he was to be here where life was so rosy. It didn't help.

He spied the first set of red masthead lights and swept in over the screen. They were tiny specks below him but in that joyful moment they seemed brighter than the lights of a Christmas tree. And he was Santa Claus. His job was done. He held the stick between his knees and pressed the mike button. "Home sweet home, guys. You're on your own now. The guys low on gas land first."

It didn't matter, he thought. If they had to ditch, the cans were there to pick 'em up, even if they had to float around until daylight. Only one damn thing. They could've turned the lights on. If the skipper had the balls he's supposed to have, he'd turn 'em on.

They circled high over the group. *Shiloh*'s flight control readied the deck and thirty knots of wind whipped across the boards. The first plane to break off and enter the landing circle was an SBD with portions of its wing sections riddled with bullet holes and chewed to ash by thermite. The pilot had reported himself and his gunner wounded and his gas to fifteen gallons. Two, maybe three times around and that would be it.

Flaps and wheels down, he wobbled into the groove, leveled off nicely and began his approach from dead astern, pointed evenly between the tiny hooded flight deck lights ahead. He was too high and angled to starboard as he closed. The lighted wands in the landing officer's hands swung frantically to correct him but it was no go. The wands shot high, crisscrossed in a wave-off. Maybe the pilot never saw it. He veered to starboard. One wingtip cleared the deck by inches. The other slashed through both barrels of the after five-inch mount and dove nose first into the sea. The tail rose high and shook like a whale's fluke and fell. The shattered hulk disappeared in the night.

The landing officer held the next bomber steady and she looked good in the groove. On she came, overtaking the fantail and he gave the cut. The dry engine sputtered and died and the SBD, almost sighing, settled and splashed heavily in *Shiloh*'s wake.

LeClair distraught in flight control found Paige at his side with an ugly frown on his face. "Get 'em aboard, Miller. We haven't got all night."

"We need more light across the deck, Captain. Those little flight deck lights aren't enough."

"That last SBD ran out of gas is all."

"Captain, those boys up there will never make it. Give 'em a break. They're shot. They need lights."

"Can't risk it, Miller. This is Jap sub country, and we're too damn close to the Jap fleet. They fly night patrols. So forget it."

"There's only seventeen of them up there, Captain. With lights I'll have 'em aboard in twenty-five minutes."

"If the flag gives the order. I sure as hell won't." He left abruptly and went into the pilot house. Another SBD swooped over the port gun gallery after a second wave-off. The landing officer had to dive into his safety net to avoid being cut in half.

Paige stalked his narrow quarterdeck and the bridge watch stirred uneasily, not daring to approach or look at him. Once he bent to watch the radar repeater's green light sweep its arc uninterrupted except for the two blips of the picket destroyers at ten miles.

The radio messenger came on the bridge. He held a dimmed flashlight over the dispatch board. Paige read the message and signed it. Radar Midway's enemy surface contact reported earlier at eighty miles west of the atoll had now changed course and was retiring to the northwest.

Paige showed it to Catlin and Catlin nodded toward flight control. Paige scowled. "How the hell do I know the Midway report's accurate? Or that it even comes from Midway. It could be another Jap trick."

The TBS crackled suddenly and Catlin went to it. Paige recognized Flint's voice. "Hardtack from Flag."

Paige went over and pressed down the transmitting lever. "Hardtack, aye."

"How many chickens still aloft?"

"Seventeen." He heard a grinding crash from the flight deck and a tearing of steel. LeClair's bull horn boomed orders. Catlin ran to the port wing. Paige pressed the transmitting lever.

"Repeat," he said. "Could not read your last message."

"Hardtack, this is Flag. I repeat: Estimate time to complete landings."

"With ship darkened, no telling. Two crashes—erase—three crashes. Two in water. One on deck just now. Many ditched planes."

"Estimate time with deck lighted."

"Twenty-five minutes."

"Stand by."

There was heavy silence in the pilot house. Catlin came in looking relieved. "Barrier crash. No fire. Pilot's hurt bad."

The TBS came on again. The voice was not Flint's. Hardtack from Flag. "Use searchlights on flight deck at your discretion. Security of your command your responsibility. In twenty-five minutes—repeat twenty-five minutes—darken ship again. Secure from flight operations. We can remain on present course no longer than that. Screen will conform to your movements. Over."

"Roger. Wilco." He went out to flight control. Somewhere above, planes were still circling. He said to LeClair, "How long to clear the fouled deck?"

"Three minutes, Captain." He sounded more cheerful.

"Resume landing planes as soon as it's clear."

"We're turning up searchlights?"

"Negative." He started to leave. LeClair held him. "I just heard—"

"Goddam you!" Paige shouted. "You got your orders." He thrust his face against LeClair's. "Can't you carry 'em out? If you can't then get the hell below and I'll get someone up here who can."

He wheeled and stalked to the open bridge forward of the pilot house. The sound of his own voice still rang in his ears. The shrillness of it shocked him. He stood alone on the open bridge and heard the planes swing into the groove astern and the gunned engines roar after the wave-offs. A few made it. Many did not. The sea astern was strewn with floating wreckage and men crying for help in the black night.

He did not know how many had come aboard and how many had not. He did not turn to look. They had their orders. There was nothing he could do about it. He heard Tod Newell call his name from Sky One above. He ignored it.

Five minutes to go. He walked into the pilot house. Catlin stood behind the helmsman. Paige thought he saw tears glisten in his navigator's eyes. "Course?"

"Still two-four-zero, speed twenty-five knots."

Paige looked at the chronometer. "In exactly two minutes, Cat, advise Commander LeClair to secure from flight quarters. Any planes left in the air will have to ditch and do the best they can. In exactly four minutes from now, we will come right to course zero-four-five. Maintain present speed. Secure from general quarters. Put it out over the TBS to the screen. They'll conform to our movements as we execute."

"Aye, Captain."

Four minutes. Paige walked out to flight control.

Blaesing in the last plane aloft swung into the landing circle and in darkness came down the groove as though he had done this every day of his life. He held true, fighting nausea, fatigue, and his deep loathing for the way the world went. He came on in and the Wildcat's nose blotted away the deck but he knew he would make it and the lighted wands said so. The landing officer gave him a quick cut and the Wildcat's tail hook caught and Blaesing was home. He taxied forward and hands reached to help him.

Paige turned to his orderly, Shane. "Get that Commander Blaesing here. That was beautiful." Shane started and Paige said, "No, damn it, I'll go down there myself."

Catlin was already putting the course change over the TBS and LeClair had left flight control. Paige headed down through the debris of flag plot to the flight deck.

They had to help Blaesing out of the cockpit. He waved away the corpsmen and their litter. "I'm okay," he said and started across the flight deck on his own two good feet. Paige went to meet him and halfway across the deck, thrust out his hand. Blaesing ignored it. His face was stony with hate. He looked straight ahead and kept on going.

Paige went to his sea cabin. The planes, what was left of them, were aboard. Two tin cans were looking for ditched fliers. His ship was heading to safer waters. He threw off his helmet and tore the awkward battle gear from his sweaty body. All of him trembled. He poured some whisky in a tumbler and drained it and poured another. It was the drink he would have given Blaesing for leading the strike and bringing the boys back and barreling in like the pro he was. And damned if he wouldn't have given him another for the cold-cocked way he snubbed his skipper on the flight deck. I don't blame him, Paige thought. It took guts. The kind of guts all of those boys should have.

His restless mind was already engaged in estimating what Flint's next tactical move should be. If the enemy's retirement westward continued and was reliably reported as such in the morning, then there could be little doubt that the invasion plan had failed. But it also could be a feint to throw the island defenses and Flint's carrier group off guard and during the night the Imperial Fleet could reverse its course and in a high-speed run resume its attack. Nor was there assurance that more Japanese carriers were not present. With *Tarrytown* out of the fighting, the brunt of the work still rested on Paige's shoulders and on the few planes he could put into the sky.

He finished the second drink and corked the bottle and put it away. He could not stop his hands from trembling. He heard words

outside and a light scuffling sound and the door swung in and Tod
Newell pushed past Shane. "I'd like a word with you, Captain."

Shane stood redfaced and uncertain. Behind him Paige saw the
inquiring faces of the bridge watch. He nodded to Shane who closed
the door, and he turned to see what Newell wanted. He had forgotten about Newell. David had liked him and he remembered that
now. The handsome face was calm but Paige did not like the un-
focused look in Newell's eyes. "What's going on?" he demanded.

Newell breathed hard. He had climbed down from Sky One and
looked for the captain on the open bridge, pushing the crowded
watch aside. Catlin standing by the helm change could not stop
him and Newell had charged into the sea cabin. He dropped his
helmet on the deck. His .45 Colt sagged from the gun belt at
his lean waist. "You're a murderer, Captain Paige."

"Get out of here."

"Joe Allen," Tod said slowly. "Stick Wilson. Oley Olsen. Every
dead sailor off the *Gloucester*." He waved his arm. His eyes had
narrowed and his mouth was twisted in a way that made his face
almost unrecognizable to Paige. Paige glanced at the sidearm in
Newell's belt.

"Return to your cabin, Newell. You're under hack."

"Those fliers in the drink just now, you murderer. And poor
David—"

"*Not David!*" Paige swung before he knew it, an open slap in a
swift arc with every ounce of his strength and guilt and his pent-up
grief behind it. The blow threw Newell against the bulkhead. He
straightened slowly, taunting. "I'm next, right? The last one. Go
on, Captain. Murder *me*." He tugged the sidearm free and tossed
it. Paige gingerly caught it and dropped it on the bunk. He moved
into Newell with a short left jab. It caught Newell in the stomach
and doubled him. A jarring right hook against the side of Newell's
face started blood trickling from his nose. Newell sagged to his
knees and got back to his feet, half-dazed. His face bore a curious
smile. He started toward Paige again. Paige in absolute horror
dropped his fists and went to him and threw both arms across
Newell's shoulders. "Help me," he muttered brokenly. "Goddam
it, help me!"

They held each other, heads bowed, both spent. Newell led Paige
to the bunk and sat him down. Paige buried his face in his hands.

Newell wet a towel and gently sponged Paige's head and neck. "Get out," Paige whispered.

Newell dabbed at his own nose. It had stopped bleeding. He wiped away the blood and picked up his .45 and his helmet by the strap and quietly left. His flesh was racked with pain. Yet he felt curiously strong and useful, and in a way he did not quite understand, avenged.

40

With *Shiloh*'s planes aboard, Flint took Alpha force northeast in a night run. In the early morning hours he reversed course to put *Shiloh*'s planes in striking range if needed for the defense of Midway. Radio Midway's early report, however, proved accurate. The Imperial Fleet had retired to lick its wounds.

But Kaizuka was not quite through. One of his cruiser-based search planes sighted *Tarrytown* before dawn. She was abandoned and drifting in the company of two destroyers. A salvage party was aboard with power being provided by a third destroyer, *Guthrie*, alongside. Imperial Command dispatched a submarine. Visibility was excellent. Oil and debris in the water made sound detection by the destroyers difficult. The submarine slipped by the screen and fired four torpedoes. Two found *Tarrytown*'s vitals. Another struck *Guthrie* amidships and she broke in two. The surviving destroyers searched vainly for the submarine and rejoined Alpha that night at Point Oasis.

In *Shiloh* the air crews turned to the task of overhauling and repairing her planes while the combat air patrol guarded the skies overhead. Paige remained in his cabin writing his report of the battle. Commander Logan on the bridge supervised the refueling operation. The chaplain called on Captain Paige that morning to inquire what should be done with David's effects. "Over the side," Paige said. He did not look up and the chaplain finally left.

Paige was reminded of the folder of poetry Felicia had given him in San Diego. He tried but could not erase that memory. He got up and pawed through his gear until he found it in a briefcase among his penciled notes on aircraft carrier command. He sprawled out on the davenport and began to read the poems.

HERO

"Three cheers!" I yelled to the homebound hero
But he could not hear me.
He could not see and he could
not talk
And he had no arms and legs.

* * *

GI (Q. & A.)

Crawl through fields in endless dew,
(When will I see home again?)
Tread lanes mined by the wily Hun;
Wade streams swollen with bodies and rain.
(When is war done?)

Drink, fields, drenched with the brothers' blood,
Grow, grass, as never before;
Cling, bone to soil and flesh to sod,
War is within us. Curse it no more,
Leave it to God.

* * *

SHIPYARD

The brute yammers
Of steam hammers
Manglia
My
Ganglia.

* * *

Who can know when the seed is sown,
In time to come how the plant will fare?
To what odd pattern its branches grown,
Bitter or sweet the fruit it will bear?

Paige lay with the poems in his fingers. His eyes were closed. His mind was faraway, a zoo of regrets. Marine Private Shane knocked and when the captain did not answer, he peered in. "Sir?"

"Speak up, Shane."

"Message received from the flag, sir." He handed Paige the dispatch. The radio messenger hovered in the passageway. "The destroyer's coming alongside now, Captain."

"Very well." Paige initialed the dispatch and put aside David's poems and picked up his sea-tarnished cap and tunic. Nobody goes calling on neat and natty Admiral Flint without a tunic, not even a salty skipper who has just sunk four Nip flattops. He jammed the battle report into a folder and went to the fantail where the breeches buoy and sleek *Bradbury* waited. The one David loved, he remembered.

Admiral Flint's flag lieutenant met Paige at the cruiser's quarterdeck and escorted him to flag country. Flint in freshly pressed khakis sat at his desk before a stack of reports. He wore rimless glasses and Paige thought he looked displeased. You could never tell with Flint. To Paige, he always looked as though he had just sucked a dozen lemons.

Flint waved a hand. "Sit down, Harry. Let me have that report. I'll be through here in a minute."

Paige sat warily in the deep leather chair. He had seen all kinds of admiral's quarters. The setup in *Gloucester* had been lavish and had been used by two Presidents. These seemed no different from most of the others. A huge leather-framed picture of Flint's frosty-eyed wife intrigued Paige. Flint must have sent for it at the last minute before transferring his flag from *Shiloh*. Like the Nips with their Hirohito. Devotion beyond the call of duty, Paige thought.

Flint put the reports aside and pushed up his glasses. "Adds up to quite a good show, Harry. We know for sure now all four flattops went down. And the one cruiser."

"Any new word on *Tarrytown?*"

"Some of the salvage crew were picked up this morning along with a few from *Guthrie*. Messy. All in rough shape. Oil and underwater explosion. Tully's here in sick bay. He's about had it and overdue for stateside leave. They all had a bad time but they got most of the crew off. They're crowded in the corners of every ship in the group. We've got a sub tender enroute from Pearl to pick them up. Tactically, we're in good shape. Midway's beefed up with enough fighters and B-17s to handle any change of mind the Imperial Command may have. But they won't be back, not soon."

"I'm going to need a week in Pearl to straighten up the flag bridge, Admiral. That doesn't leave much cover out here."

"The Sara's enroute from Dago and will be out here in a couple of days with a well-trained air group. Wasp's working her way west but she's still in the Atlantic. Soon as we're done fueling, Shiloh'll head in." He patted the pile of reports. "CINCPAC's very eager to read these. I've radioed my own evaluation of the situation along with some recommendations." He paused and seemed to choose his words. "I want to say, Harry, that you've done well. I was stumped for a decision last night, believe me. I wanted to save those fliers if I could and yet I didn't dare bring the Jap Fleet down on us. At one point we were within thirty miles of them. If we lighted up, they certainly would have seen our loom. Yet they seemed to be retiring and I suppose we were faced with the old 'calculated risk' theory again. That's why I pretty much left it up to you. You knew the score and Shiloh was your command. It took your kind of courage, I guess, to keep those lights off."

"No need to apologize, Admiral."

"I'm not apologizing, damn you." He picked up a dispatch from his desk and with a somewhat exasperated expression said, "This should be of some interest to you." He read:

FROM: CINCPAC
TO: OTC ALPHA
SUBJ: OPERATION ALAMO

1. YOUR BRILLIANT LEADERSHIP AGAINST SUPERIOR ENEMY FORCE IS IN THE HIGHEST TRADITION OF OUR NAVY. DEFEAT OF ENEMY'S INVASION PLAN AND SINKING OF FOUR ENEMY FLATTOPS MAY WELL BE TURNING POINT OF WAR. CONGRATULATIONS ON BEHALF OF PRESIDENT, COMINCH AND GRATEFUL PEOPLE OF THE UNITED STATES.

"That's pretty fancy stuff," Paige said. "Congratulations."
"I'll read the rest," Flint said.

2. BECAUSE OF HIS BOLDNESS IN ATTACK, PERSISTENCE IN SEEKING OUT AND DESTROYING ALL FOUR FLATTOPS, COOLNESS IN FACE OF GREAT PERSONAL RISK AND

DANGER TO HIS COMMAND AND CONSISTENT EXCELLENCE
OF AND INSPIRATION TO AIR GROUP AND SHIPS
COMPANY IN FIRST ACTION, YOU ARE HEREBY
AUTHORIZED TO AWARD IMMEDIATE FIELD PROMOTION
TO RANK OF REAR ADMIRAL FOR HARRISON PAIGE,
CAPTAIN, USN, CO SHILOH.

"Well, I'll be damned," Paige said surprised.

"That all you have to say?"

"Should I stand and salute?"

Flint shook his head. "Same old wise guy." He put down the dispatch. "I'm certainly not going to kiss you on both cheeks. I can't for the life of me figure you out, Harry. I never could and I'm going to stop trying. I'll say this: We're in this war together and there's no sense in rocking the boat." He stuck out his hand. Paige took it.

"Congratulations," Flint said.

"Thanks, Amos. I mean it."

"Before you go." Flint went to his desk and took a small black box from the drawer. It held a pair of worn rear admiral's shoulder boards. "I was saving these for a son. If I ever had one." He removed Paige's four-striper boards and snapped his own old ones in place. "You deserve these, Harry."

"I'm not so sure," Paige said almost to himself.

"I am. Whatever other thoughts I may have are best left unsaid."

"Now I'm out of uniform," Paige said gruffly. "Wrong collar devices."

"Get yourself a pair at ship's service, Admiral. My duty's done, painful as it was." Flint turned abruptly and stared through the open port, his back to Paige. After a few moments, Paige shrugged and left.

After fueling, *Shiloh* was detached from Point Oasis and steamed for Pearl in the company of two destroyers. At a point due north of French Frigate Shoals, Paige took an F4F Wildcat off *Shiloh's* bow and headed south. He slid the plotting board from under the instrument panel and set a course to fly him over the spot where he knew David had been lost. He had checked the latitude and longitude in the ship's log and when he reached the area he banked and circled in narrowing arcs. At five hundred feet he had wheels

out and flaps down and dropped in a steady glide toward the sea.
He slid the canopy back along its track and skimmed the wave tops.
He knew that all it needed was one rogue wave or an antic wind
to smash him like a swift bird against a stone wall.

He had made a loose packet of David's poems wrapped round
his captain's shoulder boards. The slipstream caught it and tore
it from his fingers and whipped it apart and scattered the papers
and insignia over the sea. The shoulder boards sank at once. The
poems stayed afloat like saucy boats. He watched them drift and
dip until finally they were out of sight and then he gunned for
Shiloh.

41

"Hello, Harry."

"Nick."

"Grab a chair. Or should I get up and bow and say 'Welcome home, Admiral Paige, and give you my chair?'"

"Knock it off, Nick."

"That was a slick job you did out there, Harry."

"Amos ran the show. Give him the credit."

"Oh, he'll get it all right. Leave it to old Amos." His long finger tapped the battle reports. "I can read, Harry. Sometimes it has to be between the lines. But this time Flint spelled it out. Paige all the way."

"He's getting senile."

"How about another medal? How about a few medals? We got all kinds. Gold, silver, bronze ribbons. All colors of the rainbow." He pulled open a drawer. "Let's see now. Something in blue?"

"No more medals, Nick."

"How about a few stars? You got to have medals and ribbons and stars, Harry. That's what the game's all about."

"You feeling all right, Nick?"

"Never better in my life. I sit here with the whole damn Pacific war on my shoulders and I feel a little younger every day."

"What's the secret?"

"Just knowing port from starboard." He grinned. "Have a medal, Harry."

"You know what you can do with your medals, Nick."

"Sure. Give 'em to Flint." He shut the drawer and leaned back. "Harry, what's eating you?"

"Nothing eats me, Admiral."

"You're not the cocky Hardtack Harry who took *Shiloh* out of here last week. Who sent four enemy flattops to the bottom. Who just made admiral." His voice softened. "David?"

Paige shrugged and looked away.

"We're all hurt by it, Harry. Not nearly as much as you and Felicia, of course. But it was one of those tragic accidents—"

"No accident, Nick. He walked off the deck. He could see. He knew what he was doing. He just walked right off."

Nickelby sat in shocked silence for several moments. "How do you know, Harry?"

"Because I got to know the kid, finally—too late—and what was on his mind and the kind of guts he had. Four Nip carriers? It took ten times the guts to do what he did."

"The log reads 'Lost at sea.'"

"Who gives a damn what the log reads? The boy is gone, dead. And why? I'll tell you why, Nick. Because he refused to make the compromises you and I make. He hated war enough to do what he did. Would you? Would I?" He stiffened. "You sent for me."

"Yes." Nickelby, deeply agitated, shuffled some papers abstractedly. "I wanted you to have my old shoulder boards. I see someone's beat me to it. Was it Tully?"

"Flint."

"Be damned. That's a switch."

"Said he was saving 'em for the son he never had." He looked Nickelby squarely in the eyes. "You have sons, Nick?"

"Two. One's a lawyer back home. The other has a chain of drugstores in Chicago."

"Smart."

"How?"

"Played it safe, didn't you?"

"No, Harry. I'll ignore the nasty overtones. I didn't play it safe at all. The door was wide open for both of them if they wanted the Navy. They didn't and I never made an issue of it." He carefully looked at the ceiling. "No Rollo Blatchfords in my clan, Harry."

"Okay, Nick. Besides the shoulder boards for which I'm grateful, what else?"

"Two things. Surprises, I hope."

"Another set of barbells and a punching bag?"

Nickelby's smile was fleeting. "I'm giving you Tully's command. A carrier group. He's heading for a rest."

"No surprise. How soon?"

"Soon as we can rearm and refuel *Shiloh* and get that flag bridge fixed up for you. More carriers are on the way, as you know. The Midway deal broke Tojo's back, thanks to you, and I've a hunch, Harry, this is the beginning of the end. A long way to go yet, but the balance is shifted now, psychologically, strategically, tactically— any way you want to read it. Up to now it was hit-and-run. From now on in, it's got to be hit-and-stay. You're the boy who's going to do the hitting."

"I don't know, Nick."

"You don't know what?"

"That I'm the boy to do it."

"That'll be the day." Nickelby laughed. "You're the best we've got, Harry. You proved it out there the other day. You also got me off a very tender limb. As you know. A lot of characters here and back in Washington would have loved to cut me down. Well, never mind. It's my neck. What were you about to say?"

"You heard about the deck lights?"

"It's in the report."

"Those planes came back in darkness. Fuel tanks just about drained. Some of the boys were hit bad. None of them ever made a night landing on a carrier in their lives. Flint left me the choice to light up the flight deck or not."

"Not the wisest of decisions, between you and me, Harry. Too vacillating. But I understand his situation and all of you were under considerable pressure."

"I'm not faulting Flint this time. It's me, Nick."

"What do you mean?"

"I damn near turned up those lights. Every instinct in me said, *Get those kids back aboard. The hell with the Jap fleet. The hell with everything else. Give 'em the break they earned. Get 'em aboard.* I went through hell while they were up there. A lot of them were lost, Nick. Ditched. I kept thinking. *Now. Give the order now. Up with the lights.* I kept thinking, David's up there. Every damn one of those kids is David and I have got to save him. But something else said to me, *The hell with them! David's dead. Why not them?*"

His fingers were trembling and Nickelby pretended not to notice. "You didn't turn up the lights, Harry. That's what matters. The risk of losing your ship with two thousand men on board and priceless equipment that would take years to replace. . . . There was no choice. Amos should not have given you one. You acted properly and in the best interests of the service."

"I know all that, Nick. But you're missing the point." He pounded the desk. "I goddam near turned up those lights anyway! You understand? It *was* a choice. I made room for it. I got soft! It damn near happened." He roughly wiped his eyes. "Listen, Nick, and listen closely. You're giving me a carrier group command and I'm damned honored and proud and I'll go back out there and fight it with every ounce of skill and savvy I possess. But you better know one thing. It won't be the same man out there who took *Gloucester* into Sunda Strait. Not after David. Not after what happened to me out there. If the situation comes up again, I swear I don't know whether those deck lights will go on or not. I want you to know that."

Nickelby sat drumming his fingers on the desk. "Are you trying to tell me, Harry, that you don't want to go out again?"

"I'm telling you how things are, Nick. That's all."

"There are desk jobs. I could use a seasoned carrier man on staff here. Someone like you who's been out there and knows the score."

"Look at me, Nick. Can you see me cooling my heels behind a desk while there's a scrap going on somewhere? All I'm saying is, I'm not the same man. Can you understand that? I've changed and I felt it my duty to say so."

"You always were blunt and outspoken, Harry Paige, and I always knew where I stood with you. Now I'll be frank. What you've just told me troubles me. But it also pleases me. Why? Because deep inside, where nobody ever sees the real Nickelby, there's no love for what we do."

"Nick, there's no need . . ."

"War happens to be my business, Harry. Like my younger boy with his drugstores. He hates the lousy hours, the inventory—ever have to take an inventory in a drugstore, Harry?—but it's the way he chose to make his living and he stays with it. Same with me. I used to talk myself into believing a Navy career was noble and deeply significant. Actually, I was propping up my sagging self-confidence. But I chose this career and at times it's noble and sometimes I wonder. But the world's changing, Harry. Kids like David prove it. Inch by inch, man is crawling ahead. A single misstep flings him back a thousand years. His only hope is to keep crawling until he finds out how to settle his conflicts without the need for war. Someday wars will be won with food and jobs and tools. And love. And no shots fired. Crazy, eh? Well, we're rich enough to make it happen. Someday we will."

"It's what David was trying to say."

"He was before his time, Harry. Right now, it still takes blood and guts and professionals like you. I always kept an eye on you, Harry, from the first day you wore the gloves for the Academy. You were poor, as I was, and an object of scorn from the Amos Flint types, as I had been. But you were tough and smart and you didn't give a damn what anyone thought and I liked that. And you liked to kill, Harry, didn't you? It used to scare me a bit and disgust me. It also used to thrill me a bit, knowing a killer. And the business and the world we're in being what it is, I knew a day would come when I would call on you. Now you've shown me this other side—a Harry Paige I hardly know. You had to pay a terrible price, didn't you, Harry?"

"Never mind—"

"Yet I'm pleased to see it, Harry. Grieved and pleased."

"I never heard you say so goddam much in all the years I've known you." He got up to leave. "I don't need speeches, Nick." He was frowning, feeling in Nickelby a stranger.

"It clears the air some," Nickelby said.

"I wanted you to know how we stood," Paige said. "That was all." He slowed at the door. "You said something about another surprise."

"My God, yes!" Nickelby, deep in thought, shook himself out of it. "Down the corridor. In the waiting room, Harry. Treat her gently. She's a sweet and tender one and she's come a long way."

When Paige left, Captain Miehle came in with a stack of official papers in his hands. "We're ready to cut Hardtack's orders, Nick. Want to check them?"

"The carrier division?"

"Roger. Gets under way first of the week."

"Leave 'em on the desk, Charley."

Captain Miehle looked surprised, "You said you wanted to expedite."

"Leave 'em on the desk. I want to do a little thinking is all."

"Harry, darling." She went to him.
Oh Felicia!
They walked hand in hand into the sunshine where enlisted men in dungarees tended green grass and banks of brilliantly colored island flowers. In the midst of the vast churning machinery of war they smelled the fresh-mown sweetness of a peaceful countryside. It seemed wrong somehow. Loneliness and grief and the thought of David numbed them. They strolled aimlessly, like lovers in a cemetery. Paige named the names of ships and buildings and pointed to newly historic places. It made Felicia sad and proud to know that people knew him and nodded wherever they walked.

He told her about David's poems and the four-striper shoulder boards and how the wind had swept them like fire into the sea and the poems alone remained. She was silent for a time. Then she said it was probably best that way and they did not speak of it again. Their night together was one of love and grief and love again. In bed they watched the sun rise. "There's more to the world than Georgetown," Felicia promised.

It's going to be all right, Paige thought when at last she slept. No matter how Nick works it out, deck or desk, he knows where I stand. And I know. The odds and the choices and what I am like. Now it's up to him.

Whichever way it went, he was going to be all right. He was going to be fine and that was all that mattered now for both of them.

Felicia stirred and opened her eyes and reached for him.

Oh yes all right.